Devil's Gamble

Tess Barnett

ALSO BY TESS BARNETT

Tales of the Tuath Dé
Those Words I Dread
Because You Needed Me
To Keep You Near

Devil's Gamble

Domesticated: A Short Story Collection
In collaboration with Michelle Kay

AS T.S. BARNETT

The Beast of Birmingham
Under the Devil's Wing
Into the Bear's Den
Down the Endless Road

The Left-Hand Path
Mentor
Runaway
Prodigy

A Soul's Worth

Devil's Gamble

Tess Barnett

Pensacola, FL

ISBN: 0692691650
ISBN-13: 978-0692691656

Cover Art by Mikao S.
mikao.tumblr.com

His Princely Delicates
An Imprint of Corvid House Publishing
Fantasy and Science Fiction Gay Romance Novels

Pensacola, FL
http://www.hisprincelydelicates.com

ACKNOWLEDGMENTS

Thank you to my husband, who still cares about my books even when I keep writing about boys touching.

1

Starting at a new school halfway through the year sucks. Starting at a new school halfway through the year because the principal at your last school died in a freak crushed-by-retracting-bleachers accident and your demon uncle decided to move you out of town before anyone remembered how much you complained about your last detention? That really sucks.

What sucked the most was that Caleb was now standing in front of a way-too-cheery-looking brick and red building with his backpack over one shoulder, being encouraged to "Have a good day, don't kill anyone yet" by the demon who had driven him there.

The demon wasn't the weird part. "Uncle Andras" had been taking care of Caleb for as long as he could remember. Having an infernal babysitter was part of the gig when your demon father was in absentia, and Caleb's had been since his birth. It hadn't been all that bad, especially once "Uncle" Andras had told him the truth about who he was and explained that Caleb's mother was only half-crazy for going on and on about his father being the devil.

Whether Caleb's father was the devil or not, he wasn't some guy who picked her up in a bar. It hadn't been hard to figure out on his own that he was different. For one thing, his seventh birthday was the first day he took a breath or had a heartbeat. As far as he understood, that didn't happen to most kids, but he could remember it happening. He woke up that morning with autonomic processes he hadn't had when he went to bed. It had been kind of a drag, actually. He couldn't run forever like he had when he was smaller, because his heart would pound so hard in his chest that he was certain he was going to die in the back yard. He was used to it now, mostly, but he still didn't like it. He used to sneak out and spend the evening in the pool at the back of the house, lounging on the bottom and enjoying the heavy silence. No more of that once he had to actually hold his breath. The density was another issue. In the water, he sunk like a stone. So now that he had to breathe, he didn't spend much time around pools.

Caleb had no memories of his mother ever picking him up. Only his uncle. He'd weighed the same since he was an infant all through his childhood, Andras said. Now, as a seventeen year old who stood just shy of six feet and had only a little muscle worth speaking of, he weighed a solid 300 pounds. It made getting on the bus or the subway awkward, as people tried to figure out how the lanky teenager was rocking the entire car, but the density and weight had the advantage of giving him the ability to hit very hard without much effort. It had made for an interesting trip to the playground the first time he had shoved some kid and broken his ribs.

Growing up, Caleb spent a lot of time locked in the house. He was allowed into the back yard, but only for a few minutes at a time, and only with his mother or Uncle Andras watching him. He didn't go on errands with his mother; he never rode in the seat of her shopping cart. Even when he got sick, he never went to the doctor. He was home schooled until the sixth grade, when he asked to go to school so many times that she finally gave in. She said he was old enough then that it didn't matter as much, though she did make him promise not to use his powers for evil "until the time came." You could only hear your mother call you the Antichrist and tell you about your important destiny so many times before you started to get jaded with the whole idea. Fortunately, Andras was always quick to remind him how unimportant he was, as he was "one of any number of cambion running around."

That hadn't stopped him from getting so spooked by Caleb's murderous lashing out that he'd shipped the whole household out into the boonies of Alabama, of course. It was a big difference from Chicago, but at least it wasn't as cold. Caleb had suggested more than once that he quit school entirely, what with the whole being-half-demon thing making it really difficult to relate to classmates more worried about the last episode of The Voice than things like accidentally wishing someone dead, but Andras had insisted that finishing his education was important.

He let out a sigh that puffed his cheeks and pulled open the metal entry door to the school. The woman in the front office greeted him cheerfully and handed him his class schedule, then pointed him in the direction of his assigned homeroom and left him to his own devices. The school was a single building, so the room was easy enough to find, and he let himself in while the teacher was taking roll.

"Ah! You must be our new arrival," she said brightly. She held out a hand to urge him closer and placed it on his shoulder when he complied. "Everyone, we have a new student today. This is Caleb—Caleb, right?" He nodded. "Why don't you tell us a little about yourself, Caleb?"

He looked out over the classroom full of teenagers almost as disinterested in him as he was in them. "I'm Caleb," he said simply. "From Chicago."

"Ooh, Chicago!" the teacher gushed, clearly hoping to wring some enthusiasm from the class. "The big city, huh? Well, I hope our little town lets you slow down a little. Now," she said, her hand still uncomfortably on his shoulder, "who wants to show Caleb around today?"

Immediately, a boy's hand shot up near the middle of the room. He was fair-skinned, with dusty blonde hair clipped short in a simple style, and his pale grey eyes were clear and excitable. He had a bright smile that showed the faint dimple in his chin. He was almost pretty, Caleb thought.

"Isaac," the teacher beamed, "thank you so much! I know you'll make sure Caleb feels welcome." She urged Caleb forward with a gentle pressure on his shoulder, and he moved to take the seat next to his volunteer. The boy—Isaac, apparently—leaned on his elbows to smile at him, and Caleb caught sight of a simple silver band on his left ring finger, stamped with a cross and some words he couldn't quite read. He didn't return his smile, just turned to the front of the room as the teacher carried on.

When the bell rang, Isaac happily led Caleb down the hall toward his next class, gripping the straps of his backpack while they walked.

"So, you come from Chicago, huh? You like it there?" he asked.

"It was fine."

"What brings you all the way down here?"

"Nothing interesting."

"I didn't mean to pry," Isaac answered with a bright smile. "We just don't get too many new folks. When you go to school with the same people your whole life, a new face can be the highlight of the year," he laughed.

"Great."

Isaac stopped in front of a classroom door, seemingly oblivious to Caleb's curt answers, and he gave the other boy a friendly wave. "I'm next door, so I'll see you after, Caleb!"

Caleb didn't answer him. He took his seat in his classroom and leaned his chin in his hand while the teacher wrote notes on the board that he was clearly expected to copy. School in Alabama was the same waste of time it had been in Chicago. How could anyone expect the Antichrist to concentrate on economics? Judging from the stares he had gotten from his classmates, at least it didn't seem like he would have to worry about fending off new friends. He'd known for a long time that he gave off a certain unwelcome vibe.

Except that Isaac was waiting for him after class, as promised. And after the next. He walked beside Caleb and asked him endless questions, not seeming to mind the other boy's monosyllabic answers. He chatted about the school football team, lamented Caleb arriving too late in the year to attend homecoming, and made a list of all the places kids tended to hang out in town—which consisted entirely of a little burger hut on Main Street and occasionally the parking lot by the Dollar General. Because that was where the Red Box was, of course.

"That's it?" Caleb asked as they approached third period, the first time he'd replied with anything resembling actual interest. "There are no clubs or anything? Where do you get your liquor?"

"Liquor?" Isaac repeated in a hushed voice, as though scandalized, but then he chuckled and offered Caleb a kind smile. "You can't buy beer or liquor in Bibb County, silly. You've got to go all the way into Tuscaloosa. And anyway, you're underage!"

"Are you serious?"

"Now, come on. I know things are different in big cities, but you don't need liquor to have fun. Our youth group gets together every couple weeks now the weather's cooled off. We make a bonfire, have some s'mores, sing songs—that sort of thing. It's fun! We're set to meet up this weekend; you should come along!"

"Sounds like laughs," Caleb said dryly, and Isaac followed him into the classroom when he opened the door. After class, he cheerfully led the way to the small cafeteria, since of course they had lunch together. Isaac was like one of those sucker fish attached to Caleb's shark belly.

"Look, you really don't have to follow me around," Caleb said bluntly as Isaac dropped his tray and slid onto the bench beside him.

"Nonsense," the boy grinned. "I don't mind at all. It's hard being new." His napkin blew off the table as the door opened behind them, and he reached out to grab it and missed. "Crumbs," he sighed, quickly lifting from his seat to fetch it. "Anyway," the boy started again as he sat back down, "I know if I was starting out at a new school in a new town with new people, I'd want someone to be friendly with me." He smiled past Caleb's weary stare. "So, have you decided what church you'll be going to?"

Caleb snorted into his can of soda and focused on opening his pack of chips. "No."

"Oh, well there are a lot to choose from! There's the Methodist church up on Camellia Lane, the Church of Christ, and then there's West Baptist, Mt. Carmel Baptist, Liberty Baptist, Faith Baptist, Mt. Olive Baptist, Shady Grove Baptist—"

"Yeah," Caleb cut him off. "I see there's a whole lot of variety here."

Isaac only smiled at him. "I attend Mt. Carmel, myself. We'd love to have you. But if it's not the right fit, I'm sure you'll be able to find somewhere that suits you."

"Not likely."

The boy's smile faltered slightly, and he set down his french fry to look at Caleb with a pensive knit in his brow. "Caleb, I know it can be hard moving to a new place, getting used to new people—"

"I don't go to church," Caleb explained flatly. "Ever," he added with a pointed glance in the other boy's direction.

"Oh. *Oh.*" Isaac leaned back slightly as though he hadn't considered that answer, and for a moment he just sat quietly, tucking a single french fry into his mouth. "Well," he added just as Caleb was beginning to appreciate the silence, "I'd be happy to introduce you at mine, if you ever change your mind."

"Sure. Thanks, I guess."

Isaac didn't stay solemn for long. Another group of students approached them and sat down at his urging, and he introduced Caleb to each of them in turn. They all smiled at him and welcomed him with such syrupy sincerity that Caleb almost got up and left. He had promised Andras that he wouldn't draw too much attention on his first day, so he resisted the urge to command them away from him and solve the problem entirely. It was one of the perks of his demon half. When he tried, he could tell people what to do, and they didn't have any choice but to obey. He was still getting the hang of it, but just a couple of weeks ago, he had told John Wilkes to fuck off in sixth period, and he had actually gotten out of his seat and left the room in the middle of class. He got in trouble, of course, but when Mrs. Beecher asked him why he did it, he almost seemed like he didn't realize he'd done anything strange at all. Andras had been proud when Caleb had told him, but they were trying to keep a low profile here, or so he'd said.

Isaac waited for him after the release bell at the end of the day, and he walked beside him all the way out to the front of the school. Caleb finally stood by the curb where Andras's silver Aston Martin sat waiting, and Isaac stopped short.

"Say, I've seen that car!" he said with a laugh. "It was y'all who moved into the big house back past the pond, right? That's great! We're practically neighbors!"

"Great," Caleb agreed less enthusiastically.

Isaac bent down to smile through the passenger window. "Is that your dad? Nice of him to come pick you up."

"He's my uncle," Caleb answered as he opened the car door.

"Oh. Well, I'll see you tomorrow, Caleb! I'm real glad you're here!" Isaac waved and turned to trot for the bus as the diesel engine cranked up nearby, leaving his reluctant new friend to climb into the car with a weary grunt.

"Making friends?" Andras asked without looking at his passenger, a sly smile on his lips. Caleb thought he didn't look very much like a demon, but he didn't have any frame of reference. He just looked like a guy—mid-thirties, handsome, tan skin, brown hair. No horns or slit pupils; not even a pointed tail or hooves. The only difference was that he'd looked exactly the same for Caleb's entire life.

"Not by choice," Caleb muttered as he slammed the door shut after him.

Andras's Ray-Ban sunglasses hid his blue eyes as he finally looked over at the boy. "Who is he?"

"Just some kid. He's freakishly friendly. I guess he doesn't have enough friends here? He tried to get me to go to his church with him."

The demon let out a hoarse laugh and eased the car into the street. "Did you tell him you'd burst into flames?"

"I left that out." He paused. "Wait. I wouldn't, right?"

Andras only shrugged, smiling sidelong at the boy as they drove.

The house they'd moved into was set back from the road, up a long driveway that curved through the trees. It was a strange house made of dark wood, with the front door set above the garage at the top of a set of creaking steps. The inside was nice, Caleb supposed, wide and open, but the whole place looked as dated as the rest of the town felt. It had been furnished to Andras's liking before they'd arrived, meaning it was full of sleek black furniture and expensive electronics. That made it feel a little more like home, but it was too new and not-haunted-seeming to remind him of the house they'd left.

Back in Chicago, they had lived in his grandparents' house. They had died right around the time Caleb was born—he wasn't sure if it was before or after—and left his mother everything. "Everything" turned out to be a pretty hefty sum. So she didn't work. She hired a maid, or rather, Andras hired a maid, and Caleb ate the dinner that Andras made or cooked something himself. He wasn't really sure what she did all day. Mostly she seemed to sit in her room and mutter to herself. She had never moved out of her parents' house, and Caleb had gotten the impression she hadn't been let out much when they were alive. He had tried to get her to see a doctor, but she had always refused, and Andras had encouraged him not to press the issue. She said she was fine. She said she talked to Caleb's father. He didn't ask her what they talked about.

He didn't see her when he walked in, which wasn't unusual. She liked to knit in her room in the afternoons. Andras's dog, Nobah, bounded a quick circle around them as the demon dropped his keys and sunglasses near the door, and Caleb paused to pat its head. It looked more like a wolf, black and half as tall as Caleb was, but Andras had insisted it was only a pet. Still, it must have been more than just a dog, since it, like its master, had been the same since Caleb was born.

He went upstairs without a word and dropped his backpack by the door. The rest of the house suited Andras and his expensive tastes, but at least his room had been kept simple. He didn't like stuff. He had a bed, and a dresser, and a nightstand with a Futurama alarm clock. He'd hung up a poster he'd gotten from Lollapalooza the year before, but beyond the slate grey blanket on his bed and the iPhone speaker dock on his dresser, the room was bare. It was the way he liked it. He didn't understand his friends back in Chicago, who had piles of crap all over their rooms—magazines and comic books and old concert tickets and little pointless figurines from this video game or that anime. Why hold onto any of it?

He shut the curtains above his bed and laid down on his stomach, trying to quiet Isaac's relentlessly hospitable voice in his brain.

2

Andras panted against the sweat-slick skin of the man beneath him, tasting the salt between his shoulder blades with a long, slow brush of his tongue. The sound of his lover's trembling moan shot straight to his groin, and he bent over him to catch one earlobe tenderly between his teeth as they rocked together on the bed. His fingers intertwined with the other man's, each squeezing the other tightly to ground themselves. Andras nuzzled his lover's dark cheek with his nose until the other man turned his head, and the demon smiled at his helpless, clouded eyes in the moment before their kiss.

Andras chuckled at the sharp bite to his lip and drove deep into the other man with one forceful thrust, his breath hot against his lover's ear as he whispered, "Just say so if you're ready."

"I'm ready," he answered impatiently, and a faint smirk touched the edge of the demon's mouth.

He pulled up to his knees, letting his fingertips brush the man's parted lips as he rose, and he tugged him close against his hips, savoring the low groan that resonated from his chest. He kept him in place with a hand on the warm umber skin of his lover's back and pushed into him at a hard, steady rhythm, no longer waiting and teasing at every whimper. He moved relentlessly, his tongue wetting his lips as he felt the man's strong back arch under his palm, fingers tangled in the rumpled sheets.

"Come for me," Andras half ordered and half begged, and he reached underneath them to stroke the other man's seeping cock. He jerked as his lover tightened around him at the touch, but he kept up his pace until he could feel the familiar hitch in his partner's breath.

When the man beneath him tensed and cried out, and Andras felt the ribbon of heat hit his fingers, he brought his hand to his lips and groaned with satisfaction as the bitter liquid touched his tongue.

A soft swear escaped him as he moved again, and his lover's exhausted writhing snapped the coiled spring in his stomach, drawing his own release out of him in a tight-jawed moan. He stayed still for as long as he could, savoring every last twitch and sigh his partner made, until the other man reached back to lazily swat at him, and Andras reluctantly withdrew and dropped onto the bed beside him with a quick kiss to his shoulder.

"I missed you too, B," the demon murmured, but the other man just grunted without opening his eyes. "You aren't skipping important duties, slumming it here with me?"

He sat up with a weary sigh and padded into the attached bathroom to clean himself up. "Can't we ever just enjoy the silence?"

Andras sat up on his elbow and leaned his head in his hand to watch his lover through the open door. "What, are your ears still ringing? Or is all that heavenly choir noise stuck in your head?"

"I don't know why I came," he grumbled, and Andras slid from the bed and moved to wrap his arms around the other man's waist. He touched a soft kiss to the back of his neck with smirking lips, his fingertips brushing the dark skin of his lover's stomach.

"I know exactly why you came," he teased, drawing a reluctant grunt from the taller man. "I can show you again if you like, seraph."

"Can you not?"

"Barachiel," Andras corrected himself, and the angel turned in his loose grip to press a kiss to the demon's lips.

"Better," he murmured with a smile, letting his thumb brush the other man's stubbled cheek. He let his forehead affectionately touch his lover's for just a moment before pulling away. "So what's this I hear about your little ward killing someone in Chicago?"

"Just an accident," Andras shrugged. He sat back on the bed with his shoulders against the headboard while his partner dressed from the discarded pile of clothes on the floor. "You know how these things are."

"You told me you had it under control."

"I do. But he is what he is, B."

The angel pulled his shirt over his head with a pensive frown. "A cambion is a dangerous thing, Andras. He isn't like you or me. If he starts making deals, taking souls for his own, then he could grow too powerful to ignore. If he gets out of control, he could become human in name only—and the last thing we need is a demon on Earth unfettered by the rules of demons."

"Thanks for the reminder. This isn't my first go-round; I know what I'm doing."

"I know," Barachiel sighed. "But after the last one—"

"He did exactly what was asked of him," Andras cut in. "Bending the rules is what they're made for. He just bent them too far, and now he's dead. You want to have any more fun little recaps?"

"Andras, your master—"

"—Has done a great deal for me." The demon sighed. "Do you really want to do this again? I'm handling it."

"I just don't want to see it happen again. I know it hurt you."

"Caleb doesn't have too many world-conquering ambitions," Andras chuckled, waving away his partner's concern, and he scooted over to allow the other man to sit beside him. "He's still struggling with high school. Did you know a boy tried to get him to go to church today?"

"Lofty goal," the angel said dryly, but he nodded as he sat. "Isaac Mitchell. He's a rare case. Teenage boys aren't usually that good."

"You know him? My mistake; of course you do, Mr. Chief Guardian Angel," Andras smiled.

"His guardian actually asked for a new assignment, because he was bored," Barachiel said.

"Wow. Poor kid."

Barachiel paused and turned to look at Andras, casually brushing aside the demon's hand as it wandered over his thigh. "He could be a good influence, actually."

"What, on Caleb? Are you serious?"

"He's fast becoming a man," the angel said sternly. "Soon he'll have to make his choice. I would have him make the right one."

Andras reached out to touch his lover's sharp chin, stroking the bottom lip that he'd so often caught in his teeth. "Don't take it so seriously. You'll ruin our rendezvous with what-ifs." He sat up and edged closer to the other man, and he tilted his head with a sly smile. "How about we make a deal?"

The angel's eyebrow lifted skeptically. "I think I misheard you."

"Not that sort of a deal," Andras laughed. "A friendly one. Caleb is his father's son; there's no denying that. He has blackness in him that even you and I can't understand. You say this kid is so good even angels think he's boring? You think he could keep Caleb from the dark side, turn him nice?"

"It's a possibility."

"So, let him try. You give little goody two-shoes a nudge in the right direction, and if he's able to turn my boy toward the light, then I'll give you a gift."

He shook his head. "Why make a bet like that? Don't you want Caleb to follow in his father's footsteps?"

"It's win-win for me," Andras smiled. "If your kid fails, and Caleb takes the dark road, then I get to see him blossom into a beautiful demon butterfly. If he gives it up and goes good, then I get to see you without having to listen to your heavenly foreboding like I have every time for the last seventeen years. It'll make a nice break." He guided Barachiel closer to him and kissed him, savoring the relenting sigh the angel let out.

"And what's this gift you're offering?" Barachiel asked without retreating. He let his nose brush the demon's cheek.

"I'll let you be on top for once," he answered against the other man's lips.

The angel frowned, pulling away and staring at his lover as though waiting for the joke. "That's it?"

"What, it isn't enough?"

"You want to gamble for the life of a boy you've raised from birth, and the wager you're willing to make is to let me be on top? Once?" He held up a finger for clarification. "Once, in all of eternity. That's your offer."

Andras only smiled at him and waited, watching his lover's eyes linger on his lips until he snorted.

"Fine. But only because I was going to do it anyway."

"Mhmm."

Barachiel stood and glanced toward the bedroom window. "His parents aren't home yet."

"What, you're going now?" Andras reached out to tug at the hem of the angel's shirt. "But we've only gone once, and I'm still naked."

"And I suspect you'll still be naked when I get back." He paused. "In fact, I demand that you still be naked when I get back."

"I love it when you're commanding."

"Hush." Without another word, Barachiel vanished from the room.

Isaac sat in his room with music quietly playing from the speaker of his phone, a history textbook open on his small desk. He bounced his heel off of the leg of his chair in time to the music while he tried to focus on the dry passage about the transcontinental railroad. He was frequently alone in the afternoons. His father worked on an assembly line in Birmingham, so he was always late home, and his mother had taken the late shift at the BP station up the road. Sometimes she left late enough for Isaac to see her on the way home from school, but usually he only saw her in the mornings. She always stayed up late after her shift to have breakfast ready for him when he woke up. He didn't mind being alone; it gave him time to do his homework in a quiet house, and it meant that he had standing permission to visit friends after school.

When the words in his textbook began to blur together, he pushed back from his desk and pressed the balls of his hands to his eyes. After pausing to stretch, he scraped his chair backwards and made his way into the kitchen. He took a Coke from the fridge, and when he let the door fall shut, he jumped at the sight of a man standing in the doorway to the living room and stumbled backwards in surprise.

"Hoooly buckets!" the boy shouted, barely catching himself before cursing and fumbling to keep his soda can in his hands. The man in front of him stood almost as tall as the door frame, with a heavy cloth robe draped around his broad shoulders. Behind him, massive wings of silvery white spread to fill the room, casting a soft glow on his russet brown skin.

"I didn't mean to startle you, Isaac," the man said. His voice was gentle and warm, but Isaac didn't feel very relaxed as he looked at the stranger in his kitchen. Dark eyes were fixed on the boy's face, and his stare made Isaac tremble. Without thinking, Isaac sank to his knees, his Coke rolling away from him, forgotten as his hands went slack at his sides. He wanted to speak, but he didn't seem to have any air in his lungs.

"Be not afraid, child," the angel said as he took a small step forward, bare feet padding on the tile floor. "I am Barachiel, blessed by the Lord my Father, and I have come to give you an important mission."

"A...a mission?" Isaac whispered through a tight throat. All the hairs on his arms and the back of his neck stood up as though there was electricity in the air, but he didn't dare move to rub the tingling from his skin.

"A cambion has come, Isaac Mitchell," the angel said grimly. "The unholy child of a devil and a human woman. They are a grave danger to the balance of this world, and I need your help in making certain that he does not bring ruin to mankind."

"My help?" the boy squeaked. "What can I do that you can't do?"

"We are forbidden to interfere directly. The creature is still part human, and thus must be allowed to make his own choice. He may be a force for evil—or not. We would ask that you turn him to the path of righteousness. Should that be your choice," the angel added with a slight bow of his head.

Isaac's head spun. He tried to look up into the angel's dark eyes and felt a wash of heat on his face that swayed him on the spot. The man knelt in front of him and put a large, comforting hand on his shoulder, soft wings circling them in a faint light.

"You are not alone, Isaac," he assured him.

"But why me? I don't know how to...how am I supposed to help a...a demon? I'm just one person."

"So said Moses," the angel replied with a gentle smile, "and you are tasked with showing compassion and friendship to a teenage boy, not with toppling a pharaoh."

A quiet laugh escaped the boy despite himself. "I...of course I will. I'll do everything I can."

Barachiel rose and stepped back from him. "The boy's name is Caleb Durant," he said. "He will need your help if he is to be turned from his dark path, but he is as much human as he is devil. You must remind him."

Isaac's eyes widened. "Caleb?" he whispered.

"You may reveal this mission to no one save the boy himself, and then only if you must; if the truth is brought to light, and he senses violence, he may retaliate. But if you need me, you need only call. I will be here to aid you, as I can. Go with God, Isaac Mitchell," the angel said gently, and then in a bright flash of white, he was gone, leaving the boy to shiver on his kitchen floor and wipe the rising tears from his eyes.

Barachiel slumped back onto Andras's bed with his arm slung over his face to hide his eyes, though a smile touched his lips as he felt the demon's brief kiss.

"Laid it on a little thick, didn't you?" Andras chuckled.

The angel lifted his arm to peek up at him, then sighed and let his hand drop to the mattress. "He's a Baptist from Alabama. I showed him what he expected to see."

Andras barked out a laugh. "Then you should have been white."

Barachiel snorted and turned to nuzzle the other man's shoulder. "Now, you aren't allowed to cheat, you know."

"Cheat? How am I supposed to cheat?"

"Please. We've met." He sat up on his elbow to look into his lover's innocent face. "You have to let Caleb make his own choice."

"He will make his own choice," the demon assured him. "But you know I can't have him making uninformed decisions."

"Andras—"

"Relax, B." He ran a hand down the angel's chest and deftly unfastened the jeans that had replaced his robes as soon as he returned. Barachiel hissed softly as the demon's lips brushed his hip. "You've started the game; now wait and see how it goes. I can take your mind off of it," he promised, and he smiled as Barachiel's hand fisted preemptively in his hair.

3

In the morning, Andras let himself into Caleb's room bright and early and pulled open the curtains by his bed, shining the morning light onto the teenager's face. Caleb winced and groaned in protest as he pulled the blanket over his head, but Andras gave a sharp clap near his ear that jarred him awake.

"No rest for the wicked, Caleb," he said cheerily.

"Aren't demons creatures of the night?" he grumbled as he sat up.

"Demons are creatures of opportunity," Andras clarified. "And right now you have the opportunity to be driven to school instead of being made to walk, you lucky perisher."

"Great. Do demons get to shower first?"

"Demons are above such earthly concerns, but allowances are made for sweaty teenage boys. Get ready."

Caleb waited for Andras to leave the room, and then he climbed out of bed and stumbled his way into the shower. He scrubbed his face and body quickly, knowing from experience that Andras would come right in to hurry him up if he took too long. When he was dressed, he went downstairs and accepted the bagel Andras had waiting for him, and he let his mother kiss his cheek on his way out the door. He climbed into the passenger seat of Andras's Aston, the car creaking under his disproportionate weight, and munched on his bagel while the low-slung car lurched down the dirt driveway.

At school, Caleb climbed out of Andras's car as yesterday, but today he was early enough to see the groups of students standing around chatting on the lawn outside. He walked by them on his way to the front door, ignoring the few passing looks he got along the way, and he reached for the handle fully prepared to sit alone in homeroom and listen to music until the bell rang. When he heard someone call his name, he stopped with his hand on the door and let out a long sigh through his nose. He looked over to see Isaac approaching him, though there was something different about the boy's smile. He was fidgeting with the hem of his shirt as he stopped in front of Caleb.

"Good morning," he offered cheerfully, but Caleb could see something falter in his face as their eyes met. "Are you...settling in? At your place?"

"I guess," Caleb shrugged.

"Good," he answered with an awkward smile, and for a moment the two of them stood without speaking. Caleb was about to open the door and go inside anyway when Isaac took a step closer to him. "Hey, so I meant to get your phone number," he said in a rush. "You know, in case you wanted to hang out, or...text. You do live right next to me, pretty much, so I thought you should have my number too, in case you got...lonely?"

Caleb ticked an eyebrow at him. "You're being weird," he said bluntly, and he pulled open the door and stepped into the hallway, leaving Isaac to trot after him with both hands clutching the straps of his backpack.

"I—I'm just trying to be friendly," Isaac insisted. He walked beside Caleb down the short hall toward homeroom. "Everyone should have someone they can call a friend, and you must have left all yours back in Chicago, right?"

Caleb slid into his seat without answering, but he watched the boy next to him as he frowned and fumbled awkwardly with his backpack. Something had changed between yesterday and this morning. Isaac's brow was knit with concern, and he worried his bottom lip with his teeth while he tried to avoid Caleb's gaze. When his grey eyes finally peeked up and found Caleb still staring at him, he seemed almost flustered.

"Well I just wanted to offer," he said, defending himself against an argument Caleb hadn't made. "So that we can get to know each other. You don't seem like much the talking sort, so I thought you might like it better to text."

Caleb glanced over his shoulder as other students began to file into the room, and he snorted out a soft chuckle at the hesitant look on Isaac's face. "Sure," he said, and he scribbled his number down on a scrap of paper from his bag and slid it onto Isaac's desk. Caleb had seen this sort of behavior before, but he hadn't expected it from the sweet blond Baptist. The nervousness, the sudden push to "get to know each other" in the vaguest possible way. To protect yourself. There was a chance he was misreading it, he supposed, but he suspected he knew what was really on the other boy's mind. He almost felt sorry for him, out here in the boonies. In Chicago, there had been no shortage of other boys who had been eager to get closer, but here in Alabama, the choices must have been much slimmer. Caleb might have been the first opportunity Isaac saw that wasn't likely to end in a beating.

"Text me whenever, I guess," he said as Isaac fingered the slip of paper he'd been given.

"Thanks." Isaac beamed as he dug his phone from his backpack, hiding the screen under his desk as he sent Caleb a simple smiley as a test. Caleb felt his phone vibrate in his pocket. "That'll be me," Isaac smiled.

"Great."

They had to turn their attention to the front of the room as the bell rang. Isaac walked with Caleb in between classes and sat beside him at the lunch table, just like he had the day before, chatting about this and that and asking about life back in "the big city." Caleb gave him some of the banal answers he was clearly looking for, but Isaac seemed to be growing more and more tense as the day went on. When the final bell of the day sounded, releasing the students en masse onto the front lawn of the school, Isaac stopped Caleb with a firm grip on his bag before he could reach the waiting car.

"Hey," the boy started anxiously, taking his time looking up into Caleb's dark eyes. "So, listen. Caleb," he added purposefully, seeming to want to reassure both of them who he was talking to. "I'm...really struggling in Calculus. Do you think you could come over today and help me?"

Caleb stared at him for a beat before answering. There it was. "You want me to come over. So we can study together."

"Well, yeah. Friends help each other out, don't they?"

"And what makes you think I'm any better at Calculus than you are?" Caleb chuckled, enjoying the slight flush that appeared in the other boy's cheeks.

"Just...you know, even if you're not, if there are two of us, it's easier, right?"

"Uh-huh." Caleb paused to consider, tilting his head as he studied Isaac's waiting face. He was a little cute, in a bumpkin sort of a way. He had a delicate face, and his pale eyes were open and innocent. Not normally Caleb's type, but cute. It could be a fun way to spend the afternoon. "Sure," he agreed, and Isaac's face lit up.

"Great!" he said. "I'll, uh...give me a little bit to get home, okay? Mine's the house third from the main road on Hills Avenue, right by you. Will you come by at four?"

"Sure," Caleb answered as he moved toward the car, but Isaac's hand on his bag stopped him.

"Caleb, you'll...really come, right?"

A slight smirk quirked the edge of Caleb's lips. "I'll see you at four." He pulled away and climbed into the passenger side of Andras's car, watching Isaac rush away to his bus in the rear view mirror.

"You really did make a friend," Andras said as he started the car.

"He's persistent. I'm going over today."

"Oh, really?" The demon chuckled and revved the engine as he pulled out of the school parking lot. "Getting some Bible study in?"

"Something like that."

"Well, you know what I always say; practice safe sermons, Caleb."

"You're a riot."

"Should I drop you off?"

"I'll walk."

Andras let Caleb out of the car at the bottom of their long driveway. "Be good or don't get caught," he called through the open window as Caleb slammed the door shut behind him. Caleb stood to listen to the grinding of tires through the gravel at the end of the drive while he lit a cigarette from his backpack. He could already see Isaac's street. He wondered what the chances were that Isaac's parents would be home when he arrived. Just on the way out, maybe; long enough to introduce him and avoid suspicion. Caleb had played this game before. He'd never held onto anything like a boyfriend for very long, but he knew that he was attractive, and he knew how to give people what they wanted. That was usually enough.

He left a cloud of smoke in his wake as he began to walk, shifting his bag on his shoulder as he kicked a stone along the road with him. By the time he reached Isaac's house, it was almost four o'clock, so he dropped what was left of his cigarette and snuffed it with his shoe before approaching the door. It looked like a very average house on a very average little street. A small porch, a garage, and a screen door that probably squeaked. Exactly the sort of place he expected Isaac to live. He rang the doorbell and waited. He could practically hear Isaac's heartbeat on the other side of the door, feel the trembling in his hands as he reached for the doorknob. Maybe he really could hear it. He was still feeling out this whole demon-powers thing.

Isaac opened the door with a wide smile and a look of slight relief on his face. "You came," he said.

"Why so doubtful?" Caleb moved forward when Isaac stepped aside to let him in, and he dropped his bag on the floor near the sofa. The house was simple and homey, with a wooden cross over the entertainment center and a collection of childlike porcelain angels on a shelf.

"I—I wasn't, I just...I'm really happy you came," he said more softly, and he hesitated a moment before he remembered to shut the door. "I feel like...it's important that I get to know you."

"As a study buddy, right?" Caleb asked with a faint smirk, tucking his thumbs into his jean pockets as he turned to face the other boy.

"As a friend," Isaac clarified. He sat down on the couch behind the coffee table where he'd already laid out his textbook and notes, and Caleb sat down closer to him than was necessary.

"Sure," he said. "So your parents aren't home?"

Isaac shook his head, seeming like he was torn between scooting further away and offending his guest. "They both work late. I'm usually here by myself of an evening. Oh!" He jumped back up to his feet. "I didn't offer you anything. You want a drink, or I have some chips and stuff...?"

"If you're going anyway."

"Okay," he grinned. "Just a sec. You make yourself at home, now." He scampered off into the kitchen and left Caleb for just long enough to retrieve a couple of Cokes. He offered one to his guest and sat down again with a bit more space between them. "So anyway, this stuff from today..." Isaac bent over the coffee table and flipped through his textbook in search of the right page. Caleb watched him with mild amusement while he rattled off a quick recap of the day's lesson, spinning a pen in his fingers.

"Shouldn't we be in your room?" Caleb interrupted, and Isaac looked up with a start.

"Uh. Well, I mean, it's a bit of a mess, and I didn't know if you'd want to..."

"I want to," he said, leaning his elbows on his knees to look into the other boy's pale eyes. "Show me your room."

Isaac chewed the corner of his bottom lip for just a moment before he nodded. He let out a soft laugh to hide his nervousness. "I warned you though, it's a mess."

"That's fine."

Caleb followed Isaac down a short hallway and through the open bedroom door, waiting while he scooped up a small pile of dirty clothes and threw them into the hamper. Isaac's room was just as average as the rest of the house. It looked like a photo from some sort of All-American magazine. The bed was made, he had a few books on his small desk, and the shelf beside his bed held picture frames of friends on camping trips next to a baseball mitt and a trophy. There was even a pennant for the Atlanta Braves pinned to the wall.

"Well, this is it," Isaac said awkwardly as he gestured around the room.

"It suits you," Caleb answered, and he stepped closer to the other boy, positive now that he could hear his heartbeat. It grew faster as Caleb drew near to him, and he could see the faint, nervous hitch in Isaac's chest as they stood almost nose to nose. Caleb was slightly taller, which made it easy to bend down and cover Isaac's lips with his own. He felt every muscle in the boy's body tense, and he laid a hand against the side of Isaac's neck, fingertips brushing the soft hair at the back of his head. For just a moment, Isaac only trembled without moving, but when Caleb opened his mouth to him and pressed closer, the boy's hands shot up between them, and he pushed himself away so hard that he stumbled and had to catch himself on the edge of the mattress.

"What—" he started, but then he didn't seem to know where to go. "What are you—why would you—what—"

"Isn't this why I'm here?" Caleb chuckled, and Isaac retreated with a scrambling backwards step as he approached.

"Wh—why would...*this* be why you're here?!"

"You invited me over to study, Isaac. Just us. Alone. For a subject you didn't even think I was good at."

"But—we're both boys," Isaac pointed out, almost shouting, as though no further explanation was required.

Caleb paused, and he watched Isaac catch his breath with a furrowed brow. This wasn't how this was supposed to go. Isaac was supposed to be timid and shy, but with a longing, secret, lusty side. Caleb was supposed to show him the ropes, and they would have a few weeks of fooling around before Isaac got tired of his detached nature and moved on. That was how this always went.

"Then what the hell did you invite me over for?" he growled, not sure if he was more irritated by the loss of opportunity or his complete failure to comprehend the situation correctly.

"To study!" Isaac countered. "Jiminy Crickets, Caleb, I just want to be your friend!" But something in his voice betrayed him. Caleb frowned at him and took a step closer, trapping Isaac against his dresser drawers with a hand on either side of him. Isaac tried to push his arm to move away, but Caleb was like stone, hard and immovable.

"Then why were you afraid?" he pressed. Isaac looked up at him with wide eyes, and Caleb heard the racing rhythm of the other boy's heart. "I can smell it on you. What happened yesterday that made you afraid of me this morning?"

"Be strong in the Lord, and in the power of his might," Isaac murmured with his eyes lowered, his hands defensively between them but not quite willing to touch the other boy. "Put on the whole armor of God, that ye may be able to stand against the wiles of the devil—"

"Are you—are you praying?" Caleb asked, mild distaste in his voice. "For fuck's sake, Isaac." He sighed and pushed away from the dresser, allowing the boy to move. "What do you think I'm going to do?"

The blond took a few slow, deep breaths before opening his eyes again. "I'm sorry," he said, and Caleb hesitated at the sincerity on his face. "You...startled me, is all. I just want to get to know you, to be your friend, but you seem so...aloof, so I was...nervous, I guess. I didn't mean to—to shout at you. I just wasn't expecting—*that*," he said pointedly, as though afraid to say out loud that the other boy had kissed him.

"I'm not a crazy rapist or something," Caleb grumbled. "I thought you were into it."

"And you tasted like cigarettes," Isaac barely whispered with a hesitant frown on his face.

"Really? That's what you're taking away from this?" Caleb tilted his head as he looked at the blond. "So just...friends, then," he said skeptically. "You want to be friends with me. Even though we have nothing in common, and I've been nothing but rude to you since we met. And now I've driven you to prayer."

"I'm sorry. I just—you know, I've never done anything like that, so all of a sudden, and then it being another boy, which I never even—"

"Never done anything like what, kiss? You're joking, right?"

A flush of embarrassment reddened Isaac's cheeks. "This isn't the big city," he said defensively. "And anyway, I'm—it's not right, before marriage." He nervously fingered the ring on his left hand, and Caleb could read the words for the first time—True Love Waits.

"Wow," Caleb said, actually letting out a soft laugh as he ran a hand through his dark, messy hair. He had completely misread the situation. But that meant that Isaac really was interested in him. As a person. He was determined to be friends with the new boy, even though the new boy was brusque and standoffish and showed no interest whatsoever in being his friend in return. Isaac had friends already—he had introduced Caleb to quite a few people over the last two days and could barely stop talking about his church youth group—but for some reason was dead set on getting a new one. "Why me?" he asked after a long moment.

Isaac paused, and he let out a quiet sigh and smiled as he looked up into Caleb's face. "You say we don't have anything in common, but that isn't true. We have things in common. We may not know what they are yet, but even if it turns out we don't like any of the same things or have any of the same hobbies..." He shrugged. "It doesn't mean we can't be friends. Friends have experiences together, and they empathize with each other, and they care about each other. They can figure out Calculus together if neither of them are good at it," he added with a chuckle. "And Caleb, you...you just seem to me like someone who's in need of a friend."

"You don't know anything about me," the boy countered.

"Isn't that what I'm trying to fix?"

Caleb stared at him for a while, but Isaac only smiled and waited. There was a catch. There had to be a catch. Caleb had had friends back in Chicago, but they were school friends—people he had classes with who talked music with him or invited him to parties. He had known quite a few people, some even by name, but none of them had known him. He'd never confided in anyone. He'd used their friendliness to get free beer at parties, and he'd used their attraction to him to occupy his nights. That was as close as he got. He didn't have any plans to change now, especially not for the church-going blond.

"Whatever," he said at last. "If you just want to study, I'm going home."

"Oh. O-Okay," Isaac said. "Well, thanks for coming anyway, and sorry you...got the wrong idea," he finished in a rush. He followed as Caleb walked back to the front door and scooped up his bag along the way. "I'll see you tomorrow, okay?" he called out the door at the other boy's back and waved even though Caleb didn't turn to look. When he reached the end of the street, Isaac shut the door and leaned his back against it with his fingers laced over his mouth and his eyes shut tight.

4

Caleb left his bag on the floor by the sofa and went to forage in the kitchen for dinner. He found his mother sitting quietly at the breakfast table with a large book propped open in front of her, its pages littered with scratchy symbols and letters Caleb didn't recognize. She looked up at him with a bright smile as he approached. His mother was thin, with prominent collarbones and sharp cheeks hidden by her long mess of curly black hair. Her eyes looked sunken as she smiled up at her son, and she laid both hands on the open book.

"Oh, Caleb," she said in her soft, wispy voice, "look at what your uncle has given me. Isn't it beautiful?"

"What is it?"

"He says that I can use it to talk to your father," she answered with her fingers curling affectionately over the pages. "Isn't that wonderful?"

Caleb frowned and glanced over his shoulder as Andras padded in wearing nothing but dark green pajama pants, but the demon wasn't concerned by the boy's glare. He breezed by the table and took a can of beer from the refrigerator, and he popped it open and took a long drink before even seeming to notice Caleb's stare.

"What?"

"What is this?" Caleb asked, tapping the open book with one finger. "Why are you giving her this shit?"

Andras shrugged one shoulder. "It's harmless."

"Harmless? Summoning demons is harmless now."

"As harmless as sleeping down the hall from one for the last seventeen years. You can help her draw the circle, if you're so nervous about it." He leaned past Caleb to catch the woman's eye. "Don't you listen to him, Marian; you just do your reading and let me know when you're ready, hm? Caleb and I will make sure it goes smoothly, won't we, Caleb?" The demon slung an arm around the boy's shoulders and led him from the room. "Let's go talk about it right now, shall we?"

"Thank you both," she called out after them, and Caleb frowned up at his guardian as they passed into the living room.

"She's not going to hurt herself," Andras assured him once they were out of earshot.

Caleb tried to move out from underneath the demon's arm, but Andras leaned against him relentlessly. "Who is it she's going to try to talk to, exactly? Does she even know?"

"Oh, well she'll try to go all the way to the top, of course. She thinks you're straight from the big S, after all. There isn't an evocation circle in the world that could protect her if he decided to show up. Luckily, he doesn't really make house calls."

"So why not tell her the truth? Why let her keep believing that? Why make me sit through birthday seances and candlelit ouija boards? Why not tell me who it is?" He looked up into the demon's face with a curled lip. "It's not just you, is it? Please tell me it's not you."

"You should be so lucky," Andras chuckled, and he drained his can and left it balanced on Caleb's head as he finally pulled away. The boy snatched the empty can before it could clatter to the floor. "If you were mine, you wouldn't be so sullen and mopey." He smiled at Caleb's faint scowl. "See? Like that. How did your study date go, by the way? I expected you home much later."

"More study-oriented than anticipated," Caleb muttered, and he dropped down onto the sofa with his feet on the coffee table. Nobah padded up to lay its head on his knee, so Caleb sighed and gave it a scratch behind its massive ears.

Andras grinned and perched himself on the arm of the couch with his elbows on his knees. "How disappointing. You'll have to wait more than a day to get laid in your new town; poor little lamb. Wasn't this the overly-cheery boy who wanted you to go to church? Does your gaydar need calibrating?"

"He was flirting," Caleb insisted. He frowned down at his hands in his lap, remembering Isaac's wide grey eyes and the shine of his kiss on the other boy's parted lips. He had objected, but Caleb had felt the faint shiver in the skin under his fingers. To his surprise, he found himself wanting to feel it again.

"Well, it's a repressive sort of a town, I suppose," Andras chuckled. "So why not show him a good time?"

Caleb shook his head. "He literally started praying when I made a move. He's got one of those purity rings, even. Maybe a chastity belt. Who knows?"

"Is that so?" Andras mused. "That sounds like a challenge to me. Maybe he just doesn't know what he's missing." He leaned his chin onto his folded arms when Caleb looked at him uncertainly. "You want to get more in touch with your father's side of the family, don't you? So do what we do. Corrupt him," the demon finished with a sly smile curling his lips.

Caleb could picture the timid look on Isaac's face, his flushed cheeks, eyes squeezed shut as he panted weak protestations. The thought sent a jolt to the pit of his stomach, and he swallowed without looking back up at his guardian.

"Maybe you'll even get a deal out of it," Andras shrugged. "Wouldn't that be fun? Making a deal for a boy like that—I'm all ashiver just thinking about it."

Caleb's hands tightened in his lap. When he was thirteen, Andras had taken him out every night for weeks in search of what he had called "the right one." He had forced Caleb to practice his coercion, talk to strangers, and try to read them for what they truly wanted. When Caleb had finally found the one, when he had offered the man the fame and riches that he wanted and felt the grip of his handshake, the whole world had eased to a stop. Caleb's blood went cold and quiet, and his heartbeat slowed to a steady, distant thump in his chest. It was the closest he had ever come to feeling that calm, empty peace he'd known as a child. With life and breath and heartbeat had come complications like hunger, emotion, lust, and frustration. He had three more under his belt now. He wanted to find that cold quiet again. He could get Isaac to give it to him.

"Maybe," he mumbled while Andras watched him, and he rose and jogged up the stairs to his bedroom, thoughts of dinner forgotten. He shut the door behind him and sat down on his bed, pulling his phone from his pocket to turn it in his hand. When he turned on the screen, he could see the notification from Isaac's text that morning, the little yellow smile taunting him.

Caleb fell onto his back on the mattress with his phone held above him and stared up at the blinking reply cursor. There would be something Isaac wanted. He could play nice until he found out what it was. He wet his lips and imagined he could still taste the other boy there, trembling. Caleb knew at least one thing that Isaac wanted, even if the boy couldn't admit it himself.

Let's be friends, he typed. He dropped the phone onto his stomach and waited until it vibrated against his belly.

Of course! I'm still doing that Calculus homework. Are you having any luck?

Caleb turned over onto his side to look out the window by his bed, lifting himself up on his elbow. He could distantly see Isaac's street through the thin trees, and if he squinted, he could make out the light in the boy's window. He glanced down at his phone.

I'm distracted, he answered.

By what?

By you.

Caleb waited, imagining the flush of color on Isaac's cheeks, maybe the soft stammer as he thought of how to reply. After a long delay, Caleb's phone buzzed again.

I really am sorry. You should come to the campfire this weekend! Everyone will be there, and maybe you can get to know some of the girls. It might take your mind off this stuff.

What stuff? A faint smirk twitched at the corner of Caleb's lips.

All that this afternoon.

You mean kissing you? It's hard to stop thinking about it.

Please don't say stuff like that.

Friends are honest with each other, right? If we're going to be friends, it's only fair to tell you that I think you're cute. I'm hard just thinking about your lips. A little lie, but one that was easily becoming the truth as Caleb pictured Isaac staring down at his phone, that pink bottom lip caught in his worrying teeth. His hand had drifted to the hem of his shirt by the time the phone vibrated in reply.

OMGsh Caleb, please stop! I don't judge you for having those thoughts, but I'm not comfortable with you saying those things to me.

Caleb sighed and laid on his back, letting his fingertips brush over his stomach and the buckle of his belt. *Better get back to your homework then, he typed back with his free hand. I'll be here in bed thinking sinful thoughts.*

He set aside the phone, not expecting it to sound again, and he huffed out a small snort of frustration as he unfastened his belt buckle. Just as his hand slipped beneath the waist of his jeans, his breath hitching softly in anticipation, the phone vibrated on his nightstand. He paused and stared at it for a moment before relenting and unlocking the screen again.

I'm praying for you.

Caleb let out a humorless laugh and dropped the phone on the mattress beside him, then let his arm drape harmlessly across his stomach. What a moment ruiner. He almost got up, but as he sat on the bed, he frowned at the thought of Isaac's troubled face. He picked up his phone and tapped out another quick message.

Nobody tries this hard to be friends.

He tossed the phone onto his blanket and stood to stretch, telling himself he wasn't going to talk to the boy anymore, but when the notification chimed, he leaned to peer at the screen.

I have a good feeling about you.

Caleb picked up the phone and stared down at the message for a while, chewing the corner of his mouth as he frowned. It was bullshit. He wanted something. Everybody wanted something. He dropped the phone on the table by his bed and didn't reply.

A single knock sounded on his door before Andras opened it and leaned in to peer at him. "I thought I heard you moping up here."

"How do you hear someone mope?"

"Years of practice," Andras answered dryly. "Since you seem to have a free evening, why don't we have a little training exercise?" he suggested. "Might give you a bit of a jump start on your little church boy."

"What kind of training?"

"The best kind. We'll go into the city. Well, if Birmingham counts. Still. More city than this."

"Right now?"

"Why, is it past your bedtime? It isn't even dark. I'll have you back for school in the morning, if you're worried about your attendance ribbon."

"Fuck off," he grumbled, but then he gave a small shrug. "Sure, I guess."

"Excellent. Get in the car."

Caleb followed the demon down the stairs and out the front door, waiting for the doors to unlock before he dropped into the low car. He bounced in the seat as it struggled with the dirt driveway.

"You didn't consider downgrading a little when you decided to buy a house at the top of a wooded hill?" Caleb asked.

Andras snorted and slipped his sunglasses on as they pulled onto the road. "With some things in life, Caleb, you just don't settle. Do I look like I belong in a minivan?"

"Are those the only options?"

"What would you like to do today?" the demon asked, pausing to check for traffic that didn't exist before he turned the car onto the highway. "You're still such a little fledgling; you need practice at just about everything."

"Oh, hey, I have an idea," Caleb started with mock enthusiasm, "why don't you tell my dad that if it's so important I learn this shit, he should come and teach me himself?"

"Is that what we're going to do today? We're going to be snotty?" The demon glanced at him out of the corner of his eye. "Why so concerned about your father lately, anyway? I thought you didn't care who he was."

"I don't," he snapped back. "It's just shitty what he did to mom. Why can't you let her talk to him? Why wouldn't he show up? Why's he so goddamn important? What did he even knock mom up for if he didn't want me?"

"Oh, such a sad story," Andras said in a pitiful tone. "Poor Caleb got to grow up with a mother who loves him and a supernaturally powerful guardian; he got everything he ever wanted and never suffered from cold nor hunger nor lack of iPhone. Don't try to blame your father for you spending the last two years in a blur of alcohol and cheap sex."

Caleb slouched in his seat and stared out the windshield with a spiteful look.

Andras sighed. "Look. You really want to stick it to your father? Forget about him. Show him he doesn't matter to you. You are a powerful creature in your own right, Caleb, even if you haven't come fully into your own yet. You don't need your father's approval to make an impact on this world—or the one below, for that matter. If you wished it, if you applied yourself, you could mold the world around you to your liking, and there's not a thing in heaven or earth that could stop you." He slowed the car to take the turn onto the next stretch of highway and glanced sidelong at the boy beside him. "So, I'll ask you again—what do you want to do today?"

Caleb watched him with a stern frown for a moment. Isaac was just like everyone else. There would be something he wanted. Caleb just had to find the right angle. "Show me how to be like you."

Andras's lips curled into a smile. "Good boy." He pressed a little harder on the accelerator.

As they drove into Birmingham, Caleb watched the streets fill up through the car window. The scenery went from dirt and thick trees to concrete and steel, and Caleb felt slightly more at home. Birmingham wasn't Chicago, but it was reassuring to be someplace busy, where he could walk down the street or go into a store and reasonably expect to be left alone.

"Now, Caleb," Andras started once they were surrounded by buildings instead of foliage, "if you want to be more powerful, you're going to need to do better than three. How would you like to make a deal today?"

The boy's skin shuddered pleasantly at the thought, but he tried not to let the demon see. "I'll try."

"And how do you expect to find someone willing to make such a deal?" He waited for a response, but Caleb only shrugged, so he went on. "You know the basics. Humans are complex animals, but they're also base." Andras counted off on his fingers as he listed, "They want food, money, fame, sex. They want to get high, they want revenge. They're impulsive and emotional, but even so, there exist only a certain number of scenarios in which a human is going to be willing to trade their soul to you. You got lucky with your first one. He wasn't a believer. They're easier to convince, since they don't really think they're giving anything away. That second one, the guy with the, ah...fantasy, or whatever—it's your call how often you want to do things like that. I find it a bit sordid, personally."

"Really? *I'm* sordid?"

"It's your body. It's fairly hardy, and you clearly aren't very concerned with what happens to it, so carry on as you please."

Caleb scowled out the window. Humans wanted sex, and he had given it once before in the name of a deal—a desperate middle-aged man who leered at him on the street had offered him money for a good time. Caleb hadn't wanted his money, but he had convinced him to give something far more precious in exchange. It wasn't something he planned to make a habit of, but it didn't seem like something Andras was likely to let him forget, either.

"Anyway," the demon went on with a pointed clearing of his throat, "what you really ought to be looking for—what you really want—is not someone greedy or lecherous or what-have-you. You want someone in need. Desperation drives humans to terrible, rash things—which is exactly the sort of thing you want them to do, of course."

"That's great," Caleb scoffed, "but even Birmingham has a shit ton of people in it. Am I supposed to just introduce myself to everyone on the street and hope I find the one willing to be the ultimate sellout?"

"That's today's lesson," Andras answered. "Do you think demons are such social creatures that we want to spend all our time chatting with various flavors of unfortunate? Of course not. The right one is easy to find when you know what to look for. Well, feel for would be more appropriate, really."

"Feel for?"

Andras turned to him as they pulled up to a stoplight. "They want you as much as you want them, Caleb. Their beating hearts ache for someone to relieve their suffering—someone to show up and solve all their problems, just like that," he said, snapping his fingers for emphasis. "They want you to be that person for them. They're calling for you, whether they realize it or not. Shut your eyes, and see if you can hear them."

Caleb stared at him skeptically for a moment, but Andras nodded at him, so he shut his eyes. He had no idea what he was supposed to be listening for. He could hear the engine, the heavy thump of bass from another car nearby, and a sharp honk from the front of the line of traffic, but nothing that sounded very much like desperate hearts in need.

"This is stupid," he muttered without opening his eyes.

"Hush," Andras hissed. "Listen."

Caleb sighed through his nose and tried squeezing his eyes tighter. He heard wind through the landscaped trees along the road. He heard someone calling out on the street, and—something else. It wasn't like hearing it, really. He felt a tug, like a needle and thread pulled through his brain, and as he turned his head, it seemed to get sharper. He thought he could hear a man's quiet sob, but it was distant, like hearing it through water.

"Take a right," he said, and the car shifted under him as Andras obeyed. The pull grew stronger as they drove, and a dark, tight feeling began to build in his gut. He wasn't hearing the crying. Not really. It was desperation he was feeling. The car slowed, and he furrowed his brow.

"Here?" Andras asked quietly, but Caleb shook his head.

"Keep going."

They drove a little farther, until the thread pulling Caleb felt about to snap, and he reached out to put a hand on Andras's arm. "Here. Stop here."

"Oh, this is almost cheating," Andras chuckled as Caleb opened his eyes.

He craned his neck to look out the window. They were outside a complex of tall, white concrete buildings, each one adorned with an enormous metal cross.

"A hospital?" Caleb muttered, and Andras pulled into the parking lot without hesitation.

"Can you think of a more likely place to find people willing to give anything?" He parked the car and pulled off his sunglasses. "Lead the way."

Caleb climbed out of the car with a frown on his face, and they walked into the main building, pretending they belonged there. The tight thread pulling Caleb forward almost seemed to shudder as they approached the elevator, and he could swear he felt a tremor in the wood as he pressed the button for the third floor. The whole building was full of hopelessness, and Caleb swayed slightly on his feet as the low rumbling of pain washed over him from all around them. Everywhere, people were suffering, begging, or praying. Even the nurses who walked the floor held lingering heartaches for their lost patients. But as he turned a corner, the sound of muffled sobbing rang clear in his head. They were getting closer. To what, he didn't know, but the sharp pull in his brain turned his head as they walked the halls like a bit in a horse's mouth. A nurse tried to stop them as they went, asking them what room they were looking for and who they were there to see.

Caleb glanced back at Andras, but the demon didn't seem inclined to answer, so Caleb said, "I think it's time for your lunch break." He knew the tingling in his throat as he put force behind his words, and the nurse suddenly seemed to look past him, muttering something about the cafeteria closing as she brushed by them.

"Nicely done," Andras chuckled.

They reached a long hallway of closed doors, and as Caleb walked, he let his hand brush each metal door and the wall between them, waiting for the tug that would tell him which door he wanted. When his fingers touched a door near the far end of the hall, he stopped and pressed his palm against it. His head ached as if someone had plucked the thread pulling him. Without thinking, he turned the handle and stepped into the room.

Inside, a middle-aged man lay in the reclined bed with his head turned toward the far window. He was wearing a pale blue hospital gown, but a thick white blanket covered him up to his waist, where a tube ran out to a fluid-filled bag hung from the side of the bed. He turned to look at them as the door opened, and his brow furrowed in confusion.

"Who are you?"

Andras hung back near the door while Caleb approached the bed. "I think I can help you," he said. The man frowned up at him, clearly skeptical. Caleb looked down at the man's legs under the blanket, and he reached out to touch his knee, feeling the dead weight and useless pulse. "Paralyzed?" He knew without the man having to answer. "An accident, but not really," he murmured. He could almost see it happen, but it was blurry and disjointed, like trying to remember a dream.

"How did you know that?" he demanded, but he didn't move to brush Caleb's hand away.

"To protect them?"

The man froze, and when Caleb locked eyes with him, he could see everything. The man standing in his foreman's office, tightening his fists as he listened to platitudes about layoffs and the economy, the foreman refusing to meet his gaze. Searching on websites, attending job fairs—but he'd never done anything but factory work. There weren't enough jobs for people like him. The desperation, the shouting arguments with his wife while four frightened little faces watched and listened from the doorway. Finally, the hopeless revelation, and the speeding car honking and slamming its breaks too late to keep from hitting him. Mostly because he didn't move.

"You wanted them to claim your life insurance," Caleb said, and the man's stern face broke into a pained grimace.

"I...I did," he admitted with a rough intake of breath. "And now this...I'll never find work now. And all the medical bills—I've made things even worse." He finally lowered his head to hide his sob behind one calloused hand.

"You want them taken care of."

"Of course I do," the man sighed.

"I can take care of them," Caleb said, and the man looked up at him and reached to grasp his hand. For a while, they only stared at each other, the man seeming to search Caleb's face.

"You...you can, can't you?" he said at last. "Who are you?"

A chill ran down Caleb's spine as though he'd been doused in ice water. Maybe it was the feeling of this place, or the pleading hope of the man in front of him, but a gnawing hunger had begun to grow in his belly that he couldn't ignore. Caleb was human, wasn't he? He could feel his heart beating; he still needed to breathe. But he knew what he would get in return if he promised this man peace of mind, and he ached for it.

"It doesn't matter who I am," he said softly. "You want them to live happily, don't you?"

"Of course."

"So much that you would die for them."

"I would. I tried," the man said, as though defending himself.

Caleb hesitated. The rhythmic thump in his chest was distracting. He wanted it stilled, but he couldn't help the doubt in his mind.

"You want your legs fixed?" he asked. He could practically feel Andras lifting his hands in disbelief, but he didn't look back.

"No," the man said immediately. "We'd never pay off all these bills. If I'd died, they'd have gotten the insurance money, and that would have helped them along...my wife, her family's all dead. She's got no one to help her with me like this. I wish I'd died," he sobbed, releasing Caleb's hand to hide his face.

"Then," Caleb said, his brow knit as he took a step closer to the head of the bed, "why don't you die?" When the man looked up at him, the hunger in Caleb's gut was too much to bear. He was so close. "Your life for their comfort and safety," he murmured.

"Gladly," the man answered.

"Then let me help you." Caleb offered the man his hand and tilted his head slightly to look into his reddened eyes. He hesitated, just for a moment, and his hand shook as he placed it in the boy's, but Caleb squeezed it tightly, and it stilled. Cold rushed over Caleb like a wave, up his hand and into his chest with a sudden thud. His heart slowed almost to a stop, and he shuddered when it finally gave a single beat. He kept breathing, but it almost felt unnecessary. The room around him came into sharp focus, and he relaxed into the calm cold his blood ran through his body. He felt sated, but he knew it was only temporary—even as the man slumped back on his bed, and the beeping of the heart monitor became a solid drone, Caleb could feel his heart working again. The man's hand fell from his grip and dropped limp onto the bed. Caleb could sense him at the back of his mind, twisting and trapped there. He was in Hell, Caleb supposed, whatever that meant, waiting to be used or commanded as soon as the boy learned how.

Andras took him by the shoulder and led him from the room in a slight daze before the nurses could respond to the heart monitor's alarm. "Well done, Caleb," he said, urging the boy along beside him toward the elevator.

5

As they exited the building, Andras kept Caleb steady with one hand. His legs felt weak and slightly wobbly. He followed with an empty, longing feeling in his chest until the demon stopped him by the car with both hands on his arms.

"Don't lose this, Caleb," he said softly. "This is what it means to be one of us. That quiet, that freedom—that's what you're after. You can have it if you take it for your own."

Caleb nodded, but his mind was on Isaac. Caleb had taken souls for selfish reasons before, and it had been nice, but this—that man was sacrificing himself. He thought he was doing good. If Caleb was able to convince someone like Isaac...he shivered at the thought. Andras apparently mistook the shudder for exhaustion, because he opened the car door and eased the boy inside.

"Take it easy," he said. "Delivering on deals is going to be rough on you for a while. Especially 'take care of a family for their whole lives' sorts of deals. Maybe work on nailing down the specifics before you commit in future, hm? Let's get you something to eat."

Caleb didn't answer, but the demon didn't wait. He shut the car door and walked around to get into the driver's seat, then flicked on his lights against the dim twilight and pulled out of the parking lot.

"What do you feel like, hm? I could go for some falafel."

Caleb frowned over at him, the weight of his beating heart still heavy and cumbersome in his chest. "Why do you eat, anyway? If this...this is what you're like, isn't it? This...emptiness. Do you even need to eat?"

"Well, yes, actually. I'm rather a special case. For now, anyway.

This body is temporary."

"Temporary?" Caleb sat up in his seat. "Hold on; are you possessing someone right now? Have you had some poor asshole in there with you my whole life?"

Andras chuckled and patted his own chest with one hand. "I'm all me; not to worry. This body is a joint effort between your father and I. Mostly him, if I'm being fair. Having a truly physical form is difficult. Mostly when our kind shows up on Earth, if humans can see us at all, we're corporeal but largely useless. No substance, you understand? No function. Just a shell that happens to take up space and look like a human, or a lion, or a woman on a dromedary, or whatever."

"A dromedary?"

"A camel. Aren't you in school?" He sighed. "Anyway, this body works. I've been living with humans since well before you were born, and it's just easier if I fit in. Besides, it's usually not possible for us to stay up here for such long periods. This way, I can stick around and keep you company 24/7."

"Before I was born," Caleb repeated with a frown. "So, what, my father planted you here early because he knew he was going to ditch us?"

"Weren't we deciding where to eat?" Andras glanced sidelong at him. "Dinner sounds much better than listening to your filial lamentations. Look here; there's a nice-looking Mediterranean place. We can bring your mother some baklava."

"Whatever," Caleb grumbled, and he stared out the window as Andras drove. He managed to refrain from slamming the door as he got out of the car. He should be used to not getting straight answers out of the demon when it concerned his father. He followed his guardian toward the restaurant entrance, but almost ran into his back when Andras stopped short in front of him.

"What the hell?" he snapped, and Andras paused to look over his shoulder as another voice called out across the parking lot.

"Hello, is that Andras?" the voice shouted, and Andras groaned under his breath.

"Here we fucking go," he muttered. Caleb turned around to find the source of the noise and spotted a man approaching them from the road. He was wearing a trim grey suit with his tie loose around his unbuttoned collar, but his dark hair was tied back in a loose, low bun, and softly curling tendrils fell around his delicate face. His voice had sounded masculine, but as he drew closer, Caleb could only think to describe him as beautiful—but in a distant, fragile way, like antique gold behind museum glass. His skin was a rich amber, and his eyes were large and so brown they almost looked black.

"What are you doing here, Paimon?" Andras sighed, but he accepted the offered handshake.

"You thought you could have your little ward make a deal like that and not attract any attention?" The other demon turned to Caleb with a smile that seemed friendly, but Caleb felt like he could see through it, like there was something menacing hiding behind his teeth. "This is him, isn't it?"

"This is Caleb, yes," Andras answered quickly. "Anyway, we're just grabbing dinner, and then we have a long drive home."

"It's actually a rather short drive, isn't it?" Paimon smiled. "Would you mind company?"

"Actually—"

"Oh, who doesn't like to share a meal with an old friend?" he interrupted before Andras could finish, and he led the way to the door of the restaurant and held it open for them. Caleb followed Andras inside, and they took their place at a booth as the hostess seated them, both of them across the table from Paimon, who sat with his hands folded on the table and a pleasant smile on his lips.

"So, Caleb," the demon began while Andras slouched and opened his menu between them, "how are you coming along with your studies?"

"Fine, I guess. Who exactly are you?"

"Oh, aren't I being rude? Andras hasn't told you about me? Never heard of Paimon?"

"Can't say I have; no."

"Neglecting some parts of his education, aren't you, Andras?" Paimon looked over at him with a slight tilt of his head.

"You think I should have him memorizing lists of demon names?"

The other demon smiled. "Isn't it important for him to know the company he's in?"

Andras frowned and slapped his menu back to the table. "What good is it going to do him before he even knows how to control himself?"

"You want him to be well-rounded, don't you?"

"What's your definition of 'well-rounded?'"

"Well, shouldn't he at least know better than to make a deal without knowing what exactly he's promising?"

Andras sat up in his seat, leaning forward with what seemed like determination. "Would you rather have the job of teaching him?"

"Oh, who am I to question your place?" Paimon asked, the friendly smile never leaving his face.

"Shouldn't you be off tending to your camel?" Andras snorted.

Paimon stared across at him without faltering while Caleb looked between the demons like he was watching a tennis match. "Haven't you left your dog at home?"

"Now you're questioning how I keep my servants?"

"Do you really need to be so defensive?"

"You started it," Andras snapped, but then he pressed his lips together in a frustrated scowl.

"Aha!" Paimon laughed. "Statement."

"Fuck you," the other demon grumbled.

"What the hell just happened?" Caleb asked.

Both demons waited for the approaching waitress to take their orders, though Paimon only asked for a glass of water. When she walked away, the overly pretty stranger smiled blithely at Caleb. "Poor Andras can never resist a game of questions. How many is that to me?"

"I'm not counting," Andras said, but Caleb got the impression the demon knew exactly how many times he'd lost. Were these demons or twelve-year-olds?

"Regardless," Paimon went on, "I came to talk to you, Caleb. You made a deal today; that's important. Did you like it?"

Caleb glanced at Andras, not sure how he should answer.

"It's all right if you aren't sure," Paimon said. "You're still learning. You know, some others your age haven't claimed a single soul at all."

"If you say so. I've never met any others like me."

"Nor are you likely to," the demon mused. "Your guardian has done well, despite my teasing."

"Good to know. Do the others have fathers who passed them off on random demons, too?"

Paimon leaned on his elbows and stared across the table at Caleb. The boy held back his shudder at the blackness in the demon's eyes. There was definitely something different about this one. He wasn't like Andras at all, no matter how much he smiled.

"Quid pro quo, cambion," the demon murmured. "Answer me a question, and I shall answer yours."

"What? What could you possibly want to ask me?" He leaned back as the waitress set plates down in front of him and Andras, leaving Paimon with his ignored glass of water.

"What is making you falter?" he asked simply.

Caleb knew what he was asking. He could sense it. The demon watched him with sharp, empty eyes, like a shark, and the boy shifted in his seat. "I'm not faltering," he said, knowing it was partly a lie. He wanted to know more about what he was and what it meant, but he still had a gnawing of guilt inside him once the rush of cold wore off. "There's just this kid at school who's been super friendly, and it's weirding me out."

Paimon stared at him without blinking for a long while, and then he let out a quiet hum of agreement. "A fair, if evasive, answer. The answer to your question is no."

"No? Just no?"

"No, the other cambions do not have guardians like yours."

"Why not?" Paimon tilted his head with a sly smile, and Caleb sighed. "I don't know if I like this quid pro quo bullshit."

"I think it's enough, don't you?" Andras cut in as he swallowed a mouthful of falafel. "Give the kid a break, Paimon."

"Oh, all right." The demon sat back in the booth. "But I did come to give you a gift. Will you take it?"

"That depends on what it is," Caleb answered skeptically.

Paimon held a hand out over the surface of the table, and without a word, something began to form underneath his palm. It took a moment for Caleb to figure out what was happening, but he quickly recognized a tiny, four-legged skeleton. Pink muscles and tendons stitched themselves to the bones, and then pale skin wove itself to hide the growing organs. Finally, soft grey fur sprouted from the skin, and the eyes filled in black, leaving only pink hairless ears, a tail, and four small feet. As soon as Paimon removed his hand, the fully-formed rat lifted its head and began to sniff around, twitching its whiskers. It immediately clicked across the table to Caleb, who jumped slightly as it latched onto his sleeve and climbed up to settle on his shoulder.

"This is Greedigut," Paimon explained. "He has served many witches and cambions before you, and you will find him loyal."

"Witches?" Caleb chuckled. "Shouldn't he be a cat?" He hissed as the rat nipped at his earlobe. "Hey, no offense; Jesus. What does he...you know, what is he for?"

"A familiar will do pretty much whatever you ask it to," Andras said. "Just experiment. You'll find uses for him, I'm sure. It's a good gift," he added, though he seemed slightly reluctant about it.

"What do you want for it?" Caleb asked, but Paimon shook his head.

"Consider this a favor to your father, not to you." He scooted out of the booth and gave Caleb a small nod. "I'll leave you two to your meal. I'm happy to have met you, Caleb. And it was a pleasure seeing you again, Andras. Give my regards to the other side."

Andras hissed at him as though trying to shut him up, but Paimon smiled, and in the time it took Caleb to shoot his guardian a questioning look, the other demon was gone.

"The other side?"

"He's fucking with me," Andras said unconvincingly. "Don't worry about it. Eat your shawarma."

Caleb frowned and turned his attention to the plate in front of him. He fed the rat on his shoulder little bits of lamb until the waitress returned and let out a small shriek.

"Uh, sir," she said with a hand on her chest, "you can't have your...pet in here."

"We're just leaving," Andras said, and he urged Caleb out of the booth ahead of him.

Caleb waited just outside the door while Andras convinced the waitress to bring him some baklava, and he stared at the little grey rat curled up in his hands. "So?" he asked it, and it poked it head up to wiggle its whiskers at him. "What am I supposed to do with you?" The rat stared at him, but no answer seemed forthcoming. Caleb sighed. "Well, hopefully you're helpful, and not just some way for creepy androgynous demons to spy on me."

He rode home with Andras in silence, the rat nestled in his lap and a box of baklava at his feet. Paimon thought he was faltering. Andras was keeping things from him. He could do better. He could take what he wanted from Isaac.

6

Isaac kept his hands pressed against his eyes the entire bus ride to school the next morning. He was going to have to look Caleb in the face again, and Caleb was probably going to tease him. He had completely panicked during their entire text conversation. He had almost hidden his phone in a drawer and begged the angel to choose someone else. He hadn't expected any of that sort of talk when he had agreed to help Caleb. It was too embarrassing, too confusing, and too—Isaac didn't even know the word. But he couldn't give up. If Caleb thought he was getting to him, he would definitely tease him even worse than before. So the only solution was to rise above. He fisted his hands and thumped them determinedly on his knees as the bus approached the school. Isaac would smile, and he would chat, and he would be the best gosh darn friend that homosexual half-demon could ever hope for.

When the bus squeaked to a stop outside the building, Isaac hooked his backpack over his shoulders and followed the crowd down the aisle. He spotted Caleb shutting his ride's car door as soon as he rounded the corner, his shoulders hunched and his face deadpan as always, and he trotted up to him with a cheerful smile.

"Good morning, Caleb!" he called brightly. "I hope you got the Calculus homework done. I feel like I spent all night doing mine!" He kept the smile on his face as the other boy's dark eyes fell on him, but the same chill ran down his spine that he'd felt every time Caleb had looked at him since he found out the truth. Caleb didn't look very much like a demon, but Isaac knew that the devil came in many shapes. If he had a chance to help what was human in Caleb turn from the darkness, then he had the responsibility to try his very hardest.

"I did most of it," Caleb admitted, and Isaac let out the breath he hadn't realized he'd been holding. That was a normal answer. That was good. Caleb glanced sidelong at him as they walked toward the entrance together. "Can I copy yours? My uncle will be pissed if my grades go to shit so soon."

Isaac hesitated, twisting the straps of his backpack in his hands. "That's cheating, Caleb."

"Come on; it's completion credit bullshit. She's not even going to check the answers."

They sat down in their homeroom seats, and Isaac sighed as he unzipped his bag and dug for the right folder. "Just this one time," he said. "And only if you stop swearing so much."

"Where did you even come from?" Caleb asked with a brief chuckle. He took his own homework from his notebook and leaned his chin in his hand as he copied the other boy's equations. "I've heard the other kids in my classes; it's not like the whole town is Jesus Stepford, USA. What's with you?"

"This is just me," Isaac smiled. "I've been going to church since I can remember, and my parents always expected a lot of me. I didn't always do right; I sure took my share of rapped knuckles when I was little, I'll tell you what," he said with a good-natured laugh. "But my mom and dad are good people. They work hard for me, so I try to do right by them and by the Lord."

"Because he's done so much for you," Caleb snorted.

"He's everything," Isaac countered somberly. "You may not believe, Caleb, but Jesus Christ is alive in my heart, and I know with all my soul that there is Heaven waiting for those who follow Him, and a terrible punishment for those who don't." He lowered his eyes as Caleb turned to look at him. "I know I can come off annoying. But if I seem uptight or stupid to you, it's only because I want so much to live the life the Lord intended for me, full of love and kindness and good work. I don't know if you've ever been to church, but that feeling I get when everyone is singing, and I can feel the Lord's light filling me up inside—there's nothing like it. If I seem pushy, it's because I'm truly afraid for the eternal souls of people who...don't choose to live that way."

"Like me?"

"Well, yes," Isaac shrugged. He thought he saw a slight change in Caleb's eyes, but then the boy frowned and returned his attention to copying the paper on his desk. "But anyway," Isaac went on, "I don't mean to only talk about that. I know people don't like to hear it."

"You're passionate," Caleb muttered, so softly that Isaac wasn't sure he was talking to him. Caleb lifted his head to look at him as he passed back Isaac's homework. "But what is it you think you're going to get out of that life? Just go to church, don't swear, play baseball in the summertime? Get good grades? That's a dream. Real life isn't like that. Nobody ever gets anywhere in this world without stepping over someone else."

Isaac smiled despite Caleb's sour words. They might have been the most the other boy had ever said to him. They were honest. That was something. "I want to help people," he said. "At church, sometimes the kids who've graduated go on missions together. To South America, or Africa, or somewhere else that needs help. I'm lucky to have been born in the greatest country in the world. I feel like I ought to use what I've been given to help others."

"You're lucky to have been born here, so the first chance you get, you take off for someplace shittier? That makes a lot of sense."

"I'll always have this home to come back to," Isaac said softly. "Other people are making do with much less. If I can help, I should. We all should."

"So it's not about what you want for yourself," Caleb mused. He tucked his notebook back into his bag with a pensive hum.

"I've got everything I need already!" Isaac answered with a bright smile. "A loving family, food and shelter, and even a new friend."

Caleb leaned his elbows on his desk to peer across the aisle at him. "Even if that friend's a heathen who has lustful thoughts about you?"

Isaac couldn't help the heat in his cheeks. He zipped up his bag and looked down at it instead of meeting the other boy's gaze. "E-Everyone has their own demons," he said, and then he bit his lip at his poor choice of words and looked up into Caleb's patient eyes. "I mean—I believe that if you want to be good, you can be. Everyone can. Maybe that doesn't always mean not swearing or going to church every single week. But there's good in everyone, Caleb. Everyone has the chance for redemption, and everyone has the love and faith of the Lord, whether they accept it or not. You do, too."

Caleb watched him with a soft frown as other students began to file into the room, and Isaac fidgeted with the zipper pull on his backpack. He didn't like the anxious rumbling he got in his stomach when Caleb looked at him. He focused on listening to the teacher and answering when she called his name. When they were released to go to their next class, they walked down the hall without talking. Isaac smiled and greeted the people who spoke to him, but he kept glancing at the boy beside him. Caleb stopped him at the door to his classroom with a light touch of the back of his hand on his arm.

"Hey," he said in a quiet voice, causing Isaac to inch closer to hear him in the noisy hall. "You really think there's a place in your Heaven for someone like me?"

Isaac smiled and put a gentle hand on the other boy's shoulder. "Of course. If you want it."

Caleb frowned at him and didn't answer as he turned to enter the classroom, but Isaac couldn't keep the grin from his face as he moved through the hall. He was making a difference. Caleb had spoken to him candidly. He had shown a little bit of what he was like. Isaac made a mental list of the things he knew about his strange new friend. One, he was quiet, standoffish, and pretty sullen in general. Two, he had a little bit of a temper, if the way he had pinned Isaac against the dresser the day before was any indication. Three, he was cynical about the concept of God. Isaac wished he had thought to ask the angel whether or not Caleb knew what he was; that would have been helpful. That could make a huge difference. And four, Caleb was apparently attracted to other boys—Isaac in particular. That was the most worrying. He would have to be careful not to lead him on anymore. The last thing he wanted was another unexpected attack like the one in his room. He had been so frightened that he hadn't been able to get his heart rate down until long after the other boy had left.

Maybe if Caleb got to know some of the girls at school, he'd come around. Not that any of the girls Isaac knew were likely to want to be suddenly kissed either, but being in the right company couldn't hurt. He sat through his next class with a smile on his face. He was making progress.

At lunch, Caleb sat beside Isaac so close that their knees bumped under the table, but Isaac didn't pull away. He didn't want Caleb to feel rejected just when he seemed to be reaching out.

"So," Caleb started as he popped open his can of Coke, "which unfortunate country do you want to visit and bring your White American Civilization to?"

"I can't say I like the way you worded that, but I get what you're asking. And I don't know," he shrugged as took a bite of his unsatisfying cafeteria burger. "Wherever I can get to, I guess. I don't mind."

"And what'll you do once you get there? Pray away the malaria?"

Isaac huffed softly. "Anyone can build houses or dig wells, Caleb. But for your information, I want to go to nursing school."

"Nursing. Not doctoring?"

"Oh," Isaac said with a soft smile, "I don't know if I'm smart enough for that."

"Why not?"

"Well, you know...a doctor is something special. Besides, school is expensive. Nursing is only two, four years, but being a doctor? That's a lot of school. My parents would never be able to afford it."

Caleb frowned down at his tray as he nudged his fries around their little cardboard boat.

"What about you? What are you doing to do when you graduate?" Isaac prodded, nudging him lightly with his elbow.

"Nothing, probably," he shrugged. "Or whatever my uncle wants me to, I guess."

"There isn't anything you want to do? You must have dreams."

Caleb scoffed. "So far, my life's been all about what other people want. I...come from an important family, my uncle says. So whatever future I've got, it's pretty much already laid out for me."

Isaac's expression softened, and he put down his burger to lean in and give the other boy his full attention. "I understand feeling pressured. But you always have a choice. Whatever your uncle wants you to do, you should only do it if you really want to. You deserve to be happy, Caleb, and nobody else can decide for you what that means."

Caleb turned to look at him with a furrowed brow, and Isaac hesitated at how close the boy's face was to his. The same rapid pace started in his heart again, and his breath caught in his throat the same way it had the afternoon before. He was frightened, he told himself. When he saw Caleb's dark eyes flick down to his lips, Isaac pulled away in a panic and tried to brush off the awkwardness with a laugh that he knew sounded forced.

"Anyway," he said too loudly, "I don't mean to be so serious all the time. Sorry."

"It's fine," Caleb answered. They ate in silence for a few minutes, and when the bell rang, Caleb hesitated before standing. "Hey. Skip the bus today. Walk home with me."

Isaac paused. "I...I'd like to—really. But I have practice."

"Practice?" Caleb frowned suspiciously at him.

"Baseball practice. Every Wednesday. We don't have a game this week, but we still have to practice."

"Then never mind, I guess," Caleb shrugged, but something seemed strange as he left Isaac behind in the lunchroom.

Isaac couldn't catch up with him after class, either. Was he avoiding him? Isaac sighed as he left the classroom following the final bell, and he headed for the locker room with a frown on his face. He'd thought he was getting somewhere.

Andras hadn't bothered asking questions when Caleb called to tell him not to pick him up. Caleb lingered by the parking lot until the buses had pulled away and the yard was empty, and then he circled the school building and headed toward the baseball field. He took his time and lit a cigarette on his way, and he arrived at the field just as the boys were filing out of the locker room in their uniforms. He spotted Isaac immediately, dressed in snug grey and red, and he took up a place behind the nearby bleachers to watch him. If Caleb watched, if he listened, maybe Isaac would give something up. Some throwaway comment to a friend, or a look—anything that might give him some insight. So far, Isaac seemed content and good-natured, which did not make him a very good candidate for a deal. Caleb had hoped to pry something out of him during their walk home, but this would have to do for now.

He watched the coach bark out commands and the boys perform well-practiced stretches in unison. Isaac looked so serious. Caleb took a long drag from his cigarette as he watched them break out of formation and form a line up the field. He had never understood the appeal of baseball. Or any sport, really. He guessed they might have been fun to play, if he hadn't in general hated activities that made his heartbeat even more noticeable than normal—barring one activity, of course. But to watch? It seemed completely pointless to him.

Isaac did look a little impressive as he ran agility drills with the other boys, though—his cheeks slightly flushed from exertion and a faint glimmer of sweat forming on his brow as he sprinted from line to line. But he wasn't there to leer at the other boy, he reminded himself. Even if the pants were form-fitting. Even if Caleb had never realized that the boy's jeans hadn't been doing his ass justice. And even if Isaac's smile seemed even warmer while he panted for breath. He seemed like a delicate person, but he was holding his own with the other boys as they ran. Stronger than Caleb expected. He frowned and dropped his cigarette into the dirt, snuffing it with the toe of his shoe. This wasn't helping. He leaned against the bleachers to keep himself half-hidden and tried to watch more closely.

After a few more minutes, the boys split off into groups to run bases. Isaac was fast, but he wasn't the fastest. When they stopped running and spread out to play some sort of organized version of catch, Isaac did well, but not the best. He didn't seem to get discouraged; on the contrary, he was constantly encouraging his teammates and laughing at his own missteps. He was having fun. This was a dead end, Caleb realized with a sigh. If Isaac had seemed competitive, he might have been tempted by being the best player on the team, or in the state, or something. But he wasn't.

The boys began to play through what looked like a quick mock game, and Caleb lingered, watching Isaac run and reach to catch each hit that came toward him. When it was his turn to bat, his back twisted with such practiced grace as he swung that Caleb momentarily considered becoming a baseball fan. He leaned his head against the cool metal of the bleacher with a scowl. Who was tempting who, here? It didn't matter how attractive Isaac was—Caleb meant to use him.

Caleb almost turned away to start his long walk home, but he hesitated when the coach snapped at the boys to form up. There wasn't any harm in waiting long enough to watch Isaac's determined frown or the shifting muscles in his arms as he used the last of his energy on the push-ups the coach was counting. He could be attractive *and* useful, Caleb told himself. He finally pulled himself away when the team began to clean up their gear and head back toward the locker room. It didn't complicate things that Caleb wanted to touch him, or that he couldn't get the image of Isaac rinsing away his hard-earned sweat under the shower out of his head. It would make it easier to give the blond what Caleb suspected he really wanted if Caleb wanted to give it. That didn't complicate things at all.

7

Isaac was determined to be strong. The next day at school, he met Caleb and greeted him as usual, pretending he hadn't spent the night tossing and turning in bed trying to forget the memory of the boy's fingertips on his cheek. That he hadn't woken up thinking about their awkward kiss. It wasn't right. He shouldn't be having the kinds of thoughts he'd been having at all, let alone about another boy. Maybe it would do him some good to spend time with the girls at the campfire, too.

He talked with Caleb about anything he could think of as they walked the halls between classes, and when they sat down to lunch, he was thankful for the small break he was given by the friends who sat down at their table. As soon as he let out a soft sigh of relief, he saw the look on Caleb's face and felt guilty. Caleb had been talking to him almost normally all morning, and even smiled once or twice, but now that there were others around, he had snapped shut again, like a surly Venus flytrap. He gave them one-word answers if he answered them at all, and he mostly kept his eyes on his tray as he ate. As soon as the bell rang, Caleb was on his feet to toss his tray away without so much as a glance back at the others.

"What's with him?" Heather asked as she picked up her bag. "I know you want to make friends with everyone, Isaac, but that one might be a lost cause."

"He's just...quiet," Isaac said. "He'll open up. You'll see."

"If you say so," the girl shrugged. "He gives me the creeps."

"It's hard being new," he argued. "We just have to be welcoming."

"You're too nice," she laughed, and she pushed his shoulder as she started down the hall in the opposite direction.

Isaac twisted the strap of his backpack while he walked to his next class. Caleb was talking to him, at least. He knew that he missed the pizza in Chicago, and that his favorite band was twenty one pilots, but he also liked slightly older stuff like The Postal Service. Isaac knew that he felt pressured by his uncle and separate from the people around him. He guessed it was natural to isolate yourself when you weren't completely human. Caleb needed a lifeline, something to make him feel like he was a part of humanity, and Isaac could be that link, he knew it. He just needed to focus better on that task than on the squirming it made in his stomach when their hands happened to brush in the hall.

After school, Isaac looked for Caleb to say goodbye, but the other boy was waiting for him by the empty curb.

"Walk home with me," he said, and Isaac obeyed with a soft smile on his lips.

Caleb started walking with his bag over one shoulder, and Isaac couldn't tell if the pit in his stomach was nervousness or excitement. Talking at school was one thing, but being alone with him again—no. He couldn't be afraid. Caleb was his friend. Caleb had to be his friend. Don't think about being alone on the quiet road. Had Caleb seen through him? Did he sense a threat, like Barachiel had said? Or maybe, as soon as they were out of town and past the church, where there wasn't anything but trees empty fields, Caleb was planning to attack him again? Isaac had felt the hidden strength in the other boy's arms when he had tried to push him the day before—if Caleb decided to grab him, to pin him down, then there wasn't really anything Isaac would be able to do about it. His stomach did a little flip-flop as Caleb turned to face him on the sidewalk. He tried not to look as tense as he felt as the two of them headed down the main road together, but Caleb seemed relaxed as could be.

They walked quietly, and Isaac slowly loosened the grip on his backpack. Caleb lit a cigarette from his bag as soon as they were out of sight of the school, but he held it out on his opposite side as if to keep the smoke from blowing too near the other boy.

"So," Caleb said finally in a puff of smoke, "your family has money troubles? Can't afford to send you to school?"

"Not any more than anybody else, I guess. We get by."

"But you'd get by better with more money."

Isaac chuckled. "Wouldn't everybody?"

Caleb looked over at him as he took a long drag from his cigarette.

"If you had millions of dollars, what would you do with it?"

"Oh, I don't know," he laughed. "I'd take care of my mom and dad, I guess, so they wouldn't have to work anymore. I'd pay for my college, and...I'd give a lot of it away, probably."

"Even just a million dollars could help a lot of people."

Isaac nodded. "I don't have much need for money, myself. I'm fed and dressed. I don't need anything fancy. I'd just make a lot of charities real happy, I guess. But I'm happy to work instead. Since mom and dad don't play the powerball, I guess that's my only option." He smiled and gave a half shrug. "Hard work brings you closer to God, anyhow. That's what dad always says."

Caleb stopped walking and turned to face him, so Isaac stopped too. "So if I told you that it could be easy, you wouldn't take it?"

The blond's eyebrows knit together in confusion. "What do you mean?"

"I mean, what if I told you that I could make you rich? Overnight, and you wouldn't have to do a thing?"

Isaac laughed gently despite the sudden shudder in his chest. "I'd say it sounds like you're about to get me into trouble."

Caleb stepped closer to the other boy with a dark look in his eyes. Isaac wanted to retreat, but he stood fast while Caleb drew so near that he could smell the smoke on him. "I can make that happen for you. More money than you would know what to do with. You could go to medical school, let your parents retire...you could do anything you wanted."

Isaac faltered slightly with Caleb so close to him, but he swallowed down the nervous lump in his throat. This wasn't what he thought it was, was it? Caleb wasn't...making him an offer? He wasn't really a demon—could he even do a thing like that? Didn't they need to be at a crossroad or something? Isaac tried to smile, but he suspected it looked false.

"It's fun to think about," he said, doing his best to keep his voice steady. "But nothing like that comes for free."

Caleb slipped a step closer, and Isaac froze up as the other boy leaned into him to whisper against his ear, Caleb's thumb brushing lightly along the soft line of Isaac's jaw. "What if it's a price you want to pay?"

Isaac couldn't breathe. He felt goosebumps prickle his skin at the heat of Caleb's breath against his cheek, and his body seemed torn between pulling away and leaning into the other boy's gentle touch. "I don't..." he started, but he could barely get the words out. This was fear, he told himself. The pounding heart, the heat in his face and neck, the tight stomach—it was fear. He could overcome fear. "I don't think I like this joke," he said softly, and he reached up to brush Caleb's hand from his cheek. "There aren't any easy answers, Caleb. Even if you could do something like that, I wouldn't want you to. We can't appreciate things in this world we didn't work for."

Caleb's eyes narrowed slightly, his mouth set into a grim line, but it wasn't anger on his face. He seemed almost conflicted. They stared at each other for a long moment, until Isaac realized that he was still holding Caleb's hand between them and hastily pulled away with another forced laugh.

"This walk is a lot longer than I remembered," Isaac said as cheerfully as he could manage. He walked slowly until he saw Caleb catch up to him out of the corner of his eye, and then he hurried just a little.

"So, you don't want money," Caleb said when they had almost reached Isaac's street. "You want something more hands-on?" He took a pull from his cigarette while Isaac looked at him curiously. "Maybe you want to be the youngest doctor in your field. Nobody better than you. You want to cure some terrible disease?"

"That would be nice, wouldn't it?" Isaac chuckled. "Maybe if I work hard enough."

"But you don't have to work hard," Caleb pressed. "Let me give it to you."

"You can't just *give me* being a good doctor, Caleb."

"What if I could?"

Isaac sighed. "I don't want you to give me anything. Especially not something that seems like it might involve crimes or some kind of witchcraft to give to me," he added, hoping his laugh covered up the nervousness in his voice. "I just want to be your friend. Heather and Jon and the others, they want to be your friends too, you know."

Caleb snorted and returned his attention to the street ahead of them as he flicked his cigarette onto the road.

"I know you're still adjusting, but if you'd just talk to them a little, show them what you've shown me—"

"They don't interest me," Caleb cut him off, and he paused right at the corner where they would have to separate and put a hand on Isaac's chest to stop him. "You do."

Isaac hesitated at the sudden press of Caleb's warm hand through his shirt. "Oh," he breathed.

Caleb didn't move for a moment. He only watched Isaac with dark, piercing eyes that kept the blond pinned to the spot. "You're confusing," he admitted. "What is it that you want?"

Isaac softened slightly at the perturbed look on the other boy's face. "Hasn't anyone ever just wanted to get to know you?" he asked.

Caleb paused, and Isaac thought he felt his fingers tighten slightly in the fabric of his shirt. "No," he answered in a softer voice than Isaac had ever heard from him. It made his heart ache. Caleb stepped closer to him, the hand on Isaac's chest moving to gently grip him by the waist, and Isaac's breath hitched slightly in his chest. The blond couldn't bring himself to move as Caleb leaned in, though his hands stayed securely on the straps of his backpack.

"What can I give you?" the dark-haired boy asked, his lips barely a breath away from Isaac's. "Not money, not fame. What is it that you want most?"

Isaac gripped his straps to keep his hands from trembling while Caleb's thumb brushed slowly over his waist. He should move. He should make a joke, or run away, or tell Caleb to stop—but all he wanted in that moment was for the other boy to close the distance between them, and that frightened him more than any thoughts about the demonic nature of his new friend. He couldn't answer, couldn't move. He was frozen, too breathless to step back and too afraid to lean in.

Caleb let his hand fall back to his side as he pulled away, staring at Isaac with what looked like a mixture of curiosity and frustration. He opened his mouth to speak and hesitated, but then he said, "So where is this stupid bonfire tomorrow, anyway?"

Isaac took a moment to register what the other boy had said. He opened and closed his mouth like a fish a few times, and then he smiled so broadly that his cheeks hurt. "It's right out back of my house, almost! There's a little field behind the church where we set up. We can walk together, if you want."

"Fine. Text me and I'll come." Caleb turned to walk up the long drive to his house before Isaac could answer, but the blond waved anyway.

"O-okay! See you tomorrow, Caleb!" he called after him.

Isaac practically ran back to his house and abandoned his backpack just inside the front door. He rushed to the bathroom and scrubbed his face with cold water over and over again, then leaned his elbows on the edge of the counter and watched the water drip from his chin. This wasn't right. It wasn't right for him to—to want another boy to kiss him. It was sinful. He needed to focus. He needed to work harder.

He dried his face and went to kneel at the side of his bed, lacing his fingers together in front of him and squeezing his eyes shut as he lowered his head.

Please help. Lord, I'm trying my best, but these thoughts—please help take them from me, and show me the best way to help Caleb. I know there's good in him. I know there is. Please show me the way.

Isaac heard a soft thump on the floor behind him, and when he turned to face the noise, he saw Barachiel standing in his room, but not the angel he saw before. This man's face was the same, but he was dressed in worn blue jeans and a soft grey henley shirt, his sleeves pushed up to his elbows and his thumbs hooked in his pockets. His feet were still bare, but he was lacking his wings, and Isaac was able to look at him without flinching from the heat.

"Hello, Isaac," the angel said. Isaac felt such relief at the gentleness in his voice that he almost teared up again, but he swallowed it and let out a soft laugh instead.

"I didn't...really expect you to come."

"I told you that I would be here at your call." He lifted his elbows slightly and glanced down at himself. "I thought this might make it easier for us to talk."

"Thank you," the boy sighed, but he still hesitated on the floor. He waited for Barachiel to nod at him before he lifted himself to sit on the bed instead, and the angel took a seat beside him and waited patiently for him to speak again. Isaac took a few deep breaths. "I don't know what to do," he said softly.

"You're doing fine, Isaac. A cambion is a proud, selfish creature, and it expects others to be the same. It's going to take time to convince him of your intentions."

"I'm more worried about his intentions," the boy admitted. "He keeps—you know." He could feel the heat in his face, and he wouldn't meet the angel's eyes.

Barachiel laid a hand on Isaac's back. "There hath no temptation taken you but such as is common to man: but God is faithful, who will not suffer you to be tempted above that ye are able."

Isaac's shoulders relaxed under the angel's warm hand, and he looked up into his face with a faint smile. "I guess I just...never expected to be tempted in this way. Before him, I'd never had...thoughts like that. He's offered me wealth, and success, and—those things are easy to say no to." He twisted his fingers in his shirt over his heart. "But when he looks at me like that, I—I'm sorry," he added quickly. "I shouldn't talk about it."

"I'm here to help you, Isaac. If it helps you to talk, then you should talk. But I urge you to watch over your heart with all diligence; it is in the cambion's nature to manipulate others to get what it wants. He will offer you the world's pleasures at a terrible cost. It is your job to show him that the bonds of friendship are stronger than the lures of sin."

"I know," Isaac said, and he took a slow breath and let it out in a sigh. "I know."

"You are making good progress," the angel assured him. "He agreed to attend your gathering. You have the opportunity to show him companionship and support. To show him that he can be himself and still find compassion. I know that you can turn his heart in time."

"Thank you. I will show him. I'll do my best."

"I know you will," the angel said with a warm smile, and he gave Isaac's shoulder a gentle squeeze as he stood. "Guard yourself, Isaac, and go with God."

Isaac shut his eyes as Barachiel vanished in a flash of light, and he fisted his hands on his knees and took one last deep breath. He could do this.

"Fuck," Barachiel spat as he paced the kitchen floor, his sudden appearance startling the demon at the breakfast table into dropping a pretzel onto his magazine.

"Well, good afternoon," Andras chuckled as he brushed a crumb from his page.

"He's attracted to him," the angel snorted.

"Who, your little golden boy?" Andras laughed. "He's gay?"

"At the very least, he's seventeen and confused," Barachiel grumbled.

"And you didn't know? You didn't know."

The angel took the replacement pretzel from Andras's hand and crunched it grumpily in his mouth. "I *see* everything; I don't *know* everything. Nothing about that boy suggested he might be—liable to be smitten," he finished with a sour frown. "I know his type. He was on track for a young, hasty marriage and an awkward wedding night."

"Well, there's no accounting for natural attraction." Andras took another pretzel from the bag as he turned the page in his magazine.

"And you," Barachiel added with an accusing prod at the demon's shoulder, "having that little jackal trying to make deals with him. I told you not to cheat."

"Name-calling is beneath you, dearest," he answered without

looking up. "And it's hardly cheating to remind the boy that he has certain options available to him. I'm sure your chosen champion will prevail over Caleb's lustful temptations. Or not," he shrugged. "That's the lovely nature of free will, isn't it?"

The angel sighed through his nose. "I am going to make you beg for mercy when I win this bet, you awful creature," he promised.

"If," Andras corrected him, and he flipped his magazine shut and stood to face the angel with a pleasant smile. "If you win." He tenderly stroked Barachiel's cheek, feeling the tension just begin to leave him, and then he fastened his hand to the back of the angel's neck and tugged him in for a vicious kiss. He let his lover give one tiny grunt of acceptance before breaking the kiss with the angel's bottom lip in his teeth. "Until then," he whispered against the corner of Barachiel's mouth, "shall I show you how merciful I can be?"

"Andras, I have things to do—"

"So do I," the demon chuckled, and he turned the other man and forced him face down onto the breakfast table in one smooth, powerful movement.

8

The next evening, Caleb walked down the long dirt driveway toward the road where Isaac said he would be waiting. He shifted his bag on his shoulder, kicking a rock ahead of him as he went. Isaac was a lower middle-class kid from a lower middle-class town who had big dreams of growing up and helping the world. He should have been the prime candidate for a deal. He should have leapt at the chance to get ahead—to get rich, or to get famous, or to cure cancer, or whatever. What hadn't Caleb thought of? Should he have actually pursued the baseball angle? This was the South; maybe he should have offered to teach him to play guitar. But with Isaac, Caleb never felt that rush, that look into someone's heart that told him how to answer their need. Isaac, apparently, wasn't desperate enough to be read. Self-righteous little prick. Caleb had never been so angry at another person before.

He'd never wanted to kiss someone to badly before, either. When Isaac had looked up at him with those soft grey eyes, his lips just slightly parted and his cheeks flushed pink, Caleb had wanted to devour him. There was something about the other boy that drove Caleb insane—he was just so relentlessly *good* that it made Caleb's head hurt. Nobody was that nice. The friends he'd made in Chicago only kept him around because he always had money. They let him buy their booze and cigarettes because he could command the clerk into giving it to him, and they let him come to their parties because he kept to himself and drank in their back yards. He went because it got him out of the house and it occasionally meant sex. Even when he had sex, he did it because it was something to do and because it felt better than doing it himself. The people he did it with never wanted to keep him around, and he didn't really want to be kept. It was all about mutual exchange. Give something, get something.

But Isaac only wanted to give. And every time Caleb got close to him, he felt warm and alive—the opposite of how a potential deal should have affected him. It was making him crazy. All he thought about, from the time he woke up until he fell asleep, was Isaac. Isaac laughing at his attempts to be brusque, or the blissful look on his face from simple things like getting an orange soda at lunch before they ran out. But no matter how he tried, Caleb couldn't figure him out. He had tried to avoid him at school that day, but he hadn't been able to resist when Isaac looked at him with that smile on his face to ask if he was still coming to the bonfire.

Caleb spotted him at the bottom of the drive, smiling and waving as though he hadn't almost been attacked the day before. There was something he wanted. Maybe Isaac was too Baptist to know it, but there was no denying the shudder in the other boy's breath every time they got close. Isaac wanted something very specific from Caleb. Something only he could give. He could fight that hot pounding in his blood and see this thing through.

"Hey, Caleb!" Isaac called out when he got close. "I hope you're ready for some songs and s'mores!"

"Not songs I'm likely to know, right?"

"Oh," Isaac paused. "I guess not. Still, they're easy! You'll pick 'em up in no time!" He smiled brightly and led the way down the road and through a narrow patch of trees, emerging in a wide, open field bordering a distant cemetery. There was already a small group gathered near the center of the field, piling up branches and dragging more in from the woods. A few plastic coolers formed a loose circle in between the logs laid down as makeshift benches, and a mound of grocery bags sat by the cooler nearest the church.

As soon as they were spotted, people waved and called out greetings to them, and as soon as they were in range, the boys all shook Isaac's hand, and the girls all gave him chaste hugs. A couple of the boys shook Caleb's hand out of politeness, and a few girls smiled at him but didn't seem inclined to make conversation. It was fine by him. He wasn't here for them.

Caleb mostly tuned them out while they chatted amongst themselves; they didn't seem to want his help lighting the fire, and he wouldn't have known what to do anyway. He took a place on one of the logs and satisfied himself with picking blades of grass and tossing them into the fire. Isaac busied himself helping out around the site, and Caleb watched him smiling and talking with the other students. There was a single adult overseeing the whole situation—probably the pastor or someone else from the church assigned to chaperone the teenagers after dark. Caleb wouldn't be surprised if they were made to sit boys on one side of the fire and girls on the other. Everyone else set about counting paper plates, skewering hot dogs and holding them over the fire, and scooping out handfuls of potato chips, while Caleb sat with his eyes on Isaac's smile. The other boy glanced at him occasionally while he worked, but the other students seemed slightly wary of him. He was used to it; he'd been called creepy, weird, freaky, even spooky. Because of Andras's pushing and after weeks of practice, Caleb knew that he could be charming and convincing when he wanted to be—Andras had said attractiveness and persuasion were innate demonic traits—but it seemed that Caleb's natural state was more vaguely disconcerting to the average person. It kept him from having to make small talk or be bothered at school, so he didn't mind.

Well, it usually kept him from being bothered. Isaac approached him with a paper plate in each hand and sat down beside him on the log. He let Caleb take a plate from him and set the other on his knee, but when Caleb reached for the provided food, Isaac nudged him lightly with his elbow.

"Not yet."

Caleb frowned at him in confusion as the other students made their way to their various places around the bonfire, and his eyebrows lifted when Isaac slipped a hand into his. He felt an unexpected touch on his other hand and jerked away instinctively, but when he turned to look, the girl beside him was staring at him like he'd offended her.

"Caleb," Isaac whispered with a faint chuckle, "it's just grace."

"What the hell is grace?" he hissed back as he let the girl reluctantly take his hand.

"Give us grateful hearts, O Father," the pastor-or-whatever spoke up from his place in the circle, and everyone around him bowed their heads and shut their eyes. "For all thy mercies, and make us mindful of the needs of others. Make us grateful for food in a world where many are in hunger; for faith in a world where many walk in fear; for friends in a world where many walk alone." Caleb felt a warm press on his hand, and he looked over to see Isaac peeking at him with a gentle smile on his face. "We ask in Jesus' name," the pastor finished. "Amen."

The rest of the students echoed him and raised their heads, and then the noise of conversation quickly started up again. The girl at his side turned away to face her friends as she plucked her hand from his, but Isaac gave Caleb one last encouraging squeeze before releasing him. Caleb told himself it was the light of the bonfire in front of him that was making his face feel warm.

"So, usually we eat, and then we sing some songs, make s'mores, and we'll play some games," Isaac said between bites of his hot dog. "You like s'mores, right?"

Caleb snorted as he picked at his chips. "S'more of what? I haven't had any yet."

"Ugh," Isaac scoffed. "You're killing me, Smalls!"

Caleb paused with a chip halfway to his mouth and looked over at the boy beside him. "Wait, you've seen *The Sandlot*?"

Isaac laughed. "Shut the front door! You've seen *The Sandlot*?"

"Oh my gosh," the girl opposite Isaac said with a smile. "Isaac has awful taste in movies. He only ever watches old stuff."

"Not only," Isaac said defensively, but he seemed to take the accusation in good humor. "I just like what I like, that's all."

"I've never even heard of half the stuff you talk about."

"There's nothing wrong with old movies," Caleb said. Isaac smiled down at his plate, and Caleb almost said something biting just in case the other boy started to think he was being friendly, but he held his tongue and ate his hot dog instead. Isaac tried to encourage him to talk to the girls on either side of them, but Caleb didn't have anything to say to them.

The chaperone gathered everyone's attention after they'd had a few minutes to eat, and, just as Isaac had predicted, he retrieved a guitar from its case nearby and picked at it to finish tuning it. When he started to strum, and Isaac and the other students began to sing along to some vaguely Dave Matthews-ish song about loving Jesus, Caleb's hand itched to reach for the vodka hiding in his bag. Even worse, there seemed to be an endless supply of them—songs about eyes of hearts and breaking chains and majesty and kingdoms. Isaac nudged him a few times to try to get him to join in with a simple chorus, but Caleb only stared at him, hoping the other boy could hear his silent plea for the sweet release of death.

Watching Isaac make s'mores was much better. He kept getting melted marshmallow and chocolate on his fingers and licking them clean, so Caleb passed on making any of his own whenever Isaac offered. He seemed to realize how unsanitary he was being after three or four s'mores, and he apologized so profusely that Caleb couldn't keep from smiling.

"It's fine," he said, but he quickly replaced his usual scowl when he spotted one of the nearby girls peering at him.

"So, can I ask you something?" Isaac began as he handed Caleb a newly-smooshed s'more.

"I guess."

"You live with your uncle, right?"

"And my mom, yeah."

Isaac seemed surprised. "Oh. Really? So, then...I mean," he hesitated, turning the marshmallow skewer in his hand, "how come you live with your uncle, and not...you know, your dad?"

"Well, my uncle murdered my dad and took his place in my house."

Isaac's mouth hung open slightly, and he looked so horrified that Caleb almost spit out his mouthful of s'more laughing.

"Because I'm the Prince of Denmark?" Caleb pressed, and Isaac furrowed his brow for a moment before letting out a somewhat scolding laugh and shoving the other boy with his shoulder.

"You scared me!"

"Sorry." Caleb chewed his snack for a bit before answering. On the rare occasion that someone actually found out enough about him to know his unusual living situation, his standard reply was that his father was dead. It was easy, and then it became understandable that his uncle had stepped in to help raise him. No further explanation needed. But, looking at Isaac, he found himself not wanting to lie. It was a strange feeling for him. "It's just always been that way," he finally said. "I don't know my dad."

"Oh. Do you know what happened to him?"

"My mom says he was a fling," he answered, which was only half a lie. "I don't really care. Wherever he is, he never did anything for us. It's always just been my uncle."

"I'm sorry to hear that," Isaac said with a solemn frown, and Caleb believed him. "What's your mom like? You've mentioned your uncle before, but you don't talk about her."

"She's crazy," Caleb said simply. "I don't want to talk about her."

"All right." Isaac's voice was soft, and he smiled warmly when Caleb peeked up at him. "If you ever want to, I'm listening."

Caleb hesitated, momentarily disarmed by the gentleness on the other boy's face. "Thanks, Dear Abby," he muttered, hoping he sounded rude enough.

"Thank you, by the way," Isaac said as he passed over another finished s'more. "For coming. You're not very comfortable with church stuff, huh?"

"God's just got nothing to do with me," he scoffed.

"You could change that, if you wanted."

"I don't think so."

Isaac paused as though he wanted to say more, but then he seemed to change his mind. "Well, I don't mean to push you. Just...keep an open mind, okay? I promise there's more to it than singing songs."

"Christ, I hope so."

Isaac smiled and opened his mouth to speak again, but another boy put a hand on his shoulder and bent down to offer him a flashlight.

"You ready?" the boy grinned, and Isaac laughed as he took the flashlight from him.

"What's happening?" Caleb asked. Isaac was already getting to his feet.

"Oh! Flashlight tag," he explained. "The cemetery gate is the jail, and the road's out of bounds."

Caleb looked up at him with confusion on his face. "What?"

"Flashlight tag! Two teams, one has flashlights, the other hides. If you get a light shined on you, you're out, and you go to the jail. Other people can tag you back in, but they have to actually tap your hand. Game's over when everybody's in jail."

"Are you serious? What is this, summer camp?"

Isaac laughed. "Oh, no. The games we play at camp have way more people!" He offered Caleb his hand to help him up.

"Great." Caleb sighed as he stood, and he tucked his thumbs into his pockets while the others laughed and split into their teams. "So I guess I'm supposed to hide?"

"And I come and find you," Isaac nodded, lifting his flashlight. "Well, not just me, but you know."

"Sure."

Isaac turned and trotted over toward the other kids with flashlights. "You get a minute to hide!" he called over his shoulder. Caleb watched him go with an oppressive sense of boredom settling over him, but as he saw the others on his team scatter into the darkness, a faint smirk touched his lips. There were worse things than running into Isaac in the dark.

Caleb followed the rest of his team toward the tree line, but he lingered within sight of the "jail," focused on the beam from Isaac's flashlight. When all the flashlights went out at once, he assumed signaling the end of the designated minute, he waited near a thick tree and watched the distant silhouettes approach. He heard others nearby him, but he ignored them, and they didn't notice him. Andras had forced him into dark alleys his whole life—made him stand in shadows, as still as a statue, and refuse to be seen. It was the same as commanding someone, he had said. Just refuse to let them see you. Now it was second nature. Caleb may have had a heartbeat now, but the dark was still where he belonged. A girl passed by within inches of him, so close that she almost brushed his arm as she crept, but she didn't even glance in his direction.

He watched as a boy a few feet from him was spotted, and in the brief gleam of light, he saw Isaac's laughing face. He followed the boy deeper into the woods, waiting until they were apart from the others, and then he touched Isaac's arm. Isaac spun on him and immediately turned the flashlight on, illuminating Caleb's face in the black.

The blond was smiling, but something in Caleb's calm stare must have given him pause, because he kept his light on until Caleb moved close to him, covering his hand with his and switching off the light with a soft click.

"You're out," Isaac said in a timid voice. He retreated from Caleb's advance until his back hit the solid trunk of a tree, and he let out a soft sound as he was jolted into a stop.

"I'm not interested in the game," Caleb admitted. He pressed close against the other boy, one hand on the tree trunk and the other keeping a gentle hold on Isaac's wrist. "I think there's one more thing that I can offer you," he whispered. He heard the sudden hitch in Isaac's breath as he leaned in, his lips touching the trembling skin of the blond's neck. Caleb let the tip of his tongue brush the delicate dip right beneath Isaac's ear and smiled at the shivering gasp it elicited from the other boy. The flashlight hit the ground with a dull thump, the game forgotten. Easy. Caleb had been right all along—Isaac was looking for someone to test the waters with. He was afraid, but Caleb could give him what he wanted. Acceptance. Release. For a price.

Caleb slid his knee between Isaac's slim thighs, pinning him in place with the weight of his body, and he moved a hand to rest firmly on his waist. He let his hand slip under the blond's shirt, fingertips creeping up toward his ribs.

"C-Caleb," Isaac whispered, "so...someone will see." His hands were pressed tightly against the taller boy's chest, but he wasn't trying to remove him. His fingers dug into Caleb's shirt as though he thought he might fall without the support.

"Someone will see?" Caleb murmured against his ear, his own heart beating uncomfortably fast. He could feel the stirring in his belly already, and the jolt down his spine as Isaac shifted nervously against him and brought their hips together. "'Someone will see,' not 'don't do this?' Did I hear that right?"

"Caleb," Isaac said again, almost begging, but Caleb couldn't wait. He had an opportunity now. A moment of weakness—that was all he needed. His head swam with the promise of the cold quiet Isaac would bring him—the slow, thudding pulse that came so tantalizingly close to stopping. He just had to push Isaac over the edge. All it would take was one moment of weakness.

He leaned back just enough to tilt the blond's chin to him, allowing himself to take in the sound of Isaac's soft, longing breath in the instant before their lips met. Caleb's stomach tightened at the quiet whine in Isaac's throat, the hesitation and panic before the surrender. There it was. Isaac wasn't pulling back this time. But as Isaac's hand fastened instantly in the dark hair at the back of Caleb's head, a different sort of feeling turned his stomach. Not so very long ago, he had been exactly here—luring in someone who wanted him, using them for the sake of finding that peaceful cold. But then he had been distant, unsympathetic. He had forced his mind onto other things while the desperate man had taken him, panting and sweaty, clammy hands running paths over Caleb's skin that the teenager had later tried to scrub off in disgust. Now he was that aggressor. Needing, taking, while Isaac trembled in his grip. It wasn't what he wanted.

Caleb broke the kiss, Isaac's hand still in his hair, and for a few moments neither of them moved, both struggling to catch their breath. Caleb couldn't make his heart slow down. He could just barely make out Isaac's face in the darkness, flushed and dazed and waiting. The blond whispered Caleb's name against his lips with a tremble of confusion in his voice. This wasn't what he wanted at all. He didn't want a deal. The boy with the gentle smile and the kind grey eyes could never give him the cold he sought. Everything about Isaac was heat and life and laughter. Caleb's blood ran hotter than he could bear as the other boy's fingertips brushed his scalp. He didn't want a deal. He wanted Isaac.

With a sudden pressure of fear in his chest, Caleb tore away from Isaac, only pausing a moment to look at him before rushing back through the woods toward the field and the fire. He thought he heard Isaac call out after him, but he didn't stop. He scooped up his bag from near the fire and slung it over his shoulder.

"Hey there, son," the pastor said as he appeared between Caleb and his destination. "Everything all right?"

"I'm leaving," Caleb said simply, and he jerked away when the man reached out to touch his shoulder.

"Easy now. It's late; why don't you wait a bit for the others to get back, or let me get you home?"

"I said I'm leaving," Caleb growled, feeling that tendril of chill in his stomach as he put force behind his words.

"You're leaving," the man repeated with a nod. "Well, take care now."

Caleb started to walk away, but then he paused and looked back at the pastor. "You don't tell Isaac you saw me."

"I don't tell Isaac I saw you."

Caleb pressed his lips together in a frown and hurried across the field toward the road that would lead him home.

9

Isaac stood with his back pressed against the tree, his heart and his lungs struggling to regain a steady rhythm. Caleb had kissed him—again—and Isaac had wanted him to. He could still feel the burning touch of the other boy's hand on his side, and when he nervously licked his lips, he could taste the lingering bitterness of nicotine. Isaac clutched his hands to his chest and stood still, not quite sure what to do with them now that they didn't have Caleb to hold on to. His brain was still trying to process what had just happened. He felt like he'd just gotten off of a roller coaster—lightheaded and just a little queasy. He had wanted Caleb to kiss him. He had let him kiss him. He had even kissed him back. He had felt loss when the other boy had left.

"Oh, but I am in trouble," he whispered to himself, and he let his head fall back against the trunk of the tree.

He could hear the other kids in the woods with him and see the beams of their flashlights as they laughed. Right. Flashlight. He crouched down and felt around the grass until he put his hand on the cool metal. He needed to find Caleb. Something about the way he'd stopped, the way he'd pulled away so quickly and disappeared without a word—he needed to find him. He had no idea what he would say, or how he could face him without stammering, but he had to try.

Isaac made his way back through the woods with his flashlight on, and once he reached the open field, he jogged back across to the bonfire where Mr. Garrett was cleaning up and helping himself to a s'more. Caleb's bag was missing.

"Hey, Isaac," the man smiled. "Something wrong?"

"Mr. Garrett, did Caleb come back here?"

"Hm? The boy you brought with you? No; I haven't seen him. You all right, son? You look like you had a scare."

"No, I'm...I'm not feeling very well. I think I'm going to go home now."

"Well, all right. You want me to take you?"

"No thank you, sir. I can make it across the way."

"You be careful, son. Thanks for coming tonight. Tell your friend we were glad to have him, and he's welcome back anytime."

"I will. Thanks, Mr. Garrett." Isaac handed him back the flashlight and trotted off through the field toward his back yard. He ran into Heather when he skirted the woods and feigned a stomachache to get away from her. He tried to call Caleb's number, but it went straight to voicemail. He must have turned it off.

When he reached his house, he paused near the back door and looked up the hill toward Caleb's. There were still lights on. With a silent apology to his parents, he slipped by the house and cut through the trees to head up Caleb's long driveway. He didn't know if the other boy would be happy to see him, or angry, or if he would talk to him at all. He walked up the drive with his stomach in knots. What was he going to say? Why did you stop kissing me? He shouldn't have let it go as far as he did—he could practically feel the angel's disappointment like a weight upon his shoulders. He was supposed to be turning Caleb toward the light, and here he was, nothing but sinful thoughts almost since the day they'd met.

Isaac got about halfway up the dirt driveway before he heard a sound nearby and stopped to listen. He peered through the trees and saw a dark silhouette by the pond at the bottom of Caleb's front yard, dimly illuminated by the burning orange end of a cigarette. He slowly approached and recognized the hunch of Caleb's shoulders as he sat by the water, his bag discarded beside him. He saw the other boy pause as he drew near, and when Caleb looked over his shoulder, Isaac could feel his eyes on him even in the darkness.

"What do you want?" Caleb called.

"I...I was worried about you." Isaac took a few more hesitant steps forward and spotted the bottle in Caleb's hand, half full of clear liquid that he suspected wasn't water. How full had it been when he started?

"Aren't you missing your game?"

"This is more important," Isaac said softly. He moved to stand beside the other boy. "Can I sit?"

Caleb looked up at him with a skeptical frown, but then he shrugged one shoulder and took a pull from his cigarette as he returned his attention to the still green water ahead of him.

Isaac sat down next to him, not quite close enough to touch. He could smell the alcohol in the bottle, but he didn't say anything as Caleb lifted it to take another drink. He watched him for a moment in silence. He'd expected to feel afraid, or embarrassed, or maybe even ashamed, but when he looked at Caleb in the dim light of the moon, he only felt sad for the other boy.

"What...happened?" he asked, almost in a whisper. Caleb didn't answer. "Please," Isaac pressed gently. "You can talk to me."

"Maybe I don't want to talk to you," Caleb snapped without looking at him, and Isaac recoiled slightly.

"Then...I'll be here when you're ready. Please take care of yourself." He started to get up, but he stopped when Caleb reached out to take a sudden hold of his arm.

"Stay," he said simply, and the single, strained word make Isaac's heart thump. He sat back down, and Caleb released him. They waited without speaking, the ash slowly building up at the end of Caleb's cigarette. He finally turned to look at the boy beside him and let out a slow sigh.

"I don't really do...this," he said, gesturing between them with one hand.

"Friends?"

"Are you my friend?" Caleb muttered. He took another drink and let the bottle thunk down into the dirt between his feet. "I'm still waiting for what you want from me."

Isaac's stomach twisted. It felt like a lie to tell him that he only wanted to be friendly. He would have been friendly to him regardless, but without the angel's direction, he might have left Caleb to his own devices after a couple days of being completely shut down. He certainly wouldn't have tried quite this hard to make him feel included, and that made him feel even worse. He might not have seen it if Barachiel hadn't spoken to him, but Caleb was someone in desperate need. He just seemed so...alone. He must have felt very alone, knowing what he was and knowing that no one else would ever understand. He might not have thought of himself as human at all. But Caleb didn't seem like a demon to Isaac.

"What I want from you," he began carefully, "is to understand. You don't have to confide in me if it's too hard. If you want to, we...we can forget all about what happened tonight. We don't have to talk about it. But I hope you know that anything you want to say—I'm here, Caleb, and I'm listening."

The dark-haired boy let his head drop with an empty chuckle. "You don't want to hear what I have to say."

"I do," Isaac promised, and he reached out to pry the bottle from Caleb's hand and lace their fingers together. "Whatever it is, it'll feel lighter if you share it."

Caleb glanced down at their joined hands with a furrowed brow, and then he looked into Isaac's eyes through the darkness. "You kissed me back."

Isaac's voice caught in his throat, and he found himself squeezing Caleb's hand without thinking. "I...I did."

"Friends don't kiss like that."

"Well I...I—"

"Do you want to kiss me again?"

Isaac started and stopped a few times before any words came out. "I don't know," he said at last. "It's...confusing. It's a sin."

"Right," Caleb sighed. He took another drag from his cigarette and stared back out at the pond, but he didn't try to pull his hand away from Isaac's.

"Caleb, can I ask you something?" Isaac spoke up after few beats of silence. "You don't have to answer if you don't want."

"I won't. What is it?"

Isaac hesitated. He wanted to be sure he worded it right. "You...are you only att—you know, attracted to...only to boys?"

Caleb glanced at him out of the corner of his eye while he took a pull of his cigarette. "Yep," he said as he exhaled.

"How did you...I mean, when did you first know you were..."

"Gay?" Caleb finished for him, and Isaac nodded with heat in his cheeks. "I always knew, I guess. I've never been interested in girls."

"So," he started, "what...you know, happened? To you."

"What do you mean, what happened?"

"I just mean, I was just wondering what the...the root was. The reason. I understand if you don't want to say. I know that a lot of...gay people were, you know...they were abused."

Caleb stared at him with his lips pressed into a thin line. "Abused."

"I'm sorry if it's hard. I just...I want to understand you better." Isaac dropped his voice, although they were already speaking quietly. "I know you live with your uncle, and I've heard that's sometimes—"

"You're asking me if my uncle touched me as a kid?" Caleb interrupted. "And if that's why I'm gay? Are you fucking serious?"

"Caleb, don't swear," he said timidly, shrinking back slightly from the other boy.

"What the hell is wrong with you? Why would you think that?"

"That's just—the Bible says it's a sin, and in church they told us it's not natural for a...for a man to be with another man. They say that if you can work through the cause, then you can resist those urges."

Caleb tugged his hand away with a scoff. "The world isn't your Bible school, Isaac. Nobody abused me or turned me gay. It's the way I am. Some people are just born gay. You think straight people are only straight because they dodged the sexual abuse bullet? That's fucked up."

Isaac stammered for a moment. "I didn't mean—that's just what they told us, and I guess I never—" He stopped and took a short breath. "Shoot, Caleb, I—I'm sorry. I didn't meant to come off like that. I guess...I guess I don't know very much about this stuff."

"I guess you don't." Caleb put his cigarette butt out in the dirt and scowled down at his crossed legs for a moment before looking back at Isaac. "Why did you kiss me back?"

"I..." Isaac paused to fidget in his lap, feeling the flush in his face and neck. He had to steel himself before the words would come. "Ever since you kissed me that day in my room, I've...thought about you. I think about you a lot." Caleb seemed to soften slightly, but Isaac couldn't quite meet his eyes. "I think about...if you tried again, what I would do."

Caleb inched closer to him, leaning down to try to catch his eyes. "I guess you know the answer to that. And if I tried again now?"

Isaac's fingers tightened on themselves. "I—I don't know."

The other boy's heat beside him made his stomach flip, and as Caleb reached toward him, he found he didn't have it in him to brush his hand away. Caleb cupped his cheek and tilted his face up to meet his eyes. For a moment, he seemed to hesitate, and Isaac almost pulled away out of embarrassment, but then Caleb kissed him. It wasn't careless like the first time, or demanding like in the woods. It was slow, and curious, and even a little timid. Isaac's hand went up to clutch Caleb's shirt instinctively as the world disappeared around him. Caleb tasted like cigarettes and liquor, but as the other boy opened his mouth to him, his tongue peeking out to brush Isaac's upper lip, the blond couldn't help the shivering sigh that escaped him. He let Caleb explore his mouth, heart pounding uncertainly in his chest. When he tried to reciprocate and hesitantly slid his tongue past the other boy's lips, Caleb let out a groan and tightened his grip on the side of Isaac's neck. The next thing Isaac knew, he was on his back in the pine straw with Caleb's knee between his thighs, the boy's weight pressing him down almost uncomfortably hard. He fastened his arms around Caleb's shoulders like he was afraid he might fall. He could barely breathe for the sudden intensity of Caleb's kiss, and he thought his heart might stop completely when the other boy's hand slipped from his neck down his chest and stomach. Isaac's back arched slightly against his will, and he fought the pooling heat in his belly, but then Caleb's hand ran over the front of his jeans, and the blond cried out softly in alarm at the lightning that shot through him.

"Fuck, Isaac," Caleb whispered against the corner of his mouth, and then the boy's lips were on his cheek, his jaw, his neck, teeth fastening onto his earlobe and drawing a trembling whine from him.

"C-Caleb, this—" Isaac's breath left him as Caleb squeezed him through his jeans, and he panted out the boy's name again as he struggled to maintain control of himself. "This is—too much. Too much," he insisted, weakly pushing against Caleb's chest until he reluctantly pulled away. Isaac lay on the ground and tried to catch his breath, anxiously tugging on the hem of his shirt in an attempt to hide his arousal. "I—I'm sorry," he murmured, "I—I need to—it's a sin, I can't just—"

"It's fine." Caleb supported himself on his elbow and leaned in to press one more heated kiss to Isaac's exposed collarbone. "I don't mind taking my time with you."

Isaac felt his entire face go red, and he quickly scrambled to his feet, still holding the bottom of his shirt. "Well I'm glad we cleared all that up and you're not upset about tonight and I hope you had fun and Mr. Garrett said come back anytime; so anyway I'm gonna go so please don't stay out here drinking by yourself and have a good weekend bye!" He ran off as quickly as he could, not looking back for fear of seeing Caleb's dark eyes on him again.

He ran all the way back to his house and let himself in quietly through the back door, then hid himself in his room. He was almost afraid to undress for bed. He did it quickly and changed into his most uncomfortable pajamas, then slid under his blanket with his hands folded determinedly on his chest. Every inch of Isaac's skin was still tingling, and his erection persisted despite his attempt to glare at the tent in his blanket until it relented. He could be strong. He shut his eyes and said a quick prayer, but it didn't replace the memory of Caleb's lips on his. No matter how he shuddered at the lingering sensation of Caleb's hand on him, he could be strong. He would not follow sin with sin. He was stronger than lust, he told himself, though he bit his lip as he shifted and felt the electric friction even the slightest movement made.

Isaac took slow, deep breaths and silently repeated the prayers that had helped him before. *Do not let sin reign in your mortal body so that you obey its evil desires. Do not offer any part of yourself to sin as an instrument of wickedness, but rather offer yourself to God. Resist the devil, and he will flee from you.*

He opened his eyes and stared up at his ceiling with a strange sense of sadness in his chest. "Resist the devil, and he will flee from you," he whispered. He rolled the fabric of his sheet in his fingers. He had been sent after a devil, but the thought of making this devil flee from him just made his stomach ache. Isaac pulled the blanket up to his chin and tried to force his thoughts to less sinful things.

10

Andras was on the sofa watching *The Exorcist* on television when Caleb came through the living room.

"Have a good time?" he called, and Caleb snorted as he leaned his elbows on the back of the couch. He reached over the demon's shoulder to take a handful of popcorn from the bowl on his knee.

"How can you watch this shit?" Caleb asked instead of answering. "Doesn't it drive you nuts?"

"Should it?"

"I dunno; all this 'the power of Christ compels you' and 'your mother sucks cocks in hell' crap seems over the top. Real demons aren't like that, right?"

"Depends on the demon. What, you can't picture me telling priests to put their cocks up people's asses, things like that?"

"Yeah, I'm gonna go with no."

Andras shrugged. "Some of us are more delicate than others. Now if you aren't going to give me the juicy details, go to bed and let me get back to watching your family home videos."

"Fuck off," Caleb muttered, but as he pushed away from the couch and moved toward the stairs, Andras lifted a hand and snapped his fingers twice to get his attention.

"Ah ah. Give it back." The demon held out his hand to wait while Caleb huffed, and he accepted the half-empty bottle of vodka as Caleb shoved it into his hand. "There's a good boy." He leaned back in his seat and propped his feet on the coffee table as he unscrewed the cap. "And stop leaving your damn cigarette butts all over the yard!" he called out as Caleb disappeared up the stairs.

Barachiel stepped into the flickering light of the television as soon as they were alone, and he dropped onto the sofa with his head in the demon's lap and his legs hung over the arm of the couch.

"You're looking optimistic, B," Andras chuckled.

"They kissed," the angel grumped. "They properly kissed. And now Isaac is lying in bed trying to pray away the powerful teenage urge to masturbate about it. This isn't going as well as I'd hoped."

Andras took a small drink from the bottle and offered it to him, but Barachiel shook his head. "Well, some things just aren't meant to be, hm?"

"Oh no," Barachiel said, tilting his head up to look at his lover's face. "There's hope yet. Your little jackal had a positively lovesick smile on his face this evening as Isaac left. He's going soft."

"Well, it sounds like they have opposite problems, don't they?"

"You're perverse."

"You're the one talking about teenage boys and their erections."

Barachiel sighed. "I'm sure the only reason Isaac hasn't called me tonight is because he doesn't want to risk me showing up and seeing him in his fragile state. I expect he'll want to talk tomorrow, and he'll expect me to tell him that sodomy is a sin and that he's going to Hell if he doesn't stop fantasizing about broody smokers."

"Are you going to tell him that sodomy is a sin? I thought you two already had this conversation."

"I may have...skirted the issue." He sat up when Andras frowned down at him in disapproval. "I didn't want him falling for your deal-making little ward," he said defensively. "Either way, it's only a complication. Progress is being made."

"Sure. It's only been a week, and already golden boy is on the verge of getting handjobs in the woods. What will the future hold?" He laughed and took another drink, but Barachiel snatched the bottle from his lips and set it down on the coffee table with a heavy thunk. "Oi," the demon protested, but then his lover was in his lap, his hands on both sides of Andras's face as he kissed him. Andras hummed his approval and promptly slid his hands down the back of the angel's pants to squeeze his bottom and tug him closer.

Barachiel broke the kiss and moved back just far enough to look into his lover's blue eyes. "You are absolutely insufferable," he murmured, and he placed a second, softer kiss on the demon's lips.

"I've been called worse," Andras chuckled. "Killer of men, author of discord, spirit of death," he listed with a sly smile.

"Sixty-third of seventy-two," Barachiel continued for him, and the demon frowned.

"They're not in order of importance," he muttered.

"Riding upon a strong black wolf," the angel went on, kissing his lover's chin, "and wielding a sword, sharp and bright. A demon who seems in an angel's shape," Barachiel smirked. He slipped his hands under Andras's shirt and ran his palms up his lover's stomach and chest.

"Now you're just flattering me," the demon said as he arched into the heated touch. "Great and honored angelic prince of the Chora Orientis," he added with a low chuckle.

Barachiel nipped at the corner of the demon's lips. "Aren't you supposed to have a bird head?"

Andras frowned at him. "Aren't you supposed to be scattering rose petals?"

"Forgive me, Great Marquis," the angel hummed, and he untied the drawstring of his lover's pajama pants with a slow, purposeful tug.

Andras grunted as Barachiel's fingers dipped below his waistband. "You're forgiven—seraph," he taunted.

"You're going to regret being such a smartass," the angel promised. He raised himself on his knees enough to pull Andras's pants down as the demon lifted his hips, but then he let his weight rest on his partner's thighs to keep him in place. He removed Andras's hands from him and placed them on the couch cushions instead with a pointed look. He slipped long, slender fingers around his lover's swiftly stiffening cock, and he leaned in close enough to feel the demon's breath on his lips as he whispered, "You will not touch me."

Andras smiled and ran his tongue over the angel's bottom lip. "We've played this game before, B. You always lose."

Barachiel didn't seem perturbed by the caress. He gave his lover a squeeze and smirked faintly at the soft hiss the demon made. "We'll see."

11

When Isaac woke up on Saturday morning, he sat up in his bed for what felt like a long time, staring at his blanket. The night before seemed like a dream. He had kissed Caleb. He couldn't put it all on the other boy anymore—Caleb might have initiated it, but there was no denying that Isaac had definitely been kissing him, too. And he had enjoyed it, which made the guilt in his stomach twist even tighter. He turned the ring on his finger, frowning at the taunting inscription—TRUE LOVE WAITS. Isaac had made a promise, and he'd skirted the line of breaking it. Lust was a sin no matter who it was toward. And even if what Caleb had said was true, that some people were just born gay, and there wasn't anything they could do about it—that didn't mean it wasn't still a sin to act on those feelings, right? It was like—like wanting cake, but knowing you couldn't have it. Isaac pulled his legs up to his chest and put his forehead on his knees with a groan. Caleb would be angry with him for comparing being gay to having a sweet tooth, but Isaac had been told all his life to resist the devil's vices, and they said that was one of them.

"Lord, help me," he sighed without raising his head. "Please give me guidance. Help me fight these desires. Help me reach Caleb without giving in to lust. Help me find the right path."

"Isaac," the deep, now-familiar voice spoke up beside his bed, and the boy looked up to see Barachiel standing by his nightstand. Isaac immediately got down from his bed to kneel on the floor at the angel's feet, but Barachiel knelt with him and put a warm hand on his shoulder.

"I'm so sorry," Isaac said, his throat tight as he fought the tears prickling his eyes. "I'm so sorry I didn't resist. I wasn't—I wasn't strong enough."

"Isaac, you're fighting against man's very nature," the angel said softly. "Men are passionate, earthly things, and you are very young."

The boy didn't look up. He tightened his hands into fists in the carpet and shut his eyes. "Can—can you tell me if it's true? Are some people just...that way? From when they're born?"

Barachiel seemed to hesitate, but he kept his hand gently on Isaac's shoulder. "Man isn't the only animal on this earth who...sometimes has that inclination. Many creatures do. But man has been given a higher reasoning, and has been called to a higher purpose. Man has been given the ability to rise above his base desires and live a righteous life."

"I want to," Isaac hiccuped, wiping at his eyes with the back of his hand to keep his tears from spilling down his cheek. "I want to, but when I'm with Caleb, I feel—I feel different. I don't want him to go to Hell for what he is. I don't want to go to Hell. But when he—when he kissed me, it didn't...it didn't feel like a sin."

He heard the angel take a slow, deep breath beside him. "Isaac," he began gently, "do you know what God is?" Isaac looked up at him with reddened eyes. "He that loveth not, knoweth not God; for God is love." Barachiel squeezed his shoulder and bent slightly to look into his face. "God is *love*. He loves you, Isaac, as He loves all the Earth's inhabitants. He even loves Caleb Durant. The most important thing in a man is his capacity to love. When you love someone, God is in your heart, and there is no act that can be sinful when love is its source. That being said," he added when Isaac sniffled hopefully, "you've known this boy for a week. Love and lust are often confused, especially at your age."

"So..." Isaac furrowed his brow. "So it's not...sinful because of...what it is, but because it doesn't come from love? So...so all I have to do is figure out if I really love him or not!"

Barachiel looked mildly taken aback. "Well—"

"Thank you," the boy said, and he looked up at him so earnestly that the angel only softly smiled.

"Good luck, Isaac."

Isaac's mother shouted from the kitchen to call him to breakfast, so he turned to reply, and when he looked back, Barachiel was gone. Isaac got to his feet and rushed to the bathroom to wash his face, then hurried to the kitchen, where his mother waited with a plate of bacon and eggs for him.

"Thought you were gonna sleep right through," she chuckled as he sat down at the table.

"Sorry. Still a bit tired on account of the bonfire."

"Did you have a good time?" She hid her yawn in her elbow and smiled at him. His mother usually had bags under her eyes, but she never complained. She still wore her uniform from the convenience store, and her blonde hair was done up in a bun that looked like it had been tidy a few hours ago.

"Yeah. Caleb came, too. I don't know how much fun he had, but he liked the s'mores, at least."

"Well who doesn't love a good s'more? You should ask him to service with us tomorrow."

Isaac prodded his eggs with his fork. "I don't know if he'd come."

"Either way, you ought to ask. It can't hurt for him to feel welcome with us."

"I know. I'll ask him."

"All right. I'm going to get some sleep now; you keep it down out here."

"Yes ma'am," Isaac said as she bent to lean his head toward her and kiss his hair.

"I'll see you tonight, pumpkin."

"Good night, mom." He ate his bacon and watched her disappear down the hall to the bedroom, listening for the quiet click of the door. He could see his father's plate cleared away already and waiting by the sink; Isaac had slept too late to see him off to work. When he finished his breakfast, he took his plate to the sink and washed the dishes, then dried them and put them away in the cabinet. He went back to his room to change out of his pajamas, and he even made it through his hot shower without too many thoughts of being pressed underneath Caleb's body. He had dealt with lust before. Now that he knew that the feelings he was having for Caleb weren't necessarily going to damn him—which would be difficult to explain to his parents without also revealing that he'd heard it straight from an angel—he could deal with the rest of it. He just had to keep his mind clear, and he was sure he could figure it out. He just felt a connection to Caleb, and he was probably mistaking that friendship for romantic feelings.

His phone rang on his nightstand while he was pulling his shirt on, and when he glanced down at the screen, he felt a little jump in his chest as he saw it lit up with Caleb's name. Definitely just friendship feelings. He picked up the phone and tapped the screen as he lifted it to his ear.

"Hello?"

"Hey." Isaac smiled at the familiarity in the other boy's voice. Just a few days ago, he didn't respond at all when Isaac greeted him. "What are you doing today?"

"I didn't have any plans. Some homework, probably."

"So come over."

Isaac paused. "You mean, to your house?"

"Sure. You forget where I live?"

"No," he laughed. "I just...didn't figure you'd like company."

"I like your company."

Isaac swallowed, and he put a wary hand on his suddenly tense stomach. "I...thanks. I'd like to come."

"So come. I'll be here. Don't worry about the dog."

"Dog?" Isaac asked, but Caleb had already hung up. He looked down at his phone for a moment before tucking it into his pocket. These were friendship feelings. Nothing strange at all about going over to a friend's house on the weekend.

He checked himself in the mirror, running a hand through his hair to straighten it, then scribbled a short note for his mother in case she woke up before he got home. He shut the door quietly behind him and made his way across the road and through the trees lining Caleb's driveway. He purposely averted his eyes from the pond as he passed it, focusing on the looming wooden house at the top of the hill. The sleek silver Aston Martin looked a bit out of place beside the aging house, but Isaac supposed it had been right at home in Chicago. He wondered how much Caleb was missing having access to all the conveniences of the city.

Isaac put a foot on the bottom step leading up to the porch and was immediately faced with a set of sharp teeth that snapped inches from his face. The mass of black fur snarled so close that he could feel the heat from its breath, and he stumbled backwards into the grass with a startled shout. The animal glared at him from the steps with pure black eyes, its lip curling to bare its teeth as it growled. It was easily half as tall as Isaac himself, and twice as bulky. This was the dog Caleb had told him not to worry about? Isaac flinched and threw his hands up as it drew a step closer and snapped at him, but then he heard the creak and slam of a screen door at the top of the stairs.

"Nobah, maspeek," a man's voice called sharply, and when Isaac lowered his arms, he saw the dog—which was clearly actually a wolf despite what Caleb had said—padding pleasantly around the legs of a tall man with a paintbrush and a rag in his hand. He was wearing simple blue jeans and a hunter green v-neck shirt, and his brown hair had been pushed back into a stylish mess. "Sorry," he said with a smile, showing teeth that were just a little too white. "We don't get many guests. She's just excited."

"Uh. Yeah, no—no problem," Isaac answered as he tried to calm his racing heart. He made his way up the stairs and kept a wary eye on the prowling animal.

"You must be Isaac," the man said. He offered his hand when Isaac reached him and gave him a gentle shake. "Andras. I'm Caleb's uncle."

"Pleasure to meet you, sir. I've heard a lot about you. Caleb said you help take care of him and his mom. It's real nice of you to look after your sister that way."

"Sister? Oh, Marian? Oh no. I come from Caleb's father's side of the family."

"Oh," Isaac said, but then he froze as cold realization washed over him. He looked up into the man's smiling face and couldn't find his voice. This wasn't a man at all. Someone from Caleb's father's side—this was a demon. Not someone like Caleb, who was human too—the person standing in front of him was a creature of Hell, plain and simple. But Andras just stood there with a curious smile on his face, waiting for Isaac to stop staring.

"Caleb's inside," Andras said when Isaac didn't seem inclined to speak again. "Mind the paint on the floor; it's still wet."

"S-Sure," Isaac squeezed out through his tight throat, and he edged his way past the demon without turning his back on him. Andras held the screen door open for him as he slipped inside. In the living room, all of the furniture had been pushed against the walls, and Caleb stood to one side of a massive ring painted onto the wooden floor, overseeing a woman on her hands and knees. The paint almost covered the entire room—a giant circle, surrounded by four pentagrams and filled with a spiraling snake made of Hebrew letters. In the center of the spiral were a few Stars of David with letters in the points along with more symbols Isaac couldn't recognize, and off to the side, nearly in the kitchen doorway, was a triangle with another circle inside lined with letters. It was surprisingly colorful for what looked like some sort of ritualistic circle—blue, yellow, red, green, black—but the whole thing ran a gruesome chill down Isaac's spine.

Caleb reached down to take a broad paintbrush from the woman on the floor and help her to her feet, and she immediately hugged him, forcing him to hold the wet brush out at arm's length to avoid getting paint on her.

"Caleb," Andras spoke up, "you have a guest."

"I hope I'm not...interrupting anything," Isaac said warily, but before Caleb could answer, the woman turned to the door and moved toward Isaac with an airy smile.

"Hello," she said in a soft voice. Her hands and legs were covered in paint of all different colors, and her hair hung in a mass of black curls down past her shoulders, but even with her slightly gaunt cheeks and the distant look in her eyes, there was no mistaking her. She and Caleb had the same straight nose and the same dark, slightly sunken eyes. Isaac could even tell where Caleb had gotten the faint cleft in his chin. But there was something off about her. She seemed to look through Isaac more than at him. "Are you a friend of Caleb's?" she asked, and Isaac smiled at her.

"Yes ma'am. I'm Isaac."

"Isaac," she echoed. "He laughs," she said, her lips twitching into a faint smile. "Did you know that's what your name means? You have brought laughter to my son, Andras."

"I thought he could use some, Marian," the demon said with an indulgent smile, and he winked when Isaac looked up at him in confusion.

"My son is very special, you know," she went on. "His father—" Before she could continue, Caleb stepped between them and pulled Isaac to the side by his hand.

"Bye mom," he said pointedly, and he tugged the other boy up the stairs without waiting for a response, dropping the paintbrush into a tray as he passed it. He led Isaac down the hall toward his room and shut the door behind them.

Isaac wanted to ask what all that had been about, but his eyes were on their laced fingers, on Caleb's hand clutching him so tightly. His heart couldn't seem to keep a steady rhythm. Caleb turned to him, opening his mouth as if to speak, but then he shut it and pulled his hand away.

"Sorry about her," he muttered.

"She was fine," Isaac assured him. "Is she...all right?"

"I told you she's crazy," Caleb answered.

Isaac really wanted to know what she would have said about Caleb's father, but the topic clearly made the other boy uncomfortable, so he let it go. He opened his mouth to speak again and spotted a large wire cage on the floor. It was half as tall as Isaac, and filled with tubes, ladders, hammocks, toys, and a large wheel. As

Isaac stepped closer and bent down, he saw the large grey rat nestled in one of the little fleece hammocks.

"I didn't know you had a rat!" he said, smiling over his shoulder with his hands on his knees. "What's his name? Or her name?"

"Its name is Greedigut," Caleb answered.

"Oh." Isaac straightened with a faint frown. "Well that's...an interesting name."

"I didn't name it."

"Oh, so he's like a rescue rat? You should call him something cuter, like Dusty, or Mr. Whiskers. Oh, or Templeton! That was the rat from *Charlotte's Web.*"

"Call it whatever you want," Caleb shrugged.

Isaac watched him for a moment. Maybe someone had given the rat to him to try to give him some company, or empathy toward other living things, or something. A therapy rat? Was that a thing? It didn't seem to be working out so well, if that was the case. "So, what was all that on the floor?" he asked to change the subject.

"It's bullshit," Caleb scoffed, and he dropped down onto his bed with a huff. "My mom is...she's big into this occult stuff," he said without meeting the blond's eyes. "My uncle got her this book that's supposed to let her talk to—spirits, or something," he finished unconvincingly. "So she's got it in her head to try it out. I wish he wouldn't encourage her."

"That's dangerous, Caleb," Isaac said with a frown. He moved to sit, but the only place would have been beside Caleb on the bed, and heat rose in his cheeks far too quickly at the thought of being on a bed with the other boy, so he stayed where he was. "I'm not sure you all should be messing around with that stuff, are you?"

"Andras says it isn't going to work anyway," he shrugged. "He'd know."

Isaac tilted his head and pressed his lips together. He wanted to tell Caleb that he didn't have to dodge questions—that Isaac already knew his secret. But it felt like such an invasion, and Barachiel had said that if Caleb felt threatened, something bad might happen. The last thing Isaac wanted was to scare Caleb off just when he'd started to open up. He would wait for him to tell him on his own. "Well, if you say so," he said, and he looked down at his feet and forced his hands to stop fidgeting.

"Look," Caleb sighed, "could you stop looking like I'm going to eat you?"

"I'm sorry. I'm just—after last night, I...I don't want you to get the wrong idea. I'm not—like that."

"Like what? Gay? Your dick sure seemed—"

"I meant—I meant promiscuous!" Isaac cut in, and he touched his cheeks to hide the sudden flush in them. "I'm not—promiscuous."

Caleb ticked an eyebrow at him. "Are you saying I'm promiscuous?"

Isaac paused. "Well, I mean, you—you acted like—and then last night—"

"You think I'm slutty; is that it?"

"No!" he blurted out immediately. "No, I would never say—I just meant—you know, for me, personally, the level of...and then you seemed ex—experienced, and...oh, cookie crumbs," he sighed, and he looked so hopeless that Caleb's frown broke into a faint smile.

"It's fine," he said. "I am a little slutty."

"Caleb, I didn't mean to—"

"It's fine," he pressed. "I was just teasing you."

Isaac let out a heavy sigh as his hands finally dropped from his face, and he found himself smiling at tiny quirk on the other boy's lips. "A—anyway, did you have anything in mind to do today?"

For a moment, Caleb looked up at him with a faint furrow in his brow, and a shudder touched Isaac's spine as the dark-haired boy chewed his lip. Then he shifted on the bed and shrugged one shoulder. "I just...wanted to hang out, I guess. It was a little crowded for talking at the bonfire thing."

"You could have talked to other people too, you know."

"I told you, I'm not interested in them."

"Well how do you know, if you never talk to them?"

"What's it to you how many friends I have? I was fine at zero until you came along."

Isaac's stomach fluttered, and he couldn't help the smile on his face. "Are you...you're saying we're friends?"

Caleb hesitated as though he hadn't realized what he'd said, and he pressed his lips together and pretended to care deeply about a knot of thread in his blanket. "Whatever, I guess," he muttered.

Isaac chewed his bottom lip for a moment, and then he sat down on the bed beside the other boy with a timid smile. "You said you'd let me listen to that twenty one pilots album," he said, and he thought he saw another ghost of a smile on Caleb's face before he looked up.

Isaac stayed in Caleb's room until dark, listening to music, talking about classes, and exchanging stories. Caleb's were mostly about strange 2 a.m. happenings at parties, and Isaac had a variety of Bible camp memories. But every time Caleb made that little noise that Isaac grew to understand was his version of a laugh—he let out the tiniest snort and looked down at the ground to keep Isaac from seeing the soft twitch of his lips—it made the blond's heart thump in his chest. In the middle of the day, Andras knocked on the door and brought them some snacks and drinks, but the rest of their time together slipped away unnoticed. Isaac wouldn't even have realized the sun had set if his father hadn't called to ask why he wasn't home for dinner. He apologized profusely, promised to talk to Caleb later, and called out a swift goodbye to the lounging demon as he passed through the living room. Caleb was his friend, he thought with a smile on his face as he jogged back down the lane to his street. Caleb had said they were friends. His smile faltered slightly. Why did that thought suddenly make him a little sad?

12

Caleb watched Isaac run through the yard from his bedroom window, his chin on his folded arms. Being next to him all day and not touching him had been torture, but Caleb was determined to figure out what the hell was going on with himself. Most importantly, why he had jerked off twice the night before and still fallen asleep thinking of Isaac's flushed face looking up at him in the darkness. It wasn't just that he wanted him; he knew that. He wanted to see the blush on his face, wanted to see him bite his lip, beg Caleb to stop but not really mean it. But there was something else, too, and he'd thought that if he could hold off on the sexy parts, that 'something else' might become clear. It hadn't. All he knew was that when Isaac was nearby, he grew hot, and he could almost feel the blood running in his veins, scorching him from the inside out. It was the complete opposite of the quiet, calm cold he was looking for. It made his head hurt. He hated it, and he wanted more.

Andras opened his bedroom door without knocking and leaned against the door frame. "So, how did your little stay-in date go?"

"Ugh, can we not?" Caleb sighed as he turned away from the window.

"Suit yourself. Come downstairs; there's dinner. And then you can help your mother."

"Great." Caleb pushed himself off of his bed and followed the demon into the hall. "Why go to all this trouble if you aren't even going to let her talk to anybody?"

"It isn't a matter of letting. Your mother wants to talk to the adversary himself, and he doesn't take collect calls."

"So tell her who my dad really is. Tell me."

"You know I can't, Caleb. Those are the rules."

"Some fucking demon," Caleb scoffed. "Isn't breaking rules sort of what you guys do?"

"On the contrary; demons are more bound up in technicality and bureaucracy than anyone else you're likely to meet. How do you think we have such a reputation for making all those sneaky deals? Everything is in the wording. Your very existence is a technicality."

"But why? What's he doing that's so important he can't show his face even once? I don't care—but, you know, for mom."

"Mhm." Andras paused at the top of the stairs and put a hand on Caleb's chest to make him pause. "Caleb, your father...you ought to know that you may just never meet him. Once you're fully realized, maybe he'll come, but before that, it's impossible. Or maybe he's just waiting for you to stop being such a broody little shit and vacuum every once in a while."

"Wait, what does that even mean, fully realized? You mean making deals?"

Andras shrugged one shoulder as he folded his arms. "Well, four isn't exactly impressive, Caleb. And you've had almost a week to work on your little friend." He sighed at the scowl on the boy's face. "Look. This may not be the best time to talk about this."

"Why?"

"Well, you're a bit in flux at the moment, aren't you? That boy is making you sentimental."

"That's none of your fucking business. Tell me what you mean."

"Easy there, little lamb. You want the truth? Fine. You're of two minds by nature. How could you not be? One foot in the realm of man and the other in the realm of demons. They aren't compatible. Right now, you're in limbo—you feel, and you hunger, and you do all those things that men do, but you long for that peace of the unliving you had before. You felt it when you made your deals, didn't you?"

Caleb nodded but wouldn't look at him.

"You can have that again. You can have it always. But to get it, you give up what makes you human. The more deals you make, the more you separate yourself from humans and hone your powers, the more you become like me. Like your father. Like you asked me to show you how to be," he added pointedly. "But if you go too far, you'll find yourself another creature entirely from what you are now." He shrugged. "Maybe that's something you want. But you can also choose humanity. You'll never be one of them. They'll never understand you, and if they knew the truth, they'd probably try to kill you. But there are things about humans that are worthwhile, if you care to look for them. You have the option. Trade the souls you've taken, or release them, and never take another. Find something to ground you here. Something that makes you feel alive instead of cold." He gave the boy a sly smile. "Obviously, you know which road I'd prefer you take, but that's the beauty of the gift your mother's given you—it's your right to choose."

Caleb picked at the edge of his long sleeve and stared at the floor without answering. Other kids didn't deal with these problems. Isaac didn't go home and worry about whether or not he was going to become a "fully realized" demon or not. Caleb would take questioning his sexuality over this bullshit any day.

Andras put a hand on his shoulder. "Luckily, it isn't a decision you have to make today. Come and have some supper."

Caleb nodded, and he followed his guardian down the stairs to the dining room. His mother picked at her dinner like a child eager to be excused, and when they were finished, they all filed back into the living room for some light after-dinner demon summoning. Somewhere between his mother's chanting and Andras flicking the lights off for "atmosphere," Caleb's phone vibrated in his pocket, and he pulled it out to check the screen while his mother read Latin from the open book in front of her. It was a text from Isaac.

I forgot to ask! Would you come to service in the morning? My mom said we could pick you up.

Caleb snorted and dropped down on the displaced sofa to answer. Andras glanced at him, but he seemed more concerned with making sure Caleb's mother didn't accidentally manifest anything in the living room.

Service like church? Caleb typed back. *I'll pass.*

I think it would do you good. And it would mean a lot to me if you'd try.

Caleb let his head fall back against the couch cushion with a frustrated grunt and lifted his phone over his head to see the screen. *Church isn't the place for me. I'm going somewhere with my uncle anyway. I'll see you after.*

I'll ask again next week.

Caleb hid his faint smile as he slipped his phone back into his pocket. Something to make him feel alive.

His mother didn't manage to summon any infernal beings into the house—any more than were usually there, at least—and Caleb sat on the couch to comfort her for a while before he went to bed. He laid awake staring at his ceiling for a long time. He could still hear her down the hall. He hated it when she cried. Caleb might have had some resentment about his absent father for his own sake, but what really made him angry was the way his mother longed after some asshole who had clearly abandoned her. If Caleb ever did meet his father, he couldn't be sure he wouldn't punch him in the face.

In the morning, he texted Isaac to ask what he was doing before he remembered that the other boy would be in church. By the time Isaac answered, Caleb had done his weekend homework, eaten a late breakfast, and listened to the entirety of the *Give Up* album while lying on his bed. He almost wished he had gone to church after all, just so that he wouldn't have been alone. He sat up when his phone buzzed and stared at it until the screen went dark again. Since when did he care about being alone? He almost ignored Isaac's text out of spite, but then he frowned and opened the message.

We're having lunch out with some of dad's friends. Want to come over after? Your dog is scary.

Caleb chuckled softly and slipped his headphones from his head before he answered, letting them hang around his neck. *Just tell me when.*

He sat on the back porch with Nobah's head in his lap and a cigarette in his hand while he waited for Isaac to text him again. This kind of anticipation was new to him. He wanted to see Isaac again, but he didn't *want* anything from him. Sure, Caleb was attracted to him, and he wanted to pursue that, but that wasn't all there was. He thought. Nothing had happened between them the day before, and it had been...nice. If he was going to Isaac's house today, they probably wouldn't have to worry about that kind of opportunity arising. He would be able to see if there was anything to this...friend-you're-also-attracted-to thing. He wasn't sure he liked the feeling of waiting around, anxious to see someone, but he still jumped to answer when his phone sounded. He put out his cigarette, leaned his head through the back door to yell to Andras that he was leaving, and headed off down the driveway.

Isaac answered the door when he knocked and invited him inside. A man who Caleb guessed was Isaac's father was sitting on the couch, and someone was moving around in the kitchen.

"Dad, this is Caleb," Isaac said, and the man rose to shake his hand. He was tall, with broad shoulders and rough, calloused hands that gripped Caleb's hard enough that it should have hurt. His mouse-brown hair had been slicked back with something or other, and he smiled at Caleb, but it didn't quite reach his eyes.

"Nice to meet you, son. Isaac's told us all about you. Pity you couldn't make it to service this morning," he added pointedly.

"For who?" Caleb asked, and Isaac quickly forced in a laugh and came between them.

"So, dad, can we watch a movie while Caleb's here?"

"S'pose so. I've got to change the oil in the car. But you help your mother if she wants you, hear?"

"Yes, sir."

The man watched Caleb with a wary eye as he passed him, but Isaac was already heading for the entertainment center by the time the front door swung closed. Caleb stared with mild awe as Isaac tugged open the cabinet doors to reveal a small, ancient-looking television sitting on top of a VCR. Along the shelf beside it, there was a short row of VHS tapes, some with worn covers and some with peeling handwritten labels.

"Holy shit," Caleb snorted as he approached, and Isaac put a panicked finger to his lips and gestured toward the kitchen.

"Don't swear," he whispered.

"How old is this thing?"

Isaac shrugged. "We don't watch much television. Dad watches the news, and sometimes mom gets to see her soaps in the afternoon. Mostly it stays on *The 700 Club*."

"Is it in color?"

"Of course it's in color!" Isaac answered defensively. He huffed softly. "What do you want to watch?"

"I dunno; what do you even have? Like five copies of *Ben-Hur*?"

Isaac paused. "Just the one."

Caleb bent down to check the row of movies. *Ben-Hur*, *The Ten Commandments*, *Field of Dreams*, *The Greatest Story Ever Told*, *It's A Wonderful Life*, *Stand By Me*, *Flight of the Navigator*, *Jesus of Nazareth*, *The Sandlot*, *The Bridge on the River Kwai*, *Bull Durham*, and *Full Metal Jacket*. He turned to look over his shoulder at Isaac. "So, like...are these the only movies you've ever seen?"

"What? Of course not," he answered with a soft frown. "We just...we don't spend money on things like that. We don't have to watch anything. I know this isn't the...sort of thing you're used to. We can do something else," he said in a rush, and Caleb straightened and very lightly touched the other boy's wrist.

"Isaac, it's fine." He picked *Flight of the Navigator* out of the row and offered it to him. "I always liked this one."

The blond's face brightened, and he took the tape from Caleb and slid it from its cover. "Shoot; it needs rewinding."

"Dude," Caleb chuckled, and Isaac smiled as he fed the tape into the VCR.

The machine gave a few weary whirs and clunks, then hummed as it rewound the tape to the start. Isaac stood by the entertainment center to wait, since he said the remote control was broken, and then he pressed play, and the two boys took up their places on the couch. Isaac's mother appeared during the opening credits with an overflowing bowl of popcorn and placed it between them. She smiled as she greeted Caleb, then gave a small wave with her fingers and vanished back into the kitchen, humming a soft song. Isaac definitely took after her, Caleb thought.

Isaac's father was in and out of the house, and his mother came through the room a few times while they sat and watched the movie, awkwardly avoiding each other's hands in the popcorn bowl. Even if he had intended to try anything, he couldn't do it with Isaac's parents around. Caleb tried to stop himself from looking at Isaac too much, but every time he heard the boy chuckle or happened to catch him smiling, he had to chew on the corner of his lip to keep from reaching for him. He wondered if the other boy could tell how hot his skin felt when their hands happened to brush in the bowl. His heart went a little faster every time Isaac glanced over at him, and he had a nervous tightness in his stomach. It was embarrassing.

By the time the movie ended, Caleb just wanted to get away. Isaac's mother asked if he was staying for dinner, but he lied and said that his uncle had plans.

"That's a shame," she said with a smile. "You know you're welcome here anytime, Caleb."

"Thanks," he muttered, and he offered Isaac a brief glance as a goodbye on his way to the door, but the blond stopped him with a hand on his arm.

"Mom, I'm gonna walk Caleb to the road, okay?"

"Sure thing, pumpkin. Hurry back, now; these potatoes aren't going to peel themselves."

"Yes ma'am!" he called as he urged Caleb out the front door. He walked beside the other boy toward the main road, fidgeting with his hands in silence until they reached the line of trees separating Caleb's driveway from the subdivision.

"Were you afraid I'd get lost?" Caleb asked when they stopped, but Isaac didn't look up at him for a moment. "Hello?"

"Were you just..." Isaac started, but then he stopped. He opened his mouth once more and shut it, then took a single, purposeful breath and looked up into the other boy's dark eyes. "Were you just going to leave?"

Caleb's brow furrowed in confusion. "I didn't know it was super important to you that I stay for dinner."

"Not that," Isaac sighed. "I just...yesterday, we just hung out—which was fine, I had a good time—and then I had to leave all of a sudden, and then today, you seemed like you couldn't get away fast enough."

Caleb watched him for a few beats, glancing down at the blond's wringing hands. "I don't know what the—"

"I thought you would try to kiss me," Isaac blurted out, then he covered his mouth with one hand and held his elbow with the other, his cheeks burning red. He peeked up at Caleb with nervous grey eyes and moved his hand just enough to speak. "Why didn't you try to kiss me?"

Caleb's mouth dropped open against his will, and for a moment, he thought his lungs had stopped working. Then, without thinking, he pulled Isaac with him behind the nearest tree and caught him in a fierce kiss, his hands on either side of the other boy's face. Isaac reached up to clutch at Caleb's sleeves. He didn't fight or flinch away; he willingly opened his mouth when Caleb's tongue sought entry, and Caleb groaned at the blond's soft whimper and pressed him back against the trunk of the tree. He kissed Isaac until he couldn't breathe, until everything around them went dull and unimportant. He broke away to take a single breath and then kissed him again, his arms moving to wrap around the other boy's waist while Isaac's fingers tangled themselves in Caleb's hair. Isaac's tongue was warm and wet against his, and he could still taste the salt on his lips. The blond's soft panting breaths were intoxicating, drawing Caleb back in every time he thought to pull away. He only stopped when Isaac turned his head, and even then he wouldn't let him go. He held the other boy tight against him while Isaac laid his head on his shoulder and fought to catch his breath.

"I will kiss you," Caleb promised in a whisper, his cheek brushing the other boy's hair, "anytime you want me to."

"I didn't...I didn't know I wanted you to," Isaac admitted, so softly that Caleb barely heard him. He fingers curled into the back of the taller boy's shirt. "But I think I...I think I like you."

Caleb could practically feel the boy's blush against his shoulder, but he couldn't bring himself to tease him—not when his own heart thumped so painfully at the words. "I like you too," he said instead.

Isaac lifted his head to look up at him with a faint, shy smile. "I don't...really know what to say next," he laughed. Caleb's grip tightened around his waist.

"Nothing," he said, and he bent to cover the other boy's lips with his own. Isaac let out a small squeak but immediately returned the kiss. Caleb pushed closer to him, desperate to taste as much of him as he could have. He shifted down just enough to hook his hands under Isaac's thighs and easily lifted him up, forcing the boy to scramble to hold on with his legs around Caleb's hips. Isaac panted out the other boy's name, half panicked and half eager as Caleb drew his teeth down his neck and placed a hot kiss at the hollow of his throat. Isaac's fingertips dug into Caleb's shoulders, and he let out a strained whine at the touch of the other boy's tongue on his collarbone. Caleb could feel the blond's growing arousal against his stomach, and he pushed him back hard against the tree with a growling groan, rolling his hips against the hard press of the other boy's erection.

Isaac cried out softly and clamped his hand to the side of Caleb's neck for balance. "C-Caleb, don't—"

"Don't what?" he whispered against the blonde's ear as he tugged him firmly forward. He felt the longing shudder run over Isaac's skin, the twitch of his cock beneath the restraining denim, and he sighed as he pressed a kiss to the tender flesh just below his ear. "I want you," he murmured, and Isaac's fingers tightened painfully on his neck and shoulder.

"Please stop!" the boy shouted, and Caleb was so startled that he almost dropped him. Isaac pushed gently on his shoulders until he let him down, and the two of them stood inches from each other, panting. Isaac covered his cheeks with his hands, but they did nothing to hide the deep flush of red. "I—I'm sorry, I—"

"What happened?" The blond's helpless eyes looking up at Caleb knotted his stomach.

"I can't...Caleb, even if I do like you—and I do—I do," he repeated in as sincere a tone as he could manage in his breathless state. "This…this is too fast. I don't want to get…lost. Because of lust. I made a promise to wait. I need to...to wait."

"Wait for what?"

"For...for marriage, I thought, or..." He shook his head. "Anyway,

I…kiss—kissing is one thing, but...I'm sorry if you were expecting more," he finished, and he looked up at Caleb as though he expected to be scolded.

Caleb sighed through his nose as he looked at the other boy. "I'm not usually good at waiting," he said.

"Y—you said you didn't mind taking your time."

"Yeah, but I meant, like...fucking slowly."

"Oh, gosh," Isaac whimpered, and he sank back against the tree and peeked up at Caleb over his fingers.

Caleb took a deep breath and held Isaac by the shoulders, then leaned in and pressed a slow, warm kiss to his lips. "I like you, apparently," he said softly. "And you're the one who's new at this. So you set the pace. Just don't get pissed at me if I get hard when we kiss, because you're so fucking hot when you whine like that," he added, cupping the boy's chin and letting his thumb brush his lower lip.

"Geez, Caleb," Isaac murmured, chewing his lips in embarrassment, and he lowered his eyes and let his fingers brush the other boy's wrist. "What am I supposed to say when you say stuff like that?"

"How about, 'you're right, let's do it right now?' That's an option. Unless you'd really rather go peel potatoes."

"Potatoes!" Isaac shouted suddenly, and for a moment, Caleb wasn't sure if he was worried about the actual potatoes, or if this was another food-based faux-swear. "Oh," he fussed, pulling away from the other boy and hurriedly trying to straighten his hair and shirt. "My dad's gonna have my hide. I—I'll see you at school, okay?"

Before he could leave, Caleb grabbed his hand and pulled him back for one last lingering kiss. "I'll see you tomorrow."

Isaac smiled at him with red in his cheeks, and he almost seemed like he wanted an excuse to wait, but then he released Caleb's hand and took off back down the road at a jog.

13

Isaac's mother only scolded him gently for taking so long, even though she had already started peeling the potatoes herself. Isaac immediately took the peeler from her and set about slicing the skin from the rest.

"I didn't know Caleb lived so far away," she teased him, and he frowned guiltily up at her.

"I'm sorry. We just got to talking."

"It's all right. I'm glad he came over. He seems like a boy who needs a friend."

"I think he is," Isaac nodded. He helped his mother finish prepping for dinner and then hid in his room to finish his homework and not think about Caleb. It had been bad enough trying to will his erection away at the front door of his house; he didn't need his mind to wander right before supper.

When his mother called him to the table, he sat with his parents and held their hands while his father said grace, just like every other night. Unlike every other night, Isaac said his own private prayer begging forgiveness for the line he'd—again—almost crossed with Caleb. He made an effort to keep from blushing while he ate.

"That boy smelled like cigarettes," his father said unprompted. He looked across the table at Isaac while he cut his piece of chicken. "He smokes?"

"H—His uncle smokes," Isaac answered without thinking, and a guilty weight formed in his stomach as soon as the lie was out of his mouth. He never lied to his parents. What was he thinking?

"Hm," his father grunted skeptically. "And why didn't he come to service?"

"He's...I don't think he's a Christian, dad. He told me he's never been to church at all."

"What kind of family is that? You were over there yesterday; are they...off?"

"They were very nice to me," he said, glad that wasn't a lie, at least. He didn't have to mention the demon-summoning circle painted on the living room floor or the giant killer wolf-dog.

"Well, you just mind yourself around him, you hear? I don't like the look of him."

"Oh, you just don't trust anyone from any city bigger than Atlanta," his mother chuckled. Isaac was glad for the ease in tension. "He's a teenager."

"He's just quiet, that's all," Isaac added. "He's real nice once you get to know him." That felt a little like a lie, but he was sure there was something in Caleb that could be legitimately called "nice." Somewhere. Isaac was positive that with just a little more coaxing, Caleb would let him see behind the thick wall he'd built around himself.

"I'm sure he is, pumpkin," his mother said before his father could argue. "Have you finished all your homework?"

"Almost."

"Well then you scoot back to your room and finish up," she said. "I don't want to hear about you missing any work because of your new friend."

"Yes ma'am." He shoveled the last of his potatoes into his mouth and excused himself. His mind drifted back to Caleb while he tried to write his paragraph for English class—the heat of his kiss, how easily he had scooped him up, as if Isaac weighed nothing—but he bit his cheek, spun his ring on his finger as a reminder, and hunkered down over his desk to write.

Later in the night, his mother came in to kiss his head and wish him good night, and he happily shut his bedroom door behind her. The best thing he could do would be to turn in early and try not to think about it. In the morning, he would have school to worry about, and chores, and he and Caleb could talk innocently between classes. That would be good. Except...he had admitted to the other boy that he liked him, and they both knew he didn't mean as a friend. Caleb had said he liked him too, and they had—kissed. Isaac flopped face down on his bed and hid his face in his pillow. He hadn't expected to have such a reaction. He could hardly breathe when Caleb kissed him, and when he had picked him up, and Isaac had felt the other boy's—he shut his eyes and pulled his pillow tighter around his head, trying to ignore the tingling in his belly. He let out a soft, helpless sound as he felt a throbbing in his groin, but he refused to give in to the urge to press his hips into the mattress. All of this was clouding his head.

He didn't know what any of it meant. If Caleb had been a girl, would it be so complicated? If Isaac said he liked her, and she liked him too, and then they kissed...Isaac would have asked her on a real date, maybe? He couldn't do that with Caleb, could he? He would have asked a girl to be his girlfriend, he thought. They could have hung out together, talked on the phone and texted, and watched movies together—all the things he'd been doing with Caleb all week, he realized with a sigh.

Isaac lifted his head just enough to put his chin on his arm, and he stared at the phone on his nightstand. He slowly reached out to pick it up, and he opened his messages with Caleb and stared at the screen in consternation for quite some time. Then he tapped out his message and frowned at it for a while longer before finally scrunching his face up in reluctant anticipation and tapping "send."

Am I your boyfriend?

He waited with his phone in both hands and his lips pressed together, so focused on the black screen that he actually jumped when it finally vibrated.

What are you talking about?

Isaac deflated. That wasn't quite the answer he was hoping for. Or was it? Did he want to be Caleb's boyfriend? The whole thing felt so confusing. He typed his reply and sent it with his brows knit together. *I mean, are we dating?*

Do you want to date? The reply came quickly this time.

I don't know. I've never done anything like this before. How did you know you wanted to date your other boyfriends?

I haven't had any other boyfriends.

But you said you—Isaac stopped typing. He had assumed that because Caleb had admitted to being experienced sexually, that meant he'd had lots of boyfriends before, but—it had never occurred to Isaac that Caleb might have just been sleeping around. His face went hot at the thought. *Oh,* he typed instead.

You're thinking I'm slutty again, aren't you?

Isaac hid his face for a moment and only peeked back at the screen. He hadn't meant anything by it, but the thought of Caleb doing the sort of thing they'd been doing, and more, with other people—it made him feel slightly sick. Before he could answer, the phone buzzed in his hand again.

I've never dated anyone before because there's never been anyone I could put up with. But I've put up with you for a whole week already, and I still want to see you tomorrow.

Isaac's throat closed up as he read the message over and over again, and he bit his lip to keep from smiling like an idiot. *I want to see you too,* he typed back.

Well, I really want to see you right now, because I can't stop thinking about kissing you.

Sorry. Isaac didn't know what else to say. He couldn't bring himself to admit that he'd been thinking about it too, or how just reading that line of text had sent another jolt through him.

You could apologize in person if you wanted to sneak out with me.

I can't do that! I'd get caught, and dad would kill me.

Then you could at least send me a snapchat of you touching yourself.

Isaac stuffed his phone under his pillow and covered it with his hands as though he could bury the message itself. He could hear the heavy thump of his heartbeat in his ears, and his cheeks were so hot that he felt sunburned. He heard the phone vibrate again through the pillow, but he was afraid to look. He slowly pulled back the pillow and checked the screen, but it was only another text.

I know you're not going to. But think of me when you do it.

Isaac almost dropped his phone more than once as he fumbled to reply. *I don't do that.*

What do you mean, you don't do that? Everybody does that. Never?

Isaac chewed his lip for a moment. *It's lust. I've done it before, a few times, but I try not to.* He waited for a reply, but instead the phone buzzed violently in his hand, and the screen lit up with a phone call. He hesitated, staring at Caleb's name, and then he answered quietly, "Hello?"

"Dude," Caleb said without bothering to greet him. "How many is a few times?"

"I don't—I don't know, not that many, maybe—"

"You know what? Never mind. If you can even hope to count, it's too few. How do you survive?"

"It's not that big a deal," he said in a hushed voice. He crept out of his bed to peek through his door and found the house dark and quiet, so he clicked the door shut again and curled up on his bed. He should have been getting into his pajamas, but he didn't dare get undressed with Caleb's voice in his ear.

"Are you kidding? I jerk off almost every day. Why are you whispering?"

"I'm not supposed to have calls this late."

There was a pause. "Look at you, little rule-breaker. So everybody's gone to bed, huh? Are you in bed too?"

Isaac didn't think his skin could feel any warmer. "I—I'm on my bed," he clarified.

"What do you wear to bed, Isaac?" Caleb's voice was soft and low, and it ran a slow shiver up the blond's spine.

"Pajamas, I guess," the boy whispered back.

"Pants, or shorts?"

"P-Pants, mostly, and...and a t-shirt. Why do you want to know?"

"I just want to have the most accurate image I can of you lying in bed."

"Geez," Isaac sighed. "Do you say this stuff just to embarrass me?"

"I want to know how to picture you," Caleb murmured.

Isaac huffed softly. "W-Well what do you wear to bed?" he asked defiantly, but the other boy chuckled.

"Nothing."

"N...nothing? So you're...right now, you're...?"

"Naked. And wondering if I'm not as good at this as I thought, if you're not jerking off tonight after what we did."

He held the phone with both hands and cupped them around it to whisper into the bottom. "It—it's not like I don't have...you know, urges," he muttered. "I just...it's a sin."

"Isn't making out with other guys supposed to be a sin, too?"

"Well—"

"I felt you get hard when we were kissing. And down by the pond the other night, too. I wanted to touch you."

"Caleb..."

"I still want to. Fuck, I'm so hard just thinking about you. What are you doing to me?"

"Don't...don't swear," Isaac said meekly, but his jeans grew more uncomfortably tight with every word the other boy murmured into the phone.

"If I were there, you wouldn't be saying no," Caleb promised.

"Wh-what happened to me setting the pace?" He shifted to try to find a more comfortable position, but his only option was to unbutton his jeans. He bit his lip as he undid his zipper, hoping that Caleb couldn't somehow hear it and get the wrong idea.

"You're killing me," Caleb groaned. "You didn't like feeling how hard you made me today? Just from a kiss?"

"I..." Isaac couldn't quite find any words. His stomach was in knots, but it wasn't worry—embarrassment, maybe, but also excitement. It was frightening, but a little thrilling, too, to hear the hidden plea in the stoic boy's voice. His hand flattened against his stomach almost against his will, and he took an unsteady breath as he answered, "I did."

"If you hadn't stopped me today, do you know what I would have done?"

Isaac's breath caught in his throat. "What?"

"Take your pants off, and I'll tell you."

"M-My—"

"Mhm. Take them off."

Isaac whimpered softly with indecision, but before he knew what he was doing, he had his back against the mattress and the phone cradled against his shoulder, his hips lifted as he shimmed his jeans down his hips. He kicked out of the pants and left them crumpled on the floor, and he laid very still on the bed in his shirt and underwear, the air from his ceiling fan raising prickles of goosebumps on his bare thighs.

"Are they off?" Caleb asked after a moment.

"Yes," he answered in a strained whisper. He glanced down at himself and felt a flash of heat in his face as he saw his own erection straining the white fabric of his briefs, the pearling tip just barely pushing past the waistband to brush his stomach.

"Do you have underwear on?"

"Y-Yes."

"Take them off."

"Caleb," he whined in a whisper, but the other boy tutted at him, so Isaac timidly hooked his thumb into the waistband of his briefs, attempting to avoid touching himself as he wiggled out of them.

"Are you hard?" Caleb asked, and Isaac chewed his lip uncertainly.

"Yes," he said, covering his eyes with one arm as though he could hide from the other boy's voice.

"If you hadn't stopped me today, I would have pushed you up against that tree, and I would have gotten down on my knees, pushed your shirt up, and kissed your stomach. Would you have liked that?"

"I...I think so," he answered. He wet his lips and kept his hand firmly on his stomach, telling himself he wouldn't let it wander, but his skin tingled as he imagined Caleb's lips brushing his belly.

"Then I would have unbuttoned your jeans, and I would have taken your hard dick in my hand and stroked it, hard and slow at first."

Isaac sucked in a soft gasp, and his stomach tensed as his fingers gingerly wrapped around himself. He slowly moved his hand and squeezed, wishing it was Caleb touching him.

"I would have kept touching you until you made that cute little sound, when I knew you wanted more, and then I would have put your cock in my mouth. You've never had your dick sucked, have you, Isaac?"

"No," he whispered, his back arching slightly as he quickened his pace. He could picture Caleb on his knees, those dark eyes looking up at him, hands gentle on his hips, taking Isaac into his mouth again and again as he moved. All of his shame melted away at the soft promise of Caleb's voice through the phone, and he let himself give a small moan as his hand twisted around the head of his aching cock.

"Are you jerking off?"

"Yes," he answered without hesitation. The fingers of his free hand tightened in the fabric of his pillowcase.

"God, I wish I could see you," Caleb groaned, and Isaac heard his quiet, panting breath. His stomach flipped as the other boy grunted softly.

"A-are you doing it too?" he asked, and Caleb's faint chuckle sent a shiver down his spine.

"Of course I'm doing it too," he said. "You make me so hard, Isaac." He paused to let out a quiet moan. "The next time I get you alone, what do you want me to do to you?"

Isaac chewed his lip in hesitation, but his hand didn't stop working. With his eyes closed, he could almost pretend Caleb was next to him whispering into his ear, instead of far away in his own bedroom. Isaac tried to imagine what he looked like, naked on his bed, his lightly tanned skin tingling and hot to the touch, head thrown back to bare the tender skin of his neck as he stroked himself toward climax with thoughts of Isaac in his head. The image was too much for him, and Isaac's heels pressed into his mattress as he pumped helplessly into his fisted hand.

"I—I want...I want you to touch me," he whispered, shivering at the groan Caleb gave in response.

"Where?" the other boy panted.

"My...I—" He stopped to let out a soft cry as he bucked against his grip, feeling the desperate tension coil in his belly. "I want...I want you to touch my..."

"Your dick?" Caleb answered for him, and Isaac moaned so loudly that he hastily covered his mouth.

"Yes," he sighed gratefully, half muffled by his fingers.

"Are you going to come for me, Isaac?" Caleb whispered, and the other boy could only whimper in the affirmative. "Tell me when. I want to come with you."

Isaac's brows knit tightly together as he stroked himself. He couldn't stop the soft pants escaping his lips or the timid, yipping cries that caught in his throat as he drew closer. His hips lifted from the bed, and the muscles in his thighs began to tremble.

"I'm...I—" he started, but Caleb's rough groan cut him off.

"Let me hear you come, Isaac," he said, and the gentle command in his voice pushed the blond over the edge. He grit his teeth and let his back arch as a soft, strained moan tore itself from him, and he spilled hot come onto his own stomach with the last few eager pumps of his fist. He heard Caleb through the phone, growling out his own climax, and Isaac collapsed limply onto the bed, his phone crooked between his ear and the pillow. He struggled to breathe, his skin shivering slightly as he let his hand rest on his hip.

"Fuck, you're hot," Caleb said after a long silence filled only with the sound of their breath. His quiet laugh made Isaac smile.

"Don't swear," he whispered.

"Even if I say, yes, Isaac, I want you to be my fucking boyfriend?"

Isaac bit his lip, smiling faintly as he took his phone in his hand. He brought it with him as he sat up. "I...I guess that's okay," he laughed.

"Good. I'll see you tomorrow, right?"

"Right."

"Cool. If you decide to jerk off again, call me back."

"I—I'm not going to do it again!" Isaac hissed, but Caleb only chuckled.

"Night, Isaac."

"Good night, Caleb," he answered softly, and he hung up the phone and set it back on his nightstand. He crept to his desk for some tissues to clean himself up, and then quickly pulled on his pajama pants and curled up under his blanket with a comforting heat in his chest. He was Caleb's boyfriend.

14

Isaac stared at himself in the bathroom mirror the next morning, clutching the edges of his sink until his fingers felt stiff. What had he been thinking? Not only had he given in and—touched himself, with Caleb listening in no less, he had agreed to be his boyfriend. Isaac didn't mind that part so much, despite the anxious flutters it gave his stomach every time he thought about it, but he didn't even know what it meant. Was Caleb going to want to tell people? Were Isaac's parents going to find out? He wouldn't be able to bear their shame. His father would beat him, probably, and make him swear never to see Caleb again. His mother might cry. Some of his friends might understand, but the people in his youth group, the pastor—how could he tell them? It was impossible. If he wanted to keep seeing Caleb, if he wanted to figure out how serious this was and if it was more than a passing crush, they couldn't let anyone know.

He scrubbed his face with cold water one more time, pretending it was going to cool the heat in his skin. He had jumped head first into all this, and above all, he didn't know how he was supposed to look Caleb in the face after what they'd done last night. He was certain he would shrivel up and die of embarrassment.

Isaac dried his face and puffed out his cheeks in a sigh, then went to the kitchen to greet his mother and eat a quick breakfast. He rode the bus to school with a tension in his chest somewhere between dread and excitement, and as soon as he spotted Caleb climbing out of his uncle's car, his whole body seemed to seize up. He almost got back on the bus, or hid in the bushes, or took the back way into the building—anything to give himself more time to prepare for being in front of the other boy again. But Caleb had seen him. He didn't smile or wave, but he watched Isaac take each hesitant step toward him with a stare that felt like it burned right through him.

"Hey," Caleb said casually as Isaac got close, not seeming bothered in the slightest by the monumental change that had taken place in Isaac's life over the last 48 hours.

"I need to talk to you," Isaac replied immediately. He kept an arm's length between them just in case Caleb decided to be affectionate. He needed to know what was in store before it happened, and definitely before anyone else saw them. "Right now?"

He thought he saw a faint twitch of a smile on the other boy's lips, but Caleb only shrugged one shoulder. "Sure."

Isaac led him around a quiet corner of the building while the other students filed inside or lingered in the yard, fidgeting with his backpack straps the entire way. He had no idea what he was going to say. How could he ask to keep their relationship a secret without Caleb thinking he was ashamed of him?

When they rounded the corner, out of sight of the other students, Isaac barely had time to turn to face Caleb before the other boy had him pressed against the wall, his lips on his in a hard, longing kiss. Isaac wilted into the kiss, his heart in his throat and his fingers tight around the straps of his backpack as Caleb's hand cupped his cheek. When Caleb pulled away, Isaac looked up at him with his breath escaping him in a trembling sigh, and he knew that he was blushing.

"Sorry," Caleb murmured as he let his hand drop. "What did you want to talk about?"

"I—I...I forgot," Isaac admitted, but then he shook his head and squeezed out from between Caleb and the wall. "I mean...I wanted to ask you...what you—you know, what this means."

"What what means?"

"Being your...you know, your...boyfriend," he finished, whispering the last word with heat in his cheeks.

"What do you think it means?"

"I don't know! I just...whatever it is, do you think we can...keep it secret? Just for now?" Isaac waited for Caleb to scowl at him, or snap, but the other boy didn't seem surprised.

"I didn't figure you were going to want to tell your whole congregation you were dating another guy. Besides, if we told, your parents wouldn't let you see me anymore, right?"

Isaac let out a long sigh of relief. "Yes," he said. "I just..."

"Don't worry about it. It's way easier to get time alone with you if your parents don't know anything. I can keep quiet."

"Thank you, Caleb. I didn't want you to think—that I was ashamed. This is all just so new to me, and I like you, but I...I've just never felt this way before. It's silly; I know we've only known each other a little while, but I just..." He sighed.

"I get it," Caleb assured him. "I haven't exactly done this before either, you know. I think...we both need time."

Isaac watched the faint crease in the other boy's brow, the soft frown on his lips. At least it was comforting—a little—to know that Caleb might be feeling out of his depth, too.

"That doesn't mean I want to stop making out," Caleb added, and Isaac let out a nervous laugh as he dropped his gaze. "So I'm gonna need something from you if you really want to keep this secret."

"What? But you just said—"

"Kiss me," Caleb interrupted. "Right now, because you want to. If you really want to do this, I don't want to chase you. I want you to be all in."

Isaac hesitated. Caleb watched him, waiting, while Isaac's heart threatened to pound its way through his ribs and escape. Isaac inched closer to the other boy. He didn't know how Caleb just leaned in and kissed him so easily. It seemed so natural when he did it, but as Isaac slowly leaned in toward him, he was certain he was going to screw it up somehow. All of a sudden he didn't know which way to tilt his head, or whether he should have his lips parted, or if he was allowed to touch Caleb with his hands. Finally, with a surge of bravery, he leaned forward and touched his lips to the other boy's, lingering for barely a moment before he broke away with an audible smack.

For a second, Caleb only stared at him in surprise, but then he shifted his bag on his shoulder and looked down at the ground with the first genuine smile on his face that Isaac had ever seen.

"That's...good enough, I guess," Caleb muttered, his hair a dark curtain hiding his eyes. He looked up as the school bell rang. "Well, come on."

Isaac followed him into the building with significantly less worry on his shoulders. Whatever nervousness he'd felt had melted away at the sight of the quiet boy's secret smile.

It was hard to focus in the classes that they had together. Isaac kept sneaking glances at the other boy and becoming distracted. He scolded himself and tried to keep his attention on his schoolwork, but he kept finding himself with a grin on his face. During fourth period, Heather slipped him a note while the teacher's back was turned that simply said, *You've had that stupid smile on your face all day. Got a secret?*

Isaac forced his face into a more neutral expression as he scribbled a reply. *Just having a good day.*

She shot him a skeptical look across the aisle and bent over the paper for a moment before passing it back to him. *A really good day. What happened when you and creeper left the bonfire early?*

He's not a creeper! Isaac wrote back. *He wasn't having fun so he went home, and I walked him since it was late. He was my guest. It's polite.*

In response, Heather drew a picture of two stick figures, one with a big smile being stabbed by the other, which had a scribble of messy hair that was clearly meant to be Caleb's. When Isaac looked up at her with a frown, she stuck her tongue out and tilted her head to feign death. Isaac pointedly folded the paper and tucked it under his textbook to end the conversation. He really needed to encourage Caleb to make more of an effort with the rest of his friends. It would be so much better for him to feel included. At the same time, he thought with his bottom lip in his teeth to hide his smile, it was sort of nice to have him all to himself. He at least hoped Caleb didn't realize the kinds of things the others said about him.

At lunch, he tried to urge conversation between Caleb and the others, but Caleb was as quiet as always. Heather at least sighed and asked him how his weekend was after Isaac stared at her across the table in an attempt to communicate his wishes telepathically.

"Pretty good," Caleb answered, which was more than Isaac expected, frankly, but he didn't seem inclined to elaborate.

As the two of them walked home together—which apparently was something they had both decided to do without discussing it—Isaac tried to chat about regular school things, like the coming baseball season, how difficult Calculus was, and whether or not what they served in the cafeteria could legally be called pizza. Caleb just walked beside him, one hand in his pocket and the other holding his cigarette, and he listened with a look on his face that somehow seemed softer than usual. They reached the fork in the road that separated their houses too soon, and Caleb stopped walking before he had to turn off toward his driveway.

"I'll see you tomorrow," he said, and he gently pulled Isaac toward him with his free hand and kissed him. It was so easy, so comfortable, that Isaac barely even blushed. It was a goodbye kiss between two people who were dating—that was all. Isaac beamed up at him and squeezed his hand.

"See you tomorrow," he murmured, but he lingered a moment with his fingers in the other boy's before he reluctantly pulled away.

For the next few days, it seemed like he and Caleb might be able to settle into a pattern. They talked between classes, chatted at lunch, and when they walked home together, they parted with a kiss. They texted in the evenings about music, homework, or whatever else crossed their minds. Sometimes Caleb texted him dirty things, but Isaac didn't even mind that. It became easier every day for him to adjust to the idea of having a boyfriend. It felt nice. Like having a best friend, but with the bonus of fluttery butterflies in your stomach whenever you were close to them. Caleb smiled occasionally, and he even exchanged a bit of conversation with the others at lunch. Heather had gone so far as to admit that Caleb "might not be all bad." Everything was looking up, and Isaac felt more and more certain that what the angel had told him was true, and that when something came from love, it couldn't be a sin. He refused to believe that Caleb's gentle goodbye kisses were sinful. Barachiel had told him that God is love—so love must have been why Isaac was chosen to help Caleb. He was hesitant to use the word, even to himself, but he knew the feeling in his chest when Caleb smiled at him wasn't lust.

Still, there was a lingering worry at the back of Isaac's brain. He would have to tell Caleb the truth eventually—that he knew what he was. That had to be the final step in really turning him away from the dark side of him. He was sure that he could convince him that it didn't bother him, that it didn't matter because Isaac could see the good in him, but how was he supposed to admit that he'd only pursued the friendship so hard because of the angel's urging?

On Thursday, Caleb dragged Isaac out of the building on their way to lunch and kissed him in the seclusion of the tiny courtyard, and Isaac had to push him away just to be able to come up for air.

"Let me come over today," Caleb whispered against his ear, and Isaac shivered at the implication.

"I...I have practice," Isaac answered.

"So skip it." He touched a kiss to the blonde's neck that caused his fingers to tighten in Caleb's shirt. "I can't go another day without being alone with you."

Isaac had to shut his eyes for a moment to clear his head. It would have been a lie to say that Caleb hadn't been on his mind, too. "I can't," he said softly. "We have a game tomorrow; I'll get in trouble if

I don't go today."

Caleb sighed and bit the other boy's bottom lip in protest, drawing a startled squeak from him. "Fine," he muttered as he took a step back. "But you're going to make it up to me later."

"Wh—Caleb," Isaac called, but the other boy was already heading for the door. "What does that mean?" He trotted after him and felt a flush in his cheeks when Caleb glanced back at him with a faint little smirk curling his lips.

The rest of the day was very fidgety for Isaac. He tapped his pencil and chewed his lip while his imagination ran wild at Caleb's suggestion. He frowned down at his worksheet in last period, certain that distraction had been the other boy's intention. How was he supposed to practice like this? Just focus, he told himself as his cheeks puffed out in a sigh. This sort of thing *was* lust.

He rushed from class to the locker room, knowing that Caleb wouldn't be waiting for him. He didn't have any interest in baseball. If Isaac came from the hometown of the Cubs, he might not have any interest, either. The exercise actually helped get his mind out of the gutter, which he was thankful for, though his phone was waiting for him in the locker room with a text from Caleb that he decided to wait to read. He got a ride home from one of his teammates, saving him a walk, and he leaned down to wave at him through the car window in thanks before heading for his front door. He chatted briefly with his father about the game the next day and then quickly hid in his room, feigning sleepiness.

Hiding the truth from his parents was the hardest part. Caleb had been gentle and patient, mostly, and they enjoyed each other's company now without needing to fill every silence. But they hadn't even had to do much sneaking around so far, and Isaac already felt guilty. If Caleb had been a girl, Isaac would hardly have been able to wait for the morning, to greet his mother for breakfast and tell her that he'd met someone. It tore at his stomach that he couldn't. He felt even worse about all the times he had assumed that who you were attracted to was a choice—that gay people were just living a sinful lifestyle. He couldn't imagine who would choose this, given the option. He hated secrets, and this whole situation was secrets on secrets. He wondered if Caleb had told his own mother, or his uncle. For the first time in his life, he thought, he wished his family was just a little bit different.

Isaac slumped down on his bed to finally check his text from Caleb. It was a picture. He flicked his thumb to open the message, and for a few long moments, he just stared, open-mouthed. Somehow his screen was now filled with a photo of Caleb, his bare torso visible only from shoulders to thighs. The sheets from his bed pooled around his hips, just barely revealing what was very clearly Caleb's loosely fisted hand around his erection. His back was arched, just a little, and Isaac could see the tension in the boy's flat stomach. For as easily as Caleb had picked him up the other day, Isaac would have expected him to be more muscular, but he was slim and lean, his tanned skin stretched taut over his hipbones. As his brain registered what he was seeing, Isaac's hand shot up to cover his mouth, and he dropped the phone onto his bed in a panic, then came to his senses and scrambled to retrieve it from the blanket.

He should delete it. He absolutely should delete it. He was lucky he hadn't decided to check the message with his teammates around. His parents didn't go through his phone, but if either of them happened to see the photo, or if anyone at school did—but Isaac hesitated. He pulled his feet up under him on the bed and chewed his lip as he did his best to memorize every bit of the picture. It had clearly been sent to tease him, and Isaac could feel the heat in his face as he noted the dark pink color of Caleb's nipples, but the photo also felt warm somehow. Like an offering, or a...submission. Isaac turned the phone face down on his knee and took a deep breath. Don't get carried away. He hesitantly turned the phone over again and bit his lip as he spared just one more moment before deleting the message.

He tapped Caleb's name again and paused with his thumbs over the keyboard. What was he even supposed to say to that? Thank you? He dropped onto his back and held the phone above his head with a frown creasing his forehead.

You're beautiful, he typed, and he touched send before he could regret it. The phone vibrated in his hands before more than a minute went by.

Could have used you here this afternoon. It's not enough doing this alone anymore.

Isaac pressed the phone to his face for a moment in embarrassment. *Sorry*, he replied, and he hastily added, *Will you come to my game tomorrow?* before Caleb could answer with something else flirtatious.

Baseball is really boring.

His elbows slumped back to the bed. He should have expected that answer, but part of him had still hoped that Caleb would want to attend anyway. His parents very rarely got to come to the games, since they were usually working. He understood, but it would have been nice to have someone in the stands who was there to see him. *That's okay*, he typed. *Maybe since it's Friday, we can do something after.*

Like a date?

Isaac turned onto his side to hold the phone closer to his face, biting his lip as he smiled. *Do we get to go on dates?*

I can borrow my uncle's car. We can go anywhere you want.

I'd like that.

Then it's a date. Is it your first one?

He sighed, but he couldn't fight the smile on his face. *You know it is. Unless you count taking my cousin to a dance in middle school.*

Gross. Let's not count that.

It wasn't like that! Before Isaac's message even had time to send, the phone buzzed again.

It'll be my first date, too.

Isaac smiled. He kept thinking of Caleb as a worldly sort of person, someone who went to lots of parties in the big city. But that wasn't the same thing as what they had. It made it better to think that Isaac was the first person to see this side of him.

I'm looking forward to it.

15

Caleb went downstairs when Andras called him to dinner, and he sat prodding his potatoes while his mother pored over the thick leatherbound book that seemed to be her constant companion these days. She hadn't touched the plate of food in front of her.

"I just don't understand," she said softly as she turned a thick page. "Why didn't he answer?"

"You know how these things are, Marian," Andras said as he sat with his own plate of food. "Not an exact science, evocation."

Caleb chewed a mouthful of vegetables, watching his mother frown at the open book. "We could try again," he said, and Andras shot him a disapproving look. Caleb scooted his chair closer to his mother and slid the book from under her hands. "If we can't get my father, we must be able to get someone who can tell us how to, right?"

"Caleb," Andras said as a warning, but the boy didn't look up at him.

"What's wrong, uncle?" he answered in a low voice. "You wouldn't have brought her this book just to get her hopes up, would you?"

"That isn't—"

"Then we can try," Caleb cut him off. "We don't have paint all over the floor for nothing, right?"

"Oh, Caleb," Marian sighed, and she held his hands tight. "I miss him so. I just want to hear his voice again. He'll be so proud of how far you've come; I know he will."

"Then let's see what we can do." He let her keep hold of one of his hands as he flipped through the book. It was full of crude drawings of gruesome monsters and strange sigils, each with ridiculously complex instructions and descriptions of each spirit. He skimmed each page, waiting for something to stand out, and finally he landed on a page that looked promising. "Well look here," he said. "Ayporos is a demon who knows and can reveal all things, past, present, and future. That sounds helpful, doesn't it, mom?"

"Oh, yes," she smiled.

"Caleb, you don't know what you're doing," Andras protested.

"She can do the work." Caleb stood, taking the book with him, and helped his mother from her seat. "If something happens, I can fight, right?"

"You don't understand—"

"Am I one of you or not?" he snapped, and Andras went silent, but his mouth pressed into a grim line. Caleb led his mother by the hand into the living room, and they gathered the leftover paint from the hall closet, carefully repairing the bits of the circle that had been scuffed over the last few days. Andras paced the room nearby them like a panther in a cage, and Nobah lurked at the bottom of the stairs, watching with dark eyes.

When they finished fixing the circle, Andras took Caleb by the arm as he rose.

"Don't do this," he said under his breath.

"If you won't tell us the truth, maybe someone else will."

"You think I do this out of spite? I told you; these are the rules. Nobody is going to look kindly on you trying to get around them, least of all your father."

"That's cute that you think I care. You said yourself that I don't need his approval. This isn't for me. It's for mom."

"Caleb," Andras hissed, his eyes on the woman across the room as he leaned close to the boy's ear, "your mother is not well. To bind a demon takes clarity and will, and she's lacking in both. She'll be in danger."

"No she won't. I'll be here."

"What is it you think you'll do? No demon is glad to be summoned; if Ayporos gets dragged here and you can't contain him, how do you expect to keep him from doing her harm?" He took Caleb by the shoulders when the boy scowled at the floor. "Listen to me. You do not need him. Your mother doesn't need him. But if you want to pursue this, if you really feel like you need it, then at least don't be stupid. Let me teach you. Let me show you how to do this properly."

Caleb's hands fisted at his sides. He was always being told to wait. He looked up into the demon's face, and the pleading frown he found there made him waver. Andras had never kept anything from him. Not if it wasn't related to his father. If Caleb asked, he knew that Andras would tell him how to summon safely. The boy let out a soft sigh.

"Okay," he said. Andras's shoulders slumped with relief, and he immediately released Caleb to smile at his mother.

"Marian," Andras began as he approached, reaching out to gently grasp her hands, "we're going to have to postpone. Just for a while. Caleb needs to practice, you see." Caleb's mother turned to him with a soft frown, and he couldn't look at her. "Caleb needs to get stronger," Andras assured her, "but he's working very hard. We'll try again soon. I promise."

"Oh, Caleb," she sighed. She broke away from the demon and wrapped her arms tightly around Caleb's chest, resting her head on his shoulder. "You have a great burden on you, my son. But I know when your father returns for you, you'll make both of us so proud. I know that you'll be ready to take your place at his side."

"Thanks," he muttered, but his eyes were on Andras. The demon nodded at him with a solemn sigh. "Come on," Caleb urged, prying his mother gently from him. "You should eat something."

After dinner, Andras promised to teach Caleb to defend himself, but the boy shut himself in his room and sat on the floor at the foot of his bed. He was too angry to try now. His mother had been telling him his whole life how special he was, and Andras kept insisting that Caleb was powerful, but when it came time to actually do anything, it seemed like he was always getting blocked. Greedigut climbed up his pants leg and perched on his knee, cleanings its whiskers with its little hands.

"You're not much help either," Caleb grumbled, prodding the rat lightly in its furry belly. "What is a familiar even supposed to do?"

The rat squeaked at him almost like it was offended.

"Yeah? Well how useful have you been?" He sighed and let his head fall back against his mattress. More than anything, he wanted to see Isaac. He wanted to forget about this stupid demon stuff, just for a night, and watch a movie with him or sit by the pond. It made him feel sappy to admit it, but he wanted to be with him, whatever that meant.

Caleb lifted his head and pulled his phone out of his pocket, but he hesitated. There was no way Isaac would agree to meet him this late on a school night, and texting him wouldn't be enough. Greedigut launched itself onto his shirt and peered up at him.

"What?" he asked, and the rat chittered in annoyance and bounded away toward the window. It paused with a pink hand on the glass and turned back to look at him, giving one more sharp squeak. It bent to sniff the latch, and it flipped open without the slightest touch. Caleb crawled around the mattress and crouched to stare between the rat and the window latch. "You just opened it?"

Greedigut snorted as though above answering.

Caleb paused. "Can you open other things?"

The rat twitched its whiskers, and the window shot up of its own accord, startling Caleb into falling back on his rear. He laughed, and Greeditgut seemed pleased with itself.

"You're not such a waste of space after all." He smiled faintly. "Let's try something else." Caleb held out his hand to let the rat step onto his palm, and he clutched its little body gently as he climbed out of the window. He landed on the ground outside with a heavy thump, but his body easily absorbed the shock of the fall. He spared a look back at his open window before heading off through the trees toward Isaac's neighborhood. He let Greedigut ride on his shoulder as he walked, and once he was out of sight of his house, he reached into his pocket for his cigarette pack. With the cigarette halfway to his mouth, he paused, and he could picture the little frown on Isaac's face after they kissed, gently scolding him for the taste of cigarettes on his lips. He tucked the cigarette back into the pack and hid it away in his pocket again.

The houses in Isaac's neighborhood were mostly dark, and Caleb smiled to himself as he saw nothing but black inside the windows of Isaac's house. His father would be asleep. Caleb crept to the blond's bedroom window and peeked through the break in the curtains. The lump of Isaac under the blanket shifted, awake or at least restless. Caleb let Greedigut down onto the windowsill, and the rat gave an obedient little squeak as the latch flipped open, but as soon as Caleb reached to lift the glass, it locked itself again.

"What the hell?" he whispered. "Open it."

Greedigut settled against the window with its nose toward the latch and snorted.

"What's your problem?" Caleb hissed, glancing at Isaac through the window. The rat only twitched its whiskers at him and seemed to be looking pointedly between his face and the latch. The boy hesitated. "You...want me to do it?"

Greedigut squeaked.

Caleb frowned at the window latch, not certain in the slightest what the rat expected him to do, but he bent close to the windowsill and put his hands on his knees. He'd been given this rat-spirit familiar thing by an actual demon, and he'd been told that it would be helpful and loyal, so he guessed that if it thought he could open things without touching them, he probably could. That didn't mean he knew how, but he probably could. He stared at the latch with his lips pressed into a thin line. *Just open*, he told it in his head. *Just...flip on open.*

Greedigut let out a little rodent sigh, and Caleb almost knocked him off the windowsill. He knit his brow and focused.

Open, he tried again, and the latch inside gave a tiny click as it unlocked. Caleb slipped the window open a crack and paused to glance down at the rat.

"Thanks," he whispered. "Now fuck off. This isn't for beady rat eyes."

Greedigut didn't seem bothered by the dismissal; it accepted Caleb's hand down into the grass and bustled off back toward the house. Caleb inched the window fully open as quietly as he could, but Isaac's bed was directly underneath. He would have to move carefully if he wanted to keep the element of surprise. Caleb hefted himself up through the window and managed to get his palms on the bed without disturbing the blond, but as soon as he shifted forward, Isaac was up like a shot with a grip on Caleb's arm. Caleb found himself lurched forward as Isaac heaved him through the window and onto the floor with a loud thud, and then he was on his back with the other boy's fist in his shirt. He looked up at Isaac in the dim moonlight and couldn't catch his breath. The blond had straddled his waist to pin him to the floor, and Caleb could feel the tremble of adrenaline in the boy above him and hear his shaking breath in the dark. His stomach tightened pleasantly at Isaac's weight pressing into his hips. He was sorry they were both dressed.

"You're...stronger than you look," Caleb whispered, and Isaac instantly loosened his grip.

"Caleb?" he answered in a hushed voice, but he didn't move. "Gosh, I didn't know it was you! What are you doing here? And how are you so heavy? I near about threw my shoulder out!"

"I came to see you," Caleb said. When Isaac started to move, Caleb stilled him with a hand on his waist and reached up to touch his jaw. Isaac allowed himself to be drawn down, and Caleb slid his fingers through the other boy's soft honey-colored hair as he kissed him. Isaac let out a little whimper of mild protest but soon leaned his weight on his elbow so he could press closer. Heat began to pool in Caleb's stomach immediately, and he shifted his hips under the blond's weight with a soft groan.

"Caleb," Isaac whispered against his lips, only partly breaking their kiss, "you can't be here."

Caleb smirked faintly and nipped at the corner of Isaac's mouth. "You could put me out the window again."

"If my dad wakes up—"

"If you're worried about it, stop talking," Caleb murmured, and he slipped his fingers underneath the waistband of Isaac's pajama pants and gave them an experimental tug. "Do you remember what you asked me to do the next time we were alone?" He smiled as the heat of Isaac's blush warmed his cheek. He could already feel the press of the blond's erection against his stomach, but he hesitated with his fingertips brushing the soft curls below Isaac's waistband. "You're already hard thinking about it," he teased. "Don't you want me to touch you?"

Isaac shut his eyes and rested his forehead against Caleb's to take a steadying breath. "I just...haven't ever..."

"I know." Caleb tilted the other boy's chin to kiss him again. "Do you want me to?"

Isaac didn't open his eyes, but he nodded so timidly that Caleb shuddered. Caleb slipped his hand lower, and Isaac caught him by the wrist.

"Wait," he breathed. "Can we...I mean, not on the floor?"

"You trying to say you want me in your bed?"

"I just—"

Caleb cut him off with a kiss and reluctantly released him. "You're gonna have to get up."

Isaac got to his feet, trying without success to hide his erection, but his thin pajama pants weren't doing him any favors. He climbed into the bed and scooted as close to the wall as he could to leave room for Caleb, then tugged his blanket up around his hips to protect what was left of his modesty. Caleb stood beside the bed and bent down to untie his shoes, and he pulled his shirt up over his head as he stepped out of them. Isaac was doing a terrible job trying not to look at him, and Caleb didn't mind, but as the other boy's grey eyes scanned his torso with such affection, he felt naked in a way that was altogether unfamiliar. He was much more comfortable with the way Isaac's face flushed red as he unbuckled his belt, and the nervous tension in him as Caleb slipped under the blanket beside him wearing only his boxers.

"You should take this off," Caleb murmured, picking at the hem of Isaac's white cotton t-shirt. Isaac chewed his lip for a moment, considering, and then he seemed to steel himself, and he reached behind his head to tug his shirt up by the collar. He leaned past Caleb to drop it onto the floor and then sat with his hands in his lap, peeking up at the other boy with his blush spreading all the way down his neck.

"What are you so nervous for?" Caleb asked. He leaned in to press a kiss to Isaac's collarbone, and the blond kept his mouth shut tight to hold in the soft whine that formed in his throat. "You have your shirt off all the time in front of the rest of your team, right?"

"Th-that's different," Isaac whispered. "None of them ever try to kiss me," he chuckled.

"Their loss," Caleb teased. He shifted closer and slid his hand over Isaac's taut stomach, his palm flattening against the heated skin as the blond's breath caught in his chest. Isaac was almost...Caleb hated to even think the word "disarming," but the contrast between the shy, soft-spoken boy who sat beside him in homeroom and the lean, powerful chest in bed with him was—well, slightly disarming. Caleb leaned forward and touched a kiss to Isaac's chest, smiling against his skin at the shiver it caused. Isaac was so sensitive; he would have to be careful to pace himself. Caleb let his fingernails scrape the blond's stomach as he kissed him again, but when he opened his mouth to run his tongue over the other boy's nipple, Isaac jerked away and snapped a hand up to his mouth to stifle his sudden laugh.

"S-Sorry," he whispered through his fingers. "That...it tickles."

That hadn't been the response Caleb expected, exactly, but Isaac looked so embarrassed that he let it pass without teasing. "How about this, then?" he murmured, and he let his fingers slip through the blond curls beneath the waistband of Isaac's pajama pants, fingertips brushing the base of his erection. He leaned up to press his lips against the boy's jaw. "Does that tickle?"

Isaac couldn't seem to make a noise, so he just shook his head with his hand still covering his mouth. Caleb took hold of him slowly, squeezing him tight and watching his face as his hand finally fell from his mouth to help support him. Isaac's eyes were squeezed shut, and he looked so red that Caleb wondered if he had any blood left that wasn't in his face or his dick. His lips parted in a shaking sigh as Caleb began to stroke him, and when he slid his thumb over the leaking slit, Isaac whimpered and turned his head away.

"Does that feel good?" Caleb asked, tasting the skin at the hollow of Isaac's throat as he squeezed him.

"Yes," Isaac answered with his fingers gripped tightly in his blankets.

"Better than when you did it the other night?"

"Y-Yes."

"Do you want to touch me, too?"

Isaac looked down at him in a mild panic, but Caleb saw his eyes drop to the sheet pooled at their hips. "I...don't know what to do," he admitted softly.

"Just do what you do to yourself."

The blond hesitated, giving a small groan of distraction as Caleb's grip tightened around him. He reached across and let his hand rest timidly on the other boy's hip, and Caleb leaned up to kiss him for encouragement. He leaned close and ran his tongue across Isaac's with an almost demanding urgency, releasing him just enough to press his palm against the thick vein pulsing on the underside of his erection. A strained whine slipped from Isaac's throat, and his hand finally moved, gingerly cupping Caleb over the thin fabric of his boxers. He seemed encouraged by the pleading groan his touch caused in the other boy, returning his kiss with eagerness as he explored the shape of him through the soft cotton. Caleb caught Isaac's bottom lip in his teeth and rolled his hips against the gentle touch with a soft growling moan that made the other boy jump slightly.

Caleb edged closer on the bed until their hands were almost in the way of each other, but he kept his touch light, stroking the other boy with teasing slowness. When they broke their kiss to catch their breath, Caleb leaned back enough to look up into Isaac's face again. A shot ran through him at the sight of the blond's knit brow, his flushed cheeks, the panting breath escaping his open mouth. Isaac's head fell back, exposing the soft bob of his Adam's apple as he swallowed, and Caleb shuddered. He hadn't been prepared for Isaac to look like this. Caleb's daydreams and late-night fantasies never could have done him justice. He almost forgot about the task at hand until Isaac whimpered, and he was too distracted by the line of the other boy's jaw to focus on maintaining his rhythm.

He jumped when Isaac gave a sudden, irritated sound, and Caleb found himself pushed forcibly back onto the mattress with Isaac's weight against him. He sucked in a startled gasp as the blond's hand dipped bravely beyond the waistband of his boxers, gripping him tight and stroking him at an eager pace.

"Fuck," Caleb sighed, and he shifted to better position himself and tugged Isaac's pants down his hips, freeing him from the confining fabric. The boy above him let out a barely stifled groan when Caleb squeezed him again, and he supported himself on one elbow as their hands began to move in a matching tempo.

"Don't swear," Isaac whispered against his ear, but it didn't sound like the soft, shy murmur he'd heard so many times before. It was tense and through his teeth, and it sent a spark down Caleb's spine. The blond wasn't as timid as he seemed.

Caleb lifted his hips into the other boy's touch, the heat of Isaac's breath against his shoulder prickling his skin. Their hands were frantic and desperate, and Caleb's heart was beating too fast. He could hear it, feel it threatening to break his ribs, and he fought to keep air in his lungs as Isaac's firm hand stroked him closer to the cliff's edge. He thought he might snap at any moment, that his heart might finally give out, but the blond kept him right on the border between perfect and unbearable. This was what he wanted. This warmth, this fear, the other boy panting against him so sweetly that it made him lightheaded. He wanted to stay on this brink forever, alive and tingling and afraid.

"Caleb," Isaac finally whimpered into Caleb's neck, his back arching like a cat as he pushed closer into the other boy's swift caress. "I—I...I'm going to—"

"Come for me, Isaac," Caleb whispered in return, and he drew the blond to him with a gentle hand and caught his lips in a kiss. Isaac's groan resonated into Caleb's chest, both boys focused and tense through the kiss. Isaac didn't have to say anything more—Caleb could sense the tightening of his stomach as he drew close, and the blond's hips jerked suddenly as he moaned his release into Caleb's mouth. The fluid that hit Caleb's stomach felt hot enough to burn, and the quiet, begging whimper in Isaac's throat pushed him over the cliff. He grunted at the other boy's tight squeeze and arched his back as his whole body tensed, his own semen mixing with Isaac's on his goosebumped skin.

Isaac wobbled slightly, so Caleb released him from the kiss and let him fall onto his side on the bed, both of them panting and flushed. Caleb watched Isaac with a furrow in his brow as the boy's expression slowly softened into exhaustion, the faint moonlight from the window reflecting the sheen of sweat on his brow. He bit his lip as he smirked to hold in his swear, but fuck, the blond looked beautiful. When Isaac opened his eyes, he smiled for a moment before his gaze dropped to the cooling liquid on Caleb's stomach, and then he sat up in a panic.

"Oh, gosh," he whispered, not seeming to know what to do with himself. "I—I'm so sorry, I—oh, gosh. Stay there." He climbed gracelessly over Caleb and fetched the tissues from his desk, tugging his pants back into place on his way, then sat and began to clean away the mess they'd made. Caleb smiled up at him and lifted the waistband of his boxers with his thumb.

"Don't miss under there," he teased, and Isaac pressed his lips together with determination as he wiped a few more drops of white from Caleb's tanned skin. So much for forceful, grunty Isaac.

"Sorry," he said again. He tossed the tissues into the wastebasket by his desk, and Caleb sat up and kissed him instead of answering. Isaac seemed to melt into the kiss, and when they parted, his lips curled into a warm smile. At Caleb's urging, he laid back down beside him, and they faced each other in the darkness with their hands lightly brushing between their chests.

"Sorry for surprising you," Caleb whispered. Isaac shook his head.

"It...was a good surprise," he admitted, and Caleb kissed him again.

They laid together so long that they dozed off, and when Caleb opened his eyes, he sat up sharply as he realized that the sun was rising.

"Shit," he swore, and he hastily dressed himself, pausing as he clambered over Isaac's sleeping form to press a kiss to his lips. Then he slipped back out the window, locked it behind him with a quick look, and jogged across the road back toward his own house.

16

Caleb was able to slip back into the house and into his bed without being spotted, though he regretted his lack of sleep when Andras came banging on his door right after he'd managed to shut his eyes. He almost feigned sickness, but he knew that Andras wouldn't believe him, so he pulled himself up with a groan and got into the shower instead. As he was dressing, his phone buzzed on his nightstand, and he pulled his shirt over his head and leaned down to check the screen. It was a text from Isaac.

Good morning. :)

Caleb smiled faintly to himself and tucked his phone into his pocket. Greedigut peered at him from its open cage with a look of smugness on its little rat face, somehow. Caleb bent down to stroke its head with two fingers before heading down the stairs. He made himself some toast with marmalade and munched on it while he walked to the car with Andras.

"Looking a little sleepy, there," the demon observed once they were buckled in. "Up late studying, were you?"

"I have a test," Caleb lied easily, but Andras tutted at him.

"Do you honestly think you've ever snuck out of the house without me knowing? What do you take me for?"

"Then how come you never stop me?"

The demon shrugged one shoulder as he drove. "Why should I? What, are you going to get into trouble? What trouble could you possibly get in that I wouldn't approve of?" He chuckled and glanced sidelong at the boy. "Though last night could have been spent more productively, I'm certain. You went to see him, didn't you?"

"So?" Caleb grumped with a mouthful of toast.

"So, how's that deal coming?"

"I'm not making a deal with him."

"And why's that?"

"Because I don't want to," the boy answered tersely. "It's none of your business."

Andras let some silence pass between them, but he put a hand on Caleb's arm when he stopped the car outside the school. "Keep your weekend open. We'll be practicing."

"Fine," Caleb agreed. "You're teaching me how to fight. I'm summoning that demon whether you want me to or not."

"I know," Andras said. He let Caleb climb out of the car and shut the door behind him without further argument.

Caleb slung his bag over his shoulder and weaved his way through the waiting students with a faint scowl on his face, but when he spotted Isaac near the door of the building, the irritated tension in his chest eased just a little. The blond smiled at him, a slight pinkness in his cheeks.

"Sorry I bailed," Caleb said without looking him in the eye. "I just wanted to go before you got in trouble." Why was he anxious? What he'd done with Isaac the night before wasn't serious. It was the sort of thing he'd done in guest rooms at parties a dozen times with boys whose names he didn't know. It was just fooling around. If anything, Isaac should be the one fidgeting and nervous, not him.

"It's fine." Isaac picked at a stray thread on the hem of his shirt. "I...had fun."

"You didn't wake up and pray about it?"

The flush darkened in Isaac's cheeks. "I mean, I did. It's still...you know," he said, dropping his voice to a whisper. "It's lustful. I know you don't care, but I do try. But you...make it hard to make decisions," he admitted softly.

Caleb wouldn't say it out loud, but he knew exactly what Isaac meant.

"Come on," he said instead as the students around them began to head for the door. "The bell's gonna ring."

Caleb and Isaac only had a couple of their classes together, which meant that Caleb only had to spend two periods—plus homeroom and lunch—sneaking peeks at the other boy and pretending not to. Every time Caleb looked at him, he could see his silhouette in the dark bedroom, panting and exposed, and the soft smile on his face as they laid together. Caleb had never fallen asleep next to someone. Not ever.

Even when he'd gone up to a room with someone at a party, he'd never let himself go to sleep. He always cleaned up, dressed, and went home, even if the other person was already sleeping. He didn't want that closeness. But with Isaac—he hadn't wanted to leave. He wondered what it would be like to wake up next to him and not have to go anywhere. To watch his chest slowly rise and fall as he slept, to feel his warm skin under his cheek as Caleb laid against his shoulder. He wanted to see that gentle, sleepy smile when the blond finally stirred.

Caleb leaned his elbow on his desk and lightly thumped the side of his head with his fist as he sat in his last class of the day. These thoughts weren't him. Since when did he care about getting anything from Isaac other than what he'd gone over there for last night? But he did, he realized with a worried frown. He wanted more. Now they were going on this date tonight—what did that even mean? A romantic dinner? Was he supposed to bring flowers? He let his head fall to his desk with a thunk so loud that the teacher snapped at him, forcing him to lift his head again. This was a disaster. How could he focus on school, or on training with Andras, when the only thing on his mind was Isaac and his stupidly pretty eyes?

He held his stomach and frowned at his desk. He was going to go on a date. With someone who was his boyfriend. Someone who he wanted to see all the time, even when they were just together. But Isaac didn't know who he was. Not really. He didn't know what it would mean to really be a part of Caleb's life. That left only one option. Caleb would have to tell him. He would risk Isaac not believing him, or being frightened of him, or maybe even breaking things off with him completely. Isaac was so deeply religious that Caleb wouldn't be surprised if he never spoke to him again, or tried to exorcise him, or something. But he had to tell him. Better to get it over with, for better or worse.

After school ended, Caleb watched Isaac walking with a group of other boys toward the locker rooms to get ready for his game. He had some time. With a steeling breath, he started his walk home. He would need the car, but he refused to withstand the teasing and scolding he would get from Andras if he asked for it right out. So, when he arrived at the house, he dropped his bag in his room and crept quietly toward the demon's door. Ever since he'd started walking with Isaac instead of being picked up, it wasn't uncommon for Andras to be in the middle of an afternoon nap when Caleb got home from school. The room was quiet, so he assumed the demon was sleeping, but when he pushed open the door, Andras was sitting up in bed, quite awake and clearly naked, with the sheet rumpled hastily around his middle.

"And you get snippy with me if I don't knock," Andras sighed.

Caleb paused. The demon looked slightly out of breath, but he was trying to hide it. His blanket had been pushed onto the floor, and the pillows on the bed were out of place. With a suspicious narrowing of his eyes, Caleb leaned around the door to peer into the corners of the room, but there was nothing there.

"Something I can help you with, Caleb, or are you just doing a bit of surveillance?" Andras growled, the last word seeming to jump slightly.

"What's wrong with you?"

"Other than you lingering in my doorway for no obvious reason, nothing at all."

Caleb sighed. He didn't really want to know if Andras was up here having private time. He'd rather pretend he'd been napping. At least he didn't seem in the mood for teasing. "I need the car," he said. "I'll bring it back tonight, or in the morning, or whatever."

"Fine," Andras answered quickly, and he gestured vaguely at the fob on his dresser by the door, so Caleb snatched it up and shut the door behind him without hesitation. He gave a small shudder as he went back down the stairs.

He took the car and ran his preparatory errands, but it didn't take as long as he'd anticipated. The game was probably just getting started. He didn't want to wait around at the house, and if he was honest, he didn't want to wait to see Isaac again. So he parked the car outside the school and made his way toward the baseball field. He intended to linger near the outskirts and try to catch a few glimpses of Isaac in his uniform, but before he'd even been there for five minutes, he heard a voice call his name. When he looked up, Heather was waving to him from the bleachers, and she scooted down to pat the metal bench beside her. He hesitated, but she only waved him over more fervently, so he gave a small sigh and climbed over the lower bleachers to reach her.

"Didn't expect to see you here, broodybrows," she said as he sat. "You decide you like baseball after all?"

"It's not like there's a lot to do in this town," he muttered, slouching back against the bench behind him. The stands had a fair number of students and parents in them, but they were by no means packed.

"Yeah, yeah, big city boy, blah blah."

He glanced at her out of the corner of his eye. "What about you? Big fan of amateur sports?"

"Nah," she smiled. "I'm here for the baseball butts. Michael Cochran, the third baseman? Man, he's pretty to look at."

Caleb followed her gaze to the boy standing with his hands on his knees, waiting for the next hit. He was good-looking, but Caleb found him a little generic. He shrugged rather than give her an answer, and she chuckled.

"Yeah, I don't expect you feel the same. Isaac's not bad in the butt department either, but don't tell him I said so. He gets all flustered. I don't know how he's ever going to get a girlfriend," she laughed.

"Beats me," Caleb murmured, his eyes on the blond waiting at second base. He wasn't sweating yet, but his mouth was set in a firm line, and his eyes were focused. He really was more handsome than his initial bubbly impression let on. And his ass was more than "not bad." He almost felt offended on Isaac's behalf.

They watched the game without talking for a while, which suited Caleb just fine. When the teams switched positions, Isaac spotted Caleb in the stands and brightened instantly, offering him a brief wave on his way to the dugout. Caleb raised his hand in response but shoved it back into his pocket as soon as the other boy was out of sight. He felt Heather's eyes on him and refused to look at her.

"You guys have gotten close, huh?" she asked, stretching her legs out and crossing her ankles on the bench in front of her.

"If you say so."

"Come on. You guys walk home together, like, every day. I don't believe he's stayed stuck on you for this long without you being just a teensy little bit friendly. You have that in there somewhere under all that brooding, right? Friendliness?"

He frowned over at her, but she was smiling.

"You know, you're gonna get wrinkles," she said, and she reached over and poked him lightly between his eyebrows. "It's really not so bad to admit you're doing okay here, city boy."

He grunted and leaned away from her hand. "Yeah," he admitted after a pause. "I guess I'm doing okay."

"Holy cow, something positive! You said something positive! I'm gonna call the papers."

"Shut up," he grumbled as she laughed at him.

She talked to him periodically throughout the game, and he actually didn't mind. They talked about the game, the upcoming test in their 4th period anatomy class, Isaac's endless and exhausting optimism, and a few bands they both liked. She asked him if he'd left a girlfriend back in Chicago, but he only said, "Nope" and refused to answer any deeper questions. It wasn't a terrible conversation, overall, and he got to see Isaac's back twist in that perfect way when it was his turn at bat, so he considered it a successful afternoon.

As the players shook hands with the opposite team and began to file back toward the locker rooms, Caleb pushed himself up off the bench and hopped down from the bleachers.

"Bye, Heather," he offered, but she trotted up beside him as though she meant to follow.

"Come on, let's go tell Isaac he had a good game."

"Bye, Heather," he said again, this time with force in his voice, and she swayed slightly on her feet as she looked at him.

"Bye, Caleb," she answered, and she passed by him and headed for the parking lot without looking back.

He lingered by the stands as Isaac was held up talking to a boy from the other team, and when they waved at each other and parted, Caleb slipped out from behind the bleachers and followed Isaac around the small building to the locker room entrance. Just as the boy approached the door, Caleb tilted his chin at it and slammed it shut before Isaac could step through. He was getting the hang of this. Isaac jumped with a hand on his heart at the sudden movement of the door. He glanced around to see if he'd been spotted and smiled to see Caleb behind him.

"Hey," he said brightly. "I thought you weren't going to come."

Caleb moved up to him, so close that he retreated a step. Isaac's skin was pink from exertion and sun, sweat beaded on his brow and in the little divots of his collarbone, and red clay stained his thighs where he had slid down the base line. He smelled like dirt and warm leather, and Caleb didn't want him getting cleaned up just yet. He just wanted to touch him. To kiss him and have all of him before he risked losing him. He pressed the other boy against the brick wall of the building with one hand on his chest.

"Caleb," Isaac protested as his back touched the brick, "someone will see—"

"There's nobody here," Caleb assured him, and he bent to touch a kiss to the blond's neck, but Isaac squirmed at the touch.

"Don't," he whispered with a tight grip on Caleb's sleeve. "I'm all sweaty."

"Are you?" Caleb leaned in close and tasted the salt on Isaac's skin, his tongue seeking the tender spot right at his collar. Isaac's fingers tensed on Caleb's arm as he whispered, "I hadn't noticed."

"I—I really need a shower," Isaac insisted despite his faint trembling, so Caleb released him with a short sigh.

"Well I hope you don't have any other plans," he said, "because I promised you a date."

Isaac hesitated, but then a slow smile spread across his lips, and he clutched his worn mitt to his chest and nodded. "I'll...I'll be really quick! Just—be right back." He scooted out from between Caleb and the wall and dashed into the locker room, leaving Caleb to wait near the quickly emptying stands.

There was no going back now. Isaac needed the full truth.

17

"So," Andras began as Barachiel appeared in his bedroom, "is this going well, or not? What do you think?" The demon was freshly out of the shower when he heard the angel's light step through the open bathroom door. He finished toweling off his hair and leaned to peek through the doorway.

"I'm not sure anymore," Barachiel sighed. He sat down on Andras's bed, not paying much attention as the demon padded by completely naked on his way to the dresser. "I didn't expect things to progress this way."

"What did you expect, exactly? That Isaac's down-home charms would convince Caleb that Jesus was the answer to all his problems, after all?" Andras slid open a drawer and retrieved a pair of dark red sleep pants, and he stepped into them before heading back toward the bathroom.

"Maybe?" The angel watched him run the water in the sink, testing its temperature with his fingertips before tugging up the knob to close the drain. "Not Jesus, exactly, maybe, but...I thought at least Isaac could push him in the right direction. Show him that there were good things to be had here. Caleb's always been a distant child. He was sure to choose his father's road without intervention."

Andras chuckled as he turned off the faucet. He wet the badger-hair brush beside the sink and lifted the lid from his soap dish. "It seems as though Isaac's the one having his horizons broadened, doesn't it?"

"This isn't about corruption," Barachiel protested.

Andras glanced back at him through the mirror as he scrubbed the citrus-smelling soap onto his cheeks and chin. "Isn't it? You're worried you've lost one of your sweet little sheep. The more Isaac becomes a well-rounded, thinking individual, the less he's a good candidate for Heaven, right?"

"That isn't fair, and you know it."

The demon traded his brush for a razor and leaned over the sink, tilting his head to scrape the scruff from his jaw. "Then what are you worried about? It seems to me they're getting along just fine. Caleb's making friends, and Isaac's learning that there's more to life than Sunday school. It's win-win, right?"

"Except they're going on a *date*, Andras," Barachiel noted. He rose and leaned against the doorway to watch his lover work. "A date is something else entirely. Isaac told me he needed to figure out if he loved Caleb or not. Loved, Andras, did you hear that? He needs to sort out whether or not what he's feeling is *love*." His shoulders slumped slightly as the demon paused to look back at him. "I didn't intend for actual feelings to get involved. What if this has gone too far?"

Andras paused with his razor halfway to his face. "B, are you feeling sentimental?"

"Shut up. I'm looking at the big picture."

"Best case-worst case," Andras answered. He turned his head to get the last of the soap from his cheek, and then he bent to rinse his face. "Best case, as far as you're concerned. Caleb and Isaac fall desperately in love. Caleb sees the error of his ways, gives up his claimed souls, and becomes a tie-wearing, churchgoing, functioning member of society. Has charitable donations taken out of his taxes. Right? Worst case. Isaac falls desperately in love with Caleb, but it's not returned. He falls for his demon wiles and makes a deal, Caleb spirals into evil and debauchery, and they're both lost." He reached out and waved behind his back at Barachiel, who obediently offered him the nearby hand towel. Andras turned to face him as he wiped the water from his shaved chin. "But Caleb isn't going to make a deal for that boy. I hate to admit it, but he's gone a bit soft."

"And when he finds out that Isaac knows what he is?"

"He ought to be relieved," Andras shrugged. "One less secret."

"You really think that?"

The demon sighed. He set his towel on the counter and drained the sink. "No," he said. "I think he'll be afraid."

"I caused this," Barachiel said softly. "I let you bait me, and now they're both going to get hurt."

"You don't know that." Andras stepped close to him and slipped his arms around the angel's neck. "It might not be so bad for Caleb to be a bit soft."

Barachiel let his hands rest on the other man's waist. "I like this one, Andras."

"I do too," the demon admitted. "He's a little shit, but he's the first one to have his father's spark in a long while. It's a shame; I'm so close, and if Caleb would just apply himself, he could have been the one. He could have been the last."

"You planning on giving up your day job?" Barachiel murmured. "After all this time?"

Andras set his chin on the angel's shoulder, leaning his cheek against his own bicep. "It's been almost three thousand years," he sighed. "How many more children can I raise up and watch destroy themselves? A fully realized cambion is a struck match—a bright, fast burn. If I can pay back what I owe, I won't have to light any more."

"Or your master will keep fathering them anyway, and they'll be left completely to their own devices without even the benefit of your guidance. A boy like Caleb—where would he be without you? He's too much like his father. He would have turned cruel the moment he discovered what he was capable of. He would have gone too far too quickly, and he'd be dead by twenty, just like Anthony." Andras leaned back to look at him with a frown, and Barachiel shook his head. "I'm sorry. I know you've suffered. Don't think I don't know why you've done what you've done. But maybe this has been good for you."

"It's been good for *us*," the demon clarified, "and that's what matters to me." He sighed. "Caleb would be my first technical failure in some time. I would hate to ruin my record."

"What about ruining Caleb's life?"

"Oh," Andras said with a click of his tongue, "such dramatics. Caleb's going to fall for this boy or he's not. All I can do is show him what he'll be missing if he does. But it might be out of my hands."

"You really think there's hope for them? A cambion and a human? You really think that they'll ever be able to understand each other?"

"I seem to recall hearing much the same sentiment about us, some time ago." Andras gently cupped the angel's cheek, his thumb brushing the sharp line of his jaw. "You saying you don't understand me, B?"

"You and I aren't seventeen," Barachiel answered, though his voice was gentler than before.

"They have their own choices to make. You have to let them."

Barachiel let his forehead rest against his lover's. "Can you at least try to encourage Caleb not to make any more deals?"

"Not a chance," Andras chuckled. He pressed a soft kiss to Barachiel's lips. "Not with my chastity on the line."

"Has anyone ever told you that you're completely insufferable?"

"Not today," the demon answered with a smirk, and he tugged his lover closer to him and caught his lip in his teeth.

Barachiel sighed as he accepted the kiss, his grip tightening on the demon's waist, and he let Andras lead him backwards to the bed. He sat down when he was pushed and allowed the demon to crawl into his lap.

"Do you remember," Andras murmured against his lips, fingertips scratching down the soft fabric of the angel's shirt, "when you came to me so long ago, arguing for the soul of that shepherd?" He smiled against Barachiel's cheek as he touched a kiss to the umber skin. "You were so precious."

"You tricked him," the angel argued.

"I let him choose. The fact that he chose an eternity of torment for the sake of a few mating pairs of goats is hardly my fault." He chuckled and let his hands slip under Barachiel's shirt to caress his stomach. "You're always trying to save everyone from themselves. That's how you got such a shit gig."

"I don't have a shit gig," Barachiel muttered. He leaned back on his hands to look the demon in the face.

"Don't you? All the blame, none of the say? Your guardian angels run their little feathers ragged trying to keep these humans in order, and when they screw up anyway, your boss scolds you for them not falling in line."

"That's his prerogative," the angel answered with a quick glance upwards, as though he expected to be overheard.

"But if you'd listened to him back then, we wouldn't be where we are now." Andras walked his fingers up Barachiel's chest under his shirt, smiling at the soft hiss the angel gave as he tweaked one dark nipple. "What was it Uriel said? Something something irreconcilable differences?"

"He warned me that you would try to tempt me into turning to darkness," Barachiel sighed. He reached up to put his hand over the demon's, even though the cotton of his shirt separated them. "That I risked falling every time I saw you."

"But you kept coming back anyway," he chuckled, leaning forward to nip at his lover's ear. "You found me in Uruk and let me take you by the banks of the Euphrates," he whispered, "but Alexander was in Egypt before you said you loved me."

Barachiel shivered at the heat of the demon's breath on his ear, and he reached up to slip his hand through Andras's brown hair and draw him in for a slow kiss. "And I regret saying it every day," he murmured, but Andras could see the smile in his eyes.

"You don't seem any closer to falling now than you did then," Andras noted, pressing another kiss to his lover's lips. "And if you and I can last this long, who's to say Caleb and Isaac can't come to understand each other? Whatever that means for them."

"I hope you're right."

"I'm always right," Andras smiled. He leaned into Barachiel's touch and pressed him back onto the mattress with a kiss. The angel let his palms run over Andras's bare back and down beneath the waistband of his pants to pull him closer with a firm grip. Andras shifted above him to allow Barachiel to slide the pants down his hips and onto the floor and was turned onto his back in his moment of weakness, Barachiel urging the demon's legs around his hips to keep him in place. Their kisses were unhurried, their hands running over every inch of familiar skin. Barachiel only broke away to look down at his partner's softly panting lips, and he slid an arm around the demon's waist to pull him away from the bed with a slow arch of his back. His mouth found the tender flesh covering Andras's ribs and left gentle kisses on all the skin he could reach.

He'd finally shed his own clothes and gotten Andras to make that rare, rough little whimpering sound when they heard Caleb's footsteps in the hallway. Andras sat up with a hand on Barachiel's chest to push him back onto his heels and whipped the sheet around his hips just as Caleb opened the door.

"And you get snippy with me if I don't knock," the demon huffed, making every effort to pretend Barachiel wasn't kneeling naked right in front of him. While Caleb glanced skeptically around the room, Barachiel leaned forward and brushed his lips down the demon's neck, a smirk tugging the corner of his mouth as he saw Andras's fingers tighten in the sheet.

"Something I can help you with, Caleb, or are you just doing a bit of surveillance?" Barachiel's tongue dipped into the hollow of the demon's throat, making him waver as he finished his question.

"What's wrong with you?" Caleb asked from the door as Barachiel kissed a soft line down Andras's chest, drawing dangerously near to his tense stomach.

"Other than you lingering in my doorway for no obvious reason, nothing at all." Barachiel could sense Andras's desire to shove him, but he knew he didn't dare reveal the angel's presence, so he gave one slow lick to the demon's nipple and smiled as he felt the shudder in his lover's skin.

As soon as Andras had waved the boy off, he turned on the angel with a dark glare. "I hope you enjoyed that," he muttered, fixing his hand on the side of Barachiel's neck.

"I did, actually."

"Oh, good." He tugged the angel closer to him to growl into his ear, "Now get on your fucking knees."

18

Isaac had never showered so thoroughly in his life. Well, maybe on that camping trip when he'd slipped down the hill and fallen into that huge patch of poison oak. But this was different. He was going on a date. He'd already told his parents that he had plans with Caleb, which his father was reluctant to allow, but as long as he was home by curfew, they were free. He'd meant to ask Caleb what he wanted to do after the game—it had never occurred to him that Caleb would plan something on his own.

He had such a bright smile on his face while he dressed that a couple of the other boys teased him about his weekend plans, but he didn't mind. He brushed off their questions and feigned innocence at their insinuations. It wasn't difficult to object when they suggested that he might actually have a date, but he still focused on buttoning his shirt rather than look at them.

"Come on," Michael laughed as he lifted his bag onto his shoulder, "this is Mitchell. He can't look at a Sears catalog without blushing." He playfully snatched up Isaac's left hand and shook it as though to show his ring to the other boys. "True love waits, y'all," he teased as Isaac pulled back his hand.

"Cut it out," he grumbled, but he knew his face was red. He hadn't been doing so well at waiting lately. Not that he could admit that to any of them. He needed to try harder. He needed to remember what Barachiel had asked of him—not to date Caleb, but to bring him to the light. Maybe this was the best way of doing that in the end, but Caleb was...decidedly lustful, so maybe they needed to tone that down a little. Isaac resolved to get the other boy to agree to go to service this week.

When he finally exited the locker room, he found Caleb waiting for him, hands in his pockets and a slight hunch in his shoulders, as always. He smiled as they fell into step together on their way toward the parking lot.

"So what are we doing?" he asked, unable to keep the question inside any longer.

"Well," Caleb began, "you must be hungry after your game, right? So let's find some food first." He took Andras's key from his pocket and unlocked the car doors as they approached.

Isaac almost didn't want to put his hands on the car. It was probably a hundred times more expensive than anything he'd ever ridden in before. But Caleb climbed into the driver's seat calm as anything, so Isaac followed. It still had a new car smell, and the black leather seats were smooth and soft. Caleb didn't need to turn the key to start the engine; he didn't even seem to have a key at all. He just had a little fob that he slipped into a slot on the center console and clicked into place. A GPS screen on the dashboard flipped open as the engine came to life.

"Cripes," Isaac muttered as he buckled his seat belt. There were more knobs on the console than he would know what to do with—even separate air conditioning controls for the driver and the passenger, and buttons to heat or cool the seats themselves. He looked over at Caleb uncertainly. "Caleb, you did...get permission to take this, right?"

"Maybe," the boy answered with a faint sidelong smirk that made Isaac very nervous.

"Your uncle isn't going to show up and kill us, right?"

"Nah. Don't worry about it." Caleb pulled out of the parking lot and started down the familiar road toward Isaac's neighborhood, but he turned off onto the highway before they got there. "You like Mexican, right?"

"I...yeah," he answered. This felt awkward. Why did it feel awkward? Isaac imagined the two of them sitting at a restaurant together, just the two of them, maybe holding hands on the table or sitting side by side in a booth, and he suddenly felt anxious. He wanted to do those things with Caleb, he thought, but...what if someone they knew saw them? Guilt hit him in the gut before he could even finish the thought. Caleb said he understood wanting to keep everything a secret, but it wasn't fair to him for Isaac to feel that way. He wasn't ashamed, he told himself. He just didn't want to make trouble for either of them. And if Isaac's father found out about the real nature of their relationship, it would definitely be more than trouble.

They drove in silence, but if Caleb felt uncomfortable, he didn't show it. When they parked outside the restaurant, Isaac moved to unbuckle his seatbelt, and Caleb stopped him with a hand on his arm.

"Wait here."

The boy climbed out of the car on his own, not even bothering to turn it off, and he returned just a few minutes later with a plastic bag stacked with styrofoam containers. He dropped it into Isaac's lap as he fell back into the driver's seat. Caleb smiled faintly when Isaac looked at him with a question on his lips.

"I figured you wouldn't want to actually eat out," he said. He glanced over his shoulder to back out of the parking spot and started back onto the road while Isaac stared at him open-mouthed. "We can go somewhere it's just us."

Isaac curled his fingers protectively around the meals in his lap. "Caleb, I...I don't want you to think—"

"I know," he interrupted. "It's fine. You're my little secret," he said softly, his eyes not moving from the road.

Heat rose in Isaac's cheeks, and he stared down at his knees with a smile. "So," he said after a moment, "then where are we going?"

"Surprise," was the only answer he got.

They rode for quite a while through narrow highways, away from even the meager lights of the little towns they passed. Isaac started to worry that the food in his lap would get cold, but then Caleb turned off the main highway and eased the inappropriately low car down a dirt road that snaked through the trees. He drove for a few minutes more and then parked the car at a wide curve in the road.

"You got that?" he asked as he opened the door, and Isaac nodded. He climbed out and held the warm containers in both hands while Caleb fetched a small cooler from the trunk. Caleb led the way along a footworn path and stopped at a small, grassy clearing that disappeared into the black water of a lake. The woods were perfectly quiet except for the gentle lapping of the water against the ground, and when Isaac looked up, his chest grew warm at the sight of the clear pinpricks of stars in the darkness.

"So...this is okay?" Caleb asked quietly beside him, and Isaac reached out to give his hand a gentle squeeze.

"It's great. How did you find it?"

Caleb shrugged, rubbing a hand over the back of his neck to avoid meeting Isaac's gaze. "Just some Google Maps and a little driving around this afternoon. It's no big deal." He set down the cooler and dropped into the grass beside it.

Isaac smiled at him as he sat. He did a good job not showing it, but he suspected that Caleb was just a little nervous, too. This was different than walking home from school, or even visiting each other's houses. It was private, and purposeful, and...intimate. They were dating. It was real.

Caleb unzipped the cooler while Isaac divided up the food, but the blond paused at the sight of the bottles nestled among the ice packs. Caleb lifted one of the beers from the cooler and a slightly large bottle of clear liquor, holding them up to Isaac as though offering him a choice.

"Where did you get alcohol?" Isaac asked, hesitant to reach out for either option.

"Tuscaloosa, like you said."

"But how did you get it?"

"Uh, I bought it." He seemed to realize he'd said something he shouldn't have, because he looked down at the ground instead of Isaac's face. "I mean, I paid a guy, and he bought it for me. We used to do it all the time. Back home."

"Oh." Isaac got the impression the other boy was lying, but he didn't push it. If Caleb had done something illegal, he supposed he didn't actually want to know. "Well I don't really..."

"Don't really drink? I figured," he chuckled. "I just thought since it was just us, and there's no school tomorrow or anything." He shrugged. "I promise not to take advantage of you," he added, and Isaac smiled.

"I guess one couldn't hurt." He took the offered beer and twisted it open, hesitating before his first taste. He'd had beer once before at a cousin's barbecue, but he'd only been allowed a single can, and even that had made him a little lightheaded. He would have to be careful he didn't embarrass himself. He took a sip and hid a grimace behind his wrist while Caleb drank from the bottle of vodka as easily as if it were water. They ate a few bites of their food, but neither of them were talking, and Isaac grew more anxious by the second. Dates shouldn't be silent, right?

"So," Isaac started in an attempt to ease the tension in his own gut, "I saw you talking with Heather at the game. You two are getting on finally?"

"I guess so. You said you wanted me to be friendlier. And she's all right."

"She is," Isaac agreed, a wide smile on his face. Caleb was making an effort, and it was because of him. That was definitely progress. He didn't seem to want to talk about it anymore, but suddenly silence didn't seem so bad. They finished their meal and sat beside each other in the grass, watching the lake water slosh near their feet. Isaac nursed his beer, the taste growing more bearable with each sip, but Caleb took long drinks from his bottle, thunking it down beside him each time and seeming to look anywhere but at Isaac.

"Caleb, are you okay?" Isaac asked, eyeing the swiftly emptying bottle. "I mean, did something happen today, or...?"

"I'm fine," he answered a little too quickly. "Are you okay?"

"Yeah." Isaac watched him in the moonlight with a furrowed brow. Something was wrong. If Caleb just wanted to sit outside and drink, he could have postponed their date. What was the point of driving all this way if he didn't really want to be here? He'd had almost half the bottle already. There was no way he was going to be safe to drive them home.

Caleb took a deep breath beside him and let it out in a frustrated sigh. "I liked going to your game today," he said, his tone rougher than his words.

The blond's expression softened. "I...I liked you being there. I know you don't care about the game, but...it felt good that you came to see me." He smiled down at the bottle in his hands. "I feel like I played better. Maybe you're good luck," he chuckled.

"Probably not," Caleb murmured, and he took another long drink of liquor.

"Caleb?" Isaac reached out a hesitant hand to urge the bottle back down to the ground. "Please tell me what's wrong." Caleb looked up at him with such a soft, timid frown that Isaac almost hugged him.

"Just—" Caleb huffed, and he had one more pull from the bottle before he shoved it back into the cooler without even putting the cap on. He dropped onto his back in the grass with his hands on his stomach and looked up at Isaac as though waiting for something. When the blond only stared curiously, Caleb gestured to the grass beside him with his eyes and a slight turn of his head, so Isaac smiled and laid down beside him, setting aside his half-empty beer bottle.

"Is this better?" he asked in a whisper, but Caleb still wouldn't look at him. He just scowled up at the stars like they owed him money. Isaac sighed softly through his nose and settled in the grass, tilting his head to catch sight of the moon above the trees. This was supposed to be fun, or romantic, or at least relaxing, right? It was a little romantic, he guessed, if he pretended Caleb didn't seem miserable. Just when Isaac thought they were getting somewhere, why had he snapped shut again? Had Isaac done something wrong? He had barely had a chance to adjust to the idea of dating someone to begin with. He had no clue how he was supposed to handle fights. If that's even what this was.

"I really like you," Caleb said suddenly, and Isaac turned to look over at him. He sounded slightly slurred, which wasn't really a surprise. "I like you a lot."

"I like you too," Isaac assured him. He sat up on one elbow to get a better view of the other boy's face, but Caleb still avoided his eyes and picked at the hem of his shirt.

"I...wanted you to know."

Isaac chuckled. "I thought we figured that part out already. What's bothering you?"

Caleb chewed his lip and looked down at his fidgeting hands. "I've never...been close with anyone before. You know? So I never...had to really talk to anyone."

"I like talking to you," Isaac promised.

Caleb sat up and pressed the balls of his hands into his eyes. "You don't know me," he groaned, sounding quiet and helpless, and he flinched when Isaac laid a hand on his back.

"Hey," the blond whispered, but he wasn't sure what he should say. Caleb was usually so calm and distant—seeing him worked up like this was more than a little disconcerting. Maybe something had happened with his uncle, and he was afraid to say? As far as Caleb knew, Isaac didn't know anything about the other half of his life. Isaac sat up and scooted closer to him, letting his knee nudge the other boy's.

"You can tell me anything, you know," he said softly. "I'm a really good boyfriend," he added, hoping it would lighten the mood, but Caleb only dropped his hands into his lap and peeked at him out of the corner of his eye. Isaac couldn't tell him that he already knew the truth, could he? That must be what he was trying to say. If Isaac pushed him now, when he was so close to opening up on his own, he might undo every step they'd taken. But it tore at him to see the other boy so shaken.

"I don't want to tell you," Caleb sighed. "I want to eat and hang out and have a couple of drinks. I want to give you a date," he insisted. "But this stupid bullshit—"

"Hey hey hey," Isaac stopped him with an arm around his

shoulders, and he touched Caleb's chin to urge him to meet his eyes. The boy looked up at him with uncertainty wrinkling his brow. Isaac didn't know what to do. Caleb looked so lost and so vulnerable—not at all like the scoffing, aloof city kid Isaac had first met. He looked...cute. Heat touched Isaac's cheeks, and he scolded himself for the thought when Caleb was clearly upset, but he couldn't help it. Caleb was cute.

Isaac let his hand move from Caleb's chin to his cheek and leaned close, covering his frowning lips with a soft, slow kiss. He wasn't embarrassed this time. He just wanted the other boy to smile again. Caleb returned his kiss with a clinging, desperate hand in the blond's hair, and he pulled Isaac down with him as he laid back in the grass. It didn't feel like the other times they kissed. Caleb was asking, not taking, and he waited for Isaac to brush his lip with his tongue before he opened his mouth. Isaac was so used to Caleb taking the lead, to being pushed forward every step, that to have the dark-eyed boy underneath him and needing him caused an entirely different sort of twisting in his stomach. Caleb's fingernails dug into the backs of his shoulders through his shirt, tugging him closer, and Isaac shifted to lean his weight on one forearm so he wouldn't have to give up touching the other boy's face.

As Isaac edged forward, one knee in the dirt between Caleb's legs, the other boy suddenly turned away from the kiss with his hands fisted in the back of Isaac's shirt. Isaac leaned back to look down at him.

"Are you okay?" he asked softly. "I'm sorry, you're—you're upset, I shouldn't have—" When he tried to pull away, Caleb clung to him tighter, hiding his face in the crook of Isaac's neck.

"I really like you," Caleb whispered against his skin.

Isaac stayed perfectly still with Caleb's arms wrapped around his neck, not willing to move and risk disrupting the boy's slow, shaking breath. After a long while, Caleb seemed to relax, and he allowed Isaac to move back enough to look him in the face.

"Caleb," Isaac started, his thumb brushing the boy's cheek, "whatever you're trying to tell me, you can tell me when you're ready, okay? I'm not going anywhere." He bent close enough to nudge Caleb's nose with his. "Okay?"

Caleb's lips pressed together as though he was trying not to speak, and he nodded with his eyes lowered.

"Okay," Isaac smiled. "Why don't we head home? This was a really great date, but I'm a little tired."

Caleb pushed him away and sat up with a scowl, clearly recognizing when he was being placated, but after a moment, he gave a soft sigh, peeked back at Isaac, and nodded.

"Go on and get in the car. You're not driving," Isaac pointed out quickly, and he held his hand out for the key fob. Caleb slapped it into his waiting palm and pushed himself to his feet with the help of his hands, then made his way carefully back to the car. Isaac packed up their trash, fastened the cap back on the vodka bottle, and zipped up the cooler, securing everything in the trunk before he took his place in the driver's seat. He made sure Caleb was buckled in properly and eased the car back onto the road, praying that he didn't put any scratches on the very fancy car that belonged to an actual demon.

Caleb slouched in his seat and reached out for him, so Isaac held out one hand with a puzzled frown. Caleb laced his fingers with the other boy's and squeezed him tight, his head drooping against the back of the seat as his eyes drifted shut. Isaac glanced at him when he stopped to turn onto the main road, but Caleb's breath had already taken on the slow rhythm of sleep, so Isaac smiled faintly and drove the rest of the way home one-handed.

At the top of Caleb's driveway, Isaac panicked. Caleb didn't seem to be rousing despite Isaac shaking his shoulder. But he couldn't just leave him, and his own curfew was approaching, so he climbed out of the car, dropped the cooler near the porch to pick up later, and opened the passenger door. He bent down to pull Caleb's arm over his shoulder and lift him out of the car, and he had to stop short with a startled, strained grunt. Caleb had barely moved. Isaac frowned down at him, remembering how heavy the other boy had seemed when Isaac had pulled him through the window. He'd put it down to the awkwardness of the maneuver, but this was different. Caleb was just way, way heavier than he looked. Were demons...heavy? If angels could fly, it would make sense for demons to not be able to, so maybe—this wasn't the time. Worry about demon and angel physics when there isn't a boy passed out in front of you.

Isaac planted his feet and heaved, hauling Caleb out of the car and nearly stumbling backwards as the boy's weight landed on his shoulders. He scrambled to grab him around the waist and just barely managed to keep both of them from hitting the ground. It took very slow, very purposeful walking to get Caleb to the porch, and Isaac looked up the steps in despair. He was only halfway up when he started to feel the sweat forming at his temples. When he reached the top, he dropped Caleb as gently as he could on the wooden deck and fell onto his back beside him to catch his breath.

"Why is your room on the second floor?" he asked the unconscious boy, squeezing his eyes shut as he steeled himself for the second half of the journey.

Before he could even get Caleb situated on his back again, the front door opened ahead of him, and Andras appeared on the porch in pajama pants and a loose-fitting t-shirt.

"You boys have a good time?" he chuckled as he took in Caleb's limp body.

"Y-Yes sir," Isaac answered. "Caleb just—he fell asleep, so I was trying to—but—"

"Fell asleep?" the demon snorted. "That's kind. It looks like he's drunk."

"Well—"

"Don't worry about it." Andras took a step forward and bent down to take Caleb by the wrist, easily lifting him from the deck and settling the boy over his shoulder like a rag doll. Isaac's mouth dropped open, and Andras glanced over his shoulder at him. "Come inside, kid."

Isaac followed obediently as soon as he'd fetched the cooler from the bottom of the stairs. He waited in the living room, avoiding stepping on the painted marks on the floor while Andras carried Caleb effortlessly up to his room. He heard the door click shut upstairs, and Andras padded back down the steps and tilted his head to urge Isaac into the kitchen with him.

"You want anything?" Andras asked with a brief gesture toward the fridge, but Isaac shook his head, letting the demon take the cooler from him and set it on the counter. "So," he said as he leaned against the kitchen island, "he didn't give you any trouble, did he?"

"Oh, no sir," Isaac said immediately. "We were just hanging out, you know, celebrating after my game today, and I guess he got a little carried away. Oh!" Isaac reached into his pocket and offered Andras the heavy glass key fob. "Sorry I drove it without asking, but Caleb...you know."

Andras weighed the key in his palm, pursing his lips slightly without looking up. "So you two are going out, hm?"

Isaac's face and neck flushed with heat. "H—He...he told you?"

"No," the demon chuckled, "you did, just now. But I had my suspicions." He looked up into Isaac's panicked face. "I'm not big on telling other people's secrets, kid. You want to keep in the closet, it's not my business." He glanced at the clock over the stove. "It's pretty late. You want me to take you home so you don't get in trouble?"

"Oh, no sir, thank you." Isaac smiled, relieved of the tension that had built instantly in his chest. He wasn't going to tell. "I'll make it if I hurry. Dad's probably asleep by now anyhow."

"Your call." Andras walked him to the front door and held it open for him, and Isaac could feel the demon's eyes on him as he stepped onto the porch. Isaac hand his hand on the railing to head down the stairs when Andras spoke again.

"You know," he said, leaning against the screen door to keep it propped open, "Caleb talks a big game about parties and late nights, but he drinks when he's nervous. Isn't that strange?" Andras straightened, and Isaac felt nailed in place as the demon's sharp blue eyes focused on him. "I wonder what he would have to be nervous about with you?"

Isaac didn't move until Andras shut the door and turned the deadbolt, and not for a while after that, either. He finally realized how long he'd been standing there, and he took the stairs two at a time on his way down and jogged the long driveway toward his house. Caleb had been nervous. To go on a date. Before, when Isaac had found him after the bonfire, he'd been nervous. Caleb was capable of feeling nervous, and it was because of Isaac. Maybe the thought should have worried him, but the blond had a smile on his face as he crept into his dark house.

19

Caleb woke up with a headache. It wasn't helped by the loud music that reached him all the way from downstairs. Pulling the blanket over his head didn't even help. Each clang of pots and pans from the kitchen below sent a sharp pain right through his ear. He tried to roll himself up in a cocoon of blankets and pillows, but nothing helped. He had to pee, anyway. He unraveled himself with a grunt of defeat and clamped his hands over his ears as he walked to the bathroom. The second door didn't help block out the noise, either. He noticed when he stood at the toilet and reached down that he was still wearing pants. And a shirt. And he'd been put to bed, he realized with a groan. He leaned on the wall and let his head thump against the tile. He'd ruined everything.

Not only had he failed to tell Isaac the truth and ease the gnawing guilt in his gut, he'd made a complete fool of himself while he was failing. It made him sick to think how he'd clung to Isaac, pouted, and acted like a scared little boy. What did he have to be scared of, anyway? That Isaac would leave him? So what? A month ago he'd had no idea who Isaac even was. Caleb sank down into a crouch with his back against the wall and his arms around his knees. But he knew now. And he was afraid. Was this what Andras had meant by finding something to ground him? Something to connect him to his human side? If so, it felt like shit. Caleb didn't want to ever feel that exposed again.

He pushed himself up, finished his business, and went downstairs. The music blaring from Andras's iPhone dock on the counter was some sitar-heavy Bollywood pop with a woman singing in a high, piercing voice. The demon himself was multitasking, flipping a pancake with one hand while he spun Marian in a breezy circle with the other. Caleb's mother smiled as she turned, and she released Andras at the sight of her son.

"Good morning, darling," she said brightly. "Did you sleep well?"

Caleb turned the music down to a more bearable level but left it on for her sake. He didn't know why she liked this stuff so much. "Fine," he answered her.

"Your uncle's made pancakes! Isn't that lovely? And he got that strawberry syrup you like so much."

"Gee, thanks, uncle," he muttered, but Andras only smirked at his sarcasm.

"I hope for your sake you're well rested," the demon said, and he followed Caleb to the breakfast table and dropped a plate of pancakes in front of him. "Today you're going to try to keep me from kicking your ass." Marian stopped twirling long enough to offer some brief, excited applause, and Andras reached across to the island and placed a small plastic bottle of strawberry syrup next to Caleb's plate. "You do still want to learn, right? Unless you're feeling a bit...grounded?"

Caleb glared up at him. He wasn't about to be taunted. Not today. Not after the night he'd had. "I'm ready."

"I thought you might be. Eat your breakfast."

Marian sat beside him with her own plate of pancakes and happily ate with him, periodically pausing to brush the hair from his eyes and tell him for the millionth time how proud his father would be. Caleb didn't feel like he was making anybody particularly proud at the moment.

As soon as his plate was clean, he dropped it in the sink, and Andras led him out into the back yard with Nobah right at his heels. Marian came right behind them, taking a place on the back deck swing to watch. The sky was dark even though it was mid-morning, and Caleb craned his neck to peer up at the rumbling clouds.

Andras put a hand on Caleb's shoulder to position him in the yard, then stepped back a few feet and gestured to the ground. "This is your circle," he said, drawing it in the air with one finger, "and this is mine. If either one breaks, this space between us is all the time you'll have to defend yourself and your mother. You think you can stop me?"

"I dunno; are you gonna tell me what the hell to do, or are you just gonna make vaguely threatening comments?"

The demon smiled. "Let's start small." He clicked his tongue once, and the massive black dog sat down next to him and looked up as though waiting for instruction. "Nobah, hakshivi ahkhshahv, hm?" He tapped the dog on the nose with one finger and then pointed it at Caleb. "This boy is not your master. You understand?" The animal gave a little growl of acknowledgment as it peered across the yard at Caleb.

Caleb took a half step back at the slight twitch in the dog's ears. "So, what exactly is the goal here?"

"Nobah is a demon too," Andras said. "Just like me; just like the ones you're hoping to summon and bind. She might not be as strong, but she follows all the same rules." He put out a hand and idly scratched the top of the beast's head. "So, if you think you're one of us—command her. If your will is stronger, she will obey."

Caleb watched the dog staring at him, and he tried to focus. It was the same principle as unlocking windows, right? Just make it happen.

Nobah, come.

The dog's ear gave a single twitch, but it didn't move. Caleb glanced back at Andras, who was waiting patiently with his arms folded, and then pressed his lips together and returned his eyes to the animal in front of him. He wasn't going to embarrass himself. He wasn't going to be weak again. He'd had enough of that feeling.

Nobah, he tried again, a dark weight growing around his heart. The stubbornly constant beat seemed to slow, just slightly, and Caleb let out a soft breath. *Come.*

The beast shifted forward, wavering for just a moment before lifting to its feet and padding over to lick Caleb's waiting hand.

"Not bad," Andras muttered.

Sit, Caleb commanded, and the dog obeyed.

"It's the same as telling a human what to do," Andras said. "You feel it, don't you? All your being centered on that single thought. You hold onto that, and you can bend anyone to your will. Of course, if you're set on summoning Ayporos, don't expect to have him eating out of your hand, but you might just be able to stop him from taking anything out on those close to you." He threw a pointed glance at Marian and lifted his eyebrows at Caleb as if to ask if he understood. The boy nodded. "Good. Now, a fight isn't just two people staring at each other. Push me." Caleb looked at him in confusion, and Andras smirked at him. "Don't be coy. If you can unlock windows, you should be able to move me."

"You know about that?"

"You've no secrets from me, little lamb," Andras chuckled. "Come along."

Caleb stumbled backwards as though he'd been hit in the chest, and he glared across at Andras, but the demon hadn't moved.

"Come on, boy," he taunted. "Or does precious Isaac still have you all aflutter?"

Caleb's lips twisted into a scowl, and before he knew what he was doing, Andras slid backwards in the grass, struggling to keep himself upright.

"Like you mean it!" the demon snapped as soon as he found his footing. He pushed back against Caleb so forcefully that he fell to the ground, but the boy pulled himself back up with his jaw set. Caleb didn't think about it. He didn't have to. The blood in his veins seemed to grow thick and still, finally quieting the constant rushing in his ears, and he tore Andras from the ground, the demon's body colliding with the far fence. He was vaguely aware of his mother's excited voice, but everything around him seemed dull except for Andras. The demon was laughing as he rose from the grass.

"That's more like it," he growled, and when he rushed the boy, Caleb reacted instinctively. He was pushed, and he pushed back; Andras laid hands on him, and he flung the demon away like he weighed nothing. It was strange and exciting to let loose—to feel the strength of a demon gripping him and be able to stand his ground. More than that. To be able to fight. Andras taunted him at every exchange, urging him to do better, try harder, be faster. Caleb's whole body felt cold, from his weakly thumping heart to his unwavering grip on the demon's shirt.

"Enough," he heard himself say, and then Andras slammed backwards into the porch, crashing through the wood and almost bringing the whole structure down on top of him. Marian gave a small cry of surprise as the deck wobbled underneath her, and she hurried down to the grass.

"Caleb!" she shouted, almost scolding, and something snapped just inside his ears. There were birds in the trees again; traffic passed on the distant road, and the blood in him began to flow hot. He was standing in his back yard, his shirt torn at the collar where Andras had grabbed him, and the porch fell with a loud crack of wood, hiding his guardian from sight.

Caleb rushed across the yard, bending to lift the floor of the collapsed deck with barely a grunt of exertion. Andras looked up at him with a smile on his face and blood dripping from his chin. His arm was torn open from a stray nail, blood poured from a wound at his temple, and a broken piece of wood had planted itself in his gut, but he didn't seem concerned.

"A hand, please, Marian?" he said in a rough voice, and the woman ducked under the porch while Caleb held it. She eased Andras to his feet, the demon wincing as he tried to straighten, and as soon as they were both clear, Caleb let the wood drop back into its pile.

He turned in time to see Andras tugging the broken board from his stomach with a low grunt. The demon tossed aside the bloody wood and stuck his fingers into the open wound, feeling around for a moment before retrieving a sizable splinter. Caleb watched with a cold sensation in his chest that wasn't at all like the quiet he'd wanted. In a moment, without even trying, he'd lashed out—and if Andras hadn't been a demon, he would be dead.

"Don't make that face," Andras said, but his chuckle was rough and caused another slow bubble of blood from his lips. "Could have been slightly gentler, though; I did tell you this body works, didn't I?"

"Andras—"

"You did just as you should have," the demon interrupted him, locking him in a steady gaze. "I'll be fine." He nodded to Marian, who helped him up the broken steps to the back door, and they left Caleb in the yard with a frown on his face and a weight in his gut. This wasn't what he wanted. Was this what his father wanted from him? To forget, to lose himself, to fight without thinking and to hurt people without even realizing it? This wasn't making a deal. It wasn't calming, and it certainly wasn't quiet.

Caleb crouched down in the grass, his eyes on the discarded board that had been embedded in his guardian's stomach thirty seconds ago. Was this what Andras had meant by becoming something else entirely? During that fight, he hadn't been himself—everything was dim and quiet and unimportant. He was instinct, not a person, and his instinct had been violent. What if he lost control like that around someone who *couldn't* afford to be tossed into buildings? What if he lost control around Isaac?

He fisted his hands in his hair and swore under his breath. He felt split in two. Andras pulled him toward his father, toward stillness and power and simplicity and purpose. But he was forced to admit that he was undeniably grounded. Isaac was a different kind of quiet, lulling him into complacency and attachment. Andras said he was a demon, and Isaac said he was a good person. Andras said he had to choose. How was he supposed to choose when everyone else already seemed to have their minds made up about him? It felt like he hadn't made a decision on his own in months.

Caleb let out a soft sigh and ran a hand down his face, pressing his knuckles against his lips and staring down at the broken porch. This was his life. It had to be about what he wanted—not what anyone else expected of him. And right now, what he wanted...he wanted to be with Isaac. If Isaac had pushed him toward a human life, he'd only done it by accepting him, by wanting to be around him and talk to him. Isaac wanted to be with him. That was all.

He hesitated and glanced up at the back door, then put his hands on his knees and pushed to his feet. He wanted to see Isaac.

Caleb started down the driveway at a jog, the steady quickening of his heart not bothering him now. He refused to be nervous. He'd made an ass of himself out of fear, and he wouldn't do it again. Isaac didn't frighten him. When he arrived at the blond boy's front door, he was lightly panting, but he didn't mind. This beating heart, the blood pumping in his ears—it meant that he and Isaac had something in common. Caleb reached up to knock on the door, the sky giving a rumbling warning above him, and waited until it clicked open.

"Help you?" Isaac's father said through the half-open door.

"Is Isaac here?"

The man seemed slightly reluctant to answer as he took in Caleb's torn shirt and messy hair, but he gave a short grunt of acceptance and opened the door wide enough to let the boy inside. He called Isaac's name over his shoulder as Caleb entered, and the blond appeared in the hallway, stopping short as his eyes met Caleb's.

"Hey," he said, a touch of pink staining his cheekbones.

"Hey," Caleb answered quickly. "I came to ask you about that project, in Mr. Whitaker's class? Do you have a minute?"

"Oh. Yeah. Uh, sure," Isaac faltered. "Come on back."

"Y'all keep that door open," Isaac's father called as Caleb followed the other boy back to his room.

"Yes sir!"

Isaac eased his bedroom door shut just a little and offered Caleb a small smile.

"I'm sorry," Caleb said softly. "About last night."

"It's fine." Isaac noisily opened a closed a couple of drawers on his desk, then opened a notebook and urged Caleb to sit beside him. He leaned in close enough to whisper. "I...thought it was cute."

"Cute?" Caleb frowned, but then he gave a short huff and let it go. "Anyway, I...look, can we go somewhere? Alone?"

"Right now?"

Caleb nodded, and Isaac paused to chew his lip in thought.

"One sec." He rose from the desk and disappeared into the living room. Caleb could hear him exchange a few words with his father, and he felt relief touch his shoulders as Isaac came back into the room with a smile. "No problem; we can go to your place to finish this, since you've got the book we need," he said a little loudly. Caleb couldn't help the faint smile on his lips.

"Great."

Isaac stuffed some things in his backpack and carried it on one shoulder as they left the house. Caleb knew the man on the couch was glaring at him while they passed, but he didn't care. Right now he only cared about being with Isaac. They walked toward Caleb's until they were out of sight of the house, and then Caleb took Isaac by the hand and led him off down the road instead.

"Where are we going, really?" Isaac asked, but he was smiling.

"I haven't decided," Caleb admitted. "I just...needed to be alone with you." He stopped walking and turned to take Isaac's face in his hands, kissing him so suddenly that the blond gave a brief squeak of surprise. When he broke the kiss, he looked down into the boy's grey eyes and sighed through his nose without releasing him. "Where can we go? I...I need to talk to you."

"Okay," Isaac answered, a soft wrinkle forming in his brow as he reached up to cover Caleb's hand with his own. "Come on."

They walked down the road, hand in hand, while Caleb's mind ran at a thousand miles an hour. He had to tell him. If he wanted Isaac to know him, and if he wanted to—to be with him, then he had to tell him. Everything. He opened his mouth a dozen times while they walked, but he didn't know what to say. How were you supposed to tell someone that you have a literal demon for a father? Especially when that someone was the kind of person who had tried to pray away his gay thoughts?

"Here," Isaac said as they approached the church, gesturing toward a small building at the back. "That's the youth center; there's nothing going on this weekend, so we're not likely to run into anyone. We can talk as much as you want." He looked up as a splatter of rain hit the top of his head. "Cripes," he sighed, and together he and Caleb jogged the rest of the way to the squat little building, neither of them willing to release the other's hand. By the time they reached the door, the clouds had opened up completely, and in the time it took for Isaac to pull the door open and let Caleb inside, they were both soaked through.

Isaac stood panting just inside the door, and he smiled up at Caleb as he set his backpack down in a nearby plastic chair. The layout was simple; the only things in the room were a circle of chairs clearly borrowed from the school, a seating area with a sofa and a couple of plush chairs, a fridge, some bookshelves, and a foosball table pushed into the far corner. It looked exactly like Caleb would have imagined a church youth center looking like, actually. Boring. He took a small step toward Isaac, and with an easy thought, he turned the deadbolt in the door with a tiny click. He wasn't going to risk being interrupted.

20

"Is everything okay, Caleb?"

Caleb ran his fingers through the boy's blond hair and kissed him instead of answering. Isaac held him without resistance, his arms around Caleb's waist as he accepted the kiss. The moving air from the ceiling fan chilled their wet skin, bringing up goosebumps on Caleb's arms, and he clutched the boy tighter to him. Isaac gently tried to pull away, so Caleb let him break the kiss but refused to release him, keeping them close with a gentle hand on the back of his head.

"What do you want to talk about?" Isaac asked softly. Caleb had to tell him. He had to take the risk. He knew it. But no matter how many times he tried to speak, no sound would come out. If it meant Isaac never had to see what was inside of him, never had to know the things he'd done—Caleb could keep that secret, couldn't he? If it meant Isaac would never pull away from him in fear, he could keep that secret.

"I'm sorry about our date," Caleb said. He let his thumb brush Isaac's cheek and reached to hold him by the hip. "I guess I just...got worked up over nothing. I've never done this sort of thing before, and...I was nervous."

"I was too," Isaac assured him. "It's okay. Really. We can go on more dates."

"I'm not nervous now," Caleb murmured, lightly bumping his forehead against Isaac's and inching his fingers under the hem of the blond's damp shirt. "Let me make it up to you."

"It's—you don't have to do that," Isaac objected, but he let Caleb lead him backwards, and he started slightly as his ankles hit the couch. Caleb pushed him into his fall and straddled his hips, supporting his weight on his knees as he unfastened the top button of Isaac's shirt. "H-Hold on, C-Caleb, I...I thought you wanted to talk."

"I want you, Isaac," he whispered, tenderly biting the other boy's chin as the next button came loose. "I want all of you."

"Caleb, please—" Isaac put his hands on Caleb's chest in an attempt to slow him down, but the boy had already undone another button and slipped a hand inside his shirt, Isaac's wet skin cool underneath his palm.

"I don't want to wait anymore." Caleb rolled his hips against him, a shudder running down his spine as Isaac gave a soft, timid gasp. The blond might have been arguing, but he was already hard.

Isaac breathed his name once more, and Caleb smoothly unbuttoned his shirt, bunching it at Isaac's shoulders as he pushed it open and bent to lock a biting kiss on the blond's collarbone. He whimpered in response, fingers tightening in the other boy's shirt. "Please, I—we can't. It's not right, it's—it's lust, and I made a promise—"

Caleb leaned back just enough to take Isaac's hand in his, and he lifted it to brush his lips over the polished silver ring. "This promise?" he whispered. He lightly kissed the tip of Isaac's ring finger.

"Y-Yes."

"Hm." Caleb nipped once at Isaac's knuckle, feeling the shiver run through the boy underneath him. He drew his finger into his mouth, slowly, with his dark eyes locked onto Isaac's wide, clear grey, and tasted the cool metal. A soft groan formed in his throat as he ran his tongue over the band; his teeth fastened gently around the boy's finger, and he slowly eased the ring off, holding it on his tongue as he let Isaac's hand slip from his lips. Caleb reached up to take the ring from his mouth, and he dropped it onto the floor with a sharp clink that seemed to shatter the blond's resolve. Isaac sat up and snatched Caleb close to him, crushing a kiss against his lips, and Caleb wasted no more time. His hands quickly worked on Isaac's belt while his tongue explored the blond's mouth, finding his kiss returned with unexpected eagerness. Even if Isaac couldn't admit it, he wanted this as much as Caleb did.

Caleb shifted onto the floor as he unfastened Isaac's jeans, leaving soft bites all down his stomach as he went, and the blond obediently lifted his hips to allow Caleb to tug the pants down his legs. Isaac's knuckles went white as he gripped the couch cushion, his face burning red at the sight of Caleb on his knees, nipping kisses along his inner thigh. Caleb ran his hands up his skin, calming the trembling flesh, fingertips hooking into the waistband of his underwear as a devilish smile touched his lips. He could hear the hitch in Isaac's breath, the shiver in his gasp as Caleb tugged his briefs down just far enough to free him. He kept his eyes on Isaac's, a satisfied heat pooling in his gut at the clouded look on the blond's face. He took Isaac into his mouth slowly, his own grip tightening on the edge of the couch as he steadied himself. His tongue ran over the silken skin, his tiniest movement drawing tender whimpers from the other boy. He didn't want to rush, but it took everything he had to resist taking him to the hilt.

When Isaac's hips bucked up, and he let out a soft, tense little cry, Caleb let him go. He stood and tugged his shirt up over his head, abandoning it on the floor along with Isaac's, and he unbuttoned his jeans with the blond's eyes on him.

"H...Hey," Isaac started, his voice thick with arousal, "Caleb, I...I'm not sure I—I mean, I..." He was watching Caleb's jeans slide down his hips, and red flushed his cheeks when the other boy stood naked in front of him. "I'm...not sure about...you know, the...the actual..."

A smile pulled at Caleb's lips, and he slid back into Isaac's lap, scratching one slow fingernail down his jaw to lift his gaze. "Don't worry about your chastity," he chuckled. He bent to press a hard kiss to Isaac's lips and slipped his fingers around his cock as he whispered, "I'm going to show you how to take good care of me."

Isaac's brow furrowed as though he had questions, but Caleb's hand around him was too distracting. Caleb leaned back, careful to keep his weight on his knees, and he let Isaac watch him slip two fingers into his mouth. When they were slick with saliva, he reached back to press them against his entrance with a soft, wanting hiss.

"Put your hands on me," he murmured, still stroking the trembling blond beneath him. Caleb leaned close and let his head rest against Isaac's shoulder as he shifted his legs apart, his back arching at the first intrusion of his own fingers. Isaac's ragged breath was hot against his ear, each little whimper sending a pulse through Caleb's stomach. He squeezed Caleb's hips and ran his palms up the boy's sides, and Caleb let out a soft groan as Isaac's thumb gingerly brushed his nipple. Caleb pushed back against his own fingers and shut his eyes, his breath just as desperate as Isaac's as he worked himself into readiness. It would take too long to get Isaac to do it; he would be too timid, and Caleb didn't want to wait.

Caleb shuddered each time he brushed the sensitive spot inside of him, conscious of his own moans mixing with the soft yelps Isaac gave when Caleb squeezed him. He leaned back with the intension of removing his fingers, but as he moved, Isaac moved with him, the blond's mouth closing over Caleb's nipple and drawing a startled cry from him. Isaac's tongue was burning hot against his skin, and he pressed his hands against Caleb's back, keeping him close. Caleb heard the other boy's name escape his lips, but he hadn't meant to say it. He slid his fingers free with a growl and held himself up by the back of the couch as he shifted, his hand around Isaac's cock giving one last squeeze as he rolled his hips forward.

He didn't ask if Isaac was ready. He couldn't wait anymore—not with those hands on his skin and the slow, hot caress of Isaac's tongue on him. He lifted up on his knees and positioned Isaac at his entrance, a helpless moan slipping out of him as he sank down onto him. Isaac's hands tensed painfully on his waist, and Caleb heard the other boy's sharp intake of breath as he took him deep inside him. For just a moment, they stayed still, Caleb allowing himself a few scant seconds to adjust to Isaac stretching him, but he was out of patience. He ground down against Isaac's hips to make sure he was getting everything the blond had to give, and then he lifted himself up again, setting a quick, demanding pace. He had to be careful not to let too much of his weight onto the other boy, but he squeezed his shoulder for balance and kept his rhythm.

"God," Isaac whispered, his head falling against Caleb's chest as they moved. Caleb was doing the work, twisting his hips and leaning to make sure Isaac brushed against him just right, but having the blond's hands on him, tender kisses on his chest when Isaac could focus enough, was like being touched by lightning. Isaac was trembling, fighting to keep his breath steady, but Caleb didn't let up. He needed more, and each moan Isaac gave just spurred him on harder, faster.

"Touch me," Caleb said against Isaac's ear, his fingers in the other boy's hair, and he obeyed, doing his best to stroke Caleb in time with the rhythm he set. Caleb let out a growling groan and tilted Isaac's head up to kiss him. "Tell me when you're going to come," he demanded in a harsh whisper. "I want you to come inside of me."

"J...Jesus, Caleb," he whispered, and Caleb could feel the burning heat in Isaac's face against his skin. His hand tightened, and Caleb bucked against him, knowing neither of them was going to last. Isaac was hesitant and gentle, but eager, and when Caleb caught his mouth in another kiss, Isaac was the one to open his mouth and slip his tongue past the other boy's lips. Caleb covered Isaac's hand with his, helping him keep the pace and firm grip that he liked, and once he heard the blond give a shuddering cry, he rolled his hips over and over, trying to master the movement that had caused such a delicious sound. Isaac clutched him tighter, barely leaving room for his hand to move between them, but he didn't let up despite his desperate moans.

"Caleb, I—I'm going to—"

"Do it," he whispered, pressing down against Isaac's hips as hard as he dared. "Come for me."

The boy's fingernails dug into Caleb's side as he pulled him close, his attention to the other boy's erection temporarily forgotten as his body tensed. A rough cry tore itself from Isaac's lips, and Caleb could feel the burst of heat deep inside him, each pulse matching the helpless jerks of the boy beneath him.

"Shit," Isaac hissed against his neck as he held him, and Caleb couldn't help his smile. He took over where Isaac left off, bottom lip caught in his teeth as he stroked himself, and his practiced hand soon pushed him over the edge, spilling his climax onto Isaac's still twitching stomach.

They both sat panting, neither one willing to move. Isaac leaned back first, his hand carefully unfastening from Caleb's waist, and he reached up to cup the other boy's cheek.

"Don't swear," Caleb murmured with a smirk as he turned his head to kiss Isaac's palm, but the blond only looked up at him with a tense frown and worry darkening his brow.

"I love you," Isaac said, and Caleb froze. He almost asked him to repeat it, but he didn't have to. "I love you," he said again. His thumb brushed Caleb's cheek. Caleb's heart was painfully loud, but Isaac almost seemed on the verge of tears.

"Isaac," he muttered, uncomfortably aware of the blush rising in his face, "just because we did it, you don't have to—"

The blond gave a single strained sigh as though steeling himself, and then he said in a rush, "Caleb, I know. I know what you are. A cambion. I know. I always knew."

Caleb stopped, and in that instant, the blood drained from his face so quickly that he thought his heart had actually finally stopped. He stared down at Isaac's tortured face, his whole body numb and cold. "You knew?" he whispered. "You knew, and you still—"

"I...I was afraid, at first, but then I got to know you, and I saw how much it hurt you, and I just...I wanted to be your friend, and then I wanted to be more, and it didn't matter who your parents were, I...I wanted to be with you. I want to be with you," he corrected himself. "I love you, and I don't care what you are."

"How? How could you know? All this time, I—and you—"

"An angel came to me," he said, a faint smile on his lips as his hand settled gently at the side of Caleb's neck. "He came to me and told me about you, and he told me that you needed help, you...that you needed someone, and that if I helped you, you could be saved. That all you needed was the right person, and you could be turned away from the darkness inside of you."

Caleb paused. "An angel. Told you to *save* me?"

"Yes," Isaac sighed, and Caleb's heart twisted in his chest. "He said that you didn't have to be evil, and that I could help you be—"

Caleb pushed away from him, flinching slightly as he removed himself from the other boy's lap, and he snatched up his clothes without looking back at him. Even Isaac, he scolded himself as he hastily pulled his pants back on. He'd been right all along. Isaac had wanted something from him. He hadn't just been friendly; he hadn't really been interested. He'd been commanded. One more person to push him, change him, make his decisions for him. Isaac hadn't cared about him. Everyone had a motive. *Isaac* had a motive.

"Caleb?" Isaac said softly, confusion in his voice. "What are you doing? Did I do something—"

He pulled his still-damp shirt over his head, but he couldn't bring himself to look the other boy in the face. "What I am is none of your fucking business," he said, glad at least that he could keep his voice steady. "And what I do with this darkness in me has nothing to do with you. Tell your fucking angel I don't need saving. Especially not by you." He unlocked the entry door and flung it open without touching it, and he didn't stop at the sound of Isaac calling his name. He didn't look back. He just ran, and for once, his heart seemed to stay slow and steady.

Caleb threw open the door to his house and went straight upstairs without stopping. He turned his shower on as hot as it would go and stripped out of his clothes, leaving them in a heap on the bathroom floor. He needed to get Isaac's scent off of him. He could smell the other boy's sweat, his shampoo. He stood under the scalding water and scrubbed his skin until it was raw, but he could still smell him. Stupid. Stupid to get so close. Stupid to think Isaac wanted him. None of them cared what Caleb wanted. None of them cared about *him*. Not his mother, not Andras, not Isaac, and not—whatever stupid angel had decided to make Isaac pretend to like him.

He should have just ignored Isaac, just like he ignored everyone else. Or he should have slept with him and forgotten him. He'd actually let himself think that this was more, and he'd...he'd let it feel like more than sex. It had been more. He'd let Isaac kiss him so softly, hold his hand, whisper his name in his ear and lay beside him in the grass under the moonlight. If Isaac had just said 'I love you,' and ended there, Caleb might have—he flinched as he finally broke the skin on his arm, the hot water stinging his scrape. Stop. Stop thinking his name. Just forget it.

Caleb's phone was ringing where he'd left it on his nightstand. He wouldn't answer it. He wanted to throw it out the window. He didn't want to hear Isaac's voice again or think about his smile. Isaac had been using him, just like everyone else. He'd lied every time Caleb had asked why he was interested in him. It wasn't because he'd had a good feeling, or because he was interested, or because he was attracted to him. Of course Isaac could say he didn't care what Caleb was. It was his job to make Caleb feel wanted and human. He'd been on some fucking mission from God. Caleb finally stopped scrubbing, and he covered his mouth with one hand to stifle his hiccuping sob. Who the hell had asked God to get involved in the first place? He leaned against the tile wall and pretended it was the shower wetting his cheeks, and not his tears.

He jumped when he heard a heavy knock, and Andras's voice sounded through the door.

"Caleb, there's a very wet and distraught-looking blond asking for you."

Caleb did his best to swallow the lump in his throat and rinsed his face before answering. "I don't want to see him."

A beat passed. "You sure?"

He reached down to turn off the water and stepped out, tugging his towel from its hook. "I'm sure," he said.

"All right," the demon answered, but he sounded unsure. Caleb waited until he heard Andras's footsteps down the hall, and then he crept out of the bathroom after him with the towel around his waist, stopping once he reached the top of the stairs. He leaned against the wall, just out of sight.

"Sorry, kid," he heard Andras say, muffled by the rasp of the rain outside. "He says no."

"Please," Isaac begged. "He's not answering his phone, and I—I just need to talk to him for a minute!"

"Not my call."

Caleb heard Isaac sigh, and the sound slid through his stomach like a knife. He slumped down the wall, his hair still dripping water onto the wooden floor.

"Okay," Isaac relented from downstairs. His voice was wavering. "Will you please...please tell him to call me? Or...or text me, or...anything? Please."

"I'll tell him, Isaac."

"Okay," the boy said again. "Okay. Thank you. I'm...sorry to bother you."

The door clicked shut, and Caleb heard Andras coming back up the stairs, but he couldn't bring himself to move. He finally looked up when the demon stood over him and gave a short sigh. Andras still looked a bit pale, but his wounds seemed to have closed, at least.

"So, what's all that about?" Andras asked, his hands on his hips. "You two have a spat?"

Caleb scanned the demon's face. Andras had never lied to him. He kept secrets, but when Caleb asked, he always answered—even if the answer was that he couldn't say. "Andras," he said as he pulled to his feet, "Isaac knows what I am. He said that an angel told him to 'turn me from the darkness.'" He frowned as the demon's eyes widened, just slightly. "Do you know anything about that?"

Andras seemed to hesitate, but he answered before Caleb could press him. "It wouldn't be the first time they've tried to interfere with a cambion," he said. "They can't do it directly, so they have to get a human to act on their behalf. The whole free will thing."

Caleb gripped the towel around his waist. "Free will," he scoffed. "Free to be manipulated."

"Nobody can make your choices for you, Caleb. It shouldn't surprise you that there are forces interested in what that choice is, though. You know where I stand. Now you know where Isaac stands. But which way you go is up to you."

His skin still ached everywhere that Isaac had touched it. He could feel the other boy's hands on him, taste his kiss on his lips, hear his breath against his ear. The rapid beat of his heart that he'd come to expect whenever Isaac was near, the rush of heat that he'd come to crave and seek out—the thought of it made him sick. It wasn't real. He needed quiet. He needed cold.

"I want to go to the city," he said. "Right now."

Andras regarded him for a moment, but then he nodded. "All right. Maybe put some pants on first. I'll be downstairs."

Caleb went back to his room and finished drying himself off, then hastily dressed himself in the first clothes he could find that didn't have Isaac's scent lingering on them. Andras was waiting for him at the door, as promised, and together they climbed into the car and rode down the highway toward Birmingham.

"Have any activities in mind?" Andras asked, casting a sidelong glance at the boy in his passenger seat.

"I want more," Caleb said simply. It didn't matter how he found that stillness again, just that he did. Every time his heart moved in his chest, it was another reminder of Isaac's warmth. He looked across at Andras. "Show me how to get more."

"You're the boss," Andras chuckled.

The city seemed different now. As soon as they drew close to the tall buildings of downtown, Caleb could feel the sharp threads in the back of his mind, pulling him in every direction. Desperation was everywhere. Everyone wanted something, and everyone thought they deserved it. Whatever they wanted, Caleb would give it to them. And whatever he asked in return, they would pay.

21

Andras drove where Caleb directed him, following the trail of each cry for help as the boy sensed it. Caleb was more focused than last time; he wasn't humoring Andras or acting out of spite toward his missing father. He was actively seeking the souls that reached out to him. When he asked Andras to stop the car outside a house on the outskirts of the city, he didn't even let the demon out of the car with him. Andras sat in the driver's seat and watched with a frown on his lips, but the woman at the door let Caleb inside almost the instant he spoke to her. The boy reappeared ten or fifteen minutes later, calmly shutting the front door behind him, and he slid into the car without looking at the demon beside him. That was number five.

"There are more," Caleb said, and he gestured ahead of them down the street, so Andras pulled the car away from the curb again. They stopped at the Summit shopping mall, and Andras followed a few steps behind his ward as they walked. Caleb was more upset about his tiff with Isaac than he was letting on, but if it meant the boy was going to apply himself, Andras didn't mind. They would make up in their own time—or not. He wouldn't exactly be upset to see Caleb fully realized. As much as his mother said so without understanding, his father really would be proud. As long as he was smart. A hundred years ago, Anthony hadn't been smart. He'd used his commanding voice to trap people into deals, and he'd used violence to coerce them, and the angels hadn't been able to ignore him any longer. Making a deal was one thing, but interfering with the free will of humans wasn't something they would stand for. There were rules, and if there's one thing an angel can't abide, it's breaking the rules. So

Gabriel had come for him. Anthony had been strong, but no cambion Andras had ever seen could hope to stand against the angel at God's left hand. A life cut short, and all those claimed souls wasted, released on a technicality. He wouldn't see Caleb go down the same road.

Andras stood in front of the popsicle shop where Caleb had directed him to wait, and he watched the boy stalk a young woman who sat crying on the curb outside the movie theater. He sucked on the raspberry lemon treat he'd bought himself while Caleb sat down beside the woman, talking to her without looking at her. Andras didn't bother trying to overhear them. He knew well enough what the story would be. Either a distant or abusive partner, a woman desperate for some honest companionship—who didn't realize that the loyalty Caleb would promise her was anything but honest. Number six didn't take long.

When Caleb returned to him, he looked slightly drawn, and Andras put a hand on his shoulder.

"Let's get you home for now," he said. "You'll exhaust yourself. You want a popsicle? They're really good actually."

"Pass," Caleb muttered, but he obediently followed the demon back to the car.

"How are you feeling?" he asked once they were back on the road.

"Quiet," the boy murmured, his head leaned against the passenger window.

"You aren't afraid your boyfriend won't approve of this little field trip?"

"He's not my boyfriend."

"Oh, yeah? Since when?"

"Since he told me he'd been lying to me since the day we met."

Andras looked over at him with a furrowed brow. Caleb's voice was distant and soft, without a trace of the biting, brooding teenage sarcasm Andras knew too well, and he stared out the window with a faint, blank sort of frown on his face. Maybe this was more than a tiff, after all.

"I think we need to have a little talk about the rules," he said, "if you're going to use this for your escapism instead of liquor. Are you listening?" Caleb gave a small grunt of acknowledgment. "A deal is exactly that—a deal. If you're tempted to try to turn someone who doesn't want to agree, you stop and think twice. A little coercion here and there can be overlooked, if it's innocent enough, but there's nothing I can do for you if you push it too far. Do you understand?"

"There are enough saps in the world without me having to force anybody into anything," Caleb grumbled. "They just want you to talk nice to them and tell them you'll fix all their problems, and they'll agree to anything. You just have to give them a little hope. Hope makes people stupid," he finished quietly.

"Glad you're catching on," the demon chuckled.

"Can we come out again tomorrow?"

Andras paused. "If you're sure you're up for it."

"I'm sure," Caleb answered right away. "I need more."

"Well, I'm not going to argue with you."

At home, Caleb stayed in his room with the door shut. He came out when Andras called him for dinner, but he barely ate anything before retreating back to his bedroom. Andras had seen this stage before. The transition was the hardest. Caleb was still human, and part of him would always be human, but the more souls he claimed, the less human he would feel. He'd get that cold stillness that he seemed to want—but Andras wondered if he knew what he was really giving up. Caleb had stopped smoking because of Isaac, for God's sake. He'd been smiling. When had he ever seen Caleb smile?

"How did he do, Andras?" Marian asked when it was just the two of them at the dinner table. "Is he getting stronger?"

"He is," the demon answered, and she reached out to cover his hand with both of hers.

"How much longer, Andras? How much longer until his father comes for him?"

"Marian," Andras sighed. "I've told you that day may not come."

"No," she said with a smile. "He'll come. He'll come for our child when he's old enough. When he's strong enough."

Andras gently patted her hand, but he didn't answer. He distantly heard Caleb's cell phone ringing upstairs, and then the sharp crash and clatter of something suspiciously electronic-sounding hitting the wall. That was an expensive little outburst.

"Marian," he said, tilting his head as he looked at her, "do you love him? Caleb's father."

"Of course. He came to me when I was loneliest, and he gave me my beautiful boy."

"If Caleb continues this way, he won't ever love anyone. He won't feel anything but hunger, and only soul after soul will sate him. Is that what you want for him?"

"That's his destiny. His father needs him to be strong."

"I'm not so sure," the demon mused, but he only spared a glance at the stairs before he smiled at the woman beside him and rose to clear their plates. "Don't mind me. Do you want me to draw you a bath?"

"Have you seen my book? I thought I had it just here."

"I'll look for it," he assured her, and he pushed her chair back in for her as she stood. "Go on to your room. I'll run your bath."

The woman smiled up at him with that glassy, distant look she'd always had and brushed by him toward her bedroom. He let out a small sigh as he watched her go. It wasn't his place to decide what Caleb needed. No matter which way he pushed him, he risked upsetting someone. All he could do was help the boy, whatever that meant for him.

The next day, Caleb was awake early, and they drove to the city at the boy's insistence. Seven, eight, and nine came even easier than the others, and Caleb wanted to stay out, but Andras could see the exhaustion on the boy's face.

"You're not going to run out of people, Caleb," he promised as they sat across from each other at a small diner between Birmingham and home. "You're going to be no use at all at school tomorrow if you don't get some rest."

"I'm not going back to school."

"Are you kidding? Of course you are."

Caleb stirred the ice in his soda with his straw. "There's no point. I don't need to have read *Moby Dick* or know how to do calculus to do what I'm meant to do."

"What about Isaac?"

"What about him?" Caleb growled. "He's got nothing to do with it."

"I think he probably feels differently, don't you?"

"I don't care how he feels."

Andras noisily sipped the last remnants of his water through his straw, his eyes on Caleb as the slow gurgling sounded between them. He carried on until the boy scowled at him. "I'm sorry, what did you say?" he asked when he finally lifted his head. "There was this overwhelming sound of bullshit."

"What the hell do you know?" Caleb grumped, and he slouched in his chair.

"Quite a lot, actually, thank you very much," the demon laughed. "I know that you like that kid no matter what you say, but I can't make you talk to me. I can tell you I think you're an idiot for wanting to quit school in March of your senior year, but I can't make you go. So, you're an idiot. Eat your food."

Caleb picked at his meal, but he didn't have anything else to say. Even as they drove home, he sat quietly in his seat, and Andras only heard him make a sound when they pulled up the long driveway to the house. Isaac sat on the bottom porch step with his elbows on his knees and looked up as Andras parked the car. He stood when Caleb stepped out of the passenger door.

"I—I came right after church," he said. "Your mom said you weren't here, but—" He stopped as Caleb brushed by him without looking at him, and he watched the boy start up the steps. "Caleb? Please, just wait!"

Caleb pulled the front door open and let it drop shut behind him, not once looking back at the boy calling to him.

Isaac's shoulders slumped as Andras stepped around the car.

"I don't know what to do," the blond said softly.

"Caleb's always been a bit dramatic," Andras answered. "Give him some time. Go on home, kid." He gave the boy a light pat on the shoulder and followed Caleb into the house with a quiet sigh. Why did cambions coming into their power always have to coincide with them being teenagers?

When Andras tried to wake Caleb for school in the morning, he was met with flat refusal. Caleb sat cross-legged on his bed with Greedigut on his knee and his laptop open in front of him, refusing to even look up when the demon addressed him. There wasn't any point in arguing. Either Caleb would get over his little snit in a couple of days, or he could get his GED when he eventually realized what an idiot he was being. He seemed to be continuing under the delusion that making deals for souls would somehow pay his rent when he was older.

Caleb didn't come out of his room all day, no matter how many times Andras knocked on his door to remind him to eat. In the evening, Andras heard him drop down from his window, and he looked out the front door in time to spot his Aston's taillights heading down the driveway. He almost went after him, but then he leaned his elbow against the door frame with a quiet snort of laughter. The little lamb wanted to strike out on his own. Andras just had to hope he wasn't stupid.

He still waited up on the couch until the boy came home, of course.

He could count while Caleb was gone. He could feel them. Ten. Eleven. Then a distant twelve. He let Nobah rest her head in his lap, idly scratching behind her ears, and he sighed as he leaned his head against the back of the couch. If Caleb went too far, it would be his fault. He couldn't blame himself for Anthony—he'd warned him over and over again to be careful, and the boy had only laughed at him. But Caleb had been pushed. What had they been thinking, pulling an innocent boy into a cambion's life and using him to bait Caleb into emotion? He didn't know whether to be angrier at Barachiel or himself.

Caleb finally came back through the door close to two in the morning, smelling of cigarettes and a dingy bar. He paused as he spotted Andras on the sofa, but he only gave him a brief nod before trotting up the stairs and shutting the door to his room behind him. Twelve. Twelve, and only seventeen. Andras had never had to worry before if there was a limit to the angels' patience with his wards.

Andras went with him to Birmingham the next day, and the day after that, each morning forcing Caleb to eat and each afternoon sending a desperate Isaac gently on his way. More days passed this way; if Caleb wasn't asking to go out, he was holed up in his room. Andras occasionally peeked in on him and usually found him asleep, but sometimes he was hunched on his floor with Greedigut in front of him, whispering to himself and snapping a glare over his shoulder at the intrusion. Once he asked Andras to train him again, and he'd been vicious. Andras had taken it easy on him the first time, hoping to scare him into good behavior and do away with any demon-summoning plans, but he'd been forced to take the boy seriously when he'd found himself thrown through the rear windshield of his car. He'd been more pissed about the car than the shards of glass in his skin, if he was honest. Caleb hadn't been overly concerned; he actually seemed satisfied.

By the time they came home late at night that weekend, Caleb had claimed nineteen all together, one of which required a very liberal interpretation of the concept of an agreement. They'd been returning to the car and cut through an alley, where a man threatened them with a gun and asked for their money. Andras had half expected Caleb to lash out, or even just punch him, but he walked up to the stranger without hesitation, drew close enough to whisper in his ear, and tilted his head, his lips moving in words Andras couldn't hear. Whatever was said, the man let his gun clatter to the ground, and for every step he backed away, Caleb followed, until he had him pressed tightly against the adjacent building. He never raised a hand to him, but the stranger trembled, and when Caleb calmly offered his hand, the man took it with a look somewhere between terror and relief. Caleb glanced over his shoulder to make sure Andras was following, and then they left the man in the alley and carried on back to the car in silence.

He was too good. He was going to push too hard; Andras could see it. Already, there was very little sign of the boy who had complained about his classes or rolled his eyes at the demon's teasing. Caleb looked older and harder, and the smiles Isaac had given him may as well have been a dream. Andras suddenly didn't very much like the person he'd raised.

22

Caleb sat on the floor of his bedroom with his chin on his windowsill, looking out between the trees separating his house from Isaac's street. He wanted to be in the city again, to be hunting again, but he'd barely been able to pull himself out of bed. Andras had warned him more than once about overexerting himself, and the week's worth of practice and promises had finally exhausted him. The rest wasn't unwelcome; with every deal he'd made, his heart had seemed to beat a little slower, his blood flow a little thinner, and as he sat still on the hard floor, if he shut his eyes, he could almost pretend that his body wasn't working at all. He still needed more, but this was good enough for now. He idly scratched between Greedigut's shoulders with one finger, tilting his head to peer at the squat grey rodent on his windowsill.

"Boring day," he muttered, and the rat squeaked at him in what he almost took as a disdainful tone. "Still better than school." He didn't want to say out loud that it was better than having to see Isaac. He'd finally managed to stop crying himself to sleep like an idiot, but it hadn't been any easier to keep the blond off his mind—especially since he'd been making a nuisance of himself by showing up after school every day this past week. He was at least determined to finish his holy mission, or whatever. Caleb shook his head to clear it and snorted out a sigh.

"So? What do you want to do today?" he asked, prodding the rat in its round belly. "Got any other handy tricks to pass on?"

Greedigut nipped at his fingertip. It craned its neck to stare up at him with one round, black eye and wiggled its whiskers. While Caleb watched, the rat seemed to phase out of existence right in front of him. He turned his head to check the room behind him, his brow furrowed in confusion, but the rat immediately appeared near the bedroom door, grooming itself as if nothing out of the ordinary had taken place.

"What, seriously?" Caleb scooted around to face the creature again. "Are you just showing off, or that's something I can do, too?"

Greedigut chittered at him and popped out of sight again, reappearing on his shoulder. It nibbled his earlobe and nudged his neck with its cold little nose.

"Show me how."

The rat clambered down his sleeve to the floor and sat up on its hind legs to look at him. Greedigut couldn't speak to him—or didn't, at least—but he'd begun to be able to sense what it wanted from him. Caleb pulled to his feet and tried to listen. He shut his eyes and felt the familiar's approval as a hot, tugging sensation began in his gut. His muscles grew tense and heavy, and just when he began to flinch from the contraction at his core, the ground seemed to give way. His skin went searing hot, and the air around him was suddenly acrid and sharp as he scrambled for balance on a floor that wasn't there. He landed in the front yard with a crash, crushing the recycling bin underneath his weight and sending the lid rolling off down the hill toward the road.

For a few long moments, Caleb just laid there, staring up at the sky as he tried to catch his breath. He hissed as he tried to pull himself out of the wreckage. Part of the bin had splintered and lodged itself in his bicep, and he had to sit in a pile of empty bottles and cardboard, gritting his teeth as he pried it free of his skin.

Andras poked his head out of the front door and leaned to look at him, his lips pursing slightly as he took in the sight. "Take a little tumble, did we?"

"I'm fine," Caleb grumped. He pressed a hand to the wound as he got to his feet and headed up the porch steps. He had always healed a bit faster than normal, but this would still need washing out. Andras stopped him at the door and nodded down at his arm. He followed the demon's gaze and frowned. The blood had stopped. He wiped at his arm, smearing away the blood, and the skin underneath was smooth.

"Perks of having some claimed souls of your very own," Andras said. "Not a very human trait, though, is it?" he added in a softer voice, watching the boy as though expecting him to feel guilty.

"I thought that was the idea."

"Just an observation. That little rat's just full of surprises, isn't he? Anyway, if you're going to be practicing like that, maybe don't start on the second floor of a building, hm?"

"Thanks for the tip," Caleb muttered, and he brushed by Andras to return to his room. He shut the door behind him and leaned against it with a snort. Not a very human trait. Being too human was what had gotten him in trouble in the first place.

Caleb took Greedigut onto his shoulder and went to the back yard instead, and he spent the rest of the afternoon moving back and forth across the grass, pushing himself farther and farther with each hot snap in his belly until he could take the length of the yard in one go. By the time Andras appeared to call him in for dinner, sweat was dripping from the boy's chin, and he had doubled over with his hands on his knees to support himself. His whole body ached, and his lungs strained for oxygen, but it was still better than sitting next to Isaac in homeroom and having to see that warm, carefree smile.

Just stop thinking about him, he scolded himself, wiping the sweat from his eyes with the back of his hand. *Just forget him. I don't need saving.*

He picked at his dinner, but despite his exhaustion, the thought of food made him sick. His mother preened him while he sat beside her at the table and whispered to herself about his incredible progress. At least someone was pleased.

When he was back in his room, he reached under his bed for the heavy book he'd hidden a few days ago. His mother had left it on the coffee table, and he'd secreted it away while Andras was cooking. Greedigut had helped him decipher the writings inside, and he'd been online looking at all sorts of websites—some obviously more New Age stupid than others—for anything he could find about summoning and binding demons. He'd even done some searches on his uncle. "Andrainayas, demon killer of men, the warrior-god whose smile is the lightning" didn't seem very much like the man who'd been putting chocolate chip smiley-faces in his pancakes since he was a kid, but he guessed everyone had their secrets. He just wondered when Andras was going to get around to that "teaching those whom he favors to kill their enemies, masters, and servants" thing he'd seen mentioned more than once.

If Caleb could finish what his mother had tried to start, maybe he could actually get some answers. About his father, about the angel who'd forced Isaac into his life, about himself—all the things that Andras wouldn't tell him. If he bound a demon, it would have to answer him. Like Andras was always telling him, there were rules.

He read late into the night with Greedigut on his shoulder, taking notes and saving pages in his book. He practiced drawing chalk triangles on his floor and trapping Greedigut in them, which the rat didn't suffer in good humor, but Caleb accepted the bites he got in exchange for the rehearsal. He tucked the book back under his bed and crawled onto the mattress with his arms around his pillow, trying to avoid wondering what Isaac was doing. He'd actually sounded worried when he came to the house, but was he worried about Caleb, or the risk to his own soul if he failed a command from an angel? Caleb had thought he was the one luring Isaac in, testing his limits, but Isaac had been just as manipulating. He'd tricked Caleb into caring about him.

The boy's grip tightened on the pillowcase as he hid his face in it with a sigh. So much work, so many deals, and he still got that anxious heat in his belly when he pictured the blond's face. Maybe he could at least talk to him.

He shook his head and curled up closer around his pillow. He couldn't let him in again. He'd just give him more platitudes, claiming that he loved him and that none of the things that made Caleb's life difficult mattered. Isaac only wanted one thing from him, and it wasn't his affection. Or maybe it was, but not because he returned it, but because he'd been trying to soften him up. Make him go to church and be good. But it wasn't that simple. How could Caleb give up what he was? Didn't his father's blood make him beyond help anyway?

He peeked up at the moonlit window by the foot of his bed and let out a long, slow breath. He needed to see him. If only to prove to himself what he already knew.

"Greedigut," he muttered, his mouth half-muffled by the pillow, and the rat clawed its way up the back of his shirt to sit on his arm. Caleb turned his head to look at it. "Can you bring me back a report, or something?"

The rat's whiskers gave a slight twitch, and Caleb started as he realized he was suddenly looking at his own face, blurred around the edges and tinted slightly grey. He could feel the rat moving on his arm, but all he could see was the fabric of his own shirt and the soft puff of the blanket as Greedigut climbed back down the bed. A moment later, he was looking down at the rat again as it trotted toward the window, scratched its way up, and unlocked the latch with a short sniff.

"That...definitely works," Caleb murmured. He sat up in bed and shut his eyes, hoping that would be a little less disorienting. "Show me Isaac," he said. "And don't get caught."

Greedigut squeaked at him in irritation, as if it found the mere suggestion insulting, but began its climb down the ridges in the side of the house. Caleb could see the grass parting in front of him and hear the soft shifting of dirt under tiny paws as the rat hurried down the driveway toward Isaac's house. After a brief pause at the road to let a pair of headlights pass, Greedigut passed through Isaac's yard and found a hidden hole in the masonry. It squeezed its fat little body between the walls until it emerged in what looked like a bathroom cabinet, then it crept across the brown carpet to Isaac's open bedroom door.

The boy was kneeling at his bedside with his hands clasped in front of him, murmuring to himself. Caleb willed Greedigut closer and strained to listen.

"Lord, dispel my fear," Isaac whispered, his brow furrowed as he leaned his head on his tightly-laced knuckles. "End my anxiety, wipe worry from my mind. May I know the power of Your love and the wisdom of Your word. Grant me a peaceful sleep tonight and bring me back tomorrow to a place of safety, security, and right-minded thinking. Please hold those I love as they sleep. Bless them with peace that surpasses understanding, sow in them hope that can not be put out, grow in them dreams and visions for their future and protect them with your unconditional love." He hesitated and let out a soft sigh. "Lord, Caleb needs that hope the most," he added in a quiet, strained voice. "Please help him see the good in himself, and heal him of the hurt I've done him. I tried my hardest to do right, and...Lord, I know you always have a plan, but if Caleb was a test for me, I failed it. I failed it," he whispered, shaking his head slowly against his hands. "If loving him goes against Your will, Lord, then...then I'm a sinner. Heaven forgive me; I just want him near to me again." Isaac's breath hitched as though his throat had gone tight, and he seemed to slump against the side of his bed, his head falling to the mattress while he fisted his hands in the hair at the back of his head.

Caleb's heart was beating too fast. This wasn't what he'd wanted to see. He'd expected Isaac to be apologizing for letting Caleb get away, or for having sex outside of marriage, or whatever, but—not this. He didn't want to see this. He didn't want to hear the boy's quiet, ragged breathing in this private moment. He shouldn't have done this.

He pressed his hands against his eyes and shook his head to break away from the familiar's vision. He was back in his room in empty silence, his heart clamoring in his chest so hard that he felt sick. It was a lie, wasn't it? That Isaac loved him. He'd been leading Caleb on, teasing him with friendship, trying to turn him away from the demon part of him—that was all. That was easier to stomach than the thought that Caleb had actually hurt the other boy that badly. That he'd made him feel like a sinner. That Isaac was suffering because of him.

Caleb fell back onto his bed with the pillow stuffed around his ears, trying to block out the sound of his living heart. It didn't matter. He'd broken things off with Isaac, and they should stay that way. For his own sake, and apparently for Isaac's, too. If they stayed apart long enough, Isaac would forget him, and he could go back to the carefree, happy life he had before Caleb ruined everything. This was the path Caleb was on now, and it felt much safer to stay on it. Besides, he still owed his mother some answers.

23

Andras kept accompanying his ward into the city, as he was asked, but Caleb was less enthusiastic than before. He almost seemed resigned. He left Andras behind to talk to likely targets, as usual, but despite spending all day at it, only claimed one soul by the time they were back in the car to head home.

"Something on your mind?" the demon asked while he drove. He glanced over at Caleb, whose temple was resting against the window, his head lolling with the motion of the car.

"If I keep doing this," Caleb began softly, "how long until I can't go back? You said I would 'find myself another creature entirely.' When does that happen?"

"There isn't a set number you're trying to reach, if that's what you're asking. But you've got a long way to go yet."

"How long until I get it back?" he asked, his eyes focused on the passing scenery. His voice was weary, and the circles under his eyes had grown even darker over the last day. "That quiet. I've taken so many; when do I get it back?"

"Caleb," Andras sighed, "are you sure there isn't anything you want to talk about?"

"Do you know or don't you?"

The demon frowned and kept his focus on the road. "I told you it doesn't work like that. It's not about the number so much as...loss. I know that doesn't make much sense. You're not gaining being a demon. That's already who you are. It's about shedding your human attachments. But you don't need to be in a hurry," he assured him. "You're not going to like hearing this, but you're still a kid. Give yourself some time to grow up. The kind of power you've inherited, without maturity, it...well, I've seen it go bad before. So just pace yourself, all right?"

"Whatever," the boy grumbled. He didn't speak again, but Andras could see his fingers clenched tightly into his sides as he folded his arms around his stomach.

Caleb stayed home the next day, shut in his room and refusing even to answer the demon's knock. Around the middle of the day, when Andras opened the door anyway and peeked in at him, he was curled on his side on the bed, fast asleep, which was actually a relief. At least he was getting some rest. Marian kept asking after her lost book, but Andras was too distracted to care much where she'd misplaced it, until he laid in bed that night and felt a tingling static at the back of his brain—something he hadn't felt in close to a thousand years. His eyes shot open, and he flew from his bed and down the hall to Caleb's door, turning the locked handle in an easy movement.

Caleb was on his hands and knees in the center of a painted circle, his mother kneeling beside him with her hands clutching his shoulders. Every tiny hair on Andras's arms and neck stood straight up from the electricity in the air, but when he tried to move forward to stop them, he found himself unable to take another step. He looked down at the chalk triangle on the floor, marked with the symbols and words to bind him in place.

"You little shit," he said through gritted teeth, but Caleb didn't look up from the book. He was reading aloud, oblivious to Andras shouting at him to stop, and then a growl sounded that shook the foundations of the house. A small hole opened up in the very air in front of Caleb's circle, heavy black smoke pouring out of it like deadly water, and as it widened, a lion's paw the size of a man's head appeared at the edge. The stench of sulfur and pitch belched into the room, turning the air rancid and thick. The beast climbed through the opening, first its sharp, hooked beak leading its dark leathery head and dead, black eyes. Oily black wings grew from its muscular shoulders, scattering ash and grit as they twitched, unable to settle over the lion's massive body. The creature paced its cramped circle, its blank eyes locked onto Caleb's as the boy finally lifted his head.

"You think to command me, mongrel?" the demon said, more a rumbling of gravel than a voice. It shook its head on its filthy vulture's neck, claws scraping into the wooden floor. It seemed liable to break free of its prison at any moment, its muscles quivering just under its skin.

"You will answer my questions," Caleb snapped with more conviction than Andras thought would really be considered wise, but there was a sheen of sweat on his brow. "Who is my father? How can I find him?"

The demon let out a laugh, but it was a rough, low sound that went straight to Andras's bones. This was not good. What on earth had Caleb been hoping to accomplish? After everything Andras had told him—if this demon didn't kill him, Andras just might.

"Shlamaa, Ayporos," Andras called, and the creature turned its head to catch him in its empty gaze. "Hino yeled. Shlamaa."

"For your sake, paidagógos," the demon growled, and it snaked its head in a jerking motion to turn its eye on Caleb again. "Cambion," it said, creaking the floorboards under its weight as it shifted toward him, "your father is closed to you by ones greater than I. Your brethren are the lawless ones, who teach man to know war and lead him to wickedness and impurity. When you join them, you shall know him, and not before. Now release me," it commanded, its voice rattling the glass in the windows, and Andras pressed against the barrier of the mark binding him.

"Caleb," he called as a warning, but he could see the boy's hands gripping the book in front of him, his knuckles white. "Caleb, do as he says!"

With a cry of frustration, Caleb tossed the book aside and spat out the Latin passage freeing the demon, who peered at Andras for just a moment before vanishing into a thick pile of filth and ash. Marian stroked her son's back with a tender hand until he gently brushed her aside and pulled to his feet.

"All of that, and I still couldn't make it tell me," Caleb muttered. He looked up at Andras with a look so pathetic that the demon almost touched his head, but he couldn't let him think this was acceptable. "What's the point of all these deals if I still can't do anything?"

"Are you insane?" Andras snapped. "I warned you. You think you can compete because you've claimed a dozen souls?"

"Twenty," Caleb corrected indignantly.

"Ayporos commands thirty-six legions, Caleb," his guardian hissed in irritation. "Do you know how many a legion is? It's six thousand. I'd ask you to do the math and figure out how many that is, but you're probably too fucking stupid, because you decided to drop out of school!"

Caleb clicked his tongue at him as he helped Marian to her feet. He scuffed the chalk triangle on the floor, and Andras stumbled forward slightly as he was released.

"And if you ever think to bind *me,* little lamb," Andras growled, stepping close and bending down to Caleb's face, "I'll very happily remind you of the vast difference between what I am and what you pretend to be." He reached out for Marian's hand, guiding her gently toward the door while Caleb scowled at him. "Give me the book."

Caleb didn't argue. He bent to scoop the book up from the floor and shoved it into the demon's waiting hand.

"Go to sleep," Andras said, the tone of his voice brooking no argument. "And don't you take one step out of this room. We'll talk in the morning."

He shut the door on the boy's frowning face and folded arms, and Marian squeezed his hand.

"Wasn't he incredible, Andras?" she said airily.

"Incredibly stupid." He led the woman downstairs and to her room, bidding her a soft goodnight as he shut her door. He walked back upstairs with a weary step, pausing outside Caleb's room. He could sense the boy's stormy mood even though the door. Had he really been pushing himself so hard just to distance himself from Isaac? And now he thought being a demon wasn't working out, either. The kid was tearing himself in two.

Andras let him be for now and returned to his own bedroom, sitting at the edge of the mattress with his head in his hands. He'd lost his temper. He hadn't helped him at all. He should have been softer with him and told him that it was going to be all right. It was easy to forget that something like a cambion can be afraid, too. He relaxed only slightly when he felt a warm, heavy hand on his shoulder, and he let out a slow sigh.

"I'm losing him, B. We have to do something."

"I know," the angel said, and he sat beside the demon and let him lay his head on his shoulder.

24

Isaac sat in his room with his phone in both hands, knowing it was hopeless to wait for it to ring. Caleb hadn't answered his calls for the rest of the weekend, and though he'd prayed his hardest for forgiveness and guidance at service, he hadn't heard anything from Barachiel. Now another week was almost over, and Caleb hadn't even been at school. Isaac had gone by his house every afternoon asking for him, but Andras turned him away every time.

He didn't understand what he'd done. He thought that Caleb would be relieved that he knew the truth. What did it matter why they had started talking in the first place, now that they were here? Now that they had—Isaac dropped his phone into his lap and put his face in his hands. He just wanted Caleb to talk to him. If they could just talk, Caleb could tell him what was wrong, and they could work it out, he knew it. The other boy hadn't answered a single phone call or text, no matter how many apologetic messages and voice mails Isaac left. He was probably starting to look like a stalker. But what else could he do? He couldn't sleep, and he could barely eat, he was so worried.

Isaac set down his phone with a sigh and laced his fingers together in front of him, pressing his knuckles to his forehead as he shut his eyes. He needed help, and he didn't have anyone to ask. But before he could even form a thought, he heard the soft thump of bare feet on his bedroom floor.

"We need to talk, Isaac," Barachiel said over his shoulder, and the boy looked up at him with relief flooding his chest as he dropped his hands. Barachiel would know what to do. He had to know what to do.

"I'm so sorry," he said quickly. "I thought that if I told him, he'd be happy, that—he wouldn't have to worry about telling me, but now he's—"

"I know." The angel sighed, his arms crossed loosely over his chest. He looked less bright, somehow, and he had a frowning, weary expression on his face instead of his usual placid calm. He looked almost…normal. "There's more that you need to know. Do you mind letting in a friend?"

"A friend?"

The doorbell rang, and Isaac glanced between Barachiel and the empty hallway, but the angel only stepped back to allow the boy to pass. When Isaac opened the door, Andras was standing on the porch with his thumbs in the pockets of his jeans.

"Got a minute, kid?" Andras let himself into the living room while Isaac gaped at him. Barachiel stepped into the room and stood beside the demon as if that were a completely normal thing to happen.

"Uh, this...is the friend...?"

"Andras and I are well acquainted," Barachiel said. "You don't have to be afraid of him; he's here to help."

Isaac slowly shut the door, more glad than words could say that he was alone in the house in the afternoons. "Help?"

"Caleb's slipping," Andras said simply. "Normally, I'd be pleased with his progress, but he's getting reckless. And I think it's because of you."

"What do you mean, reckless?"

"A cambion's only purpose is to make deals," Barachiel explained. "To claim souls for its father. A demon can't spend much time on Earth, usually, but they need new souls to increase their strength and influence, so a cambion is a handy way to have an agent topside. For each one they take, they and their parent grow more powerful, and they lose what makes them human."

"Souls?" Isaac breathed. "You mean, as in someone selling their soul...? So he really was trying to offer me things, back then? In exchange for my—" He pressed his lips together to force himself to breathe. "He's done a thing like that?"

Andras snorted. "He's claimed sixteen in the last five days."

"Sixteen?" Isaac's heart seemed to sink into his stomach. "Sixteen people? What—what does that mean for them?"

"It means they get what they asked for, and when they die, they go straight to Hell; do not pass Go, do not collect $200. Unless that's what they wished for, I guess."

"Classless," Barachiel sighed, and Isaac paused at the angel's casual tone. This was a much different person than the bright being that had appeared in his kitchen that day. Was this the real one, maybe? "The point is," Barachiel went on, "that Caleb is growing too powerful too quickly, and he's not minding the rules."

"He summoned a demon in his bedroom last night thinking he could bind it," Andras added. "And not a cuddly one like me. He's taking stupid risks, and I think he's using his coercion on people to push them into deals. That's a big no-no. The kind cambions get killed for."

"Coercion?"

"Sure. You know, telling someone to do something, and they have to do it. All cambions have it." He glanced over at Barachiel. "You didn't warn him about that?"

"He...he hasn't done anything like that to me, has he?" Isaac asked softly, and the angel shook his head.

"No. That's why I've been staying out of it so much. Caleb really seemed like he cared about you, Isaac. I think you can still save him."

The boy's brows knit together in confusion as he turned to Andras. "But you're...you're a demon, aren't you? Shouldn't you be...not wanting me to stop him? If I even can?"

"Sometimes the good guys really do know what's best, I suppose," Andras answered with a dry chuckle. "Caleb isn't suited to the life his father wants for him. It's strange to say since he's such a little prick, but I really think he's too sensitive. One little spat with you, and he's given himself over completely to a life he doesn't even want, just because he thinks it'll keep him from being hurt. He thinks I can't hear him when he cries at night, but I know he's in a bad way."

"He...he cried?" Isaac sank down onto the sofa with a hand over his heart, his chest almost too tight to breathe. He'd made Caleb cry. He'd hurt him, when all he'd ever wanted to do was see his secret smile.

"He's too tender for this work," Andras said. "I think he's likely to live longer, and be happier, if he's with you. It's true I'm a demon, and I have a job to do, but Caleb's still my son. My responsibility," he corrected, seeming to realize what he'd said, and he looked down at the floor with a faint grimace of embarrassment.

"We're pushing the boundaries of what's considered intervention at this point," Barachiel said, graciously picking up the conversation, "but Andras and I are responsible for you getting involved to begin with, so we think it's only fair that you understand the situation."

"What? How are both of you responsible? I thought—"

"B's being coy." The demon smirked sidelong at the frowning angel beside him. "We may have had a friendly wager going as to the outcome of this little misadventure."

"A w—you mean a bet?!" Isaac stared up at them open-mouthed, hoping Barachiel would argue or show any sign that the demon was lying, but the angel only scowled across at Andras.

"That isn't really what's important here."

"You made a bet with a demon about whether Caleb would turn evil or not? Wh-what kind of angel are you?" Isaac slapped a hand over his mouth as Andras laughed. The boy half expected to be struck by lightning on the spot.

"Just come clean, B. Tell him or I'll tell him."

"Tell me what?"

Barachiel snorted in irritation, which startled Isaac slightly. Was this even really an angel? "The truth is that Andras has been raising cambions for centuries. I've been keeping an eye on them for just as long. And in that time, we've...grown accustomed to each other."

"Accustomed?" Andras echoed. "That's the best you can do, you feathery asshole?"

"What do you expect me to say?" Barachiel snapped back.

The demon let out a soft sound of revulsion. "Angels. Do you all have your very own stick you keep up your asses, or do you share the same one and just pass it around?"

"That's disgusting."

"You're disgusting."

"For the love of—can we focus?" Barachiel pinched the bridge of his nose, then sighed and dropped his hand. "Andras and I are—involved. But all that means to you is that we're both invested in Caleb's future, and so we're invested in yours."

Isaac stared at them both, not quite able to make his brain start working again. Barachiel, the angel, and Andras, the demon, were...together? "Together together?" he whispered, not even realizing he'd said it out loud. Was that even...possible? Allowed?

"Oh, the poor dear's broken," Andras chuckled. "You're not so innocent anymore, right?" Isaac tensed as the demon leaned down close to his ear and whispered, "Together like you and Caleb were together on that couch. At the church, even. You naughty thing, you."

Isaac wondered if it was possible for him to just disappear into the ground. His whole body could have caught fire in that moment, and it still wouldn't have been as hot as his face felt. Maybe if he hurried, he could pray for forgiveness for his sins before he died of embarrassment.

Andras retreated with a laugh as Barachiel thumped him on the arm. "What?" he chuckled.

"This isn't why we're here," the angel reminded him.

"But look at his face!"

"Andras."

"Oh, fine." He gave a short sigh and looked down at the boy. "Listen, kid. The fact of the matter is, everyone in this room wants Caleb to come out the other side of adolescence content and not dead, right? If you want to wash your hands of it, now's the time to speak up. Knowing what he is, and knowing that that means—do you still want to be with him?"

Isaac couldn't bring himself to speak. He'd been thinking of Caleb as a boy at a crossroads—someone who didn't have to go down a dark path just because of who he was. But Caleb wasn't at a crossroads at all. He'd taken so many steps down the dark path that Isaac wasn't sure if he'd be able to turn back. So many people, damned because of Caleb. Because of what Isaac had done to him. Could he really be with someone who could knowingly condemn innocent people to Hell? Someone who would force people to do things against their will? Isaac wrung his hands in his lap and looked up at Barachiel.

"You...you love a demon, don't you?"

The angel softened, and even Andras stayed quiet as Barachiel took a seat beside the boy. "I do."

"But he's...done awful things, hasn't he?"

"He has."

"Then how can you...how do you love someone like that? Knowing that he's—that people are in Hell because of him?"

Barachiel gave a small sigh through his nose, and he leaned his elbows on his knees while he seemed to ponder his answer. "I didn't choose him," he said at last. "Andras is crass and sarcastic, and in his time, he's been violent, ruthless, and manipulative. But I've also seen the depths of his caring for the boys he raises. I've seen him walking circles around a sofa in the dead of night because the motion kept a baby sleeping soundly, and I've seen him patch scraped knees and lay awake nights out of worry for his charges. No matter what he's done, there's gentleness in him, and it's that gentleness that I love."

"You're making me blush," the demon muttered, and Isaac caught a whisper of a smile on the angel's lips. Could it really be that simple?

Isaac frowned down at his hands. What mattered, he thought, was that he'd set out with a mission to turn Caleb from the dark, and he'd failed miserably. He'd been the one to push him to this. He told himself that he couldn't have known that it would hurt him so much to find out Isaac knew the truth, but he felt in his gut that he should have. He should have known. The way Caleb talked about his uncle pressuring him into the "family business," how uncomfortable he'd seemed showing any real feelings...most importantly, how frightened he'd been to reveal the truth himself. The look on the other boy's face when Isaac had finally told him how he knew—it hurt his heart to picture it. He must have felt manipulated and lied to, after Isaac had spent so long telling him that he simply enjoyed his company. Isaac folded his arms to hold his stomach as he doubled over on the couch, his head almost touching the coffee table. He was such an idiot.

Despite everything, all Isaac could think about was the flushed, anxious look on Caleb's face that night at the lake. He'd wanted so badly to be accepted, and he'd been so afraid to expose who he really was, but Isaac knew him. Caleb was soft-spoken and thoughtful; he was lonely, and he hid it with sarcasm. He held Isaac so tightly because he was afraid of being left behind. It didn't make any difference what he'd done.

"I love him," Isaac said softly. "I want him to smile again." He slowly lifted his head to look the angel in the face. "But it's...a sin, isn't it?"

Barachiel reached out a warm hand and squeezed his shoulder. "Isaac, when someone loves as completely and as honestly as you do, God doesn't mind who it is that you love."

Isaac smiled and lowered his eyes, a sweet sense of relief heating his chest. "But Caleb won't even talk to me. What can I do?"

"Since standing outside his window with a boombox doesn't seem likely to work," Andras cut in, "why don't you just come with me?"

Isaac frowned faintly, but Barachiel touched his shoulder and nodded.

"Don't think this applies broadly to demons in the slightest, but you can trust Andras. Go with him."

25

Isaac half expected something incredible to happen as he followed the demon out the door, but Andras simply gave him a quick lift in his car up the long driveway to Caleb's house and led him upstairs. He opened Caleb's door without knocking on it, and Isaac peeked around him to see Caleb lying on his bed. The dark-haired boy scowled as Andras entered, but when the demon urged Isaac into the room, his eyes widened and he sat up in a panic.

"What the hell is he doing here?" Caleb snapped.

Andras raised a threatening finger at him. "Don't be a shit. If you have a problem with someone, the least you can do is let them apologize." He nudged Isaac's shoulder and murmured in his ear, "Go get him, kid," as he shut the door after him.

Caleb glared across the room at him, but he didn't move to get up. The room smelled rotten, like eggs and burned matches, and a broken phone lay shattered near the doorway, but Isaac's eyes were drawn to the pattern of deep gouges in the floor around the chipped paint markings. From the demon he'd summoned? Caleb's face seemed drawn and pale, and he visibly recoiled when Isaac took a step forward, so he kept his place across the room instead.

"I know you don't want to see me," he started quietly, and Caleb snorted. "I just...I have to say that I'm sorry. I didn't know how to tell you about the angel. But no matter why I started talking to you, I...that's not why I'm here now. I'm here now because I—I love you."

"Don't lie," Caleb growled, his fingers tightening in his blanket. "It's a sin."

"Caleb, please. What's the point of lying to you now? I came because I want to be with you—I love you," he said again.

"Don't lie!" the boy shouted, and Isaac thought he felt the floorboards tremble slightly beneath his feet. Was this Caleb? This person was cold and hunched, and he wouldn't meet Isaac's eyes.

Isaac held his hands together in front of him to still their shaking. The Caleb in front of him was more demon than man. He'd damned over a dozen people to Hell, and he didn't even look like he felt bad about it. The way he stared across at Isaac felt like ice water in his spine. But this was his fault. The Caleb he loved was hiding under that darkness, crying in secret and covering it with spite.

"What do you want me to say?" Isaac whispered. "When we met, I talked to you because you were new. If Barachiel hadn't talked to me, maybe I would have given up after the tenth time you told me to leave you alone. I don't know. I know that if I had, I would have...I would have missed out on knowing the most important person in my life," he finished in a strained voice. Caleb kept his eyes on the rumpled blanket. "Caleb, I don't care what you are."

"Of course you do," he muttered. He pulled himself out of bed and took a single step toward the blond, and the air in the room seemed to grow thick and close. The dresser near the door rattled softly as though it was an earthquake moving through the room instead of a boy. Isaac's heart raced in his chest, and he flinched slightly against the pressure building in his ears.

"Look at you," Caleb said. "I haven't even done anything yet, and you look like you're going to piss your pants. This is what I am. You think you can look me in the face and tell me you don't care?"

"I...I'm afraid," he admitted, and Caleb paused. "I'm afraid of what you've done. I'm afraid of what you might do. I'm afraid of what will happen to you if you keep going like this."

"So you're here to change my mind?" Caleb murmured. "Here to finish your mission for your angel, turn me good?"

"I don't care about that!" Isaac snapped back. Both boys hesitated, and Caleb looked into Isaac's eyes for the first time since he'd arrived. "I don't...I don't care." He reached for the other boy's hands and squeezed them tightly. "No matter which path you choose, I want to stay with you. If you stop and never make another deal, or if you go out every night looking for them, I...I don't care. You're still Caleb." He tried to steady his breath, hardly believing the words coming out of his mouth. But it didn't matter. Only being with Caleb mattered. "And if you go too far, or you get in trouble...I'll be there with you."

Caleb grit his teeth to keep from letting out a pitiful sound. Isaac didn't really know what he was getting into. He could come here and say that he wouldn't mind what Caleb was, or that he could look past things, but in the end, he didn't know what he was saying. Saying he was "still Caleb" didn't mean anything when he hadn't known Caleb to begin with. He had to show him, or it wouldn't be fair. He had to give him the chance to run. Caleb looked up at him, and behind them, the window shot open, making Isaac jump.

"Did...did you—"

"I did," Caleb said. "That's how I got into your room that night. I can move other things, too. Does it bother you?"

"No," Isaac insisted. "This is...it's just more things I don't know about you." He paused and squeezed Caleb's hand in his. "I know I can't really understand what you're going through. It's...it really is scary to think about the things that you do. I won't lie about that." He lowered his eyes. "They told me that you can...force people to do things. But that you hadn't done it to me."

"Of course I didn't!" Caleb pressed his lips together as he realized he was shouting, and he sighed through his nose. "I didn't want that from you." He had to look away from the other boy's patient grey eyes.

"I've done it to other people," he said suddenly, his eyes still on the floor. "And I don't feel bad about it. I used to do it all the time back home to get stuff for free. It's how I got the booze for our date before. I just told the cashier to give it to me. And," he added before the other boy could comment, "I'd already made three deals before you met me. Two of them were normal, just for money and success, but the other one, the guy wanted to have sex with me, so I did it. I didn't care. Back in Chicago, I slept with a lot of people. None of them meant anything to me." His stomach tightened at the soft furrow in Isaac's brow, so he rose from the bed and reached his hand into Greedigut's cage, allowing the rat up into his palm as Isaac took a step after him.

"This isn't a rat," he said. "It's a familiar. A spirit. A demon named Paimon gave it to me. I can see through its eyes if I try. And it's been helping me learn to do things like this." Caleb shut his eyes and felt the pull he'd been practicing, the tug in his gut that twisted his insides. He heard Isaac give a small shout as the tension snapped, the scent of burning tar in his nostrils, and when he opened his eyes, he was standing behind the other boy. He tapped him on the shoulder, his heart giving a painful thump at the panic in Isaac's eyes as he spun to face him.

"I can't go far yet," he went on, unable to keep the words from spilling out, "but it's easier than before. And this." He moved over to his nightstand and let Greedigut down onto the bed, then dug in his bedside drawer for his pocketknife. In one motion, he flipped the blade open and dragged it down the skin of his forearm, his blood dripping onto the floor in heavy splatters. Isaac gasped and rushed to him, but Caleb touched him on the chest to still him and urged the boy to watch as the skin knit itself back together without leaving a mark.

"It barely hurts," he said. "And it's a lot faster than it used to be." Caleb dropped his bloodstained knife onto the nightstand while Isaac watched him in confusion, and he bent to hook his hands underneath the other boy's thighs, lifting him effortlessly. He looked up into Isaac's face as the blond clutched his shoulders to keep his balance. "I can lift much heavier things than you, too. And—"

"Caleb!" Isaac finally interrupted him. He looked pained, and Caleb's fingers tightened slightly as he held him. "What are you doing?" the boy asked in a whisper.

"You're not—" Caleb stopped himself, focusing on the buttons of Isaac's shirt rather than his face. His brow furrowed, and the boy's warm hands on his shoulders were agony. He didn't deserve this touch. "Even though you're afraid, you'll still stay?"

"Even though I'm afraid," he said. "I'm more afraid to think of going back to a life that doesn't have you in it."

"Even if I keep doing this," Caleb went on. "Even if I take more and more?"

Isaac couldn't hesitate. If he wavered now, Caleb might never believe him again. "Even if you never stop."

"Bullshit," the other boy scoffed, averting his gaze from Isaac's pleading stare as he let him down to the floor, but he seemed to pause.

Caleb frowned at the floor for a moment before raising his eyes. He only had one card left to play. One more thing to make him leave. "Then promise me. Make a deal with me."

Isaac's heart skipped more than a few beats, he was sure. His hands clenched tighter around Caleb's, and he tried to still the swell of fear in his gut. Caleb was asking him to go to Hell for him. Not some metaphor, or a pit of red, horned monsters to scare children into good behavior, but a place where his eternal soul would be bound to the will of a demon. But...this demon. This boy. All of it—Caleb's shouting, his threats, his insistence that Isaac understand—it was all just the lashing out of a scared boy who was trying to prove himself right. Prove that he was alone and unloved. But it wasn't true. Isaac's stomach unknotted itself, just a little, and he realized he was faintly smiling.

"If it means being bound to you," he said, brushing his thumbs over the other boy's knuckles, "then...it's okay. You...you give me your forgiveness, and...I'll do it."

Caleb stared at him, his stern expression wavering, and then he pulled his hands free of Isaac's grip so suddenly that the blond almost stumbled. Caleb gave a single, half-sob of a sigh, and before Isaac knew what was happening, the other boy's arms were around his neck, clutching him so tightly against his body that Isaac could barely breathe. Caleb hid his face in Isaac's neck, his breath coming in ragged hiccups.

"You're so...fucking stupid," he hissed against Isaac's skin.

Isaac held the other boy as close as he could as he felt the heat of tears on his shoulder.

"Why would you agree to that?" Caleb whispered, his voice thick and strained. "Don't you know what Hell is? Hell is forever. You'd do that, just because I...you're so fucking stupid," he said again. Isaac smiled as the boy's fingers curled into the back of his shirt.

He ran a hand through Caleb's dark hair, just letting him breathe against him until he went still. "I love you," he whispered once Caleb began to relax. "And I'm sorry. I shouldn't have kept it from you. I won't keep any secrets, ever again. I swear."

"Aren't you a sinner because of me?" he asked weakly against the boy's shoulder. "I'm not human. I'll never be human. Even if I was, I'm a guy, right?"

"You know," Isaac said, keeping his voice soft as he let his cheek brush Caleb's hair, "I think an angel would know more about it than my pastor. The angel that came to me, Barachiel...he told me that God is love. And I love you." He held the other boy a little tighter, wishing he could squeeze the doubt out of him. "That's all."

Caleb clutched Isaac like a lifeline. "After I was so shitty, you still came back, and...even though I'm this—"

"Caleb," Isaac sighed, and he tried to lean back to look him in the face. The other boy seemed reluctant to lift his head, and when he did, he turned away so that Isaac wouldn't see him wipe the tears from his face with the back of his wrist. "Come here," he said, and he pulled Caleb down to sit beside him on the bed.

"You remember when we were at the lake?" he asked, and Caleb nodded without looking at him. "I know you were trying to tell me the truth then, right? That's why you were so nervous?"

Caleb still couldn't meet his eyes, but he nodded again.

"If...if you'd told me then, I would have had to act surprised. I couldn't possibly have told you about Barachiel. I would have taken that secret to my grave, because it wouldn't have mattered anymore. I would have told you that it was scary, but that I knew you would never hurt me. You could have told me all your problems and all your worries, and I would have listened. I'll still do that," he added, reaching up to touch the other boy's cheek. "I'm still here."

Caleb's whole body seemed to give out in front of him. He clung to the other boy, gripping him by the shoulders and touching the soft blond hair at the back of his head. "I want that," he whispered, hating how pathetic he sounded. But it didn't matter. He'd embarrass himself a thousand times if it meant he could undo what he'd done and make Isaac smile again. "And I'm going to listen too, okay? To whatever you have to say. So...even if you're afraid, you have to tell me. You have to tell me everything, and I'm going to listen."

"I promise," Isaac murmured into Caleb's hair. "Does this mean you'll let me be your boyfriend again?"

Caleb let out a small laugh despite himself, and he pulled back enough to wipe at his eyes again. "Yeah, I...sorry I broke up with you like such a dick."

"It was...bad timing all around," Isaac admitted, his face slightly red as Caleb peeked up at him. Suddenly he jumped, seeming to startle himself.

"Jiminy Crickets, is that the time?" He leaned around Caleb to double check the clock on his nightstand. "Oh, my dad's gonna kill me! I—I'm sorry, Caleb, I—I have to go." He paused. "Are you...gonna come to school tomorrow? You missed a lot of days already—"

Caleb didn't want to say that he thought it was pointless. Isaac would want him to go, and he wanted to be able to see him. He didn't want to hear Andras yell at him anymore, either, so he just nodded. "I guess so."

Isaac hesitated with the other boy's sleeve caught in his fingers, seeming like he wanted to say more, but then he offered Caleb a faint smile and stood to head for the door. "Then I'll see you tomorrow. Plan on walking home with me, okay?"

Caleb nodded, and he listed to Isaac hurry down the stairs and out the front door. He turned his head to watch Isaac through the window as he jogged down the driveway back toward his own house. He was determined not to complicate things this time. He liked Isaac, and he believed it when Isaac said he loved him. He had to believe it.

That wouldn't make it any easier to go back to school like nothing had happened. Caleb could distantly hear the whispering at the back of his mind, one rasping, muffled voice for every life he'd claimed, and he furrowed his brow as he looked over his shoulder, half expecting someone to be in his room. It was going to be difficult to focus on a history lesson.

26

It felt strange to have Andras drop him off at school again. A few students gave him curious looks as he walked from the curb to the door—the school was small enough for his absence to be noted, and he was sure people would have ideas about where he'd taken off to for two weeks. He didn't care. They could think what they wanted. The only thing that mattered was Isaac waiting for him in homeroom, beaming up at him when he entered like everything was the same as always.

Caleb took his seat beside him, and he hesitated as he set down his bag. What was he supposed to say? They'd agreed that everything would be like before, but that was easier said than done. He smiled faintly to himself at the sudden warmth in his chest. Now it was like they had two secrets, wasn't it? Two things that just he and Isaac had, and no one else. He could live with that.

"So," he started awkwardly, not quite meeting the other boy's eyes, "you're gonna let me copy all the homework I missed, right?"

Isaac laughed, and a stronger heat touched Caleb's stomach. When had that become the best sound in the world? "I think that might be a little more than you could copy during homeroom. I'm sure they'll let you make it up if you ask."

Caleb grimaced as he dug in his bag for the paper he was supposed to hand in to the homeroom teacher, and he unfolded it to read the note in Andras's scrawling handwriting.

Please excuse Caleb from missing classes from March 7-18. He was sick with a fever and needed time to recover. I will ensure any makeup work is completed in a timely manner.

A. Durant

Having a sick note like a little kid was bad enough, but for the claim to be that he was so delicate that he took two weeks to get over a fever was too much. The condescending pat on the head Andras had given him as he handed him the note hadn't helped, either. "He couldn't have said I got into an accident or something?" he grumbled, but when Isaac tilted his head at him curiously, he folded the note back over and covered it with his folded arms.

Isaac shifted in his seat, looking a little uncomfortable, and Caleb frowned at him.

"Is this...okay?" Caleb asked. "Me being here."

"What? Oh, no, it's not that. Of course it's okay." The blond gave him a reassuring smile. "I just..." He paused and shook his head. "We can talk about it later, okay?"

Caleb leaned forward on his desk. He opened his mouth to speak, but the rest of the class began to file in as the bell approached, so he stopped. Hadn't he just told Isaac yesterday that he'd listen to everything he had to say? He sat back in his seat and watched the other boy out of the corner of his eye. Isaac smiled when he caught him looking, but he looked like he had a lot on his mind.

Between classes, they walked together like always, and Heather even greeted Caleb at lunch and asked where he'd been. He kept up the facade that he'd been sick and left it at that. Caleb had never been more eager for their walk home. When they were alone, he could ask Isaac anything. He wanted to know what was bothering the other boy that could possibly be bad enough to compete with all the demon crap that had happened over the last couple of weeks. And he really did want to know, he realized with some heat in his cheeks. He wanted to hear what was wrong, and he wanted to help. When the final bell rang, Caleb rushed out of the classroom and waited anxiously by the curb for the other boy to appear. Isaac smiled and waved at his other friends on his way out, but his expression softened when he caught sight of Caleb waiting for him.

They walked together down the same road they'd walked over and over again, Isaac picking at his backpack straps and Caleb with his hands snugly in his pockets. Caleb waited for Isaac to speak, to pick up where they'd left off that morning in homeroom, but he stayed quiet. They reached the main road, and Caleb could see Isaac's street in the distance, but neither of them said anything. Maybe it should have been comforting that they would still just walk quietly side by side, but it didn't feel very comforting today.

Finally, Caleb huffed and reached out for Isaac's hand, lacing their fingers together between them. Isaac looked up at him with startled eyes, and then he smiled faintly and squeezed the other boy's hand.

"So tell me what's bothering you already," Caleb said without looking at him. "Did your dad give you shit last night or what?"

"Oh—no, not really. I just..." He chewed his lip and slowed his pace, like he wanted their walk to take just a little bit longer. "I love you," he said, and Caleb expected to see a blush on the other boy's face when he looked back at him, but Isaac was calm. "I love you, and I want to be with you, for...forever, you know?"

"You don't have to say it so much," Caleb muttered, and Isaac smiled at his faint grimace.

"Sorry," he laughed. "So, last night, my dad was waiting for me, and he wasn't mad about me being out, but he had a...letter for me. An acceptance letter."

"Acceptance? What, like for college?"

Isaac nodded. "I...got accepted to Cornell. I applied without telling my parents, but I figured I didn't have any chance of getting in. But then yesterday this whole packet came, and dad's asking me how in the heck we're supposed to pay for me to go to some fancy school up in New York, and why I want to live so far away from home, and..." He sighed. "I got accepted to UAB up in Birmingham, too, and I guess that's where dad figured I should go. It's close enough I wouldn't have to live in a dorm and pay all that money. UAB has a good nursing program, anyway, and Cornell's for...you know, people who want to be doctors." He tugged at his backpack strap and gave a short sigh through his nose. "I looked it up, and even a single year at Cornell can cost upwards of seventy thousand dollars. Even with the financial aid I got approved for, there's just...no way my parents can pay that. And anyway, all that got me thinking about...you know, we're graduating in just a couple months, and...what you were going to do when we did."

Caleb hesitated. "All that, and you're asking about me?"

"Well there's no choice for me," Isaac said simply, though he sounded a little sad. "UAB's the place we can afford, so I'll go there. That's the easy part. But I guess I realized that you've never mentioned anything about what you might want to do after school."

"I never thought about it," he answered. It sounded stupid to say, but Caleb had never given any thought to his future. Andras had never urged him to think about college, only to go to school and try not to kill anyone by accident. Maybe he always expected him to either follow in his father's footsteps or die too young to worry about it. Maybe Caleb had expected that, too. "I haven't applied to any schools or taken any tests or anything, so I guess I'm not going anywhere." His hand tightened around Isaac's. He was the only person who had ever bothered to ask him about having a life beyond his demonic side.

"I'm sorry," Isaac said with a nervous laugh. "With everything that's happened to you, I'm going on about something as normal as college."

"No. I want you to tell me the normal stuff. I want you to tell me everything. And...wherever you end up, I want to be there too," he said suddenly.

Isaac opened his mouth to speak and then shut it again, watching the road in front of him as he bit his bottom lip in a smile. "I'd like that." He looked up when they reached the fork in the road that would separate them, but neither of them wanted to go any farther.

"Can I ask you something else?" Isaac said softly as they stood at the edge of the road.

"Yeah."

"Do you think...you're going to keep going? I mean, with the...you know, the deals."

"I don't know," he admitted. "I kind of feel like...there's no point now. Like I just—it's stupid," he grumbled, but Isaac squeezed his hand.

"I'm listening."

Caleb sighed, worn down by the other boy's endless patience. "When...when I was a kid," he started, "I wasn't really alive. Not until I was seven. That was the first time I had to breathe, and the first time my heart started beating. Before that, everything was...still, and quiet. Andras says it's always like that for demons. I could feel it, a little, when I made my first deals. But with you, it's been...it's been so loud, and so...hot. Everything is so...crazy with you. So I just...I just wanted that back. Like I had before you."

"But Caleb, those people...you understand what you've done to them? I'm not trying to convince you. I just want to understand. How can you do it, knowing you're sending them to Hell?"

"They agree to it," he said defensively. "They know what they're doing."

"Do they?"

"It's not my fault if they don't think it through." He frowned. "And sometimes it's a good thing, right? This one guy, he...he wasn't going to be able to hold down a job anymore, and he just wanted his family taken care of. So I made him a deal, and now his wife and kids will be happy instead of homeless."

Isaac couldn't keep his hand from lifting to cover his mouth. "Caleb, that..."

"What? They'll have whatever they need. They'll be fine."

"But don't you think she would have rather had her husband? That those kids would have rather had their father?"

The boy stopped, and he looked at Isaac with a mixture of confusion and guilt. "I...I guess so." He groaned in frustration and leaned his head heavily on Isaac's shoulder. "I've been so stupid. This is what I am, and my mom and Andras have been telling me my whole life that it's what I'm meant for, but...what if I made the wrong choice?"

"What do you want to do, Caleb?" Isaac asked softly. "Don't worry about me, or Andras, or your father, or anybody. What do you want to do?"

Caleb shut his eyes, soaking in the warmth of the other boy through his shirt, and he let out a faint snort of laughter without looking up. "I'd...I think I'd like to sit at a stupid bonfire with you and listen to you sing stupid songs. Or watch you bite your lip and get down real close to your paper while you're taking a math test. I don't care about...souls, or...what my father wants. I don't care about proving some angel right or wrong. I just...I just want you." He peeked up at him.

Isaac felt a warmth in his cheeks, but it wasn't embarrassment. Even like this, when Caleb looked at him with that timid, uncertain expression, he just looked so...undeniably cute. He cupped Caleb's cheek and drew him up, feeling the startled jump in the other boy as he pressed a kiss to his lips. "I'm not going anywhere," he promised. "Maybe there's something you can do. If you want to try to fix it."

"Fix it," Caleb murmured, looking down at Isaac with a pensive frown. "Maybe." He brushed his knuckles down Isaac's jaw, studying his pale eyes. "You know, there might really...be something to ground me here."

"Ground you?"

"Something Andras said. Let...let me talk to him about it, okay? I need to figure some stuff out."

Isaac picked at the hem of the taller boy's shirt, not sure if he should give out any more secrets. "You know, if it's—if it's about not doing demon things anymore, maybe Barachiel knows something. I don't know what the rules are, if you...I mean, if he'll come if you pray, but you could ask Andras."

"Why would Andras know anything about how to talk to an angel?"

"Well—" He peeked up at Caleb and chewed the inside of his lip for a moment before answering. "I guess you don't know that he's...your uncle, that is, Andras—that he's...in a relationship?"

Caleb scoffed. "What?"

"With...the angel that asked me to talk to you in the first place?"

The boy's expression darkened. "*What*?"

"They said they had a—a bet going, about which way you were going to go, and that's why Barachiel came to me, to give me the push to try to turn you away from the...you know, all the demon stuff."

Caleb broke away from the other boy, running a hand through his hair as he let out an empty laugh. "Oh, perfect. Perfect, perfect. Of course they did. Fuckers," he swore in a harsh voice, and he took off toward his driveway at a swift pace without looking back.

27

Isaac ran after him, barely keeping up, and he almost ran into Caleb's back when the other boy had to stop to fling open the front door. He peeked around Caleb's shoulder as the screen door creaked shut behind them. Caleb stormed through the room to where Andras sat lounging on the sofa.

"What the fuck is this about a bet?" he snapped, and the demon lifted his hands and let them thump back against the couch cushions in exasperation.

"Fuck's sake, Isaac; can't keep a secret, can you?"

"So, what," Caleb interrupted, standing between the demon and the stammering blond, "you think you can just sit around with your fucking boyfriend deciding my future for me?"

"You think no one gets to have an opinion about your life but you? Christ, but I'm sick of this shit." Andras got to his feet and leaned down to look Caleb in the eyes. "I've gone blue in the face telling you that you have a choice to make. When have I ever twisted your arm? When you skip lessons to go flirt with Isaac, I let you. When you demand to be driven to the city, I take you. When you decide to stop going to school, I don't force you. Dragging Isaac here has been the first decision I've made for you since I stopped packing your goddamn lunches, and still I have to hear about poor pitiful Caleb, so tortured by his destiny. You're practically a man now. So make your choice. Be one of us or be one of them, but stop acting like anyone's made the decision but you."

Caleb stared up at him with a defiant jut of his chin, his hands in tight fists at his sides. He wanted to tell Andras to fuck himself, but the demon looked so weary. Andras had never lied. He knew that. No matter how pressured Caleb had felt, if he was honest, he knew that none of it had been because the demon had forced him into anything. Caleb had been acting like an ass. He didn't know if he'd ever be able to admit it out loud, but seeing Andras stare at him with frustration and worry made him feel like everything that had happened over the last two weeks had been nothing more than a demon-sized temper tantrum. He set his mouth into a line and turned his face away with a grunt that he hoped the demon took as begrudging acceptance rather than embarrassment.

"Well why didn't I even know this asshole existed, anyway?" he grumped.

"Oh, what, now we're sharing every detail of our sex lives? Pass," Andras scoffed.

"There's not a little more to it than that?"

"Is there?"

"Uh, maybe that you're supposed to be my uncle and you've lived here my whole life, and I didn't know you were with somebody even though you constantly remind me that you know everything about me? And he's an angel! How does that even work? Aren't you supposed to be, like, mortal enemies?"

"Angel or demon is mostly a political difference," a new voice said from behind Caleb, and he spun to seek the source. Barachiel stood beside Isaac with his arms folded across his chest, and Caleb paused to look him up and down. He took in Barachiel's worn jeans, bare feet, and soft hooded sweatshirt, and he turned back to Andras with a look of disbelief.

"This is an angel?"

"Caleb," Isaac scolded, "be respectful."

"It's all right," Barachiel said. "It's been an eventful few days."

"So you're the one who thinks it's all right to just butt the fuck into my life?"

"Caleb," Barachiel began softly, taking a step forward. "If you want to blame someone for all this, blame me. But I only saw you starting down a dark path and thought there might be someone suited to guiding you down a better one."

"What the hell do you care what path I'm on? Do both sides of this shitty coin have quotas, or what?"

The angel's faint smile was so warm that Caleb almost felt like he shouldn't look at it. "You not knowing me doesn't change the fact that I've always been here," he said. "I've watched you grow up just as

Andras has. No matter what you think, we both only want what's best for you."

Caleb scowled as a matter of habit, but he softened when Isaac moved forward to put a hand on his arm.

"I know you feel pulled from every side, Caleb, but...think about how lucky you are," he said. "To have so many people who care about you."

"Great, two fucking asshole gay dads."

"You know it means more than that," Isaac said gently.

Caleb sighed almost in time with Andras.

"Getting pretty sentimental in here," the demon muttered. "If you're all done with your little fit, and you two are made up, can we all just go back to staying out of each other's private business, please?" He tilted his head. "What's it going to be, Caleb? Shall we go out tonight, or do you plan to do your corrupting a bit closer to home?" He glanced at Isaac with a small teasing smirk, and the blond flushed as he gripped Caleb's sleeve.

"Fuck off," Caleb grumbled. He hesitated for a moment, watching the demon's face. He felt awkward with so many people staring at him. He chewed his lip before opening his mouth to speak. "You won't...be disappointed?" he asked in a quieter voice than he intended.

Andras seemed surprised by the question. His mouth curled into a knowing smile, and he took a step forward to put a hand on the boy's shoulder. "It's always been your decision," he said. "Make more deals, quit now and keep the souls you have, release them altogether—it makes no difference as long as it's what you want. That's that whole free will thing, remember?" He tilted his head to look into Caleb's face. "You don't need permission to do what makes you happy, little lamb. Mine or your father's."

"I know that," Caleb said, but there wasn't much bite in his voice. The idea that just choosing to "be happy" was an option at all seemed strange to him. He glanced at Isaac out of the corner of his eye. He guessed "happy" had never really been on the table before, either. "So then...what do I do? If I'm...feeling grounded?"

"If you intend to live your life as a human," Barachiel spoke up, drawing the boy's attention, "then you must give up the lives you've taken."

"Well, *must* is a bit—" Andras cut in, but he was silenced by a short, sharp hiss from the angel.

"It's the best way to calm your heart," he rephrased. "As you are now, you're still between two worlds. Giving up the power you've gained from your claims will help you be more alive than you are. You can be as human as you want to be."

"Of course, B and I already have the rest of your life planned out based on whichever option you choose," Andras chuckled.

"Har de fucking har," Caleb muttered. He looked back at Isaac and caught the boy's pinky finger in his, the tension of embarrassment threatening to crush him completely. "So...how do I let go of them?" he asked, and the blond boy's smile made his stomach twist in a much more pleasant way.

"Letting go of them is stupid," Andras said quickly, putting a quieting palm on Barachiel's lips and pushing him backwards to remove him from the conversation. "Twenty isn't a legion, but it's not nothing. If you release them, they'll just be snatched up by whoever's close enough to get their hands on them."

"Then what do I do?" Caleb paused. "Can I give them to you?"

"Well, you know, technically they're your father's. I don't know how pleased he'd be if you just passed them along to me."

"Doesn't he have legions of his own? Or am I helping some wannabe trying to make a name for himself?"

"Watch your mouth," Andras snapped.

Isaac's brow furrowed in concern as he looked up at Barachiel and murmured, "Did they forget they're talking about human souls?"

The angel gave a short sigh of resignation, as if he'd had this conversation before. "I think they frequently do."

"If they're his," Caleb went on, oblivious, "then why doesn't he just take them properly, or whatever?"

"He will," Andras answered. He gave a small shrug. "When you're dead."

"Oh, well in that case."

"Shut up." The demon sighed and folded his arms, his lips pressed into a thoughtful line as he stared at the boy. "It won't be easy, no matter what. Do it all at once, and it might just kill you. You aren't used to being fully human anymore."

"So I'll do it slow, or whatever. Just tell me what to do."

Andras hesitated. "Okay," he sighed. "If you're absolutely sure. You can give them to me."

Barachiel reached out a hand to touch his sleeve. "Andras, your master—"

"That's my problem." His eyes seemed to soften, just slightly, and he offered the boy his hand. "If it's what you want."

Caleb released Isaac and turned to fully face the demon, watching his extended hand. He expected to feel more uneasy. He'd done so much to gather these souls. Whispered cold promises in so many ears. Distanced himself from Isaac and from the possibility of getting himself hurt. It was possible that he and Isaac would hurt each other again. Even if Caleb did this, they would fight, or they might break up someday. It wasn't a guarantee by any means. It was a risk. But when he peeked over his shoulder at Isaac's soft grey eyes, he thought it was a risk worth taking.

He took Andras's hand in his, but the instant they touched, a deep thump sounded somewhere in his brain or his chest—he wasn't quite sure. Caleb swayed on his feet as his heart slammed to a stop, his whole body chilled by the lifeless blood in his veins. For a few seconds, he felt the cool, still silence of his childhood, and then everything seemed to move in fast-forward, his heart racing as though trying to make up the beats it lost. A trembling fear shot through him, his body tensing at the distant shout of rage that sounded somewhere in the back of his mind. His skin burned, and the sound of his own pulse in his ears was deafening. He slid from the demon's grip and dropped to his knees on the floor, clutching his stomach as he doubled over with his forehead against the wood. He was going to throw up. Was this what it had been like, before he made his first deal? This constant heat and motion churned his stomach. He distantly heard Isaac shout at him and felt the boy's hand on his back, but even the simple touch felt like a brand burning through his shirt.

"Fuck," he groaned, his own voice muffled by the blood pumping through his ears.

"Oh, yeah," Andras said somewhere above him, "probably should have warned you to brace yourself. You'll settle down shortly."

"Ugh. I'm gonna barf."

"See what happens when I try to tell you to eat and you don't? That's two weeks of turning your nose up at my home-cooked meals catching up to you, you little shit."

"You have to tease him?" Barachiel sighed, but the demon only shrugged.

Isaac looked up at Andras in a panic. "Is this normal?"

"He's fine," the demon scoffed. He bent down at the waist to peer at Caleb's scrunched face. "That was only three. It's going to take more to get rid of all of them."

Caleb's vision was just beginning to clear when he heard a woman's voice cry out in alarm. His mother's hands clawed at his shoulders, drawing him upright so quickly that his stomach lurched. She touched his chest and his face as she kneeled in front of him, searching his eyes, and her face contorted into a vicious scowl as her eyes landed on Barachiel.

"You!" she cried. "Light-filthy creature, what did you do to my son?"

"Marian, it's all right," Andras said, crouching beside her to touch a soothing hand to her back. "He's all right."

"He's less," she sobbed, her head falling against Caleb's chest as she clung to his shoulders. He could barely stay stable on his knees, but he held her to him and looked to Andras for help. "He's losing." She took an unsteady breath and sat back to look at Caleb, her cheeks stained with tears. "Start again," she said solemnly, and she put her hands on his cheeks to look into his eyes. "You must start again. He'll come for you. Your father will come for you. You just have to start again."

"Mom, I'm okay," Caleb assured her with his hands gently on her wrists. "I'm not going to be like him."

"You have to! If you don't, he'll never come, and—and what will become of us?" she finished in a tortured whisper.

"Marian," Andras said again, and at his light urging, she turned and fell into his arms, crying helplessly against his chest. He scooped her up like a child, her trembling arms around his neck and her legs dangling from his grip under her thighs. "She'll be all right," he whispered with a quick glance at Caleb, and he carried her through the house to her bedroom, her quiet sobs trailing behind them.

Caleb leaned back on his hands, his stomach full of lead as he watched Andras's back disappear around the corner. Something warm touched his arm, and he looked over to find Isaac on the floor beside him, looking fearful and unsure.

"Your mother isn't well, Caleb," Barachiel said, and if Caleb hadn't still been on the verge of vomiting, he might have spat back a 'no shit.' The angel gave a small sigh. "It isn't your fault. Some women respond better than others. She only wants to see your father again, and you taking his road was how she hoped to make that happen. But that wouldn't be a guarantee either. She'll be all right in time."

Isaac squeezed Caleb's arm, but he didn't know what to say.

"Isaac," Barachiel's deep voice sounded, startling him. "Why don't you get back before your father comes home? Caleb needs to rest."

"Y-Yeah," the blond answered, but he looked to Caleb for permission and didn't rise until the boy nodded at him. "I'll...see you tomorrow. I'm right down the road if there's anything I can do, okay?"

Caleb reached up to grab Isaac's hand as he turned to leave, and he touched the other boy's knuckles to his forehead, savoring the searing heat of his skin. This was what he'd done it for. This was worth the nausea and the aching head. He could explain to his mother, maybe. As long as he could feel this again.

"See you tomorrow," he murmured as he released Isaac's hand, and the blond smiled at him and gave Barachiel an awkward half-bow on his way out the door.

Barachiel bent to help Caleb to his feet, but when he tried to put an arm around him to support him, Caleb shoved at his chest and stumbled a step before standing on his own.

"We're not that close, feather-face," he grumped. He leaned on the banister to walk upstairs while Barachiel stared after him with folded arms.

"Little shit," he muttered, but he had a faint smile on his lips.

When Andras finally shut the door to Marian's room, he leaned against the adjacent wall and let out a slow breath. She was sleeping now, but it was exhaustion, not rest. She couldn't understand the choice that Caleb had made. Andras had no way to explain it to her that she would accept. He pushed away from the wall and made for the kitchen, walking carefully so as not to disturb the silent house. Caleb would need to eat whether he wanted to or not. He flicked on the light in the kitchen, since it had long since gone dark outside, and started at the sight of Barachiel sitting at the breakfast table.

"Fuck's sake," he hissed, "what the hell are you doing just sitting around in the dark? I thought you'd be gone by now."

"I thought you might need the company," the angel replied, his cheek resting on his laced fingers.

"What, just because I let Caleb head straight back for square one, apparently with absolutely zero intention of following through with what he started?" Andras snatched a pot from the island cabinet and held it in the sink to fill it with water. "Just because I agreed to take twenty souls that belonged to my boss instead of waiting patiently for Caleb to die and collecting my share? Or maybe because now it'll be another hundred years, another broken mother, another child begging me to tell him about his father?" He reached to turn off the faucet and paused with his hand on the knob as Barachiel's arms wrapped around his waist, and his shoulders sagged as the angel pressed a soft kiss to the back of his neck.

"Do you think you did the wrong thing?"

Andras leaned his hands on the counter and gave a weary sigh. "Did you hear him, B?" he murmured. "He was just being an ass, but...he called me his dad."

"Aren't you?" the angel chuckled, and Andras turned in his arms to face him.

"They don't usually think of me that way."

"Is sentiment catching?" Barachiel teased, nuzzling the demon's cheek with his nose. "I thought Caleb was the lovesick pup, not you."

"Fuck you," he grumbled, and he shoved him away to set the pot on the stove. He turned the switch to heat the burner and frowned over his shoulder when Barachiel embraced him again. "This was the right thing for him, wasn't it? If not for me."

"I think you know that without having to hear it from me."

Andras leaned back against the angel's chest, his head falling onto Barachiel's shoulder. "This doesn't mean you've won the bet, you know. It hardly counts since your boy got thoroughly corrupted in the process."

"Oh, I've won the bet." He leaned down to whisper into the demon's ear as his fingers tightened on his lover's waist. "You'll know when I'm ready to collect."

Andras shuddered and pushed away from him on the pretense of fetching some pasta from the pantry. "Get out of my kitchen. Brute."

"I'll be back to check on you, dad," Barachiel chuckled, but the demon didn't bother turning around to watch him disappear.

"Prick." He poured some pasta into the boiling water and leaned against the island to wait.

28

Isaac tried texting Caleb twice before he remembered that he'd seen the other boy's phone shattered on his bedroom floor. Well, whenever Caleb got around to getting a new phone, Isaac was going to have to get hold of it first or risk looking like a complete crazy person. He had left him far too many messages over the past few days.

He thought it might be hard to sleep knowing that Caleb was in his room suffering from an overabundance of humanity, but if he was honest, he was so relieved that he slept better than he had since before Caleb had left him behind at the youth center. He listened to his mother cry about not being able to afford his chosen university while he ate breakfast, the sadness in her voice making him wish he'd never applied at all. He should have known better. He promised her over and over again that it was all right, that he didn't mind going to UAB, and that he was grateful they'd let him still live at home while he was in school. He was still promising her on his way out the door to catch the bus.

He wondered if Caleb would be absent again. He'd looked pretty rough when Isaac had left yesterday, but he supposed Caleb could do worse than having an angel watching over him. If he thought about it too much, it hurt his head to try to understand the reality that his boyfriend was half demon who lived with his full-demon uncle, who was also apparently dating an angel. Did they date? Or did they just—nope, nope, nope. Stop that right there. Don't think about that. He rode the rickety bus to school with his backpack in his lap, picking at a loose string on his zipper pull. Even with everything that had happened, it had been hard to keep Caleb off his mind—the way his back had arched in Isaac's lap, his lips parted and his face flushed, lidded eyes watching him as his hips rolled in a demanding, fluid motion.

Oh Lord. I pledge allegiance to the flag of the United States of America, and to the republic for which it stands—

Isaac pressed his backpack tighter against his stomach and hoped he looked like he was sick as he curled up in his seat. He waited until he was the last one off the bus and sighed with relief as he stood. When had he become so filthy-minded? Probably somewhere between Caleb pinning him down by the pond and kneeling in front of him on that couch to—stop. Stop stop stop.

He spotted Caleb waiting for him as Andras's car pulled away from the curb, and he tried to resist running over to him. The boy was a little pale, with dark circles under his eyes; he looked tired, but...okay, all things considered.

"Hey," he offered as they fell into step on their way to the building. "Were you...able to get to sleep okay?"

"Except for Andras practically sitting on my chest to force rotini down my throat, I slept fine." He glanced sidelong at Isaac and seemed like he wanted to say more, but he just opened the main door of the school and let him in first. "I'm okay," he said instead.

Caleb stopped Isaac with a hand on his arm when they turned the corner toward their homeroom and pulled him into the boy's bathroom with him. He gave a brief glance under the stall doors, and Isaac heard the small click of the deadbolt in the door as Caleb pressed him against the tile wall and kissed him. The other boy's hands were in his hair and on his neck, sending pulses of heat through his skin and a shudder down his spine as Caleb's tongue lapped lightly over his bottom lip. Caleb kissed him until he couldn't breathe, and Isaac still didn't want to let him go. He pulled the other boy tight against him, but as soon as he shifted close enough to Caleb to feel the press of his growing arousal, the dark-haired boy retreated with a sheepish look on his face.

"Sorry," Caleb said, and he reached by Isaac to unlock the bolt by hand. "I just...missed you."

Isaac smiled at the floor to hide his faint blush. "I missed you too. Will you walk home with me today?"

"You don't have to ask." Caleb reached out to give his hand a light squeeze before opening the bathroom door.

The school day was surprisingly normal. Even more normal than yesterday, which it shouldn't have been. Caleb had made a huge decision. He'd upset his mother, given up that peaceful feeling he said he'd worked so hard for, and he'd decided to live as human a life as he could...for Isaac. The thought gave him a warm, fluttery feeling in his belly that only got worse every time he caught sight of Caleb in the hallway. Or was it better?

They walked home together, Caleb reaching for his hand as soon as they were alone on their little stretch of road, and they talked about all the homework Caleb had to do, the baseball game that he had missed, and what kinds of parties there were going to be as graduation got closer. It was almost...easy. Isaac had a hundred things to worry about—final exams coming up, how to call Cornell University and tell them thanks but no thanks, keeping the fact that he was in a relationship with another boy secret from his parents, helping Caleb deal with his decision—but none of them seemed all that important, as long as he could walk slowly beside Caleb on the way home after school.

Caleb kissed him when they had to part and promised to get a new phone that afternoon, but admitted it would probably be better for his grades to be cut off from contact for one more day. Isaac hesitated before letting go of the other boy's hand. It might have been just like before, except that Caleb was the one claiming schoolwork and Isaac the one wanting him to stay behind. Wasn't that backwards? When had Isaac become the one with kissing on his mind?

"Is Andras going to…you know, do that again today? Take souls from you?" he asked while they lingered, and Caleb touched his own stomach in anticipation.

"Probably. And then he's going to feed me. Ugh," he groaned.

"Are you going to be okay?"

"It's fine," he promised. "I already decided."

"Well just…call me if you need anything. Or want anything. Or…anything," he finished with an embarrassed chuckle. Caleb kissed him once more and lifted his hand in a wave before starting up the driveway to his house.

Isaac went home as always, had a snack, did his homework. It was the same as the last two weeks, but now his heart felt lighter. The person he loved—well, hadn't exactly said that he loved him back, but the words weren't as important as Caleb's actions. He finished his homework and left his room to do his chores, but his mind wandered. It was more difficult to keep from thinking about the other boy now that not only had they made amends, but Isaac had been told by a literal angel that what they'd done wasn't a sin. By the time he had cleaned up after supper and his father was sitting down to watch the news, Isaac had to excuse himself to his room, pretending he didn't feel well. He wanted to see Caleb again. He wanted to do more than see him. With a groan of frustration, he rolled himself up in his blanket and hid his head. He'd broken the dam by letting Caleb push him down onto that couch, he knew. He'd kept it together for years, hardly giving a second thought to things like dating, but now Caleb seemed to fill his brain completely. The stretch of his tanned skin, blunted fingernails digging into Isaac's shoulders, the heat in the silky skin as Isaac stroked his—he squeezed the blanket tighter around his face as though he could suffocate the memories. How was he supposed to focus on anything else with this aching tingle in his gut?

He had to see Caleb. But it was only Wednesday. Isaac would have to sit next to him in class, pretending he wasn't thinking about running his hands down the other boy's lean back and tasting the dark nub on his chest that put such a shiver in Caleb's skin. Even if he made it through school tomorrow, there was no way he could bring Caleb back to his room for...things like that. That would be the day his father came home early from work, for sure. But, maybe after a while, after his father went to bed—he couldn't just go to Caleb's house in the middle of the night, could he? That would be too much, especially if Caleb was still feeling ill. Although, it wasn't like Caleb hadn't snuck into Isaac's room before.

Isaac resigned himself to either breaking the rules or suffering through the night, but once the lights went out in the living room and the house was silent, he knew the choice he'd made. He waited a while, listening for any signs of life from his parents' bedroom. When he was sure his father was sleeping, Isaac crept through the house and out the back door, skirting the opposite side of the house from the bedroom window. He kept an eye on the house while he crossed the road and started up Caleb's driveway, half expecting the lights to go on at any moment, but the windows stayed dark all the way to Caleb's front yard. No going back now.

Caleb didn't have a phone, Isaac realized as he stood at the bottom of the front porch steps. He didn't have a phone, and his room was on the second floor. The third floor, really, since the house was on stilts. Isaac hadn't thought this through. He paused, then crouched down in the driveway and scooped up a few tiny pebbles from the dirt. He walked around the house to stand under Caleb's window, and he tossed one of the stones up, pinging it off the glass. He waited and listened, peering through the night up at the dark window, but there was nothing. He tried another. Nothing. He tried throwing the next one a little harder and flinched as it thunked a little too loudly against the window, but then he saw motion behind the glass, and Caleb appeared with his headphones around his neck. He pushed open the window and leaned his elbows on the sill to look down at his assailant.

"Isaac?" he called in a hushed voice. "What are you doing here?"

Isaac opened his mouth to answer and suddenly felt his face go red. He couldn't possibly say what had been on his mind when he decided to come. "I...wanted to see you," he said, which was also the truth. "Can I...can I come up?"

Caleb hesitated, throwing a quick glance over his shoulder. "Andras is still up. I'll come down." Without hesitation, he put one bare foot on the windowsill, and Isaac panicked. He was going to climb? But Caleb simply crawled out of the window and dropped down to the grass with a heavy thump, momentarily steadying himself against the side of the house as he straightened.

"Cheese and rice, Caleb!" Isaac said, and he covered his mouth when he heard the volume of his voice. "Are you okay?" he tried again more softly, his hand on the other boy's arm.

"Sure."

"But that's...what, over twenty feet!"

Caleb stared at him with that blank look in his eyes that normally was only reserved for strangers who dared to talk to him in the hallway. "And that's the weirdest thing you've seen lately?"

"Well—no, I guess not," Isaac chuckled. "I guess I'm just not used to this stuff yet. But—but you don't have to hide it from me, okay? Not any of it."

Caleb looked down at the ground to hide his faint smile. "I got it, Isaac."

"Good." Now that Caleb was right in front of him, it was a lot harder to be brave about the kinds of thoughts he'd been having all day. "A-Anyway, I...can we go somewhere and...you know, sit?"

Caleb tilted his head to get him to follow, and they walked together around to the back of the house. The porch by the back door looked cobbled together from old and new wood, as though it had recently been repaired, but the swing was intact. The chains holding it up gave a quiet creak as they sat next to each other, and Isaac briefly wondered how much they'd been reinforced to hold the cambion's weight. Isaac reached for Caleb's hand, his heart racing in his chest, and he let his thumb brush the back of the other boy's fingers. Now what? He really was happy just to be sitting beside Caleb, but he was fully aware of the heat of the other boy's body next to him, the gentle press of his thigh from sitting so close. Isaac wanted to touch him, but he couldn't just...tell him that.

"You worried about that calculus test?" Caleb asked, startling him out of his thoughts.

"Oh. Uh, not—not really; I've actually been doing okay in that class."

"Even without me there to study with you?" Caleb looked over at him with a small, quiet smile on his lips. His voice was soft, and he seemed tired. For a second, Isaac thought he'd made a mistake in coming. He should have let Caleb rest. But the moon was almost full, and the cool, pale light made Caleb's eyes seem even darker, like a void that Isaac was constantly on the verge of falling into.

Before Isaac knew what he was doing, he'd reached up to put a hand in Caleb's hair and leaned in close to press a long kiss against that private smile. Caleb's hand tightened in his as he returned the kiss, and he opened his mouth to the blond's tongue with a soft sigh. Isaac kept him close, the scent of the boy's shampoo filling his nostrils as Caleb's dark hair slipped between his fingers. The heat in his stomach that had been building all day was almost too much to bear now that Caleb's lips were on his, the other boy's hand at the side of his neck, the heat of their breath mixing between them. Isaac let his hand slip from Caleb's hair, his palm tracing the line of the other boy's waist through his shirt. His skin felt hot under the fabric, but Caleb shivered at his touch and took in a sharp breath against his lips. He clutched Isaac against him to hold their kiss and let the boy's tongue learn the inside of his mouth with eager slowness. Isaac's hand reached Caleb's hip and paused, fingertips toying with the hem of his shirt, and he felt the boy beside him shudder and tense as Isaac brushed the skin at his side.

"Caleb," he whispered between kisses, "Can I...Can I touch you?"

The boy couldn't seem to find his voice, but he pressed his forehead against Isaac's and gave a small nod. Isaac caught him in another kiss as he let his hand slip under the boy's shirt, his palm pressing into the heated skin and following the lean muscle up to his chest. His thumb found the other boy's pert nipple, and even gentle pressure caused a sudden whimper that shot straight to Isaac's groin. He rolled the tender nub between his fingers, letting Caleb moan and pant into his mouth to stifle the noise. Isaac thought, somewhere in the back of his mind, that he should have been embarrassed, but

Caleb's soft sighs and shivering skin were overwhelming. He wanted more. When Caleb's fingers clutched Isaac's shirt at the shoulder, he shifted closer, the porch swing giving a squeak as it moved, and Isaac broke the kiss to look down at him, his eyes on the boy's parted, swollen lips and the panting hollow of his throat. He drew his hand down Caleb's tight stomach to the front of his jeans, and at the first brush of his palm over the other boy's erection, Isaac felt a tight grip around his wrist and found himself forcibly pressed back to arm's length.

Caleb looked up at him with apprehension in his eyes and a nervous frown on his flushed face, and he stood suddenly from the swing and tugged his shirt back into place. "Sorry," he muttered without meeting Isaac's eyes.

Isaac fought to slow his heart so he could find the air to speak. "Did—did I do something wrong?"

"No. Just...it's late, you know? I...we've got that test tomorrow, and I'm still...pretty tired."

"Oh," Isaac whispered, his stomach churning with guilt. He must have gone too fast, or done the wrong thing. Maybe Caleb didn't like him being the forceful one. He shook his head and put on a bright smile. "I'm sorry for coming to bug you so late. I know you need your rest." He pushed himself up from the bench swing and moved toward the porch steps. "I'll...see you tomorrow then."

Caleb nodded and waited for him to leave, but when Isaac was halfway around the house, he trotted up behind him and caught the blond by the arm.

"Hey," he said, and a beat of awkward silence passed between them before Caleb took Isaac's face in his hands and pressed one last firm kiss to his mouth. "I love you," he whispered, his breath hot against his lips. Isaac's knees trembled as Caleb broke away from him, and the tension in his belly disappeared at the faint smile in the other boy's dark eyes. Caleb didn't wait for him to respond; by the time Isaac recovered, he was already standing alone in the yard with the soft closing of the back door sounding around the corner.

He pressed a hand to his mouth to hide the wide smile on his face, and he started the slow walk back to his house with soft laughter bubbling from his lips. Caleb loved him.

29

Caleb stared at his bedroom ceiling for a long time after he woke up the next morning. He would have to explain himself. He hadn't expected Isaac to suddenly be so comfortable making the first move, but Caleb wasn't complaining—he could still feel the blond's firm hand in his hair, guiding their kiss, and the heat of his thumb teasing his nipple like he'd done it a dozen times before. Isaac had looked down at him like something to be devoured, and it had sent a thrilling shudder down his spine. But Caleb hadn't realized how numb he'd become.

Ever since he claimed his first soul back when he was thirteen, just barely coming into his powers, and with every passing month since, he'd grown just a little colder, each deal draining another bit of feeling from him. By the time he was sixteen, he was having sex with anyone who caught his fancy, letting strangers take him to bed just as a way to pass the time. With Isaac, it had always been different. It was always warmer, and it always made his heart beat faster, but last night was different. His skin was on fire, and every caress of Isaac's tongue had been electric.

Was that what it was like all the time for normal people? He didn't know how they could stand it. Caleb had moaned and clung to the other boy so helplessly, just from a little kissing and touching. It was embarrassing. Plus his memory of their last time together had been soured by everything that came after. How could he let himself be that exposed again, especially knowing how pathetically sensitive his skin had apparently become? Maybe if he jerked off a couple times before Isaac got near him. Caleb was supposed to be the sexy, experienced one. That was the way this worked. And with every day that passed, with every batch of souls Andras took from him, it was only going to get worse. He had taken five the night before, and Caleb had felt like his blood was actually on fire. Could he maybe hang on to just a few souls, for the sake of his own dignity?

A prickling feeling ran up the back of his neck, a cold suggestion, and he lifted his head to make sure that his room was actually empty. He'd found himself looking over his shoulder more frequently ever since he'd given his first few souls away—he always felt as if something was watching him now.

He rolled himself out of bed with a sigh and got ready for school. Andras was waiting for him as always—with no snide remarks, though Caleb knew he must have noticed him coming back in late the night before. The demon actually seemed a little on edge. His hand gripped the steering wheel tightly, and though he had his usual casual posture, one elbow leaning on the car door as he drove, something about it seemed false today.

"What's up with you?" Caleb asked, breaking the tense silence in the car, and Andras barely glanced at him.

"Just driving a precocious little shit to school, like every weekday for the last twelve years," he said dryly.

"Have a fight with your boyfriend?"

"I'm about to have a fight with you." The demon sighed through his nose. "How are you feeling?"

"Grounded," he said simply, and he caught the slight smile on Andras's lips.

"That's not the worst answer. By the way, tell Isaac to just knock next time. You don't have to sneak around jumping out of windows."

There it was. "Yeah right," he scoffed. "As if I want him in my room with you creeping right outside."

"Who's creeping? You think I get my jollies listening to teenagers awkwardly fondle each other?"

"I guess you probably get enough awkward fondling of your own." Andras snorted, and Caleb watched him as they stopped at the single red light between their house and the school. "Hey," he started. The demon turned his head. "So, Barachiel. Has he really been...you know, around? The whole time?"

"Yeah."

"So like...how come I didn't know? It's weird for there to be a guy who acts all concerned about me and I don't even know him."

"Well, for one thing, not every generation of cambion lives in a time when two men being together is an acceptable thing to happen. For another thing, he's an angel, and it's less hassle for everyone if we keep that sort of thing discreet. You can imagine I'm a bit of a black mark on his heavenly record. And anyway, he's busy. It's not worth explaining to a little kid why someone comes and goes." Andras moved the car forward again as the light turned green.

"But you like him, right?"

"Yeah, I like him."

"Hm," Caleb mused. "Then I guess he's probably all right."

"So glad I've got your approval," Andras muttered, but he was smiling. He pulled the car up to the curb outside the school. "Now fuck off. And eat lunch," he added. "You'll feel better for tonight's trade."

Caleb sighed at him as he climbed out of the car. Isaac was waiting for him on the sidewalk, and he felt a little anxious tug in his gut as the blond drew close. He was determined not to make an ass of himself. He just walked with Isaac to class and kept his hands to himself, and the other boy smiled and chatted with him as usual. If anything, he was more bubbly than normal. Caleb did allow himself to watch him across the room during their calculus test, that tight frown on his face as he bent so low his nose almost touched the paper.

When he had handed in his own test and sat waiting for the bell to ring, the intercom clicked on in the classroom, calling him to the front office. He frowned and offered Isaac a quick shrug of confusion on his way out, and he found Andras waiting for him outside the main office door.

"Sorry to disrupt your day," he said, "but it's time to come home."

"Why? What happened? Is mom okay?"

"She's fine. Just...get in the car."

Caleb was glad it was a short ride back to the house, at least, because Andras didn't seem inclined to give him any further information. They parked at the top of the driveway, and Andras hesitated outside the front door with a firm hand on Caleb's shoulder.

"You made your choice. Remember that it was yours to make," he said softly, which wasn't comforting at all. The demon opened the door and led the boy inside, where he could hear his mother singing an airy tune from the kitchen. As Caleb turned the corner, he spotted her sitting on the island with a bag of grapes in her lap, plucking them carefully and popping them into the mouth of a barrel-chested man.

"Caleb!" she cried as she noticed him enter, and the man turned to face the door. He was tall and broad, with massive shoulders and a thick, muscular waist. He ran his fingers through his short, messy brown hair as if to tame it and smoothed the dark scruff on his jaw with a quick swipe of his hand. He took a step toward Caleb and bent down slightly to look him in the face with bright, honey-colored eyes. This. This was the gaze he'd been feeling for days. This empty, pitiless stare.

"Thought you'd be taller," he mused, and Caleb looked back at Andras in confusion.

"Caleb," the demon began, "this is...your father. My master, Azazel."

Caleb didn't have enough air in his lungs to reply. He just stared up at the square-jawed man in front of him and leaned back on instinct when he showed his white teeth in a smile.

"Don't be shy, kid," Azazel said with a low rumble of a laugh. "Sorry if I'm not enough fire and brimstone for you. If you'd gone the other way, maybe I'd play that up, but I wouldn't want to scare ya."

"Oh, Caleb," his mother sighed, "isn't it wonderful? Now your father can help you fulfill your destiny! You can just start over. He'll help you; you'll have everyone here to help you!"

"I'm not doing that anymore," he said, frowning at the demon that was apparently his father. "If that's what you came here for, you wasted your time."

"I thought you said this kid was a soft touch, Andras," he laughed. "There's bite in him." Azazel folded his arms and tilted his head as he inspected his son. "I know you made up your mind already, kid. That's why I came. I need a favor."

"A favor? Are you kidding me?" Andras gripped him tightly at the elbow, but he ignored it. "What right do you think you have to show up here and ask me for any goddamn thing?"

The demon seemed to soften slightly, and he glanced over his shoulder at Marian, who was happily humming to herself as she picked out the juiciest-looking grapes. "Not for me," he said in a low voice. "See, I've got a bit of a predicament. Marian's in a difficult spot. She had my child. There's noplace for her when she goes except for Hell. Which suits me fine, except she's going to pass by a lot of demons before she ends up anywhere I can reach her. I'm forbidden from making deals. Raphael's rules. But if, say, a certain cambion was to make her an offer," he trailed off with a shrug. "That's got nothing to do with me, does it?"

Caleb's stomach turned at the thought. Make a deal for his own mother's soul?

"I know what you're thinking," Azazel went on. He paused when Marian dropped down from the kitchen island and touched his bicep, and he bent down to bite the offered grape from her fingertips. "But you make a deal with her, and she's yours. She goes where you send her. When you're dead, she's mine. And I want to take good care of her."

"What, along with the who-knows-how-the-fuck-many other women you've knocked up?"

"No," he answered sternly. "Just her." Marian smiled up at him, turning his face to her with a hand on his jaw, and he brushed a thick curl from her face with a surprisingly gentle hand.

Caleb hesitated. He leaned forward to get his mother's attention. "Mom. You...want to go with him? With...with my father?"

"Oh, yes," she said immediately, a bright smile on her face. "Oh, Caleb, I'm so glad you got to meet him. I know he's so proud." She fed Azazel another grape and went gliding back to the island to pluck a few more from the vine.

Caleb shook his head, his brow furrowed as he watched her. "How can I? She's not even...I mean, she's not all there. She never has been."

"Grant her clarity," Azazel said. "Let her see clearly, and then let her come with me."

"You mean let her die? But she's only—"

"Time will be meaningless for her," the demon cut him off. "And you'll see her again someday."

Caleb looked back at Andras for guidance, but he only offered him a soft frown.

"It's always your choice, Caleb."

Caleb watched his mother hop up onto the island and swing her feet, bumping her heels lightly against the cabinet doors as she hummed. She seemed...happy. He pressed his lips together and looked up into Azazel's face. "You swear that you'll take care of her. Better than you have been. Better than you did me."

"Kid, if it hadn't been against the rules, I never would have left her."

He sighed, and he pulled away from Andras's grip to stand in front of his mother. "Mom?" he started, and he gently pushed her hand down when she tried to offer him a grape. "If you could...would you go with him now?"

The woman brightened. "Can we? Oh, Caleb; let's go right now!"

"Before that," he said softly, "I need you to agree to something."

"What is it, darling?" She reached out to stroke his cheek, a loving smile on her face.

"Will you let me take care of you for now? Of...of your soul. Until I can pass it to him."

"Baby," she whispered as she tenderly touched his hair, "you know I've only been waiting for you to ask."

"Yeah," he answered, unable to keep the frown from his face. He held out his hand to her, and she took it in both of hers, pulling it close to press a warm kiss to his knuckles. His heart thumped slowly, just once, running cool water down the back of his neck, and then she looked up at him again with soft focus in her dark eyes that he'd never seen before. She slipped down from the island and wrapped her arms around him, her cheek against his shoulder as she held him.

"Oh, darling," she sighed. "I'm so proud of you." Her voice sounded strange and steady, not the distracted, flighty rambling he was used to. She leaned back from him and reached out for Azazel, who took a step closer to take her hand in his. "Thank you, Caleb," she said. "You made the right choice, baby. I've never seen you look so happy as when that boy is here." She gently pulled him down and kissed his cheek. "You let him take care of you, and you make sure this is the very last deal you ever make, you understand me?"

"Yeah, mom," he whispered. Had he done this? With just a touch, just an agreement—it was like she'd been brought back to life.

"Good job, kid." Azazel patted him once on the shoulder and turned back to look at Andras. "And you," he said pointedly, and the other demon stiffened slightly. "You let this boy grow up soft, and not only do you let him give up the lives he claimed, but you take for yourself what's rightfully mine. What am I supposed to do about that?"

"He didn't do anything!" Caleb said, moving to stand between them. Andras tensed and put a hand on the boy's arm, but he shook it off.

"Caleb—"

"It was my decision, right? My choice. Isn't that free will? My mother's greatest gift to me, isn't it? So he didn't do anything."

Azazel let out a rough laugh. "Easy, kid. You really did raise a sentimental one this time, Andras." He pursed his lips as though considering. "But you, Caleb. You still carry a balance. Give them to Andras to hold onto for me."

"He still has twelve," Andras interrupted. "If I take them all at once—"

"The boy wants to be human, doesn't he?" Azazel's eyes narrowed slightly. "Don't you?"

"I do," Caleb answered. He held out his hand before the demon could even offer. "Take them. All but hers."

Andras sighed. "I hope you actually ate something," he muttered, and as he took Caleb's hand, the boy stumbled back at the sudden shock of heat. Andras held him up as he swayed, keeping him from hitting the floor as he clutched at his rolling stomach. Caleb let his weight fall against the demon holding him. He was almost afraid to try to catch his breath and risk heaving what little lunch he'd had onto the floor. Everything was loud, and the brief cool he'd felt as his mother's soul had passed to him was wiped away in an instant, replaced with a pounding head and heated blood.

"You're all right," Andras assured him, and the demon slowly helped him stand on his own. Caleb felt heavy, but it was somehow freeing to know that the only thing inside him aside from…him, was the essence his mother had entrusted to him. This was what Isaac had wanted from him all along, and it was finally finished.

"See? Not so hard," Azazel mused, and he turned to face the other demon. "But that doesn't change the fact that a debt is a debt. And your broke your contract with me."

"I know." Andras stepped out from behind Caleb, looking up into Azazel's amber eyes with a tentative frown.

"I do, however, have more important things to worry about than keeping your numbers straight." He touched Marian's hair as she leaned against his side. "So here's what we'll do. You, my friend, are not going to rise any higher than your current station. Ever. Every soul you touch, from now until the end of eternity, belongs to me. And you will continue to take them. As many as I ask for. For as long as you live."

"Are you kidding? You're making him a slave over twenty souls?" Caleb cut in, but Andras clamped a tight hand onto the boy's shoulder.

"It's fair," he said. "If that's the price for leaving Caleb be," he added in a lower voice.

"I'll trade a permanent servant on Earth for a soft touch cambion," Azazel chuckled, the sound a deep rumble in his chest. "I'm not going to be in the cambion business again for quite some time, I think. A bit turned off on the idea, honestly. If I ever change my mind, we can renegotiate, since I don't know anyone better in the business of raising difficult boys. But for now...we can leave it like this." He offered Andras his hand, and the other demon took it without hesitation. Caleb felt a pulse in the air as though something hot had burst in the center of the room before the demons parted.

"Now," Azazel said. "Let's celebrate. I haven't been on Earth in years; I want some bourbon and a nice meal. And you call that grumpy angel of yours down here. I want to make sure he knows who he owes for your freedom."

"Uh, sorry, what sort of freedom is this supposed to be?" Caleb spoke up.

"The closest thing to it," Andras answered, not seeming quite as upset about eternal servitude as Caleb might have expected. "Your father is the reason I can stay on Earth. Basically. He gave me a...soul loan, sort of. Thousands of years ago. To make me strong enough. I've been paying it off ever since." He chuckled as though embarrassed to admit it. "B can only come halfway, you see."

"So you've been doing this for that long, raising kid after kid, so that...you could be with him?" Andras gave a small, helpless shrug, and Caleb's lips curled into a smirk. "And you said *I'm* a soft touch? Some demon."

"You're lucky I'm in a good mood, you little shit."

The boy hesitated. "So then, that means...your job's done, huh?"

Andras chuckled, and he fastened a hand around the back of Caleb's neck and tugged him close enough to bump his forehead, just for a moment. "Demons are immortal, little lamb. I'm going to be bothering you until you die."

Caleb shoved his arm away with a grumpy snort, but he couldn't keep the faint smile from his face. As far as demonic punishments went, he supposed Andras had gotten off fairly easy.

"Now I'm going to take your parents out for a nice meal," he said. "We'll probably be gone for quite some time." He leaned in a little closer and lowered his voice. "You can think of some way to occupy yourself for a few hours without anyone creeping outside your room, right?"

Caleb pushed him again, and the demon tapped the side of his nose as he stepped back from him. A moment later, all three adults were gone from the kitchen, leaving Caleb alone in the empty house with a strange feeling of satisfaction.

30

Isaac texted Caleb as soon as he was in the hallway after class, but the other boy didn't answer. He was sick with worry for the rest of the day. Had something happened? Caleb hadn't seemed like he wasn't feeling well. Was something wrong at home? Isaac dragged through the rest of his classes, but as he was leaving last period, his phone vibrated in his pocket, and he almost dropped it in his hurry to check the screen.

Come over.

Isaac hesitated, glancing between the road and the bus and trying to decide which was faster. He decided on the road, and he waved a quick goodbye to Heather before taking off toward Caleb's house at a jog. It might not have been faster, really, but it would have made him too anxious to sit on the bus and wait. By the time he reached the bottom of Caleb's driveway, he was out of breath, and he wiped at the sweat on his brow with the bottom of his shirt. He started up the dirt path at a steadier pace, gripping the straps of his backpack. Andras's car was outside. He quickened his pace again without meaning to. Why did Caleb have to send him such a vague text?

He knocked on the door and slumped with relief when Caleb answered it almost immediately, not looking at all like someone who had just had an emergency.

"Did you run here?" he chuckled.

"I—I was worried! You got called out, and then you sent me that text that didn't even explain anything!" Caleb stepped back to let him in, and Isaac glanced around the living room as he dropped his bag. "Is...everything all right? It seems quiet."

"My dad came," Caleb said simply, and Isaac caught himself almost saying 'Oh, that's nice.' He froze as Caleb shut the door behind him.

"Your...*dad* dad? Like—"

"Yeah. It was...underwhelming."

"Was? He's gone already?"

"He took Andras and my mom out to go drinking, or something." He shifted his weight and held his elbow with his opposite hand. "Andras took the rest of the souls. So…I'm empty. All done. But I have to tell you that I...made a deal."

Isaac's heart dropped into his stomach. "What?" he whispered. "But...I thought you weren't—"

"It was for my mom," he added quickly. "So she could be with my dad. I know it's kind of fucked, but it's what she wanted. I wanted to tell you. This is the only one," he assured him. "I'm not doing it anymore. I just didn't want to...you know, keep a secret." He looked at Isaac with a little crease between his eyebrows, his lips turned down into a worried frown, and the blond smiled. Caleb was trying so hard to be open, even though it was difficult for him.

Isaac stepped forward and pulled the taller boy to him, warmth flooding his chest as he felt Caleb's arms around his waist. "Thanks for telling me," he murmured against the other boy's cheek. "You didn't want to go with them, though? This might be your only chance to get to know him, right?"

Caleb snorted softly. "I built him up in my head as this...big deal. I guess I thought something would happen if I ever met him, like I'd be mad, or he'd try to tell me about this great destiny I had, just like my mom. But when I finally saw him, he was just...some guy. I mean, a demon like Andras I guess, but...just a guy. And in the end, he only came for my mom. He didn't seem like someone I'd get along with, anyway."

"You're really okay leaving it like that?"

Caleb bent to rest his forehead on Isaac's shoulder. "He's not what's important to me."

Isaac's face flushed slightly as the other boy's fingers wound into the back of his shirt. It occurred to him somewhere in the back of his overactive mind that they were alone in the house, but Caleb had clearly had an emotional afternoon. And anyway, it shouldn't be all Isaac thought about when they were—

"Hey," Caleb murmured, his breath brushing the blond's neck. "Do you want to come upstairs? They're not coming back for a long time."

Isaac stammered for a moment, his cheeks hot from the other boy's light kiss. "Up...upstairs, as in...?"

Caleb tugged him closer with one hand at the small of his back and trailed his lips up Isaac's jaw, giving a light lick to the corner of the other boy's mouth. "You wanted me last night, didn't you?"

"I—I..."

"So come upstairs," he whispered against Isaac's ear, and he took his hand and drew him toward the stairway. Isaac followed with the sound of his blood rushing in his ears, but he thought he could feel Caleb's fingers trembling slightly in his. They walked the short hall from the top of the stairs to Caleb's door, and Isaac stood beside the bed while Caleb shut the door, not quite sure what to do with himself. Last time had been so sudden and so intense that he'd been able to forget himself, but this was...purposeful.

Caleb moved close to him and slid his hands under his shirt without hesitation, scratching his fingernails down Isaac's stomach and catching him by the waistband of his jeans. His movements were as sure as ever, his teeth tugging at the top button of Isaac's shirt, but when the blonde brushed his fingers over the skin beneath his shirt at the small of his back, he seemed to tense. Caleb pushed him down onto the bed and swung a leg over his hips, his hands on either side of Isaac's head. He stared down at the boy under him with sharp, focused eyes, but there was something in him that seemed nervous. Isaac reached up to him and cupped his cheek, his thumb running over Caleb's bottom lip with a tender touch, and the boy's skin grew hot under his hand. Caleb wet his lips and lowered his eyes to avoid Isaac's gaze, focusing instead on unbuttoning the blond's shirt with one hand.

Isaac couldn't imagine what he had to be nervous about, but the slight shiver in Caleb's breath and the touch of redness in his cheeks was too much. He was so cute. Isaac let his fingers slip through the boy's dark hair and pull him close, unable to resist tasting the other boy's parted lips. Caleb ground against his hips and worked at the rest of his buttons, spreading the shirt away from his chest with eager hands.

"Yours too," Isaac whispered as his palms flattened against the other boy's back, and Caleb arched into his touch but hesitated to sit up. With a huff of what almost sounded like determination, Caleb pushed up and sat back on his heels, tugging his shirt over his head and tossing it aside. The warm color of his skin was slowly returning following his exhaustion, and as he shifted to lean over Isaac again, the lean muscles in his chest and stomach moved smoothly beneath his skin.

Isaac didn't let himself get pinned again. He sat up and gripped Caleb by the back of his shoulders, keeping him in place in his lap as he pressed a kiss to his chest. Caleb's flesh was hot under his lips, begging to be kissed, and when the other boy rolled against him, his erection pressing feverishly against Isaac's bare stomach through his jeans, they both shuddered. Caleb shifted slightly so his hands could reach between them, and he worked quickly at unbuttoning the other boy's jeans, sitting up on his knees to slide the zipper down and reach a hand inside. Isaac jumped at the sudden touch, feeling like his insides were on fire as Caleb's fingers traced his shape through his underwear.

"Did you like it when I sucked your cock?" he whispered, catching the blond's earlobe in his teeth as he squeezed him. Isaac gave a short nod before he even had time to be embarrassed by the question. "You want me to do it again?" Caleb tugged at the waistband of Isaac's underwear with one finger.

Isaac's stomach twisted with indecision. If he said yes, he wouldn't be able to reach Caleb to touch him. But he really wanted to say yes. His longing for the other boy won over, and he pulled Caleb tighter against him, leaving kisses down his collarbone. He bent lower to run his tongue over Caleb's sensitive nipple, humming in satisfaction as the other boy's fingers dug into his shoulders. He broke away long enough to free his arms from his shirt and shove it away from them, and then he returned to his work, eager to taste Caleb's trembling skin. His teeth grazed the dark nub as Caleb's hand fisted in his hair, the boy hissing in a sharp breath tinged with a whimper. Isaac kissed across Caleb's chest to make sure his other nipple got equal attention, and he let his hands drift from the boy's back to unfasten his jeans. Caleb shuddered at the touch of his hand, his breath quickening, but when Isaac tried to urge him out of his lap, he wouldn't budge.

"Let me up," Isaac murmured against his skin, and Caleb's nails bit his shoulders in defiance. "I want to touch you," he whispered, his thumb pressing into the nipple his mouth had abandoned. Caleb gave a soft, relenting groan and moved out of Isaac's lap, but he refused to let the other boy help him as he shimmied out of his jeans. Isaac leaned over him immediately, catching his lips in a kiss as he tentatively ran a hand over the other boy's waist. Caleb's breath was already ragged, and his skin tightened over the muscles in his stomach as he gasped under Isaac's touch.

Isaac could feel the heat of his arousal before he touched him,

Caleb's sudden jerk brushing his hard cock against Isaac's hip. Isaac slid his fingers around him, giving a silent prayer that he wasn't going to do anything stupid, and he gave Caleb an experimental squeeze as he kissed down his neck again. Caleb's hands shook as they pressed into Isaac's arms, gripping him as if he was afraid to fall, and when Isaac started to stroke him and laved his tongue over the soft skin below his collarbone, the other boy shoved him away so suddenly that Isaac almost tumbled straight off of the bed.

He leaned his weight on his elbow as Caleb turned away from him, hugging his own arms and shuddering as he fought to catch his breath. Even Isaac's gentle touch to his shoulder made him jump.

"Caleb, what...what's wrong? I'm sorry, I didn't—"

"It's not you," Caleb interrupted him in a weak voice.

"What's the matter?" Isaac nudged slightly closer to him and leaned over to try to see his face, but Caleb curled up slightly tighter and turned his face into the pillow. The boy's whole body felt hot. "If you're still tired, we don't have to. Don't push yourself." He ran a tender hand down Caleb's arm, and he shivered and shied away. "Caleb," he whispered, "what did I do?"

"You didn't do anything," the boy answered. "Sorry."

Isaac waited, but Caleb didn't seem inclined to elaborate, so he reached out to turn the boy's face to him with a gentle hand on his cheek. The Caleb that looked up at him was flushed and frowning, his hands clutched protectively to his chest.

"Please tell me what's wrong," Isaac said, and Caleb huffed but didn't answer, his eyes anywhere but the other boy's face. "Should we stop?"

"No," Caleb groaned in frustration, one heated hand curling against Isaac's pectoral muscle.

"Then what's wrong?"

"I'm—scared, okay?" he snapped, then seemed to immediately regret it. He turned his head away again but didn't try to push Isaac off of him. "Because I only know how to have sex. And that's—not what this is. Not with you. And last time, just when I thought I..." He sighed, and his voice went quiet. "I know it's stupid. But I just keep thinking, what if—what if this is all wrong, and I screw it up, and I push too hard or I say the wrong thing, and even if I think everything's fine, you still—"

Isaac silenced him with a long, soft kiss. He let Caleb relax underneath him before he slowly pulled away and looked down at him with a gentle smile. "You really think that after all this, you can still get rid of me?" Caleb's face burned red, and he sighed with his eyes lowered.

"No," Isaac whispered, "look at me." He tilted the other boy's chin up with a light touch. "I love you. And even if one of us screws up, or says the wrong thing...I'm going to stay right here. Nothing on this Earth could make me give up on you. I promise."

Caleb chewed his lip, and he reached up to touch Isaac's hair and draw him down for a slightly firmer kiss. He touched his lips to Isaac's cheek and murmured in his ear as though he was still too shy to say the words while he looked the other boy in the eyes. "I love you, too."

Isaac slid his arm under Caleb's shoulders and held him close to his chest, taking in the scent of the other boy's hair.

"Plus," Caleb said, seeming reluctant to get the words out, "it's really...different. It's...warmer than before. Before I gave them all away. I wasn't this...sensitive. Before. It's...it's hard to think straight, and it's really annoying. I can't even—my heart goes too fast, and it's so hot, I—ugh," he sighed.

Isaac paused and leaned back from him. "You mean sensitive like..." He gingerly traced a line up Caleb's waist with his fingertips and watched the boy twist and shudder under his touch. Caleb's chest rose and fell quickly with his anxious breath, the flush in his face staining his neck and chest, and he turned away to try to hide the tense furrow in his brow. There was no chance of Isaac resisting him this way, so timid and panting and shy. He placed a soft kiss on Caleb's chin.

"Then just let me take care of you," he whispered, even his breath causing a shiver in the other boy's skin. "I'll go as slow as you like."

Caleb's hand tightened into a fist against his chest, but he was clearly doing his best to maintain his dignity as he nodded.

Isaac shifted to lean over him, touching a gentle kiss to his lips as he let his hand rest on Caleb's waist. He could barely keep his own heart steady, but his own shyness meant nothing if he could put Caleb at ease. He left light kisses down Caleb's neck to his shoulder, listening to the boy's shaking breath to make sure he didn't go too fast. Everywhere Isaac touched him, goosebumps grew on his skin, and the blond nudged his knee between Caleb's thighs to better reach him. The last time, Caleb had been calm, seductive, in control. Seeing him like this, with his lips parted, cheeks red, fingers curled against Isaac's biceps to keep them from trembling—Isaac thought he'd never known what lust was before that moment.

He lowered his head to taste the boy's skin, his tongue laying a wet trail of heat up over Caleb's ribs to his nipple. The boy's grip tightened on him as he shifted, the mattress creaking under their weight, and Isaac leaned on one arm to press his palm against the other boy's erection. Caleb let out a whine that shot right to Isaac's gut, and he squeezed him, doing his best to replicate the firm stroke the boy had shown him he liked. He peeked up at Caleb's face as his hips twitched uncertainly upwards, and the sight of the boy with his head thrown back, his throat exposed and his lip caught in his teeth to stifle his soft moans, made Isaac's cock throb painfully against the confines of his underwear. He sat up to kneel on the mattress with Caleb's legs loosely around his hips and hesitated, not quite sure how to proceed.

Before he had the chance to ask, Caleb reached out toward the nightstand and gave a soft grunt of direction. Isaac gingerly leaned over him to pull open the drawer, and his face went hot as a tube of lubricant rolled to the front of the drawer, nudging an opened box of condoms as it went.

"Oh, g...gosh, I didn't even—Caleb, last time, I should have—"

"It's fine," Caleb panted, waving his hand in a vague gesture toward the drawer. "I don't care if you use one or not. But the—here." He scooted on the mattress just enough to be able to reach into the drawer and slipped the tube into Isaac's hand. "Just...go slow, okay?" he added in a softer, hesitant voice. Isaac chuckled despite the tightness of his throat and nodded. As if he could do anything but go slowly.

His skin prickled with heat as though it was sunburned, but he flicked open the cap and squeezed a glob of the sterile-smelling gel onto his fingertips. The muscles in Caleb's thighs trembled as Isaac gingerly urged them apart, but he lifted his hips to give the blond better access to him. Isaac watched Caleb's face as he pressed a slick finger against his entrance, the other boy's sharp gasp causing a pulse under the pad of Isaac's finger. His throat wouldn't quite work, but he tried to swallow down the lump in it as he pushed forward, both of them shuddering as Isaac's finger slipped beyond the barrier of muscle. His stomach tightened as the boy clenched around his finger, and Caleb's back arched with his hands tangled in the bedsheets.

Isaac tried to move carefully, but as soon as he slid a second finger inside the other boy and saw that helpless, gasping look on Caleb's face, it was over for him. He pushed his fingers deep inside him as he leaned forward, eagerly probing Caleb's mouth with his tongue and letting the other boy cry out against him. Caleb whimpered into his kiss as Isaac teased him, and when Isaac happened to touch something firm deep inside him, Caleb broke the kiss in a shivering moan. Isaac brushed his fingertip over the spot again and let out a desperate sound of his own as Caleb flinched and panted against him.

"Is it too much?" he managed to breathe in between leaving heated kisses on the other boy's lips, but Caleb shook his head fervently and lifted his hips to allow Isaac to press a third digit into him. Isaac let his head fall against Caleb's shoulder as he pushed into him with as much restraint as he could muster, but each whimper and moan against his ear was chipping away at his resolve. "Caleb," he whispered, "will you...touch me too?"

Caleb's hands immediately slipped between them again, and Isaac's hips jerked forward as the boy gripped him. Isaac leaned back to get a breath of air, but his heart stopped short as he saw Caleb's dark eyes watching him with a clouded, longing expression. He pressed one more hard kiss to the boy's waiting mouth and then sat up, managing to be careful about removing his fingers from Caleb's body but not having the patience to do any more than push his own jeans and underwear down slightly lower on his hips. He pulled Caleb closer to him by the waist and positioned himself at his entrance, pressing against the soft, pliant muscle.

"Caleb, can...can I...?"

The boy nodded without speaking, one hand scratching down Isaac's stomach in a silent plea, but he jerked and cried out suddenly as Isaac pushed into him. He almost seemed to be retreating, but when Isaac paused to check on him, Caleb whined in complaint and ground his hips down against him. He pressed against Isaac's chest as he began to move, and his head fell to the side, the knuckles of his free hand tightly in his teeth in a vain attempt to stifle the needing moans escaping him.

Isaac could hardly breathe, the boy underneath him was so beautiful. Caleb's hair fell into his eyes as he writhed against the sheets, and a sheen of sweat began to gather into drops at the hollow of his throat. Isaac's hand ran down Caleb's thigh and stroked his leaking cock in time with his thrusts, both boys panting for breath as they rocked together on the creaking mattress. Caleb shook and cried out, and Isaac bent over him to kiss him, the taller boy's body almost doubling over and allowing him in just a little deeper. Isaac let Caleb moan into his mouth as he moved, and he gasped as Caleb suddenly clenched around him with a strangled groan, spilling hot ropes of fluid over his fingers. The pressure was too much, and Isaac only managed a few more desperate thrusts before he followed the other boy into climax, pressing into him as deeply as he could to ride out the throbs of his orgasm.

Neither of them were able to move, so they laid tangled together and just tried to breathe. When Caleb finally gave a weak grunt and squeezed Isaac's shoulder, the blond reluctantly pulled away, shuddering as he released himself from the other boy's grip. He let Caleb curl up against his chest and gently stroked his hair, touching a soft kiss to the top of his head.

"I love you," the dark-haired boy whispered against his collarbone, and Isaac smiled and held him tighter.

The next days at school seemed like a dream. Isaac had never felt so light on his feet. He walked home with Caleb every day, and sometimes they slipped away to kiss for a while before Isaac's father got home. Sometimes they did more, and Isaac was slowly learning just how far he could push the other boy before he reached his limit and begged. He hadn't expected to enjoy seeing the helpless, pleading look on Caleb's face as much as he did, but having the normally stoic boy underneath him, his arm over his eyes to hide his embarrassment while Isaac touched him, was the most addicting feeling in the world. Caleb wouldn't have trusted himself to anyone else; only Isaac could take care of him this way. It made his heart race every time Caleb put that trust in him. He never wanted to give it up.

Caleb's mother had returned long enough to say goodbye and make the boy promise to be good, and then Caleb said she had simply vanished along with his father. He said he could still sense her, in a way, at the back of his mind, but that he didn't worry for her. He knew she was in good hands. So he stayed in the house at the top of the hill alone with Andras, though Isaac had seen Barachiel in the house more frequently. He and Caleb seemed to be getting along, which had caused Isaac to catch Andras smiling more than once.

After a few weeks, Isaac stopped at the mailbox outside his house on his way home, prepared to dump out the usual junk mail, but an official-looking envelope with his name on it caught his eye. He dropped the rest of the mail on the kitchen table and slid his finger under the flap to open it, and as he scanned the page, his eyes grew wider and his mouth dropped open. He let his backpack fall to the floor, and then he was out of the house again, running full tilt for Caleb's house. He must have barely beaten the other boy to his front door, because Caleb still had his bag over his shoulder when he opened the door in confusion.

Isaac pushed the paper into Caleb's chest and leaned his hands on his knees to catch his breath while the other boy read. "It's...a scholarship," he panted. "A full ride. Tuition, housing, books—everything. At Cornell." He straightened with a smile on his face that felt like it might split his cheeks. "I don't even remember applying."

"Isaac," Caleb laughed softly, "this is—"

Andras appeared from behind Caleb and plucked the paper from his hands, leaning his elbow on the blond's head while he scanned the page. "Isn't that strange," he murmured. He offered the paper to Isaac again. "Caleb got just the same letter this afternoon."

Isaac stared up at the demon in disbelief. He knew Caleb definitely hadn't even applied to Cornell, but when Isaac opened his mouth to say so, Andras only smirked at him and ruffled his hair as he pushed away. Isaac could never have predicted that he'd one day feel grateful to a demon for interfering with his life. Before he could stop himself, he fastened his arms around Andras's middle and squeezed him tight. Andras let out a startled sound, awkwardly patting him on the shoulder.

"You're ruining the moment, kid."

"Just accept your affection," Barachiel said from the sofa without looking up from his book, and Andras sighed in Isaac's arms and offered him at least a light touch to his blond hair.

"Yeah, well you can pay me back by keeping this one in line," the demon said as Isaac released him, and he jerked a thumb in Caleb's direction. "Make him study, all right? He's going to have to get a real job someday."

"Oh, I will!" Isaac promised. He reached for Caleb's hand and squeezed him, smiling at the faint scowl on the other boy's face. Isaac was going to take very good care of him.

31
Eight Months Later

Caleb dropped his bag on his desk, the textbooks inside causing a heavy thunk against the wood. Isaac looked up at him from the desk opposite the narrow dorm and smiled as the other boy bent over him to press an upside-down kiss to his lips. Their room was small, but there was enough room for their desks, a mini-fridge and a microwave, and even a stand and a small television, since they'd pushed the two twin beds together against one wall. Adjusting to sharing living quarters had taken some time—especially for Caleb. Isaac had just had to accept that the other boy was sometimes going to sit on the bed with a book on his knee, headphones over his ears, and ignore him. He didn't mind. It was comforting just having him in the room.

Isaac's mother had cried twice because of him since graduation. The first time had been when he received the letter letting him know of his full scholarship to Cornell. That had been a happy one, at least.

The second time his mother had cried was when he'd told her about his relationship with Caleb, shortly before they left for school. His father had shouted at him, which he'd expected, but Caleb had held his hand and shouted right back in his defense. As it was, things were tense, but Isaac's mother had still called to make sure Isaac knew that both boys were welcome at the house for Thanksgiving. That was enough for now.

Caleb was settling into his class schedule; he'd decided on a degree in music, so he spent a lot of time with his headphones plugged into an electric keyboard, teaching himself to play. Isaac's classes were just as demanding since he had set his eyes on medical school, and Caleb was forgiving when the blond had to forgo movie night for the sake of studying. He was determined not to waste Andras's gift to him.

It was only a four hour drive to New York, where the demon lived now that he didn't have a secret cambion to take care of, so they planned to drive and stay the night before taking a plane to Birmingham for dinner with Isaac's parents. Thanksgiving dinner with all of Isaac's extended family—who by now must have heard about his shameful life decision—must have sounded like a nightmare to Caleb, but he hadn't argued about going. He'd kissed Isaac's furrowed brow and promised to sic Greedigut on anyone who upset him.

"Have you heard from Andras?" Isaac asked as Caleb settled on the bed.

"I'm about to call him. The last thing I want is for us to show up there tonight and he's fucked off to wherever the hell he goes when he's not at home. Timbuktu or whatever."

Isaac laughed. "Why would he be in Timbuktu?"

"I don't know his life," Caleb answered with a small smirk as he scrolled through the few contacts on his phone. He held the phone to his ear and waited while it rang, but eventually it went to voice mail, so Caleb clicked his tongue and hung up. "See? What the hell could he be so busy doing that he can't pick up the day we're supposed to drive to see his stupid ass?"

"I should really get that," Andras said through gritted teeth as his cell phone rang on the nightstand, but Barachiel kept a grip on his waist and pushed him down to the mattress again with a firm hand between his shoulderblades, forcing the demon's hips up higher. Andras was on his knees, his hands fisted painfully tight in the sheets as Barachiel thrust into him.

"Keep still," the angel commanded in a low voice, his fingers threatening to leave bruises on his lover's hips. "I wouldn't want to hurt you."

"Hurt—ugh," he grunted, letting out a tight-jawed breath as he was pressed into the blanket by the other man's demanding pace. He jerked each time Barachiel brushed the sensitive spot inside of him, but the angel didn't let up. Andras turned his head to glare over his shoulder and snapped at him, "Can you at least—ngh—slow down, you fucking tyrant!"

An unmerciful smirk curled Barachiel's lips, and he bent over the demon to leave a sharp bite on the pale, sweat-slick skin of his back.

"Settle down," he murmured against him. "Before I'm done, you're going to be begging me to do this again." He smiled as the demon shuddered under him, and he pressed a kiss to the back of his lover's neck to seal the promise.

ABOUT THE AUTHOR

T.S. likes to write about what makes people tick, whether that's deeply-rooted emotional issues, childhood trauma, or just plain hedonism. Throw in a heaping helping of action and violence, a sprinkling of steamy bits, and a whisper of wit (with alliteration optional but preferred), and you have her idea of a perfect novel. She believes in telling stories about real people who live in less-real worlds full of werewolves, witches, demons, vampires, and the occasional alien.

Born and bred in the South, T.S. started writing young, but began writing real novels while working full time as a legal secretary. When she's not writing, she reads other people's books, plays video games, watches movies, and spends time with her husband and daughter. She hopes her daughter grows into a woman who knows what she wants, grabs it, and gets into significantly less trouble than the women in her mother's novels.

FIND ME ONLINE!

tsbarnett.com
Facebook: Tess Barnett
Twitter: @TS_Barnett
Instagram: @TSBarnowl

54253025R00143

Made in the USA
Columbia, SC
30 March 2019